NOW I SURRENDER

ALSO BY ÁLVARO ENRIGUE
Translated by Natasha Wimmer

You Dreamed of Empires
Sudden Death

NOW I SURRENDER

Álvaro Enrigue

Translated by Natasha Wimmer

HARVILL

1 3 5 7 9 10 8 6 4 2

Harvill, an imprint of Vintage, is part of the Penguin Random House group of companies

Vintage, Penguin Random House UK, One Embassy Gardens,
8 Viaduct Gardens, London SW11 7BW

penguin.co.uk/vintage
global.penguinrandomhouse.com

First published in Great Britain by Harvill in 2026
First published with the title *Now I Surrender* in the United
States of America by Riverhead Books in 2026
First published with the title *Ahora me rindo y eso es todo* in
Spain by Editorial Anagrama in 2018

Copyright © Álvaro Enrigue 2018
Translation copyright © Natasha Wimmer 2026

The moral right of the copyright holders has been asserted

Excerpt from José Revueltas's *El apando*, and in English translation *The Hole*,
translated by Sophie Hughes and Amanda Hopkinson, New Directions, 2018

Book design by Christina Nguyen

Penguin Random House values and supports copyright. Copyright fuels creativity, encourages diverse voices, promotes freedom of expression and supports a vibrant culture. Thank you for purchasing an authorised edition of this book and for respecting intellectual property laws by not reproducing, scanning or distributing any part of it by any means without permission. You are supporting authors and enabling Penguin Random House to continue to publish books for everyone. No part of this book may be used or reproduced in any manner for the purpose of training artificial intelligence technologies or systems. In accordance with Article 4(3) of the DSM Directive 2019/790, Penguin Random House expressly reserves this work from the text and data mining exception.

Printed and bound in Great Britain by Clays Ltd, Elcograf S.p.A.

The authorised representative in the EEA is Penguin Random House Ireland,
Morrison Chambers, 32 Nassau Street, Dublin D02 YH68

A CIP catalogue record for this book is available from the British Library

ISBN 9781787301467

Penguin Random House is committed to a sustainable future
for our business, our readers and our planet. This book is made
from Forest Stewardship Council® certified paper.

FOR
MAIA, DYLAN, AND MIQUEL

Esta gigantesca derrota de la libertad
a manos de la geometría.

This gargantuan defeat of liberty,
all the fault of geometry.

JOSÉ REVUELTAS, EL APANDO (THE HOLE)

BOOK I

JANOS

1836

In the beginning, things appear. Writing is a defiant gesture we've long since gotten used to: where there was nothing, somebody put something, and now everybody sees it. For example, the prairie. An endless expanse of tall grasses, the occasional smoke column signaling an encampment of the original masters of the land. There are no trees. They would never survive the wind, the torpor of summer, the swirling snows of winter. In the middle of the plain, let there be Spanish missionaries and a church; then settlers, a four-street town. Somebody decided this town was something, and they called it Janos. Maybe because it had two faces, one turned toward the Spanish empire from its raveling edge, the other toward the desert and its cactuses: Apachería.

At some point, the location was strategic. There were artesian wells. Soldiers were sent. They built a fort to give a sense of fruitful security to the settlers who had once been Spanish and were now criollo; also Negro, Keralan, Lombard, Chinese, Irish. Few female settlers came, so the men married Indian women, and their children were something else again: Chihuahuans, Mexicans, God knows what. Then it occurred to someone that there was profit to be skimmed from the work of the ranchers, the traders, the baker, and the teacher, and they built a town hall. It was in the very center of town, though that didn't mean much because Janos was so small there were no outskirts. Or rather, there were outskirts, but they were never mentioned because they were goteras or rancherías, Indian settlements.

The inhabitants of these settlements were peaceful groups of Janero Apaches, Conchos, and the occasional Opata down from the mountains in the winter. The criollos called them indios de razón because they had given up being nomads and become integrated into the European-style productive cycle. Beyond the houses of the criollos and mestizos in the towns—beyond even the goteras that fed and were fed by the towns—were the indios de guerra: Apaches, Raramuris, and Yaquis, mostly, who were sworn enemies of each other and whose internecine conflicts had made it possible for the settlements to grow. It was they who had expelled from the region the Comanches, those lords of the southern plains now clustered on the far side of El Paso del Norte.

Janos still exists, with its church and town hall, but no goteras. The war there—the all-out war against the Apaches—was won, but the winners choose not to remember it, because it makes them ashamed. Today, Janos is in the Mexican state of Chihuahua.

This story begins on the prairie, a prairie that chokes the town. A land where so few people come that there are still buffalo. Let there be blue mountains in the distance, stone walls between ranches, cattle that die of thirst every few years when there's a drought. Let there be rattlesnakes, wild goats, piglike coyametl, pheasants, yellow scorpions the size of a child's hand, coyotes, all sheltered under the junipers and acacias of the chaparral, ratty yucca popping up here and there. In this harsh valley, suddenly a path appears, and the back of a woman running, a woman of grit, dressed head to toe in black. She glances back.

Still running, she unlaces the bodice of the black dress, pulls her arms out of the sleeves, and lets the garment drop as she advances in great strides. She trips but doesn't fall, keeps running. Underneath the petticoat, the cotton corset. She twists her body as she unfastens it, without slackening her pace. She slips down the straps of the petticoat and pulls the corset over her head, leaves it dangling from a bush, jerks the petticoat straps back up. She keeps running, now in just her light fawn underskirts, which blend better with the burnt shade of the vegetation, dry and stiff in the fall. She squats down to pull off her boots and hides them in the brush, losing valuable time, but with legs freed and feet bare she can go faster. The underskirts stick to her buttocks: she's so scared she's wet herself. She's running again, her jaw set, neck tense, shoulders braced. Dressed so lightly, she thinks, she can hide better in the brush, curling quietly into a ball. But she can run a little farther still, escape, save herself, as she has done so many times before.

LIEUTENANT COLONEL JOSÉ MARÍA ZULOAGA was a man of the hills, so he loved to receive orders sending him without timetable or pangs of conscience into his beloved backcountry. The moment he got the letter from the state capital, he put on his fringed Comanche jacket, his double-holster cartridge belt, and his curved-brim hat and closed up his headquarters, which were dusty and lonely and utterly useless for recruiting irregulars to join an expedition into the sierra. Back then, chasing a pack of Apaches was like going hunting: a chance to run wild on the prairie with friends, with a veneer of service in defense of the fledgling republic of Mexico.

He was about to mount his horse, a sorrel as tough and cocky as its master, when he returned to the office, folded the letter, and put it in his breast pocket to show his wife as proof that he was leaving on orders. He wiped the smile off his face, testing out woeful expressions for breaking the news: like all Chihuahuan women, his wife had a temper de la chingada. In the only photo of the two of them together, it's clear they were both handsome and fierce. He sits an inch or two behind her, his hair unruly in the way of men who enjoy themselves no matter the circumstances. She is standing: dark mantilla, severe black dress, impeccable gloves, a look of burning impatience.

The men Zuloaga usually rounded up for his expeditions were like himself, not the soldiers in uniform coats and peaked caps who had gone to defend Texas from the gringo settlers or California from a rumored invasion of the tsar of all the Russias, but ranchers in heavy serge trousers, wide-brimmed hats, flannel shirts, sharp-toed boots—needle toes, they were called, their sharpness essential for lasso handling. They brought their own rifles, bullets, and horses, enlisting in exchange for a nominal salary they knew they would never receive. Their expeditions to punish Apaches tended to be long and almost always great fun for them. Tracking their foes meant venturing into steep terrain at little risk, because except in rare cases, the irregulars could never find them. Sometimes there was a skirmish and they shot a woman or a child or rescued some captive the Apaches had left behind to sidetrack them. When they got back to town, instead of "irregulars"—or rurales, as they were called in the middle of the country—the newspapers dubbed them nacionales, an epithet they savored.

Zuloaga had the best record of his generation as an Apache fighter, maybe because his joy in the chase kept him at a remove from vulgar clichés of justice. He didn't see himself as a champion of that predatory chimera, the National State, but as a man going out to play.

He left Buenaventura at the break of day, with no rurales. All the wives in town were long since fed up with his expeditions, which were a burden on families. The men left their ranches for periods that could stretch on for weeks, not to mention that they had to be sent with provisions, always scarce. So he was accompanied only by his father, a retired soldier who was joining him mostly because it made him sad to see his son ride alone to Casas Grandes on such a cold morning. To protect the lieutenant's vanity as a tracker with a mostly imaginary post in the army of the brand-new Mexican Republic, the old man had said he would come along for a few days so that he could stop in at La Tinaja. He had delightful relatives there, half-Indian after so many dealings with the Janeros.

In the dispatch from Chihuahua City, Lieutenant Colonel José María Zuloaga had read that the attack happened months ago, and he understood that the pursuit was, frankly, pointless. By the time he found the thieving perpetrators, the cattle they had stolen would literally be shit—butchered, roasted, eaten, and turned to pulp in some bottomless Apache stomachs.

Ain't there a fort in Janos? his father asked, putting on the black dragoon's jacket he had worn in the imperial army. It still had its flared tail, gold buttons, and braid on the chest, but it was so faded it looked like the frock coat of some gentleman come down in the world. Must be empty, like this one, said Zuloaga. What about the federal troops there? Zuloaga shrugged, considering the topic a waste of saliva.

The distance was a little over twenty-five miles. They stopped at noon on a shady bank of the Santa María River to hunt wood pigeons and roast them. The horses didn't like to be ridden in the midday sun, even though winter was beginning and it was cold. They made it to Casas Grandes a little before dark, carrying the carcass of a young pronghorn that had crossed their path that afternoon. The idea was to barbecue it the next day. We'll buy sotol and hand out tacos, said the old man as they tied the carcass to one of the horses. There's your ten numbskulls enlisted, and I can go back to La Tinaja guilt-free.

SEEN THIS WAY, FROM THE VANTAGE POINT of the twenty-first century, running half-clad across the plains like a woman possessed, Camila is athletic, confident in her body, though the men of her time saw her as gaunt.

Her childhood was rather sad, but not lonely. She lived on the ranch of her aunt and uncle as their orphaned ward, which brought her close to the goteras. She slept in the master's house and ate at his table, but she played with the Jicarilla and Concho children of the ranch hands and serving girls, which was how she learned to run like a leopard and developed an ear for the tongues of the chaparral. She was always muscular and independent, as if she knew that the key moment of her life would play out in a desperate race across the plains.

Camila had married Leopoldo Ezguerra when everyone assumed she would end her days a spinster. They were married in the parish of La Soledad in Janos—a designation hardly befitting the smattering of houses that was the town in the third decade of the nineteenth century, when Mexico was a nine-year-old republic and the United States was a nervous throb on the far side of Texas.

It wasn't the most promising of marriages. Ezguerra was sixty-seven at the time and this was his third round of nuptials. I need someone to take care of me, he had said at one of the sawhorse tables that were set up every Sunday where the main plaza would have been if the town were big enough to have a recognizable center. For lack of a better place, the tables were brought out into the street in front of the church. This street was called First, though there was no Second, and it was intersected by three streets that ran not into other streets but into the plain. Ezguerra needed a woman to manage the ranch that he no longer had the strength to run, until one of his sons chose to come back to Janos to inherit it.

No one had ever shown any curiosity about Camila's body, whether in the world of notaries and doctors of Casas Grandes, the town where she was born, or at the Sacred Heart boarding school in Tepic, where she became a woman among women, or in Guadalajara, where she kept the books at a Teresian school, or in Janos, where she went to work as a tutor for a well-to-do family when she was still of marrying age. Nor did she attract any interest at the big house on the Ezguerra ranch, where she never slept with Don Leopoldo, though their everyday struggles were as poignant and exhausting as a real marriage.

Don Leopoldo had liked her ever since he noticed her toiling away as a governess, trying to corral the insufferable children of the town apothecary at the tables outside the church. He found her interesting, as only a tortoise could.

She was a tall woman, her shoulders broad from afternoons at swimming holes with the children of the Indian ranch hands—a pleasure that she continued to indulge in when she could—and she had a long back that swelled into hips belying the rather virile vigor of her legs and arms. She had small, wide-awake breasts, brown eyes, a pronounced mouth that spoke of a grandmother who'd had a dalliance with a slave and lived to tell the tale, having been rewarded in the genetic lottery with a child who could pass as Neapolitan. Don Leopoldo's calculation was that this strong-armed woman would be able to handle both his failing body and the ranch that sustained him and gave his life meaning.

He was right. As a girl Camila had liked working in the fields, and the apothecary's kids were making her miserable, so marriage seemed a fair price to pay to liberate herself from the incorrigible brats. Even at boarding school, she had chosen to live the way she had learned on the ranch. She picked fruits and vegetables in the convent gardens with the maids while the other boarders were being taught to weave brocades and make marzipan. No one complained: her uncle had put down a hefty deposit when he enrolled her, but after that he never paid the fees. The sisters thought it just as well that she earn her keep with the servants, even though she slept with the young ladies.

She came from an undistinguished line of criollos who still passed as white, though it had clearly been generations since they could make the claim. They were the kind of family who settled in the barren north because the one thing they did have was the sense that they deserved a better life, for the wrong reason: they weren't Indians. The blurring of the desert erased divides, which were more rigid the farther south you went. Anybody—except the original inhabitants of the plains—could be settlers. No one came to Chihuahua, after all, if not pursued by debt or a guilty verdict.

Early on, Camila was aware that if she wanted a chance in the courtship wars, she would have to seize it herself, because marriage wouldn't fall from the sky: she would have to earn it as she had earned her keep in boarding school, with her own hands. They were long, bony hands, darker than the rest of her body. She rubbed herbed oil into them in the mornings and at night; they could peel a ripe tomato without a knife.

Old Ezguerra imagined those hands rubbing liniment into the abscesses that formed on his legs and back during long stretches in bed, and the vision was edifying and dirty: after Camila's years at the convent and the Teresian school, there was something nunlike about her. She had the hands of a bride of Christ.

Don Leopoldo didn't have the strength to mount a woman, let alone the vigorous Camila, but he did get some satisfaction from those hands, which every so often encircled his sex, long relegated to mere plumbing. There was a certain amount of pleasure in the marriage, then, but it was the exception to the rule, and one-sided.

Give me your hand, the old man would say when he was overcome by fear of his final passage. Touch my face, he would say when he wanted to feel alive. It was the last thing he said: Touch my face. He said it in a kind of whistle from the other side, one morning when he woke knowing that his name didn't figure on the calendar's next page. When he felt his wife's cool touch on his cheek, he grasped her hand to stop his slide toward the corncob smile of the Dark Lady. Camila didn't feel the jolt of death, but she did have a hard time disentangling her fingers from his, which gripped with a force they had lacked when alive.

CASAS GRANDES WAS AS PEACEFUL as could be when José María Zuloaga and his father arrived, despite the Apache attack, which had been reported as occurring a little to the north. Maybe everything was calm, the lieutenant colonel surmised, because the people of Chihuahua chose not to work up a sweat. His father shook his head impatiently, as he always did when his son talked nonsense. It's because nobody cares what happens in Janos anymore, he said; settle in a valley already swallowed up by Apachería and it's your funeral.

They were received by the local justice of the peace, who stood in as mayor when required. Without asking for a copy of their orders, he authorized them to roast half of the pronghorn in the Plaza de

Armas. Why only half of it? inquired the lieutenant. Because the other half goes to the authorities, boys.

Lieutenant Colonel Zuloaga, whose behavior had so far been courteous, got up from his chair and planted both hands on the justice's desk. Look, Mr. Mayor, he said, you don't know it because you're a jackass, but the Republic is at war with half the world and the Apaches. He brought his stony face close to the justice, who had turned green and was shrinking down in his chair. We're under permanent curfew and martial law, and while the forts are empty, I represent the federal government. Who do you represent? It was a joke, commander, sir, said the justice, looking away. Zuloaga cuffed the side of his face, making the justice turn and meet his eyes. So how do you plan to help us? I can't leave my post to go chasing savages, and anyway I'm a lawyer, I'm from Guanajuato. But you can contribute beer to the festivities, can't you? Yes, general, sir. Zuloaga stepped back. I'm a lieutenant colonel, he said.

The lieutenant's father got up, too, and they touched the brims of their hats in parting. They were almost at the door when the justice said: There's a family waiting for you. The lieutenant colonel gave him a look. The judge continued: They don't have money, but they have a nice house. You can stay there, I'm sure, and you'll be more comfortable than at the gendarmerie. There are gendarmes here? asked the elder Zuloaga, surprised by the progress that independence had brought to the region. There's a headquarters, replied the justice, and when I have the money, we'll get some personnel for it.

THE IDEA IS TO WRITE a book about a country that still exists but was erased from the maps. A country that worked just as well or badly as any other country, and that was taken away from us like cassette tapes or incandescent light bulbs. Where Sonora, Chihuahua, Arizona, and New Mexico meet today was an Atlantis, an in-between country. And straddling it were the Mexicans and the gringos, like two children, eyes shut, their backs to each other, while the Apaches scuttled back and forth between their legs, not sure where to go with strangers bubbling up everywhere, filling their lands.

Apachería was a country with an economy, a concept of statehood, and a system for making decisions for the common good. A country that took a stand. A country of faces weathered by the sun and the wind, faces of people whose sole possession was the thing that in the end the rest of us give up to get ahead: dignity.

Dignity, the most esoteric of human virtues. It alone values the urgency of living exactly as you like above all those other slobbery, unwashed urgencies: the dispersal of genetic information, the preservation of habits or a language or a collection of objects.

When the Chiricahua—the most determined of the Apache nations—had no choice but to become part of either Mexico or the United States, they chose a third, completely unexpected path: to fight until the end. I will move to Canada, the gringos always claim, but they never do. I'd rather die, say the Mexicans, but then we all go on and accept the new state of things anyway. The Apaches said they weren't interested in integrating when the conquistadors made contact with them in 1610, and they kept on saying no until the most celebrated band of Chiricahua warriors fit into the single train car that carried the last twenty-seven of them out of Arizona.

I don't know whether there's anything to be learned from such a decision, but I find it so unsettling that I'm writing a book about it.

I make a living by writing novels, articles, and scripts based on what I read, to support my family—so that my genetic material, my language, my way of being, will live on a little longer. But if I were a

Chiricahua, I'd do nothing but read, and we would die of whatever people die of when they don't participate in the carnival of productivity: malnutrition, sixty cigarettes a day, no dental care, treatable illnesses, unpaid taxes, miseducation.

At the moment of their defeat, the Chiricahua Apaches wrote only in the symbols of death. They left messages along the road, spelled out in an alphabet of cadavers, so that no one would forget to whom this country belonged. Or to whom it had once belonged, this country that Mexicans and gringos felt the right to occupy. The country had no name, not at first.

DON LEOPOLDO WAS A GOOD MAN, father to three hardworking sons. None of them were present when death came for him, but that was normal in those days. There was no official mail delivery on the prairie, and telegraph service was still decades off. Chihuahua was at the back of beyond, never mind Janos.

Ezguerra's two sons by his first wife were in politics. One was a council member in Chihuahua City, and the other was a congressman in Mexico City. Over the six years Camila was with Don Leopoldo, she wrote them both long, rambling letters informing them of the progress of his health. Both responded, months later, with notes dictated to secretaries with professional penmanship. There was a third son, from Ezguerra's second marriage, who had gone off at twenty to study agronomy in a city of deadly winters in the heedless United States. All Camila knew about this son was what her husband had told her: his name was Hector, he had settled in Massachusetts, and he had married a Quaker woman who gave Leopoldo blond, English-speaking grandchildren he would never meet. Also: because of Hector, Ezguerra would become a gringo last name. Don't that beat all, Camilita?

When Camila was widowed, the first thing she did was send a messenger to Chihuahua City to tell her nearest stepson that his father had died.

The council member didn't return to Janos, but two months later—practically at a gallop—he sent a long letter written in his own hand, thanking Camila for the help she had given his father in recent years and asking her to stay at the ranch, managing it as wisely as he knew she had thus far, until his half brother Hector, the agronomist, arrived and could decide what was best for the family, which definitely included her.

THAT NIGHT THEY DUG THE PIT for the barbecue, in the very center of Casas Grandes, so close to the bandstand in the plaza that when the fire was lit it would be blackened by the smoke. Or rather, Zuloaga pointed out to the town's boy-of-all-work where he wanted it. Lieutenant Colonel Zuloaga may have been a down-to-earth man, generally a friend to the Indians and well-intentioned, but that didn't mean he wasn't still a criollo: it would never have occurred to him to dig the pit himself or ask the justice to do it. That's what his friends the Indians were for.

The justice showed signs of alarm at the proposed placement of the pit, but when he started to say something, the commander pursed his lips as if to kiss the air and shook his head like someone reprimanding a child. Whatever the colonel says goes, he told the boy, who griped: I just painted the dang pinche bandstand last week, Commissioner. Tell it to the colonel, replied his boss, clasping his hands behind his back.

To Zuloaga, the kid looked like a troublemaker, the kind to believe that sweeping the barracks made him a soldier. More than anything, he was strange-looking: he was very thin, his arms and legs were too long, and his head was small, but his eyes, nose, and mouth were big. When he spoke, his voice cracked. Since Zuloaga and his wife had been unable to have children, he didn't realize that this was what the passage from childhood to adulthood looked like. In addition to being contrary, the kid was long-winded: Zuloaga had time to chew a whole piece of straw as he argued his case. It has to go here, the boy concluded at last, indicating a random spot at the far end of the plaza. The commander spat what was left of the straw right on the boy's huaraches and asked his father whether the kid wasn't the very picture of a conscript. He's got a lot to learn, said the old man, and there's no better teacher than the army of the Republic.

Without rising from the bench, Zuloaga picked up another piece of straw from the ground and put it in his mouth. Squinting as if to bring the boy into focus, he asked: Is this insubordination, soldier? The boy replied: I'm the hired help, not a soldier. The old man raised his eyebrows and said: I think that's sufficient grounds to call in a firing squad. Or we could send him to clean the fort in Janos with his tongue, said the son. Or his balls, commander, if he's got any. Zuloaga turned to the recruit. What part of my orders didn't you understand, soldier? The boy gave a rather limp military salute. When you finish with the pit, the lieutenant colonel said, fill it with wood, light a fire, and keep watch over it until the embers are ready. Then you report to me to collect the pronghorn, which is being cleaned for you. It all has to be done before sunrise. The boy lowered his head.

That same night, in a gesture of boundless goodwill, the justice provided the new recruit with wood for the barbecue and a rifle, so he wouldn't have to set out unarmed on Zuloaga's campaign. It was a flintlock, so old it used buckshot, a small box of which the justice also provided. There was no powder horn: the powder had been used for fireworks the day the town government was instituted. But the justice also ponied up enough cheap sotol to put eight towns to sleep, and sufficient coffee to wake them up.

Zuloaga soon learned that he didn't have much time for carousing. Haste was needed. Later that night, the family hosting him and his father in Casas Grandes informed him that a woman who lived on the Ezguerra ranch had disappeared after the Apache attack, and no sign of her had been found.

They rode off with her, colonel, and all anybody found was her clothes scattered over the prairie, the woman's uncle had said over a cup of warm milk straight from the cow, with cinnamon and sugar. She's no good for childbearing and of no service to the nation, but she's our niece, like it or not, and our responsibility.

Like everybody in the region, the lieutenant colonel knew the Apaches didn't bury their enemies; they left them out in the open as a warning. He was already weary from travel and from wrangling with the justice, and now this. The news of the missing niece scrambled his plans for a rather leisurely expedition.

He scratched his scalp, took a wad of tobacco from the pocket of his jacket, and rolled a cigarette. In the to-and-fro of messengers between the state capital, Mexico City, and the town of Buenaventura, at least four and a half months had been lost, with no one ever mentioning that a woman was missing in Janos. Gazing with his bovine eyes past the head of the lost woman's uncle, Zuloaga decided that the rather odd fact that the Apaches had taken some cattle along with the horses gave him a certain advantage: he could follow their shit to the ends of the earth, so long as the rains held off.

He rubbed his face and explained that he hadn't been told a

captive was taken. Reaching vainly for the hat that wasn't on his head, he said with honest contrition: Look, sir, I'll tell you the truth, which you know yourself, though you may not want to admit it. By now your niece is either a pile of bones, which is the best thing that could have happened to her, or they've taken her into the mountains and they're keeping her as a slave.

Sweet Jesus, said the aunt, they'll be raping her. The lieutenant colonel lit a match, scraping it on the terra-cotta floor. He half closed his eyes as he drew in the smoke of his cigarette. Not raped, he said, I've never known them to violate a girl, but she'll be a slave, at least until she learns to be an Apache. Do you think she's alive? the uncle asked. The lieutenant shrugged his shoulders: I'm sure I'll find her, dead or alive, that I can promise you. The aunt burst into tears. So long as you give her a Christian burial, said the man of the house.

When Zuloaga went to his room, his father was in his long underwear, reading a book he had taken from the shelves over the bed. Why the long face? he asked. They took a captive. Screwed then, ain't you? Eyup. You'll have your work cut out for you. You don't say. Ride up into the mountains, do your tracking, get some trigger practice. Zuloaga inflated his cheeks and expelled the air noisily. Hardest will be turning the slobs you pick up tomorrow into the king's soldiers, said his father. The Republic's, Pop. All right then, to sleep.

IN THE TIMES I'M TRYING to write about, Chihuahua was little more than a figment of the imagination for some Mexicans, who in any case had just begun to be Mexicans. It must have been complicated for anyone alive in the year 1821 to give up being Spanish American, as they'd called themselves—no one ever described himself as a New Spaniard—and to begin to identify as Mexican, a term previously associated only with the Mexicas, the original people of the remote city that just happened to be the seat of the Republic.

Chihuahua was plains and mountains. It had been embedded in Nueva Vizcaya for centuries and it had belonged—at least nominally—to the king of Spain. There was a contract of some sort, something signed by the pope; there were books by missionaries that took its name for granted; and it was under the direct rule of the viceroy. Unlike Nueva Galicia, Nueva Vizcaya was always a loyal part of the infinite realm of New Spain, a realm whose bounds were unclear but which began somewhere beyond Lake Nicaragua and the Costa Rica, continued on past very noble and very loyal Mexico City, and then over the mountains, beyond the vague lands of Apachería, across the Colorado River.

Nobody had ever reached the end of New Spain, or if they had, they'd never told the tale, or never returned: they were eaten by bears, shot by Indians, struck down by the cold. The naming fever continued anyway. To name is to possess, to incorporate, to swallow up what's been named. The land above Nueva Vizcaya was called Nueva México, and farther north was Colorado, named for the chocolate river that ran through it. The desert that rolled down to the Sea of Cortés in the west was called Sonora, and above it was Arizona—*Ariza* plus the augmentative *ona*—because the land was red and rocky like the barrens that surrounded the town of Ariza, in Aragón, but much bigger. The infinite stretch of land bordering the Pacific was named by a soldier who was reading Garci Rodríguez de Montalvo's *Exploits of Esplandián*. He believed it to be a land of giants, so it was called California, after Montalvo's mythological gargantuan queen and her island race of warriors. Then it was discovered that the lower part wasn't an island and there were two Californias, Baja and Alta. The land bordering the gulf was originally named Nueva Filipinas, but no one called it that. It became Tejas—the Spanish word for *slabs*—because to reach it one had to pass through a canyon where the boulders were smooth and flat.

At the beginning of the horrendous nineteenth century, the criollos devoted themselves to killing Spaniards so that the country would be called Mexico instead of New Spain and the Spanish Americans would be Mexicans; twenty-six years later, the gringos set about killing Mexicans so that northern Sonora, New Mexico, Colorado, and Alta California would be called the United States. The land south of the city of Chihuahua became Durango. Tejas allowed itself the extravagance of spelling its name with an *x*, like Mexico, and became almost its own country, and Alta Sonora took the archaic name of Arizona. Apachería remained more or less untouched in this hodgepodge of vast territories where towns of twenty people killed each other in order to be called something else. The Apache land was so forbidding that no one was interested in claiming it, so it was left to its inhabitants.

What was once Apachería remains a lonely spot as I write, an extreme land where even the animals are only passing through. It has belonged to the United States for more than one hundred and fifty years, but it still goes by its Spanish name: La Mesilla. Impenetrable ravines, scorching plains, tortured rivers, stones everywhere. More than a place, it's a blank in the world's memory, a spot where the only people who could think to prosper were the stubbornest descendants of Mongols who went out hunting yaks that turned into caribou and then into white-tailed deer and pronghorns. The portable yurts they used on the steppe evolved into disposable wickiups—not tents like the tepees the Great Plains Indians moved around depending on the season, but perpetual emergency constructions, huts intended to be abandoned. In Mexican Spanish we call them jacales.

Those who build dwellings destined to be wrecked show a serious disregard for history, a steely determination, a clear resolve to live as they like, to fiddle and sing while the greedy swine sock it away. In a world that measures the prowess of cultures in pillars and bricks, such a people takes the prize for not caring. Maybe we were all like that at some point: nomadic and happy. We were just ambling along and somebody chained us to history, named us, forced us to pay rent, and banned smoking indoors. We were just the People and one day somebody turned us into something: Mexicans, Koreans, Zulus. We had to be categorized quickly so that we could be exterminated (ideally), or at least saddled with a language, taught grammar, and supplied with shoes that could later be sold to us once we stopped being used to going barefoot.

The Apaches, magnificent and mouth-filling as the name is, didn't call themselves Apaches. The way into the history books is through baptism in blood, under a name assigned to us by those who hate us or who want what we have, little though it is. The Apaches had nothing, and they called themselves Ndeé, the people, the nation, the gang. Not that it was a nice name. It implied that they were the true people and others weren't. The Zuñi thought the same way—Zuñi also means "the people"—and it was they who taught the Spaniards that the Ndeé were called 'a pacu: "the enemy." The Spanish speakers, deaf to the sounds of the desert languages, coined the harder-sounding word *Apache*.

So baptized, the Apaches entered written history at the beginning of the seventeenth century, when Spanish expeditionaries scaled the highlands of Arizona, and, on their way down, christened the land Apachería as well, having concluded the obvious: that there was nothing to be squeezed from the patchwork of woods, boulder fields, and ravines framed by the Gila, Bravo, and Yaqui Rivers.

The territory was so forbidding and the Ndeé so intractably themselves that the Spanish didn't even leave missionaries behind. To the priests of New Spain, used to baptizing crowds of hardworking naturals—as they called them—in the naves of churches raised in the heart of centenarian cities of stone and adobe, the Apaches must have seemed like pure ecosystem: cousins to the bear, eaters of thorns, frightening. In *Memorial on New Mexico*, written by Fray Alonso de Benavides in 1630, the Apaches are "a very spirited and bellicose people, ardent in war, and even their way of speaking distinguishes them from the other Indian nations, because the latter speak softly and seldom, while the very words of the Apaches strike a blow." Not a bad curtain raiser for a nation on History's stage.

By the nineteenth century there were Tarahumaras and Jicarillas, Pimas, Janeros, Pápagos, Conchos, Comanches, and Opatas. Anyone who didn't fit into one of those groups was a Yaqui or an Apache, and as the criollos liked to say, if you came across one, you had to kill him before he killed you.

The gringos were still a pale abstraction, said to be mustering troops in Tejas, buying land, setting up shop on the other side of the Rio Grande around Santa Fé, and bringing slaves they weren't prepared to free when they settled in Mexico, as the Constitution of 1821 stated they must. No one yet called them Americans, the name they'd insist upon by the late nineteenth century, to drive home the imperial nature of their Republic, nor did they call them United Statesians, an impossible name. Bestowed upon them instead was a delightful archaism: gringos, Greeks. From the early days of the Spanish language, if something was inscribed in a manuscript in a language other than Latin, a marginal note was added: "Está en gringo," "This is in Greek"—a language I don't understand. That's why in Spain a gringo is a Frenchman, and in Argentina he's a Brit.

LIEUTENANT COLONEL JOSÉ MARÍA ZULOAGA reviewed his troops at three in the morning in the yard of the house belonging to the missing woman's aunt and uncle, grand temporary headquarters of Chihuahua State's irregular forces. Roll call was quick, because for the moment the troops consisted of an officer, a recruit, and a retired imperial general who was really only there to offer his two cents. Given that no one had the courtesy to ask the recruit's name, it was over even faster: a brief inspection and the boy was sent to bury the pronghorn in the barbecue pit. Stand watch over it, Zuloaga said. I'll relieve you when the sun comes up, so you can commandeer tortillas and salsas at the market. The boy's eyes shone: "commandeer" was a sign that he might be rising in rank.

Before the squad dispersed, the lieutenant colonel asked the recruit how to reach the town's goteras. The boy told him to follow the paved road and continue along the trail leading up into the mountains, but warned that he wouldn't find anyone there. The Indians living around this presidio were all Apashees, so they left, he said, an edge to his voice betraying a generations-long hatred. Aren't you Indian yourself? I'm Mexican, the boy said, and the lieutenant colonel smiled slightly, giving a nearly imperceptible nod. The boy said: They left when rations ran out, people say they don't like to work. Was it the same in the south? he wanted to know. The same as what? The Apashee—are they all gone? That's right, not a single one left, Zuloaga concluded—and it was true.

It wasn't until the recruit was swallowed up by the darkness of the cobblestone street, pronghorn over his shoulder, that the lieutenant remarked to his father that they'd read the boy wrong. The old man, eager to return to the warm house, said: He's not a book. Zuloaga went on: He's Tarahumara, that's why he's so big. His father raised his eyebrows. How do you know? he asked. Didn't you see those paws of his? said the lieutenant. And he hates the Apaches. But he doesn't talk like an Indian, said his father. Then he must be adopted. The old man shrugged his shoulders and turned, heading for the kitchen door.

Zuloaga aimed for the mountains, following the boy's instructions. He didn't find a trail, as he expected, but a road of hard-packed dirt. He hesitated for a moment, checking the brush, picking up a fistful of dirt and smelling it. At the top of the first slope was another slope, and another, on up into the harsh mountain scrub just visible in the faint moonlight. He followed the path, cursing the Tarahumara kid who evidently considered this a short walk: a criollo would have done it on horseback. He picked up his pace, glimpsing behind him the green light of day on the horizon.

After a few more hills, he reached the abandoned Indian village. It was daylight now. Unlike the surrounding plain with its scattered huts, here was a labyrinth of mud and stone, protected by a wall. He smiled. He had been here before: it was the ruins of Paquimé, a capital of the great Chichimeca people, abandoned before the arrival of the conquistadors. He strolled around aimlessly. No matter how acclimated the Apaches of Casas Grandes had been before the great disbanding, they would never have settled within these walls, which for them would have been a teeming kettle of claustrophobia and ghosts.

On the way back it occurred to him that the boy couldn't be more than twelve or thirteen if he thought the ruins of Paquimé were goteras left by the Apaches in their flight into the mountains. He was an Indian from a criollo household who had never lived in a ranchería and didn't remember the huts of the departed Janeros.

HECTOR EZGUERRA RETURNED TO THE ranch several months after Don Leopoldo was laid in the ground. In Massachusetts he had learned that one way to worship God was to build wealth, so he came to Janos determined to apply with insect-like tenacity what he viewed as the exact science of agronomy.

Hector arrived in a military coach when the sun had yet to set on a devastatingly hot April day. He was sitting on the coachman's bench, next to an officer who plied the reins to the very door of the ranch house. The new ranch owner's buttoned-up wool jacket troubled Camila, who was waiting at the gate flanked by the maids and housemen. Hector was tall and heavyset, dressed like a city slicker, complete with fedora, watch chain, and bow tie. He had no mustache. To Camila, his clean-shaven appearance was an ominous sign. She had never seen a criollo without hair on his face.

She knew, thanks to a message from Hector's brother in Chihuahua, that the Ezguerra Parletts had gone by ship from Boston to Corpus Christi, and then by stagecoach to Laredo. They had transferred there to another coach traveling to Chihuahua City via Delicias, finally reaching Janos and the ranch in this official state conveyance. She had the house ready to receive them.

The ruminant scientist showed signs of hyperactivity from the moment the coach passed through the gate into the yard. He leapt from the driver's seat to the roof rack and removed three rather modest valises that the oldest and most venerable Jicarilla ranch hand scarcely caught in time, taken aback as he was by the spectacle of a criollo doing things for himself. Once the three valises were on the ground, the old man picked them up—one in each hand and the third under his arm—to carry them into the house. Leave them there, Pedro, said Hector, the kindly firmness of his tone making it plain that the new boss had arrived.

Still without a word of greeting, Hector climbed down the rear ladder, opened the coach door, and unfolded the steps. He held out his hand to a sturdy, scalded-looking gringa, who refused his help with a vigorous shake of the head and hopped to the ground with a blond child in her arms. Camila watched as three other gringo children followed. Their father took two of the valises and motioned to the oldest boy, who dragged more than carried the third. When Pedro moved to help, Hector shook his head. If they're going to be ranchers, he said, they'll have to learn to be real men from now on.

Camila smoothed her dress, ready to introduce herself, but Hector gestured toward the door, and the gringa and the children marched in like cattle, not even saying hello. He himself halted on the threshold, setting down the valise in his right hand, turning, and touching the brim of his hat. Nice to meet you, Camila, thanks for taking care of the place for us, he said, not even offering his hand. And turning to the oldest of the women arrayed to meet him: How are things in the kitchen, Eduviges? The children are starving, so Señora Prudence is going to rustle up a little refreshment. The cook went running into the house. He followed her, touching his hat to Camila again.

Camila exchanged glances with Pedro, then followed the others. She went to her room to read, expecting they would knock at the door to let her know when the food was ready. Her heart was wrung but not broken. Gringos, she had heard, were efficient people who didn't overthink things.

No one came to her room, so when she heard the scrape of plates and cutlery she crossed the patio to the dining room, which was empty. In the kitchen she found the new family eating not only at the servingwomen's table, but with the servingwomen. She was scandalized to see a pot of food and a big spoon sitting in the middle of the table. Even worse, there was no cloth on the boards under the dishes.

Are you joining us? asked Hector. She sat down next to the cook, confused. If you don't get yourself a plate and fork you'll have nothing to eat with, said the new master, with a condescending smile. Camila got up for her place setting, sat back down again, and held out her plate. The new mistress indicated with her gaze that the correct thing was to serve herself. Camila noted with relief that it was pork in salsa verde with greens: the gringa hadn't cooked. I made it without chile, whispered the cook, who all her life had used a tortilla to eat and was finding it impractical to fish for bits of meat with a fork.

Mistress Prudence—as she urged everyone to call her; her husband alone was allowed to address her simply by her name—was stout, more muscular than fat. She had colorless hair, pale blue eyes, and a vicious smile. The children were as gringified as could be: four disturbingly silent little towheads aged seven, five, three, and one, who drank milk as if they liked the taste of it.

No one said a word during supper. When Hector finished his meal, he carried his dishes to the sink, washed them, and thanked the cook. He asked where Pedro was. I've got to take a look at the corrals, he said. But it's getting dark, Camila ventured. All the more reason to hurry, he replied.

The women of the house waited for the rest of the family to leave the kitchen before heating up some tortillas and taking stock of the situation. What does this mean? asked the widow. You haven't seen anything, said the cook. There's a river of tears in the maids' room because the mistress doesn't want help; tomorrow they'll be sent home to their villages. There was a certain score-settling pleasure in Eduviges's smile as she ended the conversation by noting that starting the next day, Missus Camila would have to make her own bed.

MY WIFE, INÉS, TOUCHES MY FACE when she sees me looking upset. It happens a lot: being the father of three in a scattered, split-up family is upsetting. I'm taking notes for a possible book on the Apache Wars waged from Mexico—a subject no one wants to address because it's more comfortable to fob off accusations of genocide on the gringos—at a moment of transition when I'm having trouble recognizing myself. It's me in our bathroom mirror and the sour smell of my pillow; me in the voices of my younger children making their mysterious plans behind closed doors early in the morning, when they are their best selves. It's me in the mark left by the absence of my older son, Cruz, and in my wife's adorably crooked upper incisor when she smiles her first smile of the day. But I'm not completely present where I live, and my bureaucratic status weighs on me.

I never wanted to be anything but what I am: Mexican. Practical concerns have put me in a capitulatory mood, however. New York has been generous to us, and even though we only meant to pass through, now that Cruz has moved to Guadalajara to study film, any reason for returning to Mexico City is gone. To continue to support the family, then, I have to take a leap. Stop renewing visas, give up being a foreigner, become a resident of this other country, and begin to do the things that people who immigrate and acclimate do. It's hard for me to imagine myself like the Dominicans in my neighborhood, who still speak Spanish to one another but see themselves as the fathers and grandfathers of gringos and don't find it unbearable to imagine that one day they'll be buried in the vast, desolate cemeteries of Queens. And then there's Cruz, who insists over the phone that he wants to study film in Warsaw or Berlin when he finishes his degree in Guadalajara. He has suggested more than once that I stop talking nonsense about us winning the War of Independence and claim the

European citizenship I'm due, as the son of a refugee from the Spanish Civil War.

So here I am, shuffling papers and collecting documentation to become a little bit gringo (though the gringos stole half a country from us in a catastrophic, extortionate war that we lost) and fully Spanish (though the war with Spain is the only one we ever won). What a blow to the ego when even Mexico beats you on the battlefield.

I tell myself it doesn't matter: nothing is changed by having documents that better reflect the life you're leading. Inés tells me so, too, at the time of day that makes life worth living, when we talk in low voices so as not to wake the children. She touches my face as she says it. Cruz doesn't say anything when I talk to him and complain that I don't have time to read because I'm collecting papers, making appointments, printing things to prove I would be a tolerable U.S. resident and a worthy Spaniard. His response is silence, and when I ask whether he's still there, he says he's listening. (Our children don't know us at all, obviously. Or they stop knowing us as they grow up a little and become disenchanted. They believe that the rage they see as our dominant trait serves only to teach them, groom them, bestow on them the privilege of being survivors, not realizing that the same rage, given the right circumstances, would enable us to kill for them without flinching.) The gringa immigration lawyer tells me so, too, with the slight tilt of her head and the uncomfortable smile that appears on her face when she can't understand what I'm saying: it makes no sense to her that anyone would object to being a resident of the United States.

And I get it: gaining one nationality doesn't mean losing another; being resident of one place doesn't mean you can't go back someplace else. Unexpectedly, though, I feel this shift deep in my bones. Two passports and a residency card are the equivalent of citizenship in Atlantis. Something that has lasted all my life will soon cease to exist, will be classified as memory. It's not as if I'm a mariachi, a bullfighter, or center forward on the Mexico national team, but I was entirely Mexican for almost fifty years, and now, though I never wished or planned for it, I'll be something else—I know it's silly, that it's a good thing for the family, but it's also the mark of something I can't explain.

IT WASN'T A BAD HARVEST, in the end. Zuloaga rounded up nine men at the Casas Grandes barbecue, enough to spare himself the charade of a banquet in the next town. His recruits were green, to be sure. The city's older settlers, already wise to him, sent only their most witless sons to the lieutenant colonel's soiree. Everyone came out a winner. Zuloaga had underlings to boss around, and the settlers would make men of their idiot offspring.

The barbecue had begun at one. By six, after the ingestion of vast quantities of beer heavily spiked with sotol, it was a cinch to convince the group that tiptoeing for their horses and heading into the hills to fire off their rifles was a better plan than going home and getting an earful from their mothers for being drunk. With all due respect, said the lieutenant colonel, if your moms are Chihuahuan, I'd take the Apaches any day.

The lieutenant colonel, the justice of the peace, the kid, and the retired general got the brave warriors out of the plaza as best they could, and they all hit the road before hangovers and second thoughts could set in. They were about two leagues north of Casas Grandes, at the Tinajas fork, when the justice headed back to town and the retired general took his leave to visit his relatives. It was deepest night, and cold. The next ten hours will make all the difference, said the general to his son. The lieutenant colonel simply nodded, conscious of the fragile equilibrium to be maintained: the first camp had to be set up far enough away that the warmth of home was no longer a temptation, but close enough that the men could get an early start the next day. The crucial point, the old man insisted, was to wake them when they were still drunk, so that their spirits didn't flag until it was full daylight and it was too shameful to contemplate leaving the expedition under everyone's gaze.

Zuloaga knew that half of his militia had supplied themselves with extra bottles of sotol before leaving town. It was a good idea to keep them drunk, he thought. He hurried them as fast as he could to Cerros Prietos, ignoring their drinking. Once they were deep in the real badlands they would get a lesson in discipline.

It was December: dusk came early and dawn late. In Cerros Prietos he marshaled his men in an empty stable yard. But first he had the courtesy to knock at the ranch house door to attempt to inform them that the Chihuahua state irregulars were going to borrow it for a few hours, knowing no one would answer. Marching double-time through Capulín and Corralitos, he had noticed that beyond Casas Grandes it wasn't just the goteras that were empty but the settlements, too.

After sending cowboys and horses to the stable—the cold was making itself felt—Zuloaga ordered the kid to heat up the leftovers from the barbecue. He himself passed out rations, affecting a rapidly waning good cheer. His aim was to gauge the mood of the nine men. He didn't plan even to learn their names until he was sure they were staying.

The kid spread his blanket roll alongside the lieutenant colonel's, and Zuloaga didn't ask him to move over with the other men.

HECTOR EZGUERRA PROVIDED FOR CAMILA as solemnly as a man who has sworn an oath, but also with some reluctance, since it was an inescapable fact that the woman hadn't procreated with his father: in truth, she was nothing to him. He had a nice room fixed up for her and he fed her, but he stripped her unceremoniously of all the powers she had wielded during her husband's long decline, with the rigor and furtive relish she brought to everything. Camila reverted to her childhood state: the masters' table, the goteras. Relieved of her duties, she must have been as bored as any woman of means in the world in 1837.

S. M. BARRETT, SCHOOL SUPERINTENDENT of Lawton, Oklahoma, and occasional English–Spanish interpreter for the U.S. Army's 18th Cavalry Regiment at Fort Sill Military Base, was making tea on the woodstove in his office when the Apache Asa Daklugie, who was standing at the window, said in an ironic tone, as if already exasperated: Look who's coming. The gringo, who was carefully packing dried chamomile flowers and mint leaves into a little net bag, replied: It can't be.

Barrett was an inquisitive sort, but no one who knew him would have described him that way. He had learned early on that persistence and discipline were excellent safeguards for a slim, pockmarked man in a world of opportunists—namely, the towns growing up around military bases in the western United States at the turn of the twentieth century. He persisted in his task with a resolve unique to glasses-wearing gringos. Settling his spectacles on the bridge of his nose, he said nothing until the net bag was packed full and the water had boiled. He filled the teapot, dropped in the herbs, and put on the lid. Nor did he say anything as the tea steeped or when he finally poured it into two pewter mugs. Only then did he go over to the window to see the rider battling the snow falling heavily on the plain.

Your uncle? he asked Asa Daklugie. The Apache closed his eyes in assent and recognition of the rider's stubbornness, at once admirable and maddening. Barrett handed one of the cups to his guest. Vaya manera de cuidarse una gripe, he said as if to himself, in his book-learned Spanish. What a way to nurse a cold. Asa shrugged. It's as if you don't know him, he said. I don't, said Barrett. Who does? replied the other man. Barrett answered, If anyone does, it's you.

Asa Daklugie shrugged again, took a noisy sip from his cup, and went to sit in one of the rockers in the parlor, ready for the work session from which he'd erroneously thought he'd been reprieved. Barrett stood for a moment longer with his forehead pressed to the glass, his cup cradled in his hands. He nudged up his glasses again.

There was a fierceness about the rider even though he was past seventy, his head cleaving the churning snow resolutely, his legendary mane flying behind him like a giant owl, his shoulders straining forward to command the obedience of the stocky plains pony he was riding even though he could have had a regular horse. He ate up the distance at an absurd speed on the icy road.

The rider didn't pull up until he was right at the door to Barrett's house, as if he intended to mow the place down rather than simply arrive. He dismounted in a leap. Barrett scratched his face. You say he has a fever? he asked Daklugie. Maybe he'll die from sheer cussedness, said Asa.

The gringo set his cup on the table beside his rocker and went to open the door. The rider was bent over, brushing off his snow-caked clothes, slapping at his moccasins. He looked up and then stood, though he was so short it made little difference. His mouth was hard, the corners turned down. It wasn't just that he had lost all his teeth. He was a man who had killed and seen people killed countless times, a clenched fist, ghost of the longest, motherfuckingest war of all time, last survivor of the bloodbath that began in Tenochtitlan in 1521: the man who ultimately lost the last battle for America.

He fixed his right eye on the gringo; the left had been staring in whatever direction it chose for years. Barrett was thirty years younger, almost a foot and a half taller, and in good health. Even so he felt mortal fear, as he always did when the Apache's good eye plumbed the depths of his. He gave a forced smile. The old man sucked his bare gums, not smiling in return, and waved his right hand, which meant he was coming past and Barrett should stand aside. The gringo obeyed.

Geronimo, he said in greeting.

Barrett, the Apache replied, moving toward the stove as if it belonged to him. He took off his coat and hung it on a chair that he pulled out from the table.

Watching him remove the puttees, two strips of red wool wound around the upper part of his moccasins, Barrett asked in Spanish: Are those military turbans? Asa Daklugie spoke from his rocker, also in Spanish: They were part of Chato's scout uniform, and this bastard, no respect even for the dead, is wearing them as shin-warmers. Geronimo said something in Athabaskan to his godson, who cackled. And then to Barrett: Chato, Indio Chiricahua y Army Scout de los Estados Unidos. The superintendent was never sure what to read as sarcasm from the old man, so he chose to play naive. Shouldn't you be wearing them on your head? Your nephew tells me you're sick. Geronimo scratched an ear. He's my godson, not my nephew, he said, and added: If I put them on my head, I won't splash them when I piss. Daklugie laughed; the gringo didn't. I don't think you should be here, he said, you've got a fever.

We agreed to meet on Tuesdays, said the old man. For the past two months, they'd been meeting once a week to work on his autobiography, the story of the Apache prisoner of war who had become a global celebrity. Today his eyes were ringed in red, his nose raw, his skin yellow. The gringo didn't dare touch the old man's forehead. You can't work like this, he said, you're near eighty. Every single one of those years more motherfucking culeros y chingones than yours, said Geronimo. Barrett's college Spanish was no help to him here, so he turned to Daklugie, who translated: Every single one of those years interesting and beautiful. Barrett smiled; Geronimo thought him a half-wit. With a glance at Geronimo's godson, Barrett said in English: He's shaking with fever. He's Geronimo, replied the other man. Should I offer him a bed? Then, in his precarious Spanish: ¿Traigo el doctor? Daklugie raised his eyebrows and, looking at his uncle, said in Athabaskan: The gringo is asking whether you want to lie down and have him send for the doctor.

Geronimo doubled over in laughter. Aren't we going to work? he asked Daklugie in their language. The teacher says no, he doesn't want to be responsible for your health. The old man shrugged and began to wind Chato's turbans around his legs again. Asa said to the gringo: He refuses your offer, but he won't sleep in the barracks either. Stay here, insisted the gringo, I'll send for the doctor. The old man, who was already heading for the door, didn't even turn to look at him. He raised his palm in farewell. Asa Daklugie lifted the blanket from his own knees and put it around his godfather's shoulders. As Chief Juh's eldest son, he was the only human being who could get that close. Geronimo wrapped himself in the blanket.

Barrett walked to the window. The old man mounted the horse in a single leap, like a man of thirty, and set off as violently as he had arrived. If he dies on us, they'll throw me in jail, the superintendent said when Geronimo was once again a blur in the snow. Asa Daklugie opened his satchel and took out his notebook. Thumbing through it, he said: They'll probably give you a medal instead for doing what nobody else could.

IT WAS HARD FOR ZULOAGA to wake the Casas Grandes cowboys after a two-hour nap, even with the help of the kid, who had stirred the embers and put water on for coffee before the lieutenant colonel managed to separate himself from his quilt. At the delicate moment when eight half-asleep buckaroos were lined up outside the stable on their freshly saddled horses, Zuloaga noted that the kid had stationed himself and his nag in the middle of the road south, to dissuade anyone else who might seize the chance to go back. Zuloaga neither smiled nor thanked him. All he said was: We're one down.

MISTRESS PRUDENCE HAD GROWN UP on a Pennsylvania dairy farm, tending to her Quaker father's cows, so she had insufferable stores of energy and red, calloused hands. She took possession of the house as if she knew what Chihuahua was and what it was good for. Camila would have joined in her orgy of self-inflicted suffering in the name of Quaker thrift if she had been asked to, but the establishment of a utopia of milk on the Ezguerra ranch demanded her exclusion.

In the mornings, she sought refuge in the kitchen to eat breakfast with the few remaining maids. By that time, Mistress Prudence was in the corrals. From the kitchen, Camila watched her return, caked in shit. She bathed with dipperfuls of cold water, marched into the children's room, and got them up to be crammed with the milk and oatmeal she cooked for them without Eduviges's help. Is that what they have for breakfast? asked Camila the first time she saw it. Every day, the cook replied. Poor things, no wonder they never make a peep. Then, packing a lunch of bread, cheese, and more milk, the woman loaded the younger children in a wagon that she pulled behind her as she went about the rest of her chores: weeding the tomato patch, planting pumpkins in an empty field, painting swaths of the house that would likely peel in the sun even before winter came.

The oldest boy, dressed like a little rancher, trailed her and the wagon all day, helping with stoic solemnity. He was in charge of feeding his younger siblings. With their filthy faces and fingernails, they were like orphan children, climbing in and out of the wagon to play among themselves in troubling silence.

Watching them pass by on their way to the yard was by far the liveliest part of Camila's day. She took walks, wrote endless letters she didn't always send, helped make dinner before the family gathered at the kitchen table with scrubbed faces. She preferred to eat standing up by the window, observing the oppressive silence of the clan and the discomfort of Eduviges and her helper, who found the cutlery taxing: they weren't earning a peso more and they couldn't even enjoy their meal the way God intended. When Hector and Mistress Prudence shut themselves in their room after the children had gone to bed, Camila could hear them talking and laughing. She would gaze at her hands, set down the book she was reading, and look in the mirror.

Camila had brought the Ezguerra Parletts to Janos the Sunday after their arrival for a few hours of entertainment. In a community usually suffocated by the harshness of the land, it was a time when spirits briefly lifted. It didn't go well. The fact that the master and mistress played with the children outside the church instead of going in for mass; Mistress Prudence's disgust as she sank a spoon into her fruit compote before rejecting it; her ghoulish smile when she took the little mug of chocolate frothed with cool water and left it untouched; the rattlesnake-like relish with which she snatched from her oldest son the caramel-filled cone a lady had given him—all of this sparked unease among the townspeople, not tempered even by their surprise at discovering that the family spoke English among themselves. Camila, who had no idea that sugar embodied the shitstorm of slavery for Mistress Prudence, couldn't understand the Quaker woman's obsessive hatred of sugar consumption. Meanwhile, the gringa didn't understand that the Jarochos who cut cane in the fields of San Lorenzo weren't slaves—or not quite, anyway; they were just poor. Camila decided she would never bring the family back to town again. She relaxed only once they had disappeared into Don Leopoldo's buggy and clay pitchers of sotol made an appearance.

The Ezguerra Parletts didn't return to Janos the following Sunday or the next, and Camila reverted to catching an early ride to mass in a cart with the ranch hands and cooks. But no puritanism could long endure the Herculean loneliness of a ranch in deepest Chihuahua. The family began to turn up again on Sundays at the tables on First, dressed in black and white like priests instead of ranchers. The master appeared in a frilled shirt, narrow-brimmed fedora, and string tie, the mistress in a getup with so many petticoats, flounces, and trimmings that she resembled a spoiled eggplant. The little boys were dressed like miniature Quakers, the baby in an untidy white frock.

They reached the plank tables in Don Leopoldo's buggy just after midday and sat at the corner of a table eating watermelon from their own garden without sharing or talking with anyone. Hector and Mistress Prudence drank coffee from a flask; the children drank milk, also from the ranch. If Hector had matters to discuss with anyone in town, he went about it quickly, leaving his family at their table. When he was done, their departure was announced with nothing but a tip of his hat. Mistress Prudence sometimes smiled her frightening smile. By the time they left, Camila—already feeling at the back of her neck the tickle of aguardiente drunk from a small clay cup—would say that everything that gave her pleasure in life had gone to shit the day they unpacked their miserly luggage.

Toward the end of her time in Janos, Camila wrote long letters to her aunt and uncle in Casas Grandes, offering herself as governess to the grandchildren who must be multiplying in the house now that her cousins were grown and married; she wrote to Hector's half brother, pleading as tactfully as she could for a job at a school in the city where he was council member; she wrote to the Sacred Heart boarding school to see if they needed someone to help in the classrooms of Tepic.

The replies never came, or they had nowhere to go, because when the neighbor from Delicias who traveled slowly around the state delivering mail reached the Ezguerra ranch in the year of Hector and Mistress Prudence's arrival, what he found was a house burned to the ground and corrals in ruins, a nesting ground for coyotes and rattlesnakes.

AS I WRITE, IT IS 130 YEARS after Geronimo's most celebrated surrender, on March 25, 1886, in Cañón de los Embudos in the western

Sierra Madre. He surrendered in the state of Sonora, in Mexico, to U.S. Army General George Crook. The act was irrelevant: a perfunctory ceremony performed by two leaders basically powerless outside their own groups, far from anywhere that mattered. Geronimo and General Crook knew the surrender wouldn't last, but they both needed a break, and it was furnished by the mountain capitulation of the most recalcitrant of the Chiricahuas. Geronimo avoided capture by the Mexican army, and Crook chalked up a victory to boast of upon his return to the United States. The act, a pure formality, went down in history nonetheless because a secretary recorded Geronimo's official words acknowledging his defeat. He said: "Once I moved like the wind. Now I surrender to you and that is all." He turned himself in with thirty-six warriors described by General Crook's press attaché as "the best constituted group of human beings I ever saw."

In May 1885, ten months before Geronimo's surrender in Cañón de los Embudos, a relatively insignificant incident caused the Chiricahua Apaches to flee the San Carlos reservation where they had been confined for two years, living peacefully, though in humiliating and insalubrious conditions.

The Apaches were mountain people, and mountains in Arizona and New Mexico contained valuable minerals, so the United States government had resettled them at gunpoint in San Carlos, a malaria-stricken wasteland around Turkey Creek Canyon in what is now eastern Arizona. The person charged with overseeing their welfare and making sure they stayed put was an incompetent and corrupt officer, Britton Davis. Things got out of hand when he tried to punish the Apaches after the chiefs on the reservation at the time—Naiche, Nana, Mangus, Chihuahua, Loco—spent a night drinking. A couple of army scouts by the name of Mickey Free and Chato (a Chiricahua, so a turncoat) accused Geronimo of leading the drinking session.

Geronimo, who for once in his life had behaved himself but who was desperate to regain free run of the Mexican Sierra Madre, did his best to convince the chiefs to flee with him. Except for Naiche, who at fifty was a bit younger than Geronimo, the other chiefs were old men. They said no, probably knowing they were sealing his fate if it was true that Chato and Mickey Free had spoken out against him. Geronimo was a war shaman, not a chief. He didn't have a band to aid him in his flight; if he escaped alone with his family he wouldn't survive in the Sierra Madre, where most food came from raids on Sonora ranches. Like so many people in his world, the chiefs must have been sick of him.

Two days after the drinking session and one day after the council at which the possibility of escaping the reservation was discussed and dismissed, Geronimo spotted a group of soldiers approaching on the horizon. They were going about some unrelated business, but Geronimo gathered the chiefs again to report that the soldiers were coming to arrest them all because he had killed Chato and Mickey Free the night before. It was a lie: Geronimo hadn't killed anyone, and the scouts were sleeping off their own hangovers in the San Carlos barracks. But the chiefs believed him. They bolted on foot because they saw this as war, and Apache military parties demanded greater mobility than even horses could provide. All of them ran together at their legendary pace, children and old people alike.

The May 1885 escape was one of the culminating moments of Geronimo's military career. Although the soldiers heading for Turkey Creek weren't looking for a fight, when they reached San Carlos the reservation was empty. Britton Davies mustered extra mounted troops and headed straight into the mountains to hunt the Indians.

With Davies and his men within sight, the Apache chiefs broke up into small bands. Chihuahua, the big chief at the time, entrusted

Geronimo with the children in the group, maybe as a form of punishment, instructing him to take them and create a few hours' diversion that would allow the rest of the Chiricahuas to escape. If he were captured, he would be sent back to the reservation but the others would be safe; if he managed to escape—Chihuahua wouldn't have given the order if he'd thought it couldn't be done—he would catch up with them later in the safety of the Sierra Madre.

In an operation of unprecedented virtuosity, the war shaman got the soldiers to follow his trail, and—entirely on foot, accompanied only by the children—had them riding north, south, east, and west not simply for a few hours but for twenty-four days and four hundred and fifty miles. When he was sure that the rest of the Chiricahuas were in Mexico, he headed south along a path of solid rock, where his band would leave no trace. The gringo soldiers, convinced they were pursuing a lethal attack force and not a bunch of children led by a grandfather, had to accept that their enemies had bested them again.

The Apaches' military skills were so radical that there's always an air of the supernatural to the stories that are told: accounts by pursuers, terrified press reports of their deeds, anthropologists' interviews with war veterans in the 1930s. Geronimo's escape demonstrates their reliance on certain procedures. It isn't that they could endure anything, of course, as the mythology we've constructed around them suggests. It's that in some contexts the Apaches were simply invincible. One of these was flight.

At the beginning of the nineteenth century, when the balance of power between Apaches and Mexicans was tilting toward the former, it wasn't unusual for some big chief to assemble a troop of horsemen capable of challenging and defeating the Mexicans in open battle. Mangas Coloradas was the last chief able to raise a genuine

Apache cavalry. Later generations headed by Victorio, Cochise, Nana, Chihuahua, and finally Juh, Geronimo, Mangus, and Naiche, had to develop different skills because the perpetually embattled Chiricahuas couldn't compete with the capacity of the Mexicans and the Americans to raise endless new troops.

After the assassination of Mangas Coloradas, the Chiricahuas made themselves into perfect guerrilla warriors, honing the ability to attack in small groups and nimbly flee. They never fell upon a group of enemies who could beat them in pitched battle; after an attack they were nowhere to be found. It's true that an Apache could cross the mountains at astonishing speed, running at a sustained pace matched only by their mortal enemies, the Raramuris, but their greatest skill was the ability to erase their own tracks and disappear into their surroundings, sometimes lying flat on the ground mere inches from the hooves of their enemies' horses. Warrior, adolescent, child, or grandmother: a Chiricahua Apache was a defense machine. They didn't all fight, but they all knew how to conduct themselves so the warriors could do their work around them. Apache children didn't cry; Apache grandmothers could sit perfectly still for hours, hidden behind a giant cactus or mistaken for a stone. From the time a Chiricahua child was seven or eight, every move they made was focused on developing these skills.

During their final push to keep Apachería for themselves, the Chiricahuas lived on raids, in the grips of a destructive fever that devastated northern Chihuahua and Sonora, southern Arizona and New Mexico. In this blood-drenched, bullet-riddled period, in addition to stealing livestock and goods they couldn't produce as mountain nomads, they seized as many children as possible. They took women as hostages as well, in order to exchange them when they could for their own women, lest they be sent to convents in the Mexican interior to be trained as maids and sold as de facto slaves. But the children they made their own.

As soon as they were captured, the children were generally stripped naked, covered in mule grease, and tied to a stake in the sun to darken their skin. They were left for a long time without food, as if they were being cleansed from the inside out—the acclimation process wasn't pleasant. When they were brown-skinned and nearly dead of starvation, they were assigned to some grandmother, who slowly accustomed them to their new diet and taught them to speak Athabaskan. To toughen them up, they were brutally tested, and they faced the scorn of the other children if they didn't make the grade. When at last it was decided that they were more or less broken in, they were given to a family where they were treated exactly the same as the parents' natural children.

It's true that an Apache child's upbringing was infinitely harsher than that of a criollo or gringo child, but it's also true that every Mexican or American who spent time living with the Chiricahua said the same thing in the testimonies they left: that the amount of time and care parents lavished on their children was the most striking thing about Apache culture. Chief Nana, a figure of terror outside his community, was remembered by Apache children interviewed years later as the sweetest old man and a great clown who took the time to tell them stories when their parents were busy. An Apache childhood must have had its appealing side. To avoid being rescued, child captives often hid in the mountains when Mexican or gringo soldiers arrived. In the event that they were found and returned to their parents, they commonly ran away again to the mountains to rejoin their chosen people.

TEN MONTHS AFTER GERONIMO'S LEGENDARY escape with the San Carlos reservation children, the few Chiricahuas still loyal to him must have been desperate. In their haven of the Sierra Madre, the Apaches had been able to move freely and make their own choices for generations. The mountain provided them with water, shade, and grazing for the cattle they sacked from Sinaloa ranches. But by the late nineteenth century, life was hard in the highlands: there was no corn, no yucca flowers or mesquite beans, no agave root or pumpkin. Winter was brutal. The Mexican army, always crueler than its American counterpart, had become more professional with the passage of time and now was constantly on their heels. The camps were too high for foraging, and they couldn't ride down to steal cattle from the rancherías. The land that had been their refuge could be reclaimed at any moment by the insatiable Mexican Republic, which at some unspecified moment had decided it had to govern every square inch of the vast territory where it lay, as if it needed the impenetrable heights of the Sierra Madre. (It didn't. They're still unoccupied.)

The gringos were no drink of water, but living under them meant only misery and confinement on the reservation, not death. The Mexicans, who had fought a longer and bloodier war against the Apaches, were waging a rational and systematic extermination campaign in which peace talks were a thing of the past. And so the Chiricahua leaders began to return to the United States with their families, and the gringo army captured them as soon as they crossed the border and escorted them back to San Carlos. Geronimo was left with only a handful of warriors—his family had returned to Arizona with Chihuahua's family and was kidnapped like all the rest and brought to the reservation. By the time Crook offered a surrender that meant no one would have to die, Geronimo accepted it. It was a tactic typical of his strategic mind: a temporary political concession that allowed him to keep most of his people together. The warriors who followed him to the San Carlos reservation would escape back to the Mexican Sierra Madre several times before their definitive surrender and defeat.

So the surrender is remembered as a central moment in the history of the Apache Wars mostly because it was thoroughly documented: the photographer Camillus Fly captured the precise instant when Geronimo uttered a sentence so broken and sad that there's no way we can forgive ourselves for it, even though the Chiricahuas were a genuine terror: "Once I moved like the wind. Now I surrender to you and that is all."

Geronimo was an eloquent man. In his many surrenders, in his moving and hair-raising memoirs dictated to S. M. Barrett, and in the transcripts of his conversations with President Theodore Roosevelt, who I think genuinely sympathized with him, he gave proof over and over again of the soaring lyricism of his speech. He was a man of arms and a man of the mountains, but also a sophisticated orator. His statement of surrender to Crook begins with an elegiac evocation of his community's way of life, his tone the same as it must have been when he addressed his warriors as they prepared for combat, or when he told the children stories about Coyote, the Apache Ulysses. Oddly, it's the first part of his statement that's always quoted: "Once I moved like the wind," when it's the second part that matters, the moment when the declaration collapses, imitating the abrupt end of a way of life. Now I give up, that's all. It's a sentence that drops like the swift sun of the tropics; like an eagle pierced by some idiot's bullets; like Cuauhtemoc, the first towering American captain to surrender to a white man. Cuauhtemoc meant Falling Eagle, Falling Sun. No further elaboration is necessary. Geronimo's words—the words of a man of substance—are a monument in themselves: "Now I surrender to you and that is all."

A shaman, according to Claude Lévi-Strauss, is a person who has a concrete relationship with language, because he uses it for healing, as a tool and as medicine. To the shaman, words aren't just words, but a scalpel for slicing and reorganizing what's in this world, for cutting and binding; a phenomenon with power over all other phenomena—something truly sacred. In his *Structural Anthropology*, Lévi-Strauss says that scientists' problem with shamans is that they really do heal people.

The language of a man like Geronimo didn't describe reality; it transformed it. To say "Now I surrender to you and that is all" is to recognize that next comes a wall that can no longer be hurdled, and all alternatives are at an end because everything is shot to hell. Our inheritance, wrote an anonymous chronicler after the fall of Tenochtitlan in 1521, is a net full of holes. There is an arc of 350 years between the two statements. It was Geronimo's fate to realize that the net of holes was gone, too, and his people were clinging to the final threads. He belonged to an anachronism, a nation that found itself on the wrong side of the net. A nation dangling, barely attached to the world.

He let go because it was all he could do, but he didn't really surrender. What he was doing was graver and more beautiful. He was declaring the end of something vast that had begun when the first Asian voyager spied North America and saw that it was good. His brusqueness is a gesture of resistance when nothing else remains, when the earth beneath one's feet is now called something else. Saying *that is all* is to say: My silence is your curse and that will be all. America, America, that is all.

IT WAS EVENING WHEN THEY got to Janos. Zuloaga was sure the sense of outrage at the kidnapping of a local woman would make it easy to recruit a few more men to equal the dozen he judged he needed to set off into Apache territory, allowing for a few desertions.

He found that Janos had no prefect—it had almost nothing at all—but there was a local official who acted as mayor and garrison chief. He received Zuloaga sitting in a rather stark and gloomy room with the town priest. Both confirmed the story he'd been told in Casas Grandes, with a troubling addendum: it had been almost five months since Señora Camila had disappeared without a trace. No trace? asked Zuloaga, surprised. Nothing but a few bits of clothing; they carried her right off, said the priest, his eyes on the floor. And he went on: What will you need to rescue her if she's still alive? Someone who knew her well, the lieutenant replied, someone who can take me to the ranch to see her room and tell me all they know about her.

Between the two of them they told him everything they could, which was little more than what Camila's family had told him. The truth is, no one knew her well, said the priest. We exchanged words now and again and everyone thought she was clever, but she didn't have a friend among us. In Janos people seemed to have a better impression of the widow than in Casas Grandes, but maybe that was only because the terrain was harsh and she had been, too. She was a strong-willed woman, said the priest. What do you mean? asked the lieutenant, raising an eyebrow. She always walked tall, never complained about anything, got along better with the Indian women than she did with us—I think because she was half raised by the Jicarillas of Casas Grandes.

Zuloaga sighed: Are there any Indians left at the rancherías? A few, said the official. Apaches? Not a one. Will you take me to see the house? asked the lieutenant. It burned down, the other man said, everything burned, the whole ranch blazed all day and all night. Didn't you put it out? asked the lieutenant. No water for that here. What about sand? The ranch was on the prairie. Was? No one has come to claim it.

Zuloaga took out his tobacco pouch. Think on it: Who else can take me? he asked. After the attack the town emptied out, said the priest, nobody will want to go. The lieutenant, exasperated, stared at the tips of his boots, selected a paper, and piled it with tobacco. The priest said: I'm almost sure Elvira went to the ranch sometimes to see her. She's a nun, settled here for reasons unknown; she would've been making her charity rounds. Where does she live? asked the lieutenant. Just up the way, in the green house, you can't miss it. I need an Apache, too, said the lieutenant, you flat out don't have a single one? The official said: There are old folks and children in the goteras, but they're mixed, more Pima than Janero. The priest said: The fiercest ones took to the mountains when rations stopped coming from the capital.

The lieutenant focused on rolling his cigarette, licking the edge of the paper. I was told the Apaches took cattle, which means they can't have gone very fast, he said, but I don't know the terrain past Ánima: Do you have trackers? he asked. If we had, we would have gone after her ourselves, said the official. Zuloaga raised his eyebrows so high his hat twitched. No one went looking for her? The official, sweating more than was normal on a cold day, said that the Ezguerra ranch was remote and it had been several days before they realized that Señora Camila's remains weren't among those buried. What about the garrison? Weren't there soldiers at the presidio? They were called to California, explained the priest, something about protecting the coast from a Russian invasion.

The lieutenant nodded in resignation. The same thing had happened in San Buenaventura. It's been some time since there were nacionales here, said the priest. The young people leave, they don't come back, said the official, then they turn up in Ciudad Chihuahua or even Durango or Zacatecas, they send for their wives and they're never seen again.

Zuloaga lit his cigarette. Ta bien, he said. Then at least you can help me with something else: I need four or five men with guns and horses. The priest offered to call mass and ask for volunteers from the congregation. But it won't be easy, said the official. What? Calling mass? asked the lieutenant. No, said the priest obligingly, we still have bells. Don't be a fool, said the official, it won't be easy to get anyone to join up. Oh yes, of course, said the priest.

Zuloaga rose from his chair. Are there any prisoners left you could loan me as conscripts? There're two Yaquis who've been in lockup as long as I can recall, brothers, I think, I can't even remember what they did, the official said. Who has the key? asked the lieutenant. I don't. So who looks after them? No idea, must be Elvira, I guess. The nun? asked the lieutenant. The priest nodded: She brings them food, empties their little shit box, does her duty as a nun. What order is she from? The men of Janos exchanged glances. She isn't a *nun* nun, explained the official, she's a zarzuela singer from Guadalajara, she used to put on shows when we still had people here. The priest continued: She arrived with a bag of costumes and one day she dressed up in the nun's habit and now she thinks she's a nun.

Zuloaga pressed his temples. Is this the same person who was a friend of the woman who was taken? Both men nodded. They call her Elvis, said the priest. And she lives in a green house nearby? So long as she hasn't up and gone. And she's a nun but not a nun? asked the lieutenant colonel, staring at the ceiling. That's right, said the priest. Very strange, said Zuloaga. The official hurried to explain: Not really, that's how it is when towns empty out, people leave and other people take their jobs. The lieutenant looked at the priest: What about you? Me? Are you a *priest* priest? The man waggled his head a little, shrugged his shoulders. To all intents and purposes, he said.

Before Zuloaga left he asked whether it had rained since the woman was taken. Not here, said the official, this is Janos. Not a drop since she disappeared? Not a one.

THE WORST OF IT ALL is that it was foreseen; everybody knew it was going to happen and no one did a thing. One afternoon when Hector Ezguerra returned from the fields full of an unfamiliar virile energy that didn't suit him at all, Camila got the feeling she had on days when things went hopelessly off course, a hollowness between her pubic bone and navel. The master was behaving oddly, and there on the fringes of Janos where so little ever happened, this should have been enough to persuade her to throw a few things in a bag and head to town on foot, where she could wait for a coach to take her to Casas Grandes, Chihuahua, even Mexico City. But she did none of that.

Hector wasn't behaving oddly, exactly. He was voluble, excited, speaking in English to his oldest son as if seeking a comradeship he'd never looked for before, as if he'd suddenly understood that this milk-fed extension of his Quaker wife was a man and had to be urgently taught the world's rules for men in the company of men. At some point, scooping up brown beans with a tortilla, he said in Spanish: Pedro y yo matamos un salvaje. Pedro and I killed a savage. He said it in the fatuous way of someone boasting. Camila and the cook stopped eating mid-bite. What do you mean, a savage? asked the widow. An Indian, said the ranch owner, he wasn't one of ours. How do you know? she asked, insistent. We buried him by the creek, none of the field hands knew him.

Camila kept the cook company as she washed the pots. Neither of them said anything. Every so often the widow wiped her hands on her apron as if they were wet. Are you nervous? asked the cook at some point. Who wouldn't be? she replied. They went to bed without speaking about what had happened, each knowing the other knew.

In the morning Camila found the kitchen girl making coffee. When she inquired after Eduviges, the girl said the cook had gone back to town.

Camila knew she should do the same, she had thought about it all night, but she didn't. Despite it all, she had a home, a place to lay her head. She expected a job offer soon, and she could move on to her new destination with all the powers vested in her by widowhood, infinitely more respectable than she had been as an orphan. And there were the bonds of loyalty, always inconvenient: if the murdered Indian's people came back, they would discover a ranch with few hands and a single criollo old enough to handle a pistol. Somebody had to stay in case he was killed, somebody who at least spoke Spanish so those children wouldn't die of hunger, or of eating nothing but oatmeal. She had wrangled cattle on the ranch before and she could make it work, even if it meant enduring Mistress Prudence and her garden.

She made inquiries among the hands. The corral keeper told her what Pedro and his sons had told him. The savage was alone, and Hector had come upon the man as he was mounting Hector's horse. Hector drew his gun without a thought and shot him in the back of the head. Camila asked whether Pedro and his sons had searched the hills, whether they were sure the savage was alone. The ranch hand was calm: Pedro had scoured the borders of the ranch and beyond, and the only tracks he had found were the dead man's. Not the smallest leaf bent, my lady, not a twig broken, he said. Camila dared to ask the question that had been roiling her belly since the night before. The Indian, was he one of those from up there? she ventured, unable to speak the word *Apache*. The ranch hand just stood staring at her, tugging at an ear, and then he turned away, claiming he had work to do. Was the Indian buried properly? Nice and far away? she asked, out of breath now as she hurried after him. That's what they say, he replied. Pedro knows what he's doing.

Camila returned to what had been her husband's office and then hers, where the new master kept his very complicated accounts with ratlike avidity. She opened the cabinet of rifles and pistols and saw that Hector had hauled everything out for his workday on the ranch. If he had decided to put rifles in the hands of his vaqueros, either he was scared shitless or he didn't know anything about the history of Chihuahua.

Every day, Camila continued to check the gun cabinet, until on the tenth day she found it full again. Hector has Pedro, she thought, they know what they're doing. She told herself she could hold out a little longer, until the mail brought her the response she was waiting for.

KAW-TENNÉ WAS A NINETEENTH-CENTURY Mexican Apache, leader of a band of children and adolescents. He was part of a group of warriors who never came down out of the Sierra Madre and who watched Chiricahuas, Mexicans, and gringos pass through as patiently as somebody watching the neighbor kids wandering into the yard in search of a lost ball. Kaw-tenné's band was last seen in the canyons along the Bavispe River, in 1883. At that date it consisted of thirty-eight warriors—all male, nothing but adolescents and children—each on a horse or mule. They were driving branded cattle, probably stolen from a ranch in Sonora, when they rode into a stand of pine. No one ever saw them come out, or they came out one by one, dragged feet first by the proud horses of the nacionales, who must have been hunting them for years.

According to the last witness to their existence as a band—a band disturbingly reminiscent of the Children's Crusade, the Pied Piper of Hamelin, and so many other stories mistakenly labeled make-believe—they were all carrying new-model Springfield rifles with saber blades for lances, seized from the Mexican army.

Thirty-eight lances with bayonet blades imply the deaths of thirty-eight professional soldiers at the hands of a band of children. There's something righteous but also terrifying in that fact; a kind of admirable resistance, but also depravity. A soldier is sent for water, or rides with a couple of comrades carrying a message for a presidio commander in his saddlebags. Something moves on the horizon: thirty-eight children on horseback descend upon them, uttering war cries. According to the last witness to see them, the children were also carrying bows and quivers, revolvers at their waists.

Kaw-tenné's band, ghost ship in the fog, the innocence that we annihilated waking us with a cry in the night. That is all, America.

ZULOAGA DIDN'T RETURN IMMEDIATELY TO the empty town hall where he had assembled his men. He followed the traces of huarache footsteps along the only street in town and soon reached the goteras, much bigger and more sprawling than elsewhere in northern Chihuahua, though in a state of abandon like those throughout the region. For more than a century, Janos had been the Apache capital of the state. The remains of the Janeros' little mud houses were scattered over a wide, arid expanse, split by a dry creek bed through which a decent-size stream must have flowed in summer.

He crossed the whole desolate settlement with a kind of eagerness, following a thread of scattered voices. Over a rise in the ground, an old man sitting under a cottonwood stared at something indecipherable in the air. Around him ran a few children, clearly misbehaving. Zuloaga stuck his hands in his pockets and fixed something like a smile on his face as he walked the rest of the way.

Once he reached the old man, he touched the brim of his hat; the Indian nodded in reply. Zuloaga sat down beside him. The Indian kept staring into space, so the lieutenant took out his pouch of tobacco and offered it to him. The old man smiled; he was missing all his teeth. With hands so ravaged by arthritis they looked like two crustaceans, he motioned for Zuloaga to roll him a cigarette. The lieutenant did as he was asked, lighting the cigarette by scraping a match on the stone he was sitting on, then putting the lit cigarette in the old man's mouth. The Indian inhaled with relish, never touching the cigarette: one, two, three, four times. When he had finished, he flicked away the butt without using his fingers and crushed it with the heel of his huarache.

Are you a Janero? asked the lieutenant. The old man shook his head. Pima, he said, there are no more Janeros, the Apashees say working the soil is no job for a man. Zuloaga raised his eyebrows. That's what they say, he replied, feeling as if a certain trust had been established between them, but you and I know that ain't true. The Indian asked for another cigarette. The lieutenant rolled and lit it without a word. As he was about to put it in the Indian's mouth, the old man shook his head and raised one of his clenched hands, motioning for Zuloaga to put the cigarette between his claw fingers. When it was firmly in place he inhaled with puppylike pleasure. Then he waved the hand into which it was wedged. The lieutenant understood that he was being invited to smoke, too, and he would be told nothing if he didn't light a cigarette for himself.

He rolled one, lit it. I heard from the priest that they went up into the mountains, he said. The Indian shook his head: Into the mountains, but not around here. Some went to join the Chiricahua nearby and others went higher up, into the Mogollones. In Nueva México? That's where they are now: the Ojocalientes, the Gileños, the Pinaleros del Norte, the Janeros from around here, the Coyoteros from the other side of the mountains. Why is that? The old man shrugged. Do you know where they're gathering exactly? They're Apashees, they don't gather. So then? When they left they said the captains were talking about showing Sonora who's boss, they were done speaking Spanish, the Republic was all squawk and no scratch. So they do gather, said the lieutenant. They gather but only when it suits them, then they go their own way.

The lieutenant asked about the children. Pimas and a heap of Opatas from Sonora, the old man replied. They cross the mountains and come here because they don't want to be on the other side when the Apashees ride down. But is there any work here? asked the lieutenant. There are still Mexicans, they have their ranches, they need ranch hands and maids. The Mexicans, he continued, hate the Indian, but they can't live without him, and same goes for the Indian. The children were chasing a rag ball with sticks. Is there anyone left who could take me north? the officer asked. The old man took a long drag on his cigarette. He shook his head, half closing his eyes. All that's left here is fear. The Apashees' quarrel is with Sonora, not Chihuahua, but you see what they did to Ezguerra's son's family.

Who took Señora Camila? asked Zuloaga. They say it was a Gileño captain, tall as they come, and commander now of all the warriors. Did he take her or kill her? Nobody knows for sure, in town they're so scared they didn't go up to look for her. What about your people? They say if you start up toward Ojocaliente you can still find her clothes. Tell me about the Gileño. The old man glanced toward the mountains. He's no indio de razon, he said, I saw him here at the presidio just once or twice, when there were rations, he came down for his flour and beef, but he was born in the mountains and he stayed up there with his people, it only makes sense, he don't speak Spanish, he wants to show Sonora who's boss. Is he putting together an army? I tell you, the Apashees don't band together, each family is a band and the band is all there is, but they say the big man was born to be chief of chiefs. What do you mean? The old man shrugged. He asked the lieutenant to help him up. The women would be back soon and they would scold him if they found the children playing ball. What's his name? They used to call him Fuerte, because he's so big, but now they call him Mangas Coloradas, God knows why.

On his way back to the town hall, Zuloaga knocked on Señora Elvira's door, and she welcomed him in, delighted to talk to someone who wasn't a Yaqui prisoner.

THE MORNING APACHES ATTACKED the Ezguerra ranch, Camila had gone out for a walk in what the people of Janos called the hills, though it was a plain. So she never saw what the Apaches did to the people who, though not her family, had at least politely ignored her while they lived together for several months. She didn't see the fire. She didn't see the vaqueros shot in the head or Hector gutted with a knife. She didn't see the ranch hands hanging from trees or Mistress Prudence with her head crushed by a stone brought down over and over again until she was dead. Nor did she see the children—Conchos, Opatas, criollos, and gringos, it made no difference—shot. She didn't see the baby with its head dashed against the wall. She did hear the shots and shrieks, saw the smoke. She ran on, thinking of the mountains on the horizon, and when she had gone too far to turn back, she realized that she had made a terrible mistake; she should have headed south toward Janos even if she couldn't reach it: the Indians wouldn't go that way. She turned and saw the dust, felt the earth shake. This wasn't the charge of a band of Apaches, but a few warriors herding cattle at top speed, as many as they thought they could get away with before the townspeople reacted to the attack, as the poor woman believed they would.

Still running and alternately glancing forward and back, like Janus, she calculated the path of the horde behind her and turned toward the open prairie, hoping they wouldn't see her tracks, swallowed in the cloud of dust raised by cattle and horses.

Without stopping, she pulled off her black dress and removed her corset from under her petticoat. She wasted precious time unlacing her boots and hiding them in a thick patch of brush. Once she was up again and running with all her might, she didn't look back, but she clearly heard a group of horses breaking away from the herd of running cattle and swerving toward her. When the dust raised by the pounding of the horses' hooves began to sting her eyes, she threw herself on the ground and curled in a ball, hoping to be trampled to death.

Then she was yanked up by her braids, her neck wrenched, her legs kicking, her brown underskirts a flower in the wind. She wouldn't die trampled by horses' hooves. She thought: I'm a Chihuahuan, and she bore it. She dug the nails of both hands into the forearm lifting her. The pain shot down from her scalp, a hot iron splitting her spine, a spike in her buttocks. The man who had lifted her from the ground without stopping or dismounting felt the stab of Camila's fingernails and yanked harder. Raised up in the air, she bit him. He lifted her like a flag above him. For an impossible instant she was so high that she saw the head of the horse beneath her, the rider's interminable shoulders, other Apaches behind him laughing, the copper sulphate–colored heavens where she would go as soon as the son of a bitch who had lifted her so effortlessly cast her down upon the stones. She sank nails and teeth into him more fervently, so as to at least leave her mark on the bastard who'd forever had her name on his list of deaths. She tasted his blood in her mouth, warm and metallic. She felt him let her go.

Camila closed her eyes and flung out her arms to perish like a saint, trampled. It didn't happen: she dropped onto the horse's rump. The wooden frame of the saddle hurt her. The Apaches rode without seat or blanket because they wore leather pants. She wrapped her arms instinctively around the chest of the rider who had caught her. She dug in her fingernails, thinking that if he were taking her, she would get his nipples. He elbowed her in the ribs without letting go of the reins. She doubled over and thus got a second elbow in the nose that nearly made her faint. She let go of her captor's back and gripped the saddle frame, feeling a fiery throb in the bridge of her nose as her petticoat was soaked with blood. She tried to staunch the flow with one hand while clutching the saddle with the other. They were going so fast she was dizzy. Then she noticed another rider approaching; he took the reins of the horse on which she was mounted.

Her captor turned: he was so big that for a moment he seemed to absorb all the light in the desert. The giant stuck both hands down her bodice and yanked it apart. Her petticoat ripped down the middle. He pulled it off with a jerk and let it fall, doing the same with her underskirts, yanking at her drawers until they tore, throwing them on the ground. She was left naked.

WHEN MEXICAN HISTORIANS DESCRIBE the enemies of the Apaches, Mexican or American, they tend to categorize them as "white." In their eyes, all Mexicans and gringos are white—a tricky thesis to prove looking out the window of my office in Harlem, where most of my neighbors are either American or Mexican and only a few are white. U.S. historians are even more blinkered, if possible. They never refer to Mexicans as "white"; they describe only themselves that way. As they see it, the Apaches fought the Mexicans and the white man, as if the categories "American" and "white" were interchangeable, as if there had been no such thing as Black army troops—buffalo soldiers, as they were called—fighting the Apache Wars, let alone the Chinese and Filipinos who emigrated to what is today the U.S. Southwest in the nineteenth century. To divide this budding world into three ill-conceived categories—given that "Indian" is an imprecise name for the original population of an entire continent, "white" is a color, and "Mexican" is a demonym—is, to put it as cautiously and elegantly as possible, a crock of shit.

In the latter half of the nineteenth century, not all northern Mexicans were white, nor all U.S. Army soldiers. True, some settlers of Chihuahua and Sonora were the descendants of European immigrants, as were the first U.S. inhabitants of Arizona and New Mexico, and most of the Mexican army officers. But rank-and-file

Mexican soldiers included Indigenous people from all over the country, descendants of African slaves freed in 1821, and the sons of Chinese immigrants who had come to work on road crews and stayed: they weren't white.

On the other side it's the same story. Black soldiers first fought in the gringo army during the Civil War, and more than a few were posted to New Mexico and Arizona—there are plenty of pictures to prove it.

The war for Apachería was never between whites and Indians: it was between two mixed republics and an ancient nation with a single shared culture and language. The Indians didn't call the Mexicans white. They called them nakaiyé, those who come and go. They called the gringos indad, white-eyes, never white skins.

The Apaches never thought they were fighting whites. It was the white historians—Mexican and gringo—who believed the Apaches were fighting them.

ZULOAGA WOKE BEFORE THE COYOTES turned in for the night. He had chosen the room that must have been the mayor's office, because it had an armchair. When he got up, the recruit was no longer asleep on the floor, as he had been when the lieutenant got back from Elvira's house, fairly liquored up. The kid hadn't deserted: his blanket and musket were stowed in a corner. Zuloaga went into the council hall, where the rest of the vaqueros had dropped their saddles and spread their blankets. He counted six huddled bodies. Two down; not bad.

Out in the yard, the kid had lit a fire and was making coffee. The lieutenant noticed with satisfaction that it was really cold, and overcast, too; they would be able to ride all day. The kid noted the loss of a couple more nacionales apologetically. It's the musket, it's no fucking good, he said by way of explanation. Zuloaga poured coffee into a pewter mug. He didn't say that the loss of two men from a group who had signed on blind drunk struck him as paltry, but he reckoned the boy's loyalty was assured. He cradled the mug in his hands to warm them. He never put on his gloves until he'd smoked his first cigarette, so he didn't have to take them off again. You'll be my corporal, he said, and finally he asked the kid his name. Mauricio, the kid said. Mauricio what? Mauricio Corredor. The lieutenant smiled: Tarahumara. We call ourselves Raramuri, said the boy. How old are you? They took me in ten years ago. So you must be fourteen? Or thirteen, maybe. You look older. I haven't had it as easy as you, said the corporal.

They finished their coffee in a new, companionable silence. Then the lieutenant colonel rose and gave instructions: when the men got up, the coffee and whatever food there was should be warmed; they had to be given the royal treatment. Then Corredor should grab the two ugliest specimens and bring them to the local official's house to demand he help them round up provisions, enough to last to Santa Rita. It's not stealing, exactly, he said, but carry your guns where they can be seen. The Raramuri rolled his eyes. That's a long way, we'll need mules to carry it all. Round up some of those, too, said the lieutenant. I'm heading to the Ezguerra ranch. It's going to snow, the kid said, turning away. You can requisition some boots, added the lieutenant before he was gone; you can't be an irregular in huaraches. The Raramuri raised his right hand to indicate he'd heard.

Elvira was a cheerful woman in her fifties. The modest getup she'd been wearing when she answered the door the night before was at odds with her personality. She had on a very long black dress with cuffs and collar, and a bonnet that did little to hide her bowl cut. She looked like Joan of Arc, but heftier. She invited him in and served him a rather diabolical punch, poured from a stoppered flask full of fruit steeped in alcohol of unknown origin, the cinnamon barely cutting the bite. They had an almost normal conversation in which the fake nun declared herself pleased to visit the ranch with him and happy to introduce him to the Yaqui prisoners. At the end of the visit, tipsy on punch, she sang an aria or two from her repertoire, with the veiled sadness of one who once received ovations and who no longer sings, even to an all-hearing God. At the door, she bid Zuloaga good night and warned him he should talk to the Yaquis before he gave the order to free them. They're a couple of hell-dogs, she said.

He was therefore unprepared for the vision he encountered before dawn on the following day: a nun in habit, veil, and rosary, wrapped in a swashbuckler's cape out of Spanish farce and draped in a cartridge belt with a massive U.S.-made revolver hanging at her left hip. I'm left-handed, don't you know, mi general, she said when she saw Zuloaga's jaw drop. The officer just nodded, thinking: pinche goddamned Chihuahua, as he clapped his hat back on his head, murmuring that she could call him José María. Perfect, she said, and you can call me Sister or Elvis, my stage name.

They didn't talk much along the way, moving more slowly than the lieutenant would have liked in a fog that further obscured the shrouded landscape of the desert night. It was cold enough to freeze a bear. They arrived before the sun was showing on the horizon. Zuloaga took his time examining the blackened walls of the main house, removing his right glove to touch them. The roof beams had collapsed when the ceilings burned away, but the walls weren't charred. It hadn't been a raging inferno; the house was in ruins only because no one had come to fight the blaze.

It wasn't hard to find the adobe oven in the kitchen and then to divine the layout of the house. Stripped bare, it revealed its past. At first it had been one long gallery—oriented east to west to keep cool—to which a horseshoe of rooms had been added around an inner courtyard. Those pots used to hold orange trees, remarked the Sister as they looked through what had once been the kitchen windows. Zuloaga stepped out to touch one of the branches. They were only singed. If watered, the trees would put out new shoots in spring.

The biggest room, next to the kitchen in the main wing, must have been the master's office. As he examined the blackened spaces, emptied of furnishings, Elvira told him what she knew about the family. She crossed herself each time she stepped over a new threshold or mentioned someone killed in the raid. Hector and the gringa slept here, she said, making the sign of the cross in front of her face; they had some peculiar habits. What habits? asked the lieutenant. They slept in the same room, like poor people. Zuloaga was scandalized, but he didn't flinch: for this, too, independence had been fought and won. The room next door, in one of the arms of the horseshoe, was equally large. Narrow windows looked out onto the patio; there was an alcove for the washstand. It had been a bedroom for Ezguerra's successive wives, including Camila for the short time they were married, the Sister said. When the gringa arrived, they put the children here. Zuloaga examined the doorway between the two rooms. It was original to the house, but it had been recently modified. The upper part of the door opened, Elvira explained, like in a stable. Why is that? asked Zuloaga. The children slept alone, without a nursemaid. The lieutenant raised his eyebrows. I'm not surprised there was no love for them in town, he said, they didn't give jobs to anybody. The nun pursed her lips. And to think how little our Indians are paid, she said. Indeed. In a corner, twisted like something out of a nightmare, sat a single brass crib. From the marks on the floor, it looked as if two others, presumably still functional, had been stolen by someone who hadn't bothered to go searching for Camila in the mountains. Next were two all-purpose rooms used as storerooms: one for grain, the other for furniture and tools. Everything was charred; nothing of metal remained, no doubt carted off to other ranches.

On the far side of the horseshoe they found the parlor for receiving guests. The curtain rods were still in place: they were wrought iron, intended to support fabric heavy enough to keep out the summer sun. Next came the bathroom, its washstand and tub broken. Someone had stolen the woodstove for heating water. The door to the latrine, located in a little outdoor patio, had been burned, as had the shed itself. All that was left was a pit in the ground that didn't stink anymore, and some scorched nopales. In the spring they'll grow back, said the Sister. Then came a series of tiny rooms where some makeshift metal shelves still stood along with a few cots, burned to husks. The maids slept here, and so did Pedro, the ranch hand, and his children, who were like part of the family and were killed with them, said Elvira, crossing herself. The lieutenant went into Pedro's room. There was hardly space for a bedroll because of the storage shelves, built just under a meter high: the ranch hand had been obliged to crawl into his room to go to bed. Like part of the family, you say? asked Zuloaga. These rooms were separated from the final room in the house by a second bathroom, tiny and claustrophobic even though it had lost its roof, just an enclosure where you could dump a bucket of water over yourself. It hadn't had a stove. The servants' latrines were so far from the house that they had survived the fire intact.

Light was dawning on the horizon when they reached the last

room in the horseshoe. The sky, awash with orange, came in through a window stripped of glass, frame, and curtains. It was a big room, though not as big as the Ezguerras' or the children's. The floor was painted tile. Zuloaga noted that the room had recently been enlarged, a wall knocked down. This was where they put her, he said. Eyup, said the nun, rubbing her hands to warm them. They weren't bad people, the lieutenant went on, they stuck her here out of the way but they fixed the room up to make her comfortable, they weren't planning to kick her out. They could've treated her better, said the Sister. On the floor there was a rectangle where the tile still shone. Someone came to steal the bed, said the lieutenant. Then he walked to the window, at the foot of which he found a scrap of woven rattan. Part of her rocker, said Elvira, choked up.

Zuloaga sat in the window opening. The wall across from him was the only one that had truly burned. The other two were just sootstained, revealing the outline of a rather modest wardrobe. Stirring the debris with the tip of his boot, he found the locks to a chest of drawers amid the more obvious wreckage of the wardrobe. It struck him as noteworthy that it had stood in the place where there would normally have been a dressing table. He also found fragments of a frame. Was there a mirror hanging on the wall? he asked Elvira. It was always just propped on the dresser, she said. The lieutenant picked up the little piece of frame he'd found and sniffed it. Was she pretty? The fake nun shrugged. The lieutenant colonel decided that Camila must have been a woman without vanity but with self-esteem.

He sat down again in the window opening. The lady was a reader, he said, pointing to the scorched wall, look at the size of that bookcase. I told you, she used to be a teacher; I liked to visit her because she was the only person in the city with any notion of art. Janos isn't a city, said the lieutenant. It seemed like one until recently, replied the nun. And they cared about her, added the lieutenant, they gave her a giant window so she could read comfortably. More like to keep her out of the way, said Elvira, but it's true Hector sent for any books she wanted from the capital: she read them quick as a wink and loaned them to me. She was fluent in French, he said as if to himself. How do you know? asked the fake nun. There aren't enough novels in Spanish to fill a bookcase this size. Êtes-vous un lecteur de littérature? asked Elvira. He didn't understand a word, so he just put on his gloves again and said: Let's go see the Yaquis. Already? I have to get on my way north, he said, this woman might still be alive. How do you know? She had a world inside her head; people like that persevere.

Snow, when it comes, doesn't fall but simply appears. The first flakes materialized as they were mounting their horses. Though it was a long way, they galloped back. Cold as it was, Zuloaga reckoned he could work the horses harder before they were parched.

JOHN G. BOURKE, OF THE 3RD CAVALRY, Fort Craig, New Mexico, wasn't a bad guy. Born in Philadelphia of Irish immigrants, he left home at sixteen to enlist in the Northern Army during the Civil War because he hated slavery. When the war was over, he asked to be posted to the Southwest: its long history and native culture were of genuine interest to him. He reached the rank of captain under the command of General George Crook in the 1870s. Among other roles, he served as press attaché for the 3rd Cavalry. He could write very well.

Bourke was present during the Sierra Madre campaign ending with Geronimo's surrender at Cañón de los Embudos. In addition to being a competent soldier and a compulsive diarist, he was an amateur ethnologist, sometimes a great one. He wrote a humorless but brilliant volume on poop and pee called *Scatologic Rites of All Nations*.

Lately, I've been translating a few chapters of his notes on George Crook's 1883 campaign, published by the University of Nebraska as *An Apache Campaign in the Sierra Madre*.

About the Chiricahuas, for example, he has this to say: "An artist, possibly, would object to many of them as undersized, but in all other respects they would satisfy every requirement of anatomical criticism. Their chests were broad, deep, and full; shoulders perfectly straight; limbs well-proportioned, strong, and muscular, without a suggestion of undue heaviness; hands and feet small and tapered but wiry; heads well-shaped, and countenances often lit up with a pleasant, good-natured expression, which would be more constant, perhaps, were it not for the savage, untamed cast imparted by the loose, disheveled gypsy locks of raven black, held away from the face by a broad, flat band of scarlet cloth. Their eyes were bright, clear, and bold, frequently expressive of the greatest good humor and satisfaction."

Bourke's admiration for the Apaches was monolithically solid, but his manner of describing the Mexicans in his diary—he speaks of my people as a nation of miserable beasts—is particularly noxious and grating.

I won't prolong the life of his prejudices by transporting them into these notes, but I wonder whether prejudices are unavoidable no matter how we train our sensibilities. I wonder whether I myself am cruel in my descriptions of white Protestants. To lift up one thing is to tear down another, and one must remain vigilant, I suppose.

Bourke wasn't a terrible person. Probably he was simply trying to justify to himself his participation in an illegal military operation in Mexico. Probably it tormented him to think that he had been sent to fight in occupied territory that Abraham Lincoln had argued against invading when he was still a representative of Illinois's seventh congressional district. It was for Lincoln that Bourke had gone to war. Describing Mexicans as animals may have helped him grapple with this unease, which possibly afflicted a good part of his generation.

Either that or his admiration for the Apaches as fine human specimens didn't mean he considered them equals. Just as most of the soldiers who fought to end slavery would not sit down to lunch with a Black person, I guess. His description of Lieutenant Gatewood's scouts has a disturbing slant. Overall, it is very generous by the standards of its time. "The moccasins," he writes, "are the most important articles of Apache apparel. In a fight or on a long march they will discard all else, but under any and every circumstance will retain the moccasins. . . . A leather belt encircling the waist holds forty rounds of metallic cartridges, and also keeps in place the regulation blue blouse and pantaloons. The other trappings of these savage auxiliaries are a Springfield breech-loading rifle, army pattern, a canteen full of water, a butcher knife, an awl in leather case, a pair of tweezers, and a tag. . . . The tag marks his place in the tribe, and is in reality nothing more or less than a revival of a plan adopted during the war of the rebellion for the identification of soldiers belonging to the different corps and divisions [in case they are found dead]." And then he notes, without the slightest indication that what he is reporting is an outrage: "Each male Indian at the San Carlos is tagged and numbered, and a descriptive list, corresponding to the tag kept, with a full recital of all his physical peculiarities."

Not all male Indians at San Carlos were scouts. The majority weren't affiliated with the U.S. Army. They had no reason to wear the tag, except that it was imposed on them as a form of humiliation, like the Star of David on a German Jew's coat circa 1939.

THE JAIL CELL WAS A windowless hole in the wall at the back of the presidio. More than half the cell was underground, so that prisoners wouldn't die of heat in the summer. The barred opening—the only source of ventilation—was an arch at ground level, so that you had to hoist yourself in or out. It looked more like a sewer than a cell. When Zuloaga peered into the depths all he could think was how cold it must be in there on an icy morning like this.

Elvira insisted again that Zuloaga talk to the Yaquis before he enlisted them. They're twins, she said, one as bad as the other. The lieutenant shook his head. Another two and I'm back up to eight again, he explained, and he went through his calculations with her: I'll teach the Tarahumara kid to shoot and then we'll be nine, or ten counting me. Practically a federal expeditionary force of irregulars. Also, I need somebody who knows these mountains. I've never been all the way to the Gila. The nun paid little attention to these reckonings of a man who'd been spending too much time alone. She was intent on loosening the snarl of chains wreathing the gate. She unlocked them one by one, shaking snowflakes off her veil as if they were mosquitoes, and laid them on the ground. Then she turned one more key in the main padlock and opened the gate. The lieutenant laid a hand on his gun.

One of the prisoners brought over a pot of shit and held it up to the arch. Thank you, Elvis, said the Yaqui, and he retreated into the shadows. The nun set the pot aside, leaving the gate open. The lieutenant kept his hand on his gun. Won't they escape? he asked. There are those of us who still command respect, said Elvira, shaking her hands as if ridding herself of the infectious content of the pot. Then she returned to the cell and poked her head into the hole. I didn't bring you your little breakfasts, my dears, she said, but my friend José

María would like a few words with you. The two Yaquis came squinting into the light. They looked identical, except for the scars crisscrossing their faces. They rested their elbows on the paving stones of the yard like two teenagers leaning on a windowsill. What can we do for you? asked one of them. The other held out a hand, into which fell a couple of fat, spongy flakes. Real nice snow, he said to his brother. Been a while since it snowed, ain't it? the other replied. And addressing the nun: How long we been in here, Doña Elvis? Five years? God knows, said the woman, you were here when I got here. Well I reckon it ain't snowed since. His brother looked up at the sky as if calculating. He held out his own hand so more flakes would fall on it. Naw, he said, not since Sister's been taking care of us it ain't, but who's to say we'd know if it did. Zuloaga interrupted to announce that he was going to press the brothers into service. All right, said one, but don't you need papers from a man of the law for that? They looked at Elvira. No idea, she said. Zuloaga said that so long as the presidio commander wasn't here, he was the military authority in the region. He hadn't drawn his gun, but his right hand was still resting on the grip. The brothers exchanged glances. The one who usually spoke first said: Anyway, if there was a written order we couldn't rightly read it. And, turning to his twin: Give me a leg up? The other bent and interlaced his fingers at thigh height to hoist his brother.

It took him some effort to climb out: he was a stout man, tending toward fat. Once he had emerged, he stretched sleepily, as if just getting out of bed: Real sweet, he said, being set free on a snowy day. He turned to haul up his brother, who was just as big. You've fattened them up nicely, Zuloaga said to the Sister. A person gets bored, she replied. The Yaqui, bent over, offered an unsolicited explanation: There ain't no exercising inside, specially in the rains: the water comes up to here—he indicated the middle of his chest—and don't go down for days. Zuloaga considered the six señoritos probably playing cards at the town hall, his purported nacionales. Now these Yaquis are what I call men, he said to himself.

The lieutenant finally took his hand off his pistol when he saw that the Yaquis had begun to do calisthenics, something they must have learned from watching the presidio guards exercising in the mornings. Let's go, he said, we're in a hurry. The brothers ignored him, clapping their legs open and closed as they raised and lowered their arms. Gee, it's nice not to whack your knuckles on the roof, one of them said. Zuloaga let them carry on for a moment, but he interrupted them again when they started to do squats. We're in a hurry, he insisted. They ignored him, doing push-ups now. Notice how nice the ground smells? asked one of the brothers. The other replied: That's 'cause when you piss on it, it gets aired out.

For God's sake, said Zuloaga, the Apaches took a captive and she's got to be found. Still rising and falling, balanced on the palms of their hands and the tips of their toes, the Yaquis turned in perfect synchrony to look at him. What did you say? asked one of them. We have to go in search of a captive. Apashees? asked the other. Apaches, confirmed Zuloaga. The brothers bounced up like springs. Whyn't you say so sooner? asked one. Chasing Apashees is always fine by us. He looked at his brother. Narrowing his eyes, the other said: They are the ancestral enemy. The nun cracked up. What's this? asked the lieutenant, eyeing her. Ay, Don Chema, replied the nun: You wouldn't see the humor if it was dabbed with honey and handed to you on a platter. My name is José María, not Chema. Don't be angry. Both Yaquis were standing upright now, steady on their feet, their bellies poking out from under the coarse muslin shirts that no longer fit them since Elvira had taken charge of feeding them. With scathing sarcasm, one of them said: Do you really think we'd laugh at mi general Don Chemita here?

Zuloaga took stock: if he put a bullet in the man's head he would have to kill his brother, too, because he didn't know a single Yaqui whose death had gone unavenged. And he would be stuck once more with six men and a Tarahumara kid. Let's go, he said.

It had stopped snowing. As they crossed the presidio yard, one of the Yaquis remarked: You made the right decision, mi general. Zuloaga turned. I'm a lieutenant colonel, he replied, and I understand that you don't have anything to lose and you think it's funny to fuck with me, but I need all the men I can find to get across the Valley of the Moon, so tell me once and for all whether you're going to behave like grown men or whether we'll part friends, except that I'll be alive and you'll be dead. The Yaquis liked that he didn't raise his voice; if he was angry, they couldn't tell. And he was easy to read, a rare virtue among the poker-faced criollos of Mexico. It was clear that if they made one more crack he would blow their heads off. If you need somebody to fuck with, continued the lieutenant colonel, fuck with the punks in the troop. Not with me and not with my corporal, who is Tarahumara. Raramuri, the nun corrected him. What she said. The brothers looked at each other. Aw pigeon feathers, said one, another ancestral enemy. Zuloaga drew his pistol so fast that the air around it sizzled. He stuck it in the mouth of the Yaqui who had spoken. Do I have your word? he asked. The Yaqui bit down on the barrel with unexpected force. He nodded, the barrel still in his mouth.

With a jerk of the neck, he had the pistol in his hand and was spinning it on his index finger. Word, he said, not sure whether to stop the gun barrel or butt-end forward. Then he heard Elvira cock her own pistol. He turned to look at her and saw that it was aimed straight at him. It was a massive Colt, and at that range it would have decapitated him. The captive is a friend of mine, she said to the Yaqui with unexpected gravity. The man handed Zuloaga his pistol, butt forward. Just promise, he said, that if you don't need us anymore you'll shoot us instead of bringing us back to this fucking hole, mi lieutenant colonel. Zuloaga took the gun, holstering it calmly. How could I bring you back here, when you'll be armed? he asked. The Yaquis smiled. This is going to be good, said the nun as she stuck her own pistol in her belt. It was only then that Zuloaga realized something the other three already knew: his eleventh man was this zarzuela singer in a habit. He scratched his neck.

They walked on to the presidio gate. The Sister here and I are going to commandeer some horses for you, he said. With luck I'll find you rifles; you go on to the town hall. Commandeer mules if you can, they're better for catching Apashees, replied one of the Yaquis, and we still have our rifles; they're buried. Zuloaga looked at the nun, whose expression said they could be trusted. Run like the fucking wind because we need to head out, he said.

BACK IN NEW YORK, I showed up for my appointment at the Spanish consulate, where the fate of my citizenship request was at stake. The consul, a very polite young man in his mid-twenties who was being especially nice to me because he had read one of my books, assembled a packet of papers for me and declared that, once a final review was completed in a day or two, I would be a citizen of Spain and Europe. All you have to do is sign a few documents, he said, handing them over to me one by one. He explained the contents of each, and I glanced through them before signing. He checked the scrawl of my signature and then he stamped them and added his own signature. He stacked them with great care, as if the outcome of my petition rested on the perfect alignment of the sheaf of papers rather than their content, which in truth was probably the case.

Finally, he handed me the briefest document of all. The slight trembling of his hand betrayed some emotion. Printed there in ornate Castilian Spanish was a sworn statement of loyalty to his majesty the king of Spain. I set my pen down, though I didn't cap it. Looking him in the eye, I asked with all the tact I could muster whether I wasn't already pledging my obedience to the laws of Spain by requesting citizenship. He said yes, but it was also required to swear loyalty to the king. As he said this, he raised his eyebrows, looking uncomfortable. This made me think that the emotion he'd displayed upon presenting me with the paper was embarrassment, not pride, so I nodded my head, more acquiescent than sarcastic. I closed my eyes and thought of the benefits to my children if I signed. I thought of Cruz and his obsession with studying film in Europe, but then I remembered an episode from his childhood, when he accompanied me on a book tour in Madrid at the age of six or seven.

Cruz and I and Xavi, my editor at the time, were walking along Calle Lope de Vega after lunch. We were talking politics, and Xavi said something about the king. Cruz, who was monkeying around in front of us, stopped short and turned to look at him. What do you mean the king? he asked, and Xavi said he was talking about the king of Spain. There's a king? asked my son. In reply, Xavi launched into a slightly nervous disquisition on the constitutional monarchy, completely incomprehensible to a child. Cruz stared at him and repeated: So do you have a king or not? When Xavi said yes he almost wet his pants laughing.

A few hours later, after some poorly attended panel discussion, Cruz and I returned by taxi to the very modest Madrid hotel where the publishing house had put us up. It wasn't late, but he was tired, so he fell asleep almost as soon as the car pulled away. He opened his eyes as we were passing the brightly lit Royal Palace. He asked me what it was and I told him. Before he went back to sleep he noted with a wisdom beyond him in his waking state: Having a king is good if you're the king.

I capped my pen and put it away, thinking that on the outside my son was ambitious, but inside he was a republican. If he wanted to study in Europe we could save, and if I didn't follow my gut I would end up betraying other instincts. Apologizing profusely to the consul, I nearly ran from his office, the building, and the block where it stood. Once in the subway station, I sat down on a wooden bench and wrote Cruz a long text message saying that in 1815 Don José María Morelos had had red-hot coals shoved up his ass to make him swear loyalty to the king, and when he quit screaming he refused, so his balls were sliced open, the insides removed, and two lumps of salt sewn into them. Since he still wouldn't yield, he was sentenced to execution by firing squad, but not until the next day. At dawn on the morning he was to be killed, never complaining about the fierce stinging he must have felt in his testicles, he requested a cigar to smoke after breakfast and before being shot in the back of the head. He tied the blindfold on himself. That Apache-level stubbornness can't die with us, I wrote Cruz.

I don't know whether I did the right thing. I definitely didn't do the practical thing. It was more than a day before Cruz replied. In his message he said: Don't worry, we'll get a scholarship.

IT WAS CLEAR TO CAMILA that they were heading more or less directly north because she registered the arc of the sun moving implacably right to left across the long desert sky. By the scorching midday hour, her nose had stopped bleeding. The damage was apparently more dramatic than serious, but she was dehydrated. The dried blood made her breasts and stomach itch but she didn't dare touch them for fear of attracting the attention of the rider, who for a while now had acknowledged her only with the occasional grunt. Her shoulders, arms, and thighs were blistered by the sun and her buttocks and the back of her knees were raw from the saddle frame. The cantle, which on Apache saddles was upright rather than curved so that the warriors could sleep as they rode, had cut into her back. Her ribs hurt: shortly after her capture, she had decided to let go of the saddle and drop to the ground, expecting to die from the fall or trampled by the cattle. Her captor had reined in his horse for the first time since they'd left the valley of Janos and come back for her. He had kicked her in the ribs so hard she couldn't breathe or see for a moment, then he'd hauled her up and ridden on.

They didn't stop all day, even though the horses and cattle had been panting since midafternoon. She sat quiet and alert to any chance of escaping this torture, no matter how, and the chill evening wind was a balm. While there was still light, she had recognized the peaks of El Medio as they rode past, and watched the chaparral growing sparser. To Camila and anyone who wasn't Apache, beyond the Sierra de las Ánimas was the Valley of the Moon: no one ventured there without a well-provisioned military escort and a mule to carry water. She didn't know anyone who had gone this deep into the wild, because she had come to Janos when the Apache Wars were heating up again. No one was going to come to her rescue. Resigned to that fact, she was able to sleep at intervals.

The cattle the Apaches had taken were few. They were creatures of the prairie, not the desert; neither they nor the horses could go on at this speed in this heat if they didn't stop at a watering hole, and as far as she knew, there were none past Ánimas.

At some point she opened her eyes and noticed that they were veering east, toward the mountains. The landscape was so hard it seemed like something out of the dream of a stone woman. They were going faster than she had imagined. Suddenly they halted at a narrow pass, the cattle crowding together. This is the start, she thought: Apache country. And she had another thought, too. In her current state—naked, covered in blisters, sores, and scabs, her nose bloodied and one eye swollen shut—the only way to screw her enemies was to stay alive.

As if performing a well-practiced choreography, the riders began to circle the cattle, nudging them together to cross the narrow pass. Only now, when they had no interest in her, did Camila scan their faces. They were glancing nervously from the livestock to the top of the canyon, butts of rifles resting on thighs and fingers on triggers. Their nostrils were flared and their ears pricked for any sound from the hills. The youngest, armed with bows and arrows, had drawn them to guard the maneuver; they controlled their prancing, snorting horses with their legs. Her captor was the only one whose rifle wasn't at the ready. He moved more quickly than the others, giving instructions in his sharp, harsh tongue.

When the cattle finally consented to enter the pass, the riders formed a tight semicircle around them. They spun their mounts, backing them forward so that the horses spurred the cattle on with their tails, their eyes and guns trained on the path they were leaving. Delirious by now from exposure, pain, and thirst, she mused that if the Apaches ever made a lasting peace with the Mexicans, they would take the trophy at every rodeo: these were fine horsemen.

While they were stopped, she lowered her gaze to avoid making eye contact with anyone, though the riders' eyes were fixed on the canyon top. When she looked down she noticed that her shadow could fit into her captor's two or three times over.

Camila and the giant were the last to trot across the pass. On the other side there was no canyon bordered by cliffs, as it had seemed, but a valley with walls sculpted by the elements. The cattle and the other Apaches were descending in front of them at a relaxed pace now. They had truly left the world of the criollos.

When the horses and cattle returned to a gallop, she felt the frame of the saddle cutting into her like razor blades, but at least the last rays of the sun weren't pummeling her back anymore, now that they were riding in the shelter of the valley walls. At some point the giant took a shirt out of the saddlebag he kept strapped between saddle skirt and blanket. He put it on. The other Indians covered their torsos and began to talk among themselves in what sounded like a language different from the strident tongue they'd used so far, speaking to each other in looser, almost gentle tones, much more like the Janeros back home. Everything seemed to strike them as funny. None of them looked at her or even appeared to notice the bruised and battered Mexican woman on the rump of the giant's horse.

FOR MOST OF HUMAN HISTORY, a horse was a deer without antlers, a giant antelope, wild and delicious, a lode of flesh and guts. Though *Homo sapiens sapiens* and *Equus ferus caballus* must have come face-to-face for the first time in northern Europe some sixty thousand years ago, we've been riding horses for scarcely six thousand years. Their extinction in North America stems from our ancestors' continental leap twelve thousand years ago. They disappeared because we ate them, apparently. It was the middle of the Ice Age; it was cold; we needed protein.

By then, the Europeans were cultivating grain and making bread. They kept herds of cattle and goats, and put on wool sweaters when it got chilly; they fabricated objects from bronze and built two-story houses. There were chiefs, priests, and distinct trades, translators and commerce. This was the moment it occurred to someone on the Ukrainian steppe that in addition to eating horses you could put bits in their mouths and ride them.

I'm at the café of the archaeological museum in Zagreb, Croatia, where I come to read and write every morning. In the afternoons I have places to be, sometimes as audience member, sometimes as panelist, in a small, adorable festival of Central European writers with a focus on Mexico this year. Since I arrived I haven't been able to read a single sign, street name, bus stop. Croatian is impenetrable, though it's an Indo-European language like Spanish.

The archaeological museum is the perfect distance from my hotel—a vigorous but pleasant walk along a boulevard with Viennese airs, down-at-the-heels but emphatically lovely in its decay. On my first day, I visited the halls and discovered the wonderful café in the central courtyard, less frequented by tourists than by local intellectuals reading the papers in the company of dogs as shabby as their owners. I bought a book on horses at the museum shop on that first day to have an excuse to sit in this magnificent courtyard, and I've come back to read and write every morning. My stay in Zagreb has been lazy, melancholic. I was invited to the festival, I suspect, because years ago I wrote a story set on the Dalmatian coast. I agreed to come in order to get to know the place that I worked up purely as an abstraction, something out of books. If what I'm writing at this café is published, I wonder whether I'll eventually end up at a festival in

Ukraine, for no other reason than having written about the place where the first horsemen came riding into the world.

Before the fateful moment when someone got up on a horse and changed the world by traveling at its speed, things were very good, at least in what archaeologists call "Old Europe." I'm not exaggerating: it's tempting to think of it as Arcadia, because there really is a time and place where the dreamy vestiges of literary myth intersect with well-grounded facts in the concrete field of archaeology.

In just over fifteen hundred years, from 5300 to 3700 BCE, a few exquisite things were invented by a people patient and enlightened enough to sit watching birds and divining the coming year's weather in a region encompassing the vast basin of the Danube, the Balkans all the way down to the Greek peninsula, the Carpathians, the plains stretching north of the Black Sea and the Caspian Sea to the Urals, the southern Caucasus, Anatolia, northern Syria, Iran.

Living in the northern highlands and the accessible part of the steppe were hunter-gatherers, deliciously called foragers by English-speaking archaeologists because of their not inconsiderable resemblance to forage-seeking mountain elk. These foragers lived in egalitarian societies, with no hierarchy or notion of government. They shared whatever they found because there was no way to store it; they had no chiefs; they buried their dead where they lay. They are survived by hunting tools rather than weapons.

In the valleys to the south, warmer and split by rivers, the first farmers lived in dwellings on communal property with no fences or moats. Some had more jewels, dazzling garments ornamented with polished rectangles of boar's tusk, the occasional bronze object, but that was all. Archaeologists have found them buried peacefully. No ceremonial staffs, wands, or batons, no sacrificial victims, no grain for the duration of the voyage. They left the world as they came into it—elegantly attired, perhaps, but without provisions. Once dead, they all went to the same place.

Farmers and foragers coexisted peacefully where their territories intersected: there are no murder victims in the graves. They didn't often intermarry—the craniums of foragers are broad and strong-jawed, their skeletons heavier and sturdier; the farmers' bones are slender and longer, their skulls narrow—but they traded goods and knowledge. Foragers learned to make bread and to domesticate the ancestors of modern cows, becoming something like herdsmen. They didn't establish cemeteries, exactly, but they began to bury their dead in mounds.

It was around this time that the first stables were built, but captive horses shared the same fate as prehistoric cows, goats, or sheep: they were food. The horses were shorter and less docile than the *Equus ferus* familiar to us, but they provided more meat than other species, even if—based on their scarcity in grave pits—they were harder to hunt. Horses, nevertheless, seem to have been valued most. In farming towns, temples can be identified by the horse heads buried under them as offerings to gods we know nothing about.

This world, this millenium-and-a-half-long interlude that the ancients imagined as Arcadia, was destroyed around the year 3600 BCE. By then, it had grown. In the valleys of the Danube basin and the plains north of the Caspian Sea and the Black Sea there were towns whose communal dwellings had been built up layer by layer until they were a hive of courtyards, rooms, and worship spaces more than twelve meters high: four- or five-story structures.

In less than a century, all those cities of Old Europe were razed and abandoned. When new ones were founded, they were constructed differently, fortified with walls, towers, and moats. It was the dawn of war and warlords. The new cities' cemeteries harbored the skeletons of people whose only affliction was a bashed-in head, and those of others buried in great luxury, with scepters of polished stone in their hands.

Horse heads continued to be offered as sacrifices in temples, but where political and military leaders were buried, adjacent chambers began to appear, furnished with female sacrifices, child sacrifices, swords, and lances. The latter were heavier, longer, and broader than spears, used for attacking neighbors rather than for tossing at fleeing animals.

The sudden vanishing of Neolithic peace has generally and perhaps correctly been explained as the result of climate change. Measurements of pollen buried deep in the ice of Greenland and of the rings of fossilized tree trunks in Europe show that around the year 3700 BCE temperatures dropped dramatically enough to change the migratory patterns of game. Deer and elk no longer passed the camps of the foragers, wild cattle went extinct, there were no more bison, and the mountain ancestors of donkeys vanished; lean sheep with long, tangled wool appeared. Fish, which had been the main protein in the old European diet, migrated to more temperate waters. Wheat, corn, and oats stopped growing; only rye held fast. Domestic animals just barely survived.

Of all the major livestock of the period, only horses thrived. They were the sole beasts able to break ice with their hooves, and they could travel to more distant pastures when the cold prevented grass from growing in the zones where they usually grazed. A horse is a biddable migratory animal that carries and pulls a whole town with it.

Before he wrote *The Horse, the Wheel, and Language*, U.S. archaeologist David W. Anthony wondered how shepherds from the transition period between the Neolithic and the Bronze Age were able to tend to their flocks of horses. He concluded, with a deft stroke of Occam's razor, that the simplest explanation—that they rode other horses—must also be provable. He went on to study the technology of the bit, which made the revolution possible. Anyone can get up on a horse and be bumped around, but only someone who knows how to use a bit can control a mount.

Working with the modern descendants of steppe horses, Anthony noted that domesticated animals compulsively chew the bit when no one is watching, and this behavior (which must feel good on their gums) leaves traces on the enamel of their bottom rear molars.

I doubt anyone has ever collected as many teeth as David W. Anthony: new, old, petrified, American, European, Asian. He ultimately demonstrated—conclusively, it seems—that a group of foragers from Ukraine and Kazakhstan had gone from being the farmers' backwards neighbors to their new masters once they realized that a horse with a bit wasn't a source of protein but a lethal, revolutionary weapon. These men and women from the near edge of the steppe in 3600 BCE were the force that put an end to Old Europe and the happy coexistence of foragers and shepherds. It was they, too, who devised a system of political leadership based on an equilibrium between the administration of violence and the concession of benefits. They imposed this by means of a second invincible technology: the Indo-European language, whose grammar and vocabulary are the root of all languages with Slavic, Baltic, Germanic, Celtic, Italic, Hellenic, Indo-Iranian, or Anatolian roots—in other words, almost every language that a person born on my side of the world will hear or see written in their lifetime. There is a vocabulary common to nearly all of these languages, words that for better or worse have defined us. Words for things that we had during the Bronze Age and still have today: war, spear, father, mother, brother, tooth, sun, water, sow, deer, ox, yoke, burg, work, milk.

Fences and forts, surprise attacks and sackings, clubs and lances, forced migration, political assassination, patronage relationships in exchange for physical and alimentary security, genetic dispersion via the systematic violation of the enemy's women, the speaking of Latin, Greek, Hindi, or Spanish—languages that are easy to translate back and forth because they share the same essential morphology and a percentage of vocabulary—weren't imperial inventions but the unfolding or natural consequence of the original act of conjugating a verb and pulling on the reins to stop a horse.

As I write this, harboring some doubts about Anthony's exceedingly neat theory, I order tea because a third coffee would give me palpitations. They bring it to me with a little pot of milk labeled "mlijeko."

THE MORNING SNOW WAS GONE and the relentless prairie sun had lifted any trace of mist, so it was easy for Zuloaga to see that the Apaches had left behind a welter of tracks, completely out of character. They don't give a shit anymore, said Corredor, as if he knew what he was talking about. Out of the whole group, only the lieutenant colonel, the Sister, and maybe the Yaquis remembered the prosperous and playful world before the uprisings, which had begun when the government of the Republic stopped distributing rations at the presidios. Zuloaga didn't respond, but he was thinking the same thing: the very clear tracks struck him as a provocation, a captain signaling to whoever might be following him that these were no longer random attacks but a war.

Any tracks Camila might have left had been erased by the hoofprints of horses and cattle heading roughly north at a gallop.

They crept along, eyes on the path, until one of the twins shouted: Here. He had found a spot where some of the horsemen had veered off. The party dismounted, the Yaquis leading their horses by the reins. The lieutenant, used to being waited upon, handed his reins to Corredor. Zuloaga examined the tracks and shot a look at the twins. Three unshod horses had clearly turned into the bush while four others had gone on herding the cattle along the main path. They walked until they found faint traces of a woman's heeled boots. The marks were scant and soon vanished. She took off her boots, the criollo said. The Yaquis exchanged glances and separated to search the area. One of them spied a gleam of patent leather in the brush. Bull's-eye for the lieutenant, he said. Poor lady must've hid 'em, said the other, thinking she had a chance.

Too many weeks had passed since the chase for the tracks of her bare feet to survive, even though there hadn't been a drop of rain, but they soon found her corset, too. Zuloaga wrapped the shoes in it and gave the bundle to Corredor. Put it in my saddlebag, he said. What are you going to do with that? Elvira asked. Return it to her, he said. Do you think she's alive? She's a madwoman; she must be.

They followed the tracks and hadn't gone much farther when the Yaquis crouched down again by a trampled stretch of ground. Zuloaga rode up: Was it here? The rest of the troop lingered behind. Unlike Zuloaga and the twins, they didn't think tracking was the best fun anybody could have in the world. It was here, said one of the Yaquis, she was taken here. They took her for a wife, said the other; no sign of a fight, 'cause they wanted her whole. The lieutenant was not convinced. He knelt and touched the sand with his gloved hand: he could make out nothing but hoofprints. I don't understand what I'm seeing, he said to the twins. They snatched her up, said one of them. The lieutenant examined the ground again. It can't be, he said, gesturing at the horses' prints; they didn't stop. Grabbed her on the run from above, the Yaqui said, look here. Zuloaga advanced, crouching where he was pointing. There was nothing but hoofprints. What are we looking at? he asked. That's the back hooves of their fastest horse, the captain's, said the Yaqui. I get it, replied the lieutenant, but so what? The prints are deep; the lady was hoisted up here. There's no proof, said Zuloaga, knowing he had lost the argument. Go on, walk a little, said the Yaqui, and you'll find the rest of her clothes, the Apashees strip their captives right after they take 'em.

Taking advantage of the boss's momentary distraction, three of the criollos from Casas Grandes turned tail and went galloping off. Zuloaga gave them an impatient look: he was more irked that they'd broken his concentration than that they'd gone. If they're going to crack, we don't want them, he said, still searching for something on the ground. The rest of the troops shifted uneasily, and Corredor and Elvira returned to the path and cut their horses across it, just in case.

The lieutenant walked ahead. It wasn't long before he found the ripped petticoat. Lotería! shouted the twins in unison. They want her brown-skinned by the time they get to the ranchería, said one of them while mounting his horse again, I'm telling you they took her for a wife.

FOR SIX WEEKS IN JULY AND AUGUST, we trade the apartment we rent in Harlem for one in Mexico City. The children's Spanish is terrible, and though I don't think it matters much whether you lose or keep your mother tongue, I do believe that in the future it may serve them well to be bilingual. And ultimately I miss the comforting familiarity of the country I call my own, my aging parents, the food, the unnerving silence of late afternoon in Mexico City when twenty-two million people check into the godless expanse of the twilit sky. There's something mysterious, especially then, about a big, crowded, maddeningly dynamic city that can also be so very quiet.

It's a tug I've almost never felt. The occasional Sunday; every Father's Day; those March days when we're still slogging through the snow and shivering our butts off while friends in Mexico are sending me pictures of themselves at café tables drinking beer in their shirtsleeves—bastards. But now, it's as if my inability to swear loyalty to the king of Spain has stimulated some attachment-seeking urge, as if the very fact that I have run out of reasons to delay us becoming U.S. residents is calling me home.

Being separated from Cruz has also taken a toll, paid in flesh. During my first year in New York my hair and beard turned white and I lost a drastic amount of weight that I haven't gained back. The loss of him dug furrows between my eyebrows and turned me into something like a goalkeeper, alone in a small space that I rarely leave. I used to be more talkative, sometimes hard to shut up. Now I generate mostly silence.

So the pull of home is real, and we're going to obey it. The apartment that we're exchanging ours for is nice; we've spent a few New Years there. It has an office where I can keep taking notes for the Apache book. I'll go to Guadalajara. Spending a few days with Cruz is easier from there.

THE CATTLE BEGAN TO FLAG when it was almost night. Camila would have lost consciousness if the wooden saddle digging into her groin hadn't anchored her to this world. Fear, too, kept her alert in a remote and stupid way, isolated in the bubble of her torments. Nevertheless, she managed to hear the vague murmur of life from a watering hole long before they reached it. The croak of a toad roused her from the deathlike stupor she'd been sunk in for countless hours.

It was a hidden spring, feeding a small pool with no trees around it. Seasonal, she thought, because otherwise cottonwoods would grow here. Thinking reminded her that pain wasn't the only logic.

Camila wasn't sure she could move once she got off the horse, so she waited until her captor had dismounted to drop to the ground. She fell like a side of beef, hearing the Apaches' laughter. She didn't have the strength to stand. Her legs failed to respond, numb from the long ride and the chafing of the saddle. She flung herself on her belly and crawled toward the water, pulling her body along on her forearms, the stony ground scraping her stomach, thighs, knees, and the tops of her feet: every part of her body that had been more or less unscathed, not counting blisters from sunburn. She could sense coolness with the tip of her nose when she felt a sudden weight press down on her back. First she thought it was the moccasin of one of her captors holding her down. She wriggled a little, hearing more cackles as the pain in her lumbar region intensified. She couldn't move. She closed her eyes and lowered her head, listening to the horses slake themselves with water that couldn't be more than a handsbreadth from her mouth. She tried to crawl forward again and the pain grew, until it seemed that whatever was on her back was intent on grinding into the day's wounds. She reached back and touched it. They had set a stone on her kidneys, a stone bigger than she would have imagined her body could bear. She rested her face in the sand, which at least was cold.

The horses drank, then the cattle. When they had finished, the men took their time making a floating bed of grass on the surface of the water to filter it, and drank in short bursts. Then they splashed water on their faces and necks. They had what to Camila seemed an endless conversation. At some point, her captor got up and pushed the rock off her with his foot. She didn't even feel the scrape. It took everything she had left to drag herself forward and bury her face in the water. Nothing was funnier to the Apaches, apparently, than the pain of others. They laughed uproariously, though differently than Mexican captors would have done: never touching her, never pointing at her, acting as if she weren't there.

They returned to their horses and livestock, leaving her alone, so she rolled on the stony ground, lowering different body parts into the water as best she could, bathing her sores and soothing her scrapes. The experience wasn't pleasant, but at least it didn't hurt. I'll make it to tomorrow alive, she thought.

It wasn't until she was out of the water and could stand that it bothered her that she was naked. Up until now the blood and dust had made her simply grotesque. Now she was a badly beaten body with a battered, swollen face, but a body once again. She walked like the first woman on earth toward the cliff wall where the cattle were clustered, and there she crouched, her buttocks to the wall, covering her breasts and sex to the best of her ability. Her captors still weren't paying the slightest attention to her.

It was already well into the night when, to her surprise, the Apaches saddled their horses again. No one came to help her, or forced her to mount. She made her way as best she could toward the horse where the giant was waiting for her and she got up on her own, first seizing the saddle and then his forearms as if neither he nor she were there. Settling herself into the saddle again was a torment greater than anything she had yet endured.

THE YAQUIS AND THE LIEUTENANT returned to their party. If anyone else wants to go home, now is the time, said the boss. We're going to spend the night in Los Pinos. There's a little bit of civilization past that, but starting tomorrow noon it's all badlands. He hauled on the reins and shifted his feet in the stirrups, his horse nervous, sniffing the adrenaline in the air. Past that point, it's certain death to return alone.

Another criollo from Casas Grandes raised his hat and said: If you'll excuse me, and tugged his horse's reins. Elvira not only failed to move aside, she drew her revolver. Sister! shouted the lieutenant. She cocked the hammer, aiming. Go on, then, she said to the rancher, ignoring her superior, but leave us your rifle, because young Corredor here has only got a flintlock musket and it ain't fair. The man lowered his hand to the case strapped to his saddle, and as he unbuckled it the Yaquis cocked their guns. Nice and slow, said the nun. Raising one hand in the air, the criollo gingerly retrieved the rifle with the other, holding it like something contagious. He rode slowly forward and handed an almost new Springfield to Corredor. Zuloaga took off his hat and wiped away the sweat. Leave the ammunition, too, he ordered. The rancher took two boxes of bullets from the saddlebag and gave them to the Raramuri. And your boots, said the nun, because the boy's in huaraches and it will be colder in the mountains. I'll have to dismount for that, said the vaquero. She replied: So be it.

Nervous as he was, it took the criollo an eternity to remove his boots. The fame of Doña Elvis's marksmanship had reached Casas Grandes, so his hands were sweating. When he was finally able to get them off, the rancher extended them timidly to the Sister, who said, holstering her gun: Give them to the boy and God bless you.

When the criollo—or our barefoot friend, as the Yaquis called him later—was nothing but dust in the distance, the lieutenant rested his hands on the pommel of his saddle and took a long look at the nacionales he had left. One was a pudgy blond boy with almost invisible eyebrows, baby-faced and sunburned. He was wearing a yellow buckskin duster, evidence he came from money. The other was older, almost Zuloaga's own age, darker, wiry, with a close-growing beard; his eyes were black and kind-looking. Seeing him without his hat, Zuloaga had noticed that his hair was curly: he looked as if he might be the grandson of freed slaves. What about the two of you? he asked. I don't have anything to go back to, replied the older man. And you? Zuloaga asked the younger one. I'm here to stay, he replied.

Zuloaga gave his militia the pained stare he adopted when he was bothered. They looked like a traveling trapeze act, but they were heading into the world's harshest desert to snatch a captive away from warriors no one had ever been able to defeat. Let's hear your names, then, he said. El Márquez, said the bearded one. Zuloaga looked at the younger man. They call me El Gringo. Off to a bad start, noted one of the Yaquis. He's Don Renato's son from Casas Grandes, said Corredor, as if that explained anything to anybody. The Raramuri was holding his new rifle on his lap so proudly that it was clear he had never used a gun to kill anybody: he might truly be too young. Seeing that the boy wasn't about to offer further explanation, Elvira chimed in: Don Renato's sons are good people. What do you do? the lieutenant asked. We're ranchers, said El Gringo. I'm a dancing master, said El Márquez. Elvira chimed in: He lives in Janos, but he was giving lessons in Casas Grandes. El Márquez added: I speak a little Apache and I can show you the paso del perro. Where's that? asked Zuloaga. Nowhere, said El Gringo, it's a dance step. The nun explained: Doing the dog is the latest sensation in the capital.

The lieutenant colonel turned his horse north, thinking, We're fucked.

They reached Los Pinos just after nightfall. The town was deserted. They slept in an abandoned shed and continued north at dawn. Around Moscos, the tracks of the Apache's cattle and horses turned west through the chaparral. They came all this way in a single day, said one of the Yaquis, moving twice as fast as us, at least, and herding fifteen or twenty head of cattle. There were seventeen of them, corrected his brother, and they hadn't even stopped to eat.

Soon they came to what seemed like the entrance to a canyon through which the Apaches had had to funnel the cattle one by one. It was still daylight, but Zuloaga wasn't ready to venture in. They'll shoot us to ribbons, he said. He gave the order to make camp on a rise at a prudent distance from the cliffs and told the twins to explore the pass when it got dark, to see whether it could be crossed. He himself would climb up into the hills.

They made a timid fire while it was still light. On the prairie, any fire that hadn't burned down to embers by night was a call to attack. Elvira and El Márquez sang a duet as Corredor cooked up a calabaza stew. Watching them from a safe distance, Zuloaga thought they might be the most ridiculous band of irregulars in the entire history of the state of Chihuahua, but they had an impressive ability to enjoy whatever came along. Maybe that would be the key to getting through this with minimal losses.

Corredor brought him a dish of stew and a bundle of tortillas. As if he had read Zuloaga's mind once again, he said, They're happy because it's the first night we've spent out in the open, and that's what they came for. The lieutenant told him to hurry up and eat and then grab his rifle, because it would be dark soon and he wanted to teach him to shoot. I'll go right this instant, replied the Raramuri, and be back by the time you've eaten your stew.

Watching them walk off a few minutes later, the Sister said to the dancing master: Men are so sweet when they do manly things. El Márquez just said, Ay, Elvis, and took her by the waist to dance a whistled polka, prompting El Gringo and the Yaquis to join in.

I TALKED TO THE LAWYER, a routine call: checking through the list of documents I was missing, going over the endless declarations and statements to be completed before the application could be submitted to immigration services. As I was hanging up, I told her that we had to be done soon because I didn't want any unfinished business to deal with while we were away in Mexico. You can't go, she replied, after a long silence. You can't leave the U.S. until you get your green card, probably around the end of the year. But I already sublet our apartment and I have my tickets, I said, as if by arguing with my lawyer I was petitioning the government; as if there were anything she could do to help us. Anyway, it was partly a lie: I've never bought a plane ticket more than a few days in advance. I was born without the planning gene that everybody else has. You'll have to postpone the trip, she said, adding that she was sorry, she'd thought I must have known you couldn't return to U.S. territory if your immigration status was unsettled. Our visa had been canceled the moment we sent in the first papers requesting residency.

I accepted it all with Christian alacrity. I even thanked her for the time she'd spent delivering bad news, as if I weren't paying her for it.

My wife, who believes reality is more flexible than it seems and consequently almost always manages to get her way, didn't give up immediately. She consulted web pages, called friends with knowledge of U.S. immigration law, talked to the lawyer, proposed some pretty harebrained schemes. I didn't try to stop her. She's slow to give in to reality, and it's often while she's getting used to the idea that she finds a way out, but this time she was up against a wall.

Tonight, after dinner—kids asleep, second bottle of wine while we're cleaning up the kitchen—she asked the question I'd been waiting a few days for her to ask: So what will we do about the apartment exchange? Cancel it, I guess, I said. Her response was typical, the kind of thing she says that drives me crazy, in good ways and bad. Let's rent a station wagon instead, she said, and you can take us to Apachería.

THE NEXT MORNING, THE YAQUIS and the lieutenant concluded that they had to continue along the prairie: the mountains were impassable, and the canyon was a death trap.

They were drinking Corredor's strong coffee; once again, he'd been the first up, even though he'd been exploring the hills with the lieutenant past midnight. One of the twins said: The Gila River's where they took the señora; we better keep to the lowlands, and if there's trouble we can run to the Valley of the Moon, steer clear of the Chiricahua Mountains, because the Apashees are boss there now. You got that right, said his brother.

Are the Chiricahuas nearby? asked the lieutenant. Everywhere he turned lately it was Chiricahua this, Chiricahua that. They ain't far, said one of the Yaquis, over on the Sonora side. It would take too long to go that way, said the lieutenant, squinting his eyes a little as if reckoning distances, because we have to pick up the cattle tracks at the other end of the canyon, and who knows where that is. It'd be quicker through the canyon, for sure, said one of the Yaquis, but anybody with a notion to can ambush us there. Then let's take the valley, said the lieutenant.

Zuloaga prodded El Gringo and El Márquez with the toe of his boot: they were still asleep and snoring. Elvira was already on her horse.

THEY MADE THEIR LORDLY WAY in what she thought was a northerly direction: when night fell, she had lost her bearings. At some point they stopped to rest the horses and the cattle. They were in what must have been a streambed, because a group of dry cottonwoods stood waiting for the torrent to bring next summer's downpours through the ravine. Her captor unloaded her like a sack and set her on the ground beside the horse. Then he called one of the young warriors, the youngest-looking of all, and gave him a series of orders.

The boy unsaddled the horse and removed the blanket while he stroked it and talked into its ear. By now Camila had managed to sit up and was wondering how to let the boy know she was hungry. The boy took the cinches from the saddle and carried them over to her. He said something in a harsh tone, then he seized her by the hair and dragged her to the nearest cottonwood. There he pulled her to her knees and yanked her head up by the hair. She knew she should fight back, bite and kick, but her body had already settled into the servitude of pain and didn't respond. When her head was high enough, the boy wrapped the cinch around her neck, tightening it until she was almost strangled. Camila managed to get her fingers between the strap and her skin, and he removed them violently and slapped her, but he didn't tighten the strap any further. He tied the other end of the cinch to a thick tree branch. Then he bound her hands to her feet with another strap. He tied them so hard that her kneeling body arced with the pull of the two ropes. There was something terrifying about the way the boy worked her like a calf, an object. He left her there, arched and balanced on her knees, with the broad cinch around her neck. Camila soon realized that if she tried to change position or rest her body on a different part than her knees, which were already starting to hurt, she would lose her balance entirely and be hanged.

What she failed to understand through the infinite few hours that followed was that her ordeal was a diplomatic gesture. What the captain had told the boy when he ordered him to take care of her was to tie her up in such a way that she could kill herself if she chose. If Camila decided to live, they believed, it would mean she embraced her new fate. The men talked for a while longer and went to sleep. She did not.

THE NACIONALES HEADED NORTH for two more days without incident, but neither the days nor the nights were as festive as the first night in the hills had been. When the sun went down on the third day of their journey, they'd had to empty what was left in the waterskin into their hats to give to the horses to drink. Not for nothing did people call the central wasteland they were crossing the Valley of the Moon. There'll be no coffee tomorrow, said Zuloaga to Corredor. The lieutenant's lips were cracked. The Raramuri, meanwhile, seemed perfectly fresh.

Elvira was all right, though she wasn't saying much. The lieutenant's theory was that her getup involved so much fabric that no water could escape: it was like traveling with a wrapped pear. El Márquez and El Gringo had stopped talking, though they didn't seem to regret having joined the expedition. The Yaquis were transformed, but for the better. A few days out of the presidio cell they had regained their color and fine form. When they took off their shirts during the day Elvis made the sign of the cross, perhaps imagining what might have happened in the Janos jail cell if they had looked as splendid when they were prisoners as they did as free men.

They kept moving, advancing as quickly as they could from the predawn hours to midday and from late evening into the night. At noon they stopped and cooked up mesquite beans with nopal, which released its own juices. They had jerky, too, swallowed down with prickly pear water so acidic it made their eyes water and so dense it kept them hydrated through the night. In between they ate dried fruits, never realizing that it was an Apache diet that was keeping them alive.

After five days of careening through the wasteland like a ghost ship, they spotted a column of dust in the distance. There's your pinche Apashees, said one of the Yaquis, with an ear-to-ear grin. And casting a sidelong glance at the lieutenant colonel: Going to show us some firepower now, Pistolita? Corredor squinted his eyes. Those aren't Apashees, he said, they're ranchers. Zuloaga turned to look at him: Don't tell me you can see them from here, Mauricio. There are only three of them, said the Raramuri. Gringos, but they're kicking up dust because they're driving cattle. The lieutenant laughed. How do you know? Corredor couldn't understand what was so funny. They're wearing cowboy hats, he said. The lieutenant looked harder but still all he could see was the column of dust. You say there are three of them? he asked. With fourteen head of cattle, said Corredor.

The minute the boss set off at a trot toward the dust cloud, Corredor and the twins took their rifles from their cases and raced past him with whoops guaranteed to start a gunfight. They didn't hear when he ordered them to stop, and his horse was so dehydrated that no amount of spurring could make it catch up with their mules, better adapted to the grueling demands of the desert.

Everything might have ended very badly before it began if Elvira hadn't fired a shot in the air that thundered loudly enough to make the advance troops pull up their horses. Now what? asked one of the Yaquis when Zuloaga caught up with them at his insufferable bossman's trot. We're a military unit, not a gang of bandits, said the lieutenant. Ain't no way that'll work, complained the other twin. The lieutenant didn't answer until the rest of the group arrived. We're going to advance two abreast, everybody behind me, he said. Elvis and El Gringo in the middle, El Márquez and Corredor in the rear, you two—to the Yaquis—right here behind me, with rifles out to show them who's in charge and fire in a fucking hurry if need be.

If the ranchers had been wondering whether to worry about what they had probably already gathered was a band of nacionales, the nun's shot in the air made it plain that they were about to have a conversation with the law. They stopped where they were and let the livestock scatter.

Zuloaga, preferring to save bullets for when they crossed paths with the Apaches, relaxed when he saw them waiting. One of the three had even unsaddled and was stretched out on the ground, his hat over his face, apparently ready for a nap.

WHEN THE NEXT DAY THEY reached a stream after another scorching, agonizing ride, Camila, having learned her lesson, spared herself the punishment of the stone. She waited for the horses, cattle, and men to drink before she advanced on hands and knees to quench her thirst. She was in the same or worse shape than the day before, but at least she had been able to sleep along the way. She was beginning to believe that this would be her life from now on, and this thirst and pain would be all she knew.

That day they didn't eat either, but the thirst was so great that the pinch of hunger was scarcely felt, or felt as a lesser ill, part of a general assault. They didn't tie her by the neck. They left her lying on the stony ground.

When she woke the next day there was a blanket over her. The boy untied her, helped her up, and allowed her to remain covered. He offered her a leg up to the torture of the wooden saddle, but she ignored him and clambered up on her own. The boy retrieved the blanket when it slipped off her shoulders and lashed it to the saddle of his own horse. The giant didn't even turn to look at her during the process. He set off when he felt her blistered fingers take hold of the saddle fastenings.

WHEN I WAS GETTING MY DOCTORATE, I had a professor of belligerent intellect and beatific eloquence; an older man. His name was Saul. One day, as we were talking in his office, he lost patience (as he often did) with the way I read: chaotically, and perhaps trusting too much in the epistemic properties of hyperbole. He scolded me. He said: You have to read from beginning to end, understand? In the proper order. Then he opened the book I had in my hands, which was *A Universal History of Infamy*, and planted his finger on the last page. He said: From the beginning. Then he flipped backward through the pages, like a deck of cards, and pointed to the last paragraph on the first page, concluding: To the end. I was still young, cocky, arrogant. I said—probably with a shit-eating grin—that the book he was showing me was Borges, not the Torah, and Spanish was read from left to right. Saul replied: Exactly, or has an excess of hyperbole made you incapable of reading a metaphor? Literature, he said, is sacred for us, so you must read and respect every word. That day I understood something that has stood me in good stead ever since: humiliation is the price of the failure to recognize a quicker intelligence than one's own.

After a month of preparations for the trip to Apachería, so intense and exasperating that I could barely read and didn't write a thing, and a week spent cutting diagonally across the U.S., today we're approaching sacred territory: the Beef Creek Apache Cemetery of Fort Sill, Oklahoma. It was here that the story of a generation of Chiricahuas ended—and endings, as I learned from Saul, are the matrix on which everything else is ordered. Starting points are unpredictable, since our presence in the world is unidirectional only to a certain degree. It's true that we have no memory of the future, though it's already inscribed on the closed vault of time, but memory compensates for this design flaw of our brain by working back to front, in reverse, like fables. We don't know what a story is about until we finish it, even if we're the ones writing it; we have no idea why we made the trip until we're back home; a life is a sequence of actions without head or tail until it ends.

There is a journey that begins with the Oñate expedition of 1598 through the southwestern United States and ends with the burial of a generation of Chiricahuas in the Apache Cemetery of the concentration camp at Fort Sill, where a bunch of legendary warriors of America's most passionately freedom-loving first nation eventually died of old age, never declassified as prisoners of war by the U.S. government or allowed to return to Arizona and New Mexico.

The Apaches' own narrative, difficult to capture even though it's transcribed in old and new compilations of oral histories, is much greater than this cycle. It has its own, larger trajectory, prior and subsequent to the capricious Spanish, Mexican, and American historiographic record. It began on the steppe of Mongolia and had an Ice

Age apogee in Canada, where an Asiatic language took root as the American language of the Athabaskans, still spoken today. The descendants of Geronimo, Nana, Cochise, and Juh are still here, but now they are part of a different, shorter story.

We have all been written into the spectacular but narrow history of the British and Spanish empires, the shaping of the Mexican Republic and the United States, and in general we don't have the guts or honesty to recognize it as what it truly is: the story of an occupation. We have transformed the Apache chiefs and captains who lie in Beef Creek Cemetery into something they were not, something that is part of the difference-obliterating machinery of the modern nation-states, the most lethal technology for profit-making and discrimination ever designed by humankind. They are perceived as revolutionary figures now, ferocious rebels, their names and effigies stamped on street signs and T-shirts as if they were Che Guevaras. They were not. They represented something much bigger, inexpressible in our imported political language. Something we can neither see nor say. They belonged to an enormous world full of wonders—not gone, but stretched thinner and thinner—that we never had any interest in perceiving. We call it the Americas because we never cared enough to learn its true name.

The narrative of the Apaches as fearsome adversaries of the governments of Mexico and the United States, as the unfathomable Other, titans of honor and merit, is a story with a beginning and an end. It begins in 1630 when Fray Alonso de Benavides recorded that they spoke a language that "wounds with words" and ends with the quiet burial of Geronimo in the Beef Creek Cemetery of Fort Sill in February 1909. By then, the Ford Motor Company had launched its Model T, and Francisco I. Madero was preaching that Porfirio Díaz had to be removed from the government of the Mexican Republic; that the country had to be modernized; that telephone service and vaccinations should be available to all. Geronimo was a vestige of something we stole from this world long ago, and he's buried a few miles from the cabin we've rented in Medicine Park, Oklahoma, where we'll spend a night on our drive to Arizona.

Today's journey has been a long one. We left Memphis early, shaken. We had spent a night in Nashville, the thriving white capital of country and western, and another night in Memphis, the majority Black cradle of rhythm and blues. Memphis was broken, shattered, a city seemingly bombed out by its own country, which keeps opting for a monolithic racial identity and has turned resource allotment into a slow, brutal extermination campaign. Two cities, in the same country and the same state, separated by just over three hundred highway miles, a minuscule distance in a nation whose breadth has a continental feel. Yet if development strata were distributed linearly, Nashville would be in California or New York, and Memphis in Chiapas: a societal catastrophe.

Crossing the Mississippi, then, packed a double emotional punch. On the one hand we were passing over the threshold of the West, moving into the last space where the original inhabitants of America knew freedom. On the other, we were carrying in our shirt pockets the reminder that this nation—the place that has given us shelter and that we like because we don't live on its mean streets—is also a wretched third world country.

There's no ill omen, of course, that can defeat our children's ability to make a party out of anything. Belted into the back seat, they are sometimes fighting, sometimes sunk in inscrutable silence staring at who knows what out the window or napping like pashas, but almost always making a clarifying racket. They saw the steel bridge over the Mississippi between Tennessee and Arkansas as a cosmic door: the entrance to the country of Geronimo and Sitting Bull, General Custer, Victorio and Crazy Horse.

Cosme, whose musical taste at ten is pretty well-defined, demanded that we put on Paul Simon's "Graceland" to see the shine of the cradle of the Mississippi by the light of the sun's first rays. There was a hint of Saul's lesson in the act of crossing a mythic waterway listening to that song, a river that just a few hours later already seems like a dream. "Graceland" is a meditation on divorce, on the hole left by what maybe could have been avoided, though now it's forever too late; the child in the song as the witness to something dead, the steel bridge to the West as the passage to a world that endures, though it contains something that has gone. Life as war and burial ground. The West is the U.S. unconscious, and I have the sense that the Apache Cemetery at Fort Sill is its very crux.

WELL IF IT AIN'T VIRGINIA'S OWN Robert McKnight, said Zuloaga when they reached the point where the cowboys were waiting for them. He didn't get off his horse. Lieutenant, said the American, with his grim reaper's smile. He fingered his red three-day beard with his left hand, his right poised near the grip of his revolver. A few steps behind him was another cowboy, both hands resting on his hips, at which hung two long, slender pistols of a make the Mexican couldn't identify. The man wore heavy woolen trousers under his chaps, a dun-colored shirt, a sheepskin coat, and yellow gloves the lieutenant colonel liked. Both were wearing those hats with ridiculously wide brims that the gringo settlers had made fashionable in Texas. And who's that you've got back there? asked Zuloaga. A

French trapper I found on the loose in Colorado. Does he kill? When provoked. And who is that napping? asked Zuloaga. My brother-in-law, replied the Virginian; I'm a decent married man now. The lieutenant colonel kept a poker face. You looked better in your Mexican headgear, he said to McKnight: you look like a toadstool in that ten-gallon number.

The Virginian shrugged: Comes with the job, he said, tilting the brim a little more. Now that we're doing business on the Rio Grande, we have to go kitted out like wild men. Other than that, McKnight was dressed the same as ever: black three-piece suit, mysteriously clean despite the dust, a checkered shirt and purple ascot. He didn't wear gloves, so that everyone could see he had only three fingers on his right hand. Enough, in his case, to pick off a fly with a single shot. So do you like it? Zuloaga asked. I'd rather deal with Arkansas gents on the Mississippi, but it's you folks letting Texas fill up with riffraff; don't blame me. You don't say, replied the lieutenant colonel, in a relaxed tone now. He let his reins go slack.

The twins took this as consent. They leapt from their mounts with arms outstretched, as if trying to fold the entire universe into their embrace. Señor Róber, Señor Róber, they shouted. Zuloaga turned to stare at them. What's this? he asked the rest of the troop as the Yaquis hurled themselves at the Virginian. The nun brought her horse up next to his and whispered in his ear: They were in jail together in Janos. The lieutenant colonel raised his eyebrows and pulled down his hat. He dismounted calmly, without turning his back on the French trapper. The man had yet to touch the grips of his pistols, but he hadn't moved his hands from his hips either. He waited patiently with a half smile for the twins and the Virginian to finish swearing their mutual love and clapping one another on the back as if trying to dislodge the dust of the journey. When they moved apart at last, the lieutenant held out his hand, neither removing his gloves nor baring his head. I hope your memories of me aren't too bad, he said to the American. The latter extended his own hand, clutching the lieutenant's with his legendary three fingers like an eagle's claw. Cómo no, he said, in heavily accented Spanish despite more than a decade spent in Chihuahua and Nueva México. The San Buenaventura presidio is the only place I've been given a fair trial. Zuloaga narrowed his eyes. The trial had been fair, but McKnight had been found guilty and paid a fine for selling whiskey to the Apaches in peacetime—if it had been wartime, he would have been shot.

Elvira got off her horse. McKnight doffed his hat. Sister, he said, and kissed her hand. Are you still tending to the prisoners? When I'm not out and about with them, she replied. The Virginian looked at Zuloaga: You know how to pick 'em, he said. Don't poke fun at the lady, said the lieutenant. The cowboy touched his mustache and, giving her a look, said: The man hasn't seen you shoot—shall we give him a little display? The Sister cracked a pirate's smile. All right then, she said. The Virginian took a coin from his pocket, tossing it high in the air. The nun drew her gun, cocked the hammer, and shot, all in a single motion. The gringo cast a glance at the gunman, still standing impassively behind him, and gestured with his chin. At once the trapper began searching for the coin.

Zuloaga laughed. It's a good troop, no doubt, he said, but we couldn't scare up an Apache who knows the territory and we can't find water. The horses are failing, said the Virginian. Zuloaga nodded. We rode down to you because if you've got cattle, you must know where to find water. McKnight scratched his ear. He said: What will you give me for telling you where to water your animals? His bodyguard was still busy searching among the tufts of desert grass, his hands always on his hips. Will you do it for the sake of

Mexican-gringo relations? asked Zuloaga sarcastically. The forecast isn't good, said the Virginian. What do you mean? asked Zuloaga. President Jackson is crazy; if Texas leaves the Republic, Washington will gobble it up for sure, and come after Nueva México next on the way to California. Zuloaga raised his eyebrows. Well, we'll be here waiting for them, won't we? *You'll* be waiting, replied the Virginian; if they catch me they'll hang me. You know best what debt you owe, said the lieutenant colonel before getting back to what interested him. Let's say you tell me where to find water and I won't ask you for your papers, he said. Behind McKnight, the hired gun scuffed at something on the ground with the tip of his boot. He picked it up and flicked it in the air. That's no good, said McKnight, I'm Mexican now. The Frenchman tossed the coin to Zuloaga, who caught it as he asked: How's that? I married a tame Coyotero woman in Santa Rita. The lieutenant looked at the peso. Shee-it, he said. There was a bullet-sized hole through it. Still holding the coin up to the light, he replied: You lose, then. If you're Mexican now, I can conscript you. McKnight scratched his neck. I'd happily come with you, he said, but I'm on business; if you want me, there'll be a fight.

Zuloaga took his time answering. He bent down and pulled up a blade of grass, dry from the cold, and put it in his mouth. He turned to his men and ordered Corredor and El Márquez to check the livestock. McKnight came up and took him by the forearm. The lieutenant put his hand to his gun. Behind him, the nun and El Gringo cocked theirs. The French gunman drew both pistols. Zuloaga glanced around: the napping cowboy was still on the ground. If he wasn't bothered, they still had room to maneuver. He relaxed and let his weapon fall. The Virginian made a sign to the Frenchman, who returned his pistols to their holsters. Zuloaga ordered his people to follow suit. Why don't you give me safe passage? said McKnight. I'm going to trade the cattle for ammunition in Santa Fé; I'm in a hurry. The lieutenant shook his head. I think we'd better have a look at the brand on these animals you've got here, he said. Let me go, countered the Virginian, and I'll loan you an Apache. Zuloaga raised his eyebrows. That man over there is my brother-in-law Pisago, McKnight went on. Is that a fact? He speaks Spanish. Coyotero? Zuloaga asked. If you're looking for Gileños, Pisago will find them: they have a mortal hatred of each other. How do you know I'm looking for Gileños? The Gileños are from around Santa Rita, don't forget; everybody knows a captive was taken in Chihuahua. Zuloaga stood staring at him in silence, as if waiting for him to finish explaining something. He thought: She's alive, but kept it to himself. It's going to get ugly, said McKnight. Worse than this? asked the lieutenant. He went on: It's been three days since we saw a soul, and all the ranches are abandoned. Worse, said the Virginian, in Santa Rita they say the Gileños are raising a cavalry of two or three hundred braves, and they have a stronghold in the Chiricahua Mountains; the Coyoteros are even more scared than the Mexicans. The lieutenant colonel murmured: The Chiricahuas again. He turned toward his men, who were moving through the cattle without disturbing the beauty sleep of the Apache slumbering among them. Let it go, boys, he shouted to Corredor and El Márquez. The Virginian walked to his horse, which was nibbling the chaparral a few yards away. He pulled a Navajo buffalo-skin canteen out of his saddlebags, tossing it to Zuloaga. Have a drink of water, he said, we know where to get more. The lieutenant colonel caught the vessel and passed it to the nun. She uncorked it and took such a long drink that she would surely get a bellyache. Unless you want a little sotol, went on McKnight, with a truly satanic smirk. I'll take that, too, said the lieutenant.

EACH DAY WAS AS HARD as the one before, yet the boy's ministrations, harsh as they were, had returned her to humanity. She'd had time to think, and she knew the Jicarillas of Janos well: she guessed that having survived the night at the end of the rope had secured her a new place in the group. Now, on her fourth day as a captive, hunger had crystallized as the worst of her trials.

They left the canyon at last, following the bed of a dry tributary and heading north in single file at the meandering pace of the cattle. It seemed to Camila that neither the horses nor the cattle could go much farther on a minimal diet of grazing around watering holes; the lack of food must be torturing them as much as it maddened her. The Apaches didn't eat either, but they carried on imperturbably.

When, early in the day, she saw that they were emerging from the canyon, she felt that at last they were approaching someplace definite, a destination, so her discouragement was infinite when she saw that after the canyon came the real desert. A valley like the bottom of a lake, the ground so dry and hard that the animals didn't even raise dust as they walked.

Gone were the acacias and weeds and twigs that the cows and horses half cropped along the way; gone the yucca and junipers; gone the paths and any sense of moving forward in a particular direction.

Around midafternoon, one of the calves collapsed, shrieking like a madwoman. All the Apaches leapt to the ground as if at a bugle blast. Camila stayed on the horse until the giant turned steely eyes on her, shouting and motioning for her to get down and join them. It was the first time he had interacted with her since he'd jabbed her in the ribs back in Chihuahua. She obeyed, the fear of more pain keeping her fully in thrall.

She was so used to humiliation now that it hardly bothered her to be naked among all these clothed men. Anyway, they didn't see her: she might as well have been another cow. As she walked, she rubbed the calluses on her flanks, and she only shielded her breasts and sex when the giant grabbed her by the arm to pull her closer to the calf with him. Two of the warriors yanked the animal up by the head and the oldest took a knife from his belt. The giant pushed Camila to her knees and the other warrior slit the calf's neck. The blood bathed Camila's face. The chief was shouting something at her; his men were, too. It was all swift and terrifying. One of them, the oldest, opened her mouth so that the juices of the animal would flow in and the other pulled her head back to make the liquid go down. It came up again and they closed her mouth, forcing her to swallow her own vomit and smacking her to make her obey. They opened her mouth again, made her drink again, closed her mouth so she wouldn't vomit. They let her go and she crept aside. The warriors knelt to drink the hot liquid that seemed as if it would never stop welling up.

When no more blood came, the old man who had slit the animal's throat sliced its belly open and pulled out its entrails. He cut the intestines in pieces and shared them out among the warriors, who gulped down the contents with a relish that made Camila retch again. They forced her to choke down her own share of shit and then they gave her the honor of being the first to eat the rennet left undigested in the animal's belly. She vomited it up and they forced her to eat her own vomit again, twice. By the time her stomach finally accepted it, they were already chewing the raw entrails. They left her a part of the liver and a kidney, which seemed less repulsive than the rest. When her stomach began to reject this, too, they forced her again to hold steady and swallow until her body surrendered. Then they left her alone on the ground. She watched them cut up the animal like lightning, refraining from eating the strips of flesh and fat.

Sitting in the shadow of the giant's horse she could acknowledge, despite her revulsion, that for the first time in days she was neither hungry nor thirsty. She ran her hands over her body. The backs of her thighs were calloused. Her nose had healed on its own, if it had ever been broken. The sun no longer blistered her skin. Her throat was raw from vomiting, but that was nothing compared to what she had suffered the past few days.

The Apaches cleaned the calf until its bones shone. Then they scraped the inside of the skin and cut it into two pieces. With the bigger piece, they made a bundle of meat, and with the other, a kind of sack into which they urinated in orderly fashion. They gave the urine to the horses to drink, whispering into their ears and stroking their necks as if asking forgiveness. The animals, reluctant at first, drank it down.

Then they set out again, but something had changed. The giant helped Camila up on the horse, draping the skin they had used to hold the urine over the saddle frame to make the ride easier.

THE SOLDIER WHO TOOK MY ID at the entrance to the Fort Sill military base was dark-skinned and had an unfamiliar accent, though all non–East Coast U.S. accents are strange to me. When he went back to his hut to run a check on my driver's license, I told the children that his accent might be Native American, and added, thinking to interest them in our visit to the cemetery, that he was probably the descendant of Apaches and had stayed in Oklahoma to keep watch over their resting place. The kids paid close attention when he returned with my ID and explained how to get to the cemetery. When he walked back to raise the barrier and let us through, Amelia said: "Nah, he's Mexican American, he talks like you but better, Daddy."

Fort Sill is a huge training and army reserve complex. Within it stand the restored ruins of the original fort, a tourist attraction no one ever visits, given its location at the ass end of the universe. The fort also has an artillery museum and the only decent-sized hospital in southern Oklahoma. To reach the cemetery you have to pass all these buildings—countless offices and barracks, sports fields and training fields—and not give up.

The roads inside the base are named for Apache chiefs. The main one is Geronimo Road, of course. The Chiricahuas died humiliated, prisoners of war in a concentration camp on a military base, but their abasement dignifies the people living where they once lived; it's as if the U.S. Army has devoured them to usurp their powers.

All nation-states do this: they fish around in the past, borrowing the vigor of warriors of old to pass on to their soldiers. In Mexico we have the Cuauhtemoc and Cuitlahuac battalions, named for the Aztec generals who would of course have called themselves Mexica. The soldiers in those regiments today have the same skin color and facial features as the now-mythic generals; the land they inhabit is essentially the same as that governed by their forebears; the old names of the towns and cities often remain unchanged. Moctezuma's soldiers ate the same foods as their present-day successors—tortillas and squash blossom soup, salsa made from tomatoes and serrano chiles—and they did battle at Cuauhnahuac, while today's soldiers live in the barracks of Cuernavaca. There's a certain continuity that isn't merely symbolic, despite the schism of the Conquest.

The case of the Apaches in the U.S. is different: a matter of appropriation based on willful ignorance. The Chiricahua prisoners were assimilated into the national mythology of the U.S. without ever having been citizens at all. Nana, Geronimo, Loco, and Naiche, all buried in the prison camp at Fort Sill, were born before the war of 1847 in New Mexico, Chihuahua, and Sonora, where the original inhabitants were granted citizenship by Mexico in 1821. They were born Mexican and they died before the summer of 1924, when the United States at last admitted Indigenous Americans into citizenship. They all spoke Spanish as a second language, and none of them ever learned English; they all had the skin color and diet that half the U.S. population thinks will debase the country if people from Mexico and Central America continue to be allowed to immigrate.

I told this to the children, who, though gringos to the core, are also intensely Mexican, if more in theory than in practice: the roads inside Fort Sill honor the memory of Mexico's fiercest offspring. What I didn't say (I'm prey to underdog nationalism, too) is that by surrendering to the U.S. Army they were able to die of old age, prisoners though they were. The Mexican army probably would have shot them without trial, most likely after torturing them for the sole pleasure of inflicting pain on an enemy body.

At the end of Geronimo Road was a chain-link fence with a gate in it, with its own little hut. We braked even though the booth was empty and the barrier arm was up. A big red sign informed us that we were entering an artillery test range, and that visitors to the Apache Cemetery were forbidden to go off the road or to turn onto any other road in the area.

The final part of the drive felt interminable; maybe it was the excitement of approaching the original inspiration for our trip, or maybe also the periodic ungodly thunder of artillery fire. My wife turned to look at me with alarm on her face and squeezed my hand at each eruption. The children, of course, were delighted: each blast drew more nervous giggles than the last, and they laughed until they weren't scared anymore.

We continued along the road, all woods and noise, until we reached a massive wall with razor wire on top, which I took to be the far edge of the base. After another long stretch—the roar of artillery finally receding—we reached an empty parking lot. At the arch over the entrance, a wooden sign hung from an iron post like something out of a western. It read: "Geronimo's Tomb."

I parked, nervous and elated to be in a place I had read so much about, but it wasn't until I saw the bureaucratic lettering on the metal plaque used by the U.S. Army to commemorate the eradication of its enemies that I felt the thud of the sacred in the pit of my stomach: "Cemeteries," it read in white sans serif font on an olive-green background, terse and precise as a government document.

There are more than three hundred dead here. Men and women who surrendered in Mexico and Arizona in 1886, were declared prisoners of war, and could never return to their lands because the U.S. Congress didn't modify their status as enemy combatants until 1913. By then there were only 182 still alive, most of whom had arrived at the concentration camp as children: many were born prisoners.

We entered the cemetery itself, which was surrounded by yet another chain-link fence—the fourth we had passed—topped with more razor wire. It was as if the U.S. government still feared the Apaches would emerge from their tombs and escape to raise hell again.

That said, ignoring if possible the outrage that the bodies of prisoners are still captive after death—in Apache eschatology, a soul finds no repose until the body it inhabited is laid to rest where it was born—the Fort Sill cemetery itself doesn't strike me as a place that would have displeased its inhabitants in life. I've found no record of how the land was chosen for this resting place of Chiricahua bodies, but it's very likely that the Chiricahua themselves selected the spot they found most appropriate, in consultation with the military engineers making improvements to the base. They built the wall that still borders the old part of the base and dug the many ponds that supply it with water.

The cemetery occupies an almost circular bend of Medicine Creek. A dense curtain of trees hides the fence, making it feel secluded. The graves, military stones engraved with names and dates, are set in a bank that slopes gently down toward the creek, the murmur of the water interwoven with birdsong and the constant fluttering of leaves. Every so often a wave of machine-gun fire plays counterpoint: there will never be peace for the Chiricahuas.

I occupied myself on the bank, making a list of the dead. I'd never use it for anything, but I wouldn't forget it, either. The children of course wanted us to visit Geronimo's tomb before anything else. At burial grounds you don't go looking for graves, I told them, you have to wander, let the dead come to you.

My wife—for whom my obsession with the Chiricahuas is a quirk somewhere between odd and tolerable, like my taste for opera or baseball—went to sit by the creek. The children were doing whatever they do when no one is watching them: we couldn't have been in a lonelier or safer place, so neither she nor I wasted time worrying about them. I was left by myself with my names gouged in stone.

They were resounding names belonging to warriors whose lives had fascinated me for years, the names of giants. Naiche, last chief of the Chiricahua, son of Cochise. Mangas, Gileño captain, youngest son of Mangas Coloradas and half brother of Cochise's wife. Chapo and Tsisnah, sons of Geronimo, who fought alongside him until there was no more fighting. Chato, chief scout of the 6th Cavalry, taken prisoner by the officers under whom he served in the U.S. Army and left to rot in the camp at Fort Sill among the people he had betrayed; he was once kicked in the face by a horse, which is how he got his war name, meaning flat-nose. Loco, almost always chief of peace. My favorite of all: Nana, the last Mimbreño chief. Nana was the best-natured and most beloved of the warriors who joined the final band of Chiricahuas. Although lame, half-blind, and small in stature, he was the swiftest of riders and the fiercest of captains—and left the longest trail of corpses and ashes on raids that continued until he was confined to Fort Sill, when he was past ninety.

At some point I noticed that the children were higher up the bank, sitting in the shade of a tree across from a trapezoid-shaped monument that was much bigger than the gravestones scattered across the field.

When I got closer and realized what they were doing, I felt something I hadn't felt since my Catholic boyhood: the yawn of the divine. The children were lying a little way from Geronimo's tomb, making an offering of flowers, grasses, and stones for him. There was a sweet-smelling dry breeze; there was the sound of the creek, the branches, the birds; the cannon blasts. There was the light filtering through the leaves, and the taste of dust—his dust—in our nostrils and mouths. I sat with them. After a while my wife came over. Once a ballerina, she walks with disturbing lightness, as if she's returning in excellent spirits from among the dead. She sat down, touched my face: she understood.

We sat there like that until the children reached a silent agreement about how the offering should look. They picked it up and reassembled it at the foot of the tomb. Then they sat down with us. No one said anything.

OVER THE YEARS, JOSÉ MARÍA Zuloaga and Robert McKnight ended up becoming good friends. The Virginian died in 1846, as the lieutenant colonel's second-in-command at the federal army headquarters in Corralitos, Chihuahua. He never knew that Santa Rita del Cobre and all of New Mexico, where he had fled because there was no place for him anymore in the Puritan republic that his countrymen had erected, would end up becoming part of the United States as he had foretold. His children, half gringo and half Apache, grew up Mexican. The youngest studied law at the Chihuahua Institute of Science and Humanities with the aid of Zuloaga, his godfather. His name was Eduardo McKnight Cabezón and he rose to be treasurer of the state, and, later, a member of the Chihuahua delegation in Mexico City. They called him "the Persian," because he was dark-skinned and had blue eyes. He was a great friend of the novelist Manuel Altamirano, back when Altamirano was better known as an editor of literary magazines; Spanish was a second language for both of them, though Altamirano was Chontal and McKnight Apache. It's said that he served as the model for the blue-eyed Indian in Altamirano's novel *El Zarco*.

Zuloaga never grew close to Pisago Cabezón, the Coyotero who served him as guide through the Valley of the Moon and the descent through the Mogollon Mountains to the Gila River. There isn't a single note in Zuloaga's dispatches that would lead one to believe he had any differences with the man, but he frequently notes that the Apache won't talk to the nacionales or share food with them despite being, as people said with no qualms back then, an indio de razón. Ultimately, when so many Apaches had been killed in Arizona that quarrels between Gileños and Coyoteros became irrelevant, Pisago decided to shed his Mexican nationality and join the Chiricahuas in arms. He died fighting the armies of Mexico and the United States, after years laying waste to northern Sonora and southern Arizona with a diminished but ferocious band of warriors under the command of Chief Cuchillo Negro and Chief Cigarrito, whose enemy he'd been for most of his life.

The day that Pisago, Zuloaga, and McKnight met in the Valley of the Moon, none of them could have imagined that their names would appear over and over in the indexes of the dense bibliography generated by the Chiricahuas' choice to fight until the end.

Pisago woke from his nap when everyone was sitting down to drink. He sat up, his face puffy, his jet-black hair shining in the sun like patent leather until he put on the ten-gallon hat that McKnight must have convinced him to wear. He and Zuloaga and McKnight drank in moderation, being the sort of people who could not get drunk without risking giving someone the chance to kill them. After partaking of the Virginian's sotol, Zuloaga informed Pisago from the pedestal of his whiteness that he would be heading back north with them to the Gila Valley. The Apache didn't like the idea, but he didn't ask why he should have to come along; his brother-in-law's activities were always illicit, and sometimes sacrifices had to be made. He nodded in resignation and retreated a reasonable distance from the convoy, gazing at the mountains as El Márquez, the Yaquis, El Gringo, and the nun made the discovery that the French trapper could dance an unbeatable cuplé.

In addition to Spanish and English, McKnight spoke perfect Apache, and it was he who explained to Zuloaga that nobody knew the exact origins of the band of Apaches calling themselves the Chiricahua. He said they hailed from a group of families in the Gila Basin who were opposed to making peace with Chihuahua. They had gone on the warpath in the Sierra Madre when their pact with the

Spanish crown was broken, and they were uniting under the idea that no one but Apaches should live in Apachería.

There were about three hours of light left when Pisago Cabezón returned to the group to tell Zuloaga that if he wanted his horses to drink before they camped, they had to set off.

THAT DAY THEY RODE PAST nightfall again, and Camila fell asleep against the giant's back. He woke her with a jerk when they stopped beside a tiny creek, almost a stream of mud, but steady enough that the cottonwood and grasses were green. When she got off the horse and dropped to the stony ground to resume her sleep, she heard the cattle grazing, or whatever it is that animals are doing when they eat the twigs and thorns growing over the godforsaken crags of deepest New Mexico.

Soon she was awoken by the smell of meat smoking over a fire. The smell vibrated through all her glands, seeped into her from all sides, more powerful than rage, envy, memory, shame. She crawled toward the circle of men and the fire, her forearms on the ground and her head very low, like a dog. She was conscious of being naked and dirty, but she didn't care.

They noticed her immediately. They laughed, said things. The adolescent got up but the giant waved him away. He took a piece of raw meat and tossed it to her. Camila picked it up from the ground with her mouth and retreated into the darkness to clean it and chew it. She was curled in a ball, ripping at it with her teeth, when the giant approached. Beside her he dropped the calfskin she had ridden on that afternoon, the blanket, and a handful of strips of roasted meat. She bowed her head even lower in thanks.

Not caring that it smelled like piss, Camila spread the calfskin on the ground and devoured the food the giant had left her, covering herself with the blanket. From her corner of the campsite she took a careful look at the Apaches, maybe for the first time. It occurred to her to count them, and she dared to think that they were people with names, not just a mass of teeth, hair, and nails.

The band was small, at least by the standard of tales told in Chihuahua, maybe to explain why the Apaches always won. Seven hijos de la chingada against a schoolmistress.

There were two old men, one more elaborately attired than any of the others: a necklace, an embroidered shirt. They were as strong as the younger men, but the skin hung on their bellies and they had gray hair; their decades in the desert were visible in their faces and hands. There were three young men, pitilessly beautiful: bodies board-straight, shorter hair. There was her captor, the same age though maybe slightly more seasoned: he wore his hair as long as the old men. He was unquestionably the captain, his authority evident in his stature but also in his bearing, which was less tense, almost clumsy: he had the luxury of being himself whether he was riding and focused on the road or talking to the others. There was the boy, a kid still putting meat on his bones, the ugliest of all: short, big-boned and small-eyed, big-headed. He had very short hair and played the role of servant. None of them, even the old men, seemed affected at all by the ride, which had been hard on them, too, until today, even if they hadn't had to recover from beatings and sleepless nights.

She thought that if she could have, if there weren't seven of them, if they would only let her fight them one by one, she would have grabbed the giant by the hair, pulling him down and taking a bite out of his neck, jamming her nails in his eyes and her fist in his mouth, severing his dick with her teeth and crushing his testicles with a stone; she would eat the scramble of blood and semen that came out as happily as they had gobbled the rennet from the calf's intestines.

Her other thought was that perhaps they were finally nearing the end of their journey.

CONTRARY TO WHAT ZULOAGA MIGHT have guessed, Pisago Cabezón headed straight for the mountains through the chaparral, without waiting for anyone. His horse was a dapple-gray mustang that couldn't have been broken to saddle for long: you could see in the way she shook herself that she would run off again as soon as she could. She had short legs and wide haunches, her mane was as long as her master's hair, and her tail was as thick and ragged as a sudden downpour. The nacionales followed him in silence, resigned but also agonized because he was spurring on his horse—fresh and accustomed to the terrain—at a clip that might be perilous for the parched ranch horses.

The lieutenant colonel soon noticed that the twins had dropped to the rear of the procession, either from lack of trust or in open declaration of rebellion against submission to a Coyotero. Zuloaga could not afford to lose them. He slowed to let them catch up to him, then, attempting to distract them, asked them to explain why they had been in jail in Janos, information he would need to complete his report when he returned to Buenaventura. Maybe they had already served their time and had been held simply because there had been no one to give the order to free them after the regiment's soldiers were transferred to the Texas front.

The two brothers looked at each other. One scratched his mule's ear, the other pursed his lips, grimacing, and shook his head. I believe our small crime, he said, as you're so good to call it, was the hanging kind, and they only let us live because they needed somebody to clean shit out of the stables. And the latrines, added the other. Zuloaga gave a half smile. So what did you do? he asked. I don't know if it was so bad, said one of them. A little harsh, maybe, but it was an act of justice. What was it? asked the lieutenant again. Better not put it in your report, said the other brother. I'll say that I freed you for extraordinary service to the Republic, explained Zuloaga, but I want to know whether they'll court-martial me or not. The twins exchanged glances again. The quieter one said: I think we owe it to him, don't we, brother? The other responded: Just think how nice this sun feels on our backs and how cold it would be in the hole in Janos. Not to mention, added his brother, that if you'd've gone off with everybody and Mother Elvira, we'd've croaked from hunger and thirst and the stink of turds. The two of them looked at Zuloaga. Just remember your promise, said one of them. What promise? That if we're about to be locked up again, you'll shoot us first.

The brothers had happened to be on their way from Topochique to Batopilas, in the mountains. They were from Sonora and they had crossed the border into Chihuahua without realizing that the criollo government in that part of the state had instituted a zero tolerance policy against Yaqui renegades. The brothers were hunting, so they were on foot, carrying guns, shirtless, headbands holding back their hair. With them was a cousin from Bavispe. As they were crossing a cornfield at the bottom of a canyon, someone opened fire. They had no way to defend themselves out in the open on the canyon bottom, so they scattered. The twins found each other the next night at a fork in the road to Frijolar. The episode struck them as amusing until they realized that their cousin wasn't coming. The next morning they returned to the site of the gunfire and followed his trail.

It wasn't hard. They soon found the place where he had been seized, and clear signs that he'd been tied to a horse and dragged back to the road, still alive. He'd been tumbled around for quite a while and then he'd been tied to a tree and left to die; the turkey buzzards were feeding on him by the time they got there. He had suffocated to death, slowly, his balls cut off and stuffed down his throat. His hands had been burned, charred black so that anyone who saw him would know there would be no thieves in the region. His face was monstrously misshapen, brutally beaten. When they untied him they saw that his back had been cruelly lashed.

As they inspected the scene, it became clear to them that the men who'd done this had been a party of criollo ranchers: they were wearing good boots, not huaraches or moccasins; the twins counted seven horses, good ones to judge by the clean prints.

They waited, hidden among the stones, until the sun went down and they could retrieve their cousin's body. They covered him with a blanket and returned to the hills to bury him.

It's unheard of for the death of a Yaqui or an Apache not to cost a life on the other side. The next day, bad luck fell upon a criollo rancher from Chilavo who was on his way to El Vallecito with his son. The brothers picked the boy off his horse "like a sweet little pigeon"—in Zuloaga's words, poured into his diary—with a neat shot to the middle of his forehead. As for the rancher, they killed his horse and tied him up, leaving him untouched so he could watch while they hung the boy upside down from a tree, gouging out his eyes with a knife so that in the next world he wouldn't be judged as an innocent. Then they cut off his tiny white penis and threw it into the road to be taken by an animal so he wouldn't become a man on the other side. They shaved his head with a knife so that he would be an outcast and no one would speak to him as he crossed the valley of the dead. The Yaqui code of conduct did not condone the torture of children, but it had no objection to the punishment of child ghosts.

The boy's father surely couldn't understand why the body of a dead child should be the object of such rage. He must have consoled himself with the thought that none of this was hurting the boy, never considering that a person's ghost is what he is at the moment of death, not what he was in life. He must have felt a surge of terror when the twins turned to look at him.

Revenge was a technical procedure, almost bureaucratic, neither sad nor enjoyable. They pulled off the criollo's clothes, unbound his feet, and bound his hands behind his back. It surprised them that he didn't struggle. Poor bastard must've thought we were going to hang him, said one of the twins. They hit him on the head with a stone, gently, so that he would fall without losing consciousness. Once he was lying face down on the ground, one of them sat on his back and the other took his hunting knife, lifted the rancher's legs, wedged the man's feet between his armpit and his forearm, and sliced off the soles of his feet. The two strips of flesh were also tossed into the road, this time so that people would find them. The criollo didn't scream much, though he shook a lot, according to one of the twins. They fastened the same rope they'd used to bind his ankles around his neck and forced him up. They walked him all day over the roughest ground, never leaving the fringes of the Bavispe River. When they camped for the night, the man had two repulsive lumps of mangled flesh at the end of his legs and a purple blotch up his shins, but he was relatively strong. Crying quietly to himself, he was, that's all, said one of the twins. They burned the raw stumps of his feet with a torch to keep him alive. They didn't give him supper, but they did give him a little water. The next day they repeated the procedure: slicing off a strip of burnt flesh, walking aimlessly among the stones and thorns, cauterizing the wound.

How many days was it we went on like that? mused one of the Yaquis, growing emotional in the telling of the tale. The bastard wouldn't break, said his brother, but nobody was expecting us anywhere, and we just led him around, hunting quail so we wouldn't starve. In the mornings he'd be crying and begging us not to make another cut, what had he ever done to us, why not just kill him; we dried the sweat on his brow and then sliced the littlest bit more off, because the shrimp was holding out for so long that soon he'd have no feet left. One day we got tired of dragging him around behind us and we showed mercy. We broke all the little bones in his legs with a big stone and we hung him by the ankles from a branch. This time we didn't even give him water, but even so he held on for another day.

Zuloaga, who had tried to remain cool as he listened to the story, felt sick. So if we found a dead Yaqui, that's what you'd do to me, he said. One of the brothers shook his head. We'd do it to El Gringo, he said, he wouldn't fight as hard. In the end we cut the body down and left it tied to the same tree where they'd tied our cousin, doing our best to make it look exactly the same, so the ranchers would understand. And then you complain when in Sonora they're paying one hundred gold pesos for the scalp of a renegade Indian? asked Zuloaga. Maybe so, said one of the brothers, but trading for scalps is savagery.

AT AMELIA'S AND COSME'S REQUEST, we're staying a day longer in Medicine Park. They like the river. There's a wonderful walking path along the edge and a dam that makes a spring-fed pool where you can swim. The flow is strong and the water cold. The weather is so hot, it's hard to get them out. There're almost no people; the four cabins next to ours are all empty. They love the house itself: there's a big porch all around it with tables and chairs where they can play, eat, read. They call it the deck. They're sleeping in a wooden-railed loft that I told them was like the watchtower of a bluecoats fort in Lakota territory, but from what we've overheard, they see it as the cabin of a galleon. Things are all mixed up in their imagination. We've been listening to the audiobook of *Treasure Island* on the road, and now they're living in a Peter Pan adventure: pirates and Indians.

As we were playing cards on the porch after lunch—we have to keep the kids inside while the merciless sun glares down—Cosme asked if the Apaches were related to the Aztecs. No, I said, their languages have different roots. Why did they build a pyramid for Geronimo, then? he asked. What do you mean, a pyramid? I replied. In the cemetery, he said. It isn't a pyramid, I said, it's a burial mound. Amelia was eating a Popsicle, so bright red it could only have come from a laboratory. She pulled it out of her mouth, glamorous as a forties starlet, to say: It's an Egyptian pyramid. She knows everything.

I checked the photographs I'd taken on my phone at the cemetery. The cabin definitely doesn't look like a ship, whatever the kids say, but the funeral monument to Geronimo really is a pyramid. I don't know how I didn't notice it before.

It's a special grave, the only one without the traditional military stone. The others are like white dominoes, inscribed by an anonymous hand with identifying information, always in the same order: the deceased's war name, by which they were addressed in life; their Apache name, taboo once they'd been initiated as warriors; the band to which they belonged within the Chiricahua; and their dates of birth (almost always approximate) and death. Nana's gravestone, for example, reads:

CHIEF NANA
(KAS-TZIDEN)
WARM SPRINGS APACHE
1800–1896

Geronimo's vaguely Mesoamerican pyramid, meanwhile, stands more than three feet tall. It can't be very old: its four sides are concrete, with rows of river stones mounted in it for decoration, making it look stepped. On the upper platform, where the temple would be on a Mexican or Central American pyramid, there's an eagle, also concrete, clearly Aztec-inspired, though gringo tourists might well see it as a bald eagle, their national symbol. The eagle looks as if it's been decapitated, maybe by someone who imagined they could acquire some of the Chiricahua captain's powers that way. In its place a metal head has been screwed to the concrete body.

The tomb is also inscribed differently from the others. A plaque affixed to the front of the pyramid reads simply:

GERONIMO

No Apache name, no accent on the first *o*, no dates, no affiliation. He was Gileño—Bedonkohe, he would have called himself. It's as if his enemy designation has been erased, as if it were best to situate him outside of history and the waltz of languages and nations.

The prisoner of war cemetery at Fort Sill is a file with a page conveniently missing. To strip Geronimo of identifying details is to sterilize him, to pretend he was never feared, never humiliated and dispossessed. It is to ignore that although he was already an old man when he arrived in Oklahoma, he was allowed to leave the military base only under escort—to be displayed as a trophy at the head of Theodore Roosevelt's 1901 inauguration parade, as a captive beast at the 1904 St. Louis World's Fair, as an Indian for rent at Wild West shows.

There is a rumor, too, that the grave itself was robbed. In the book *In Geronimo's Footsteps*, Harlyn Geronimo, the shaman's great-grandson, claims that when Captain Prescott Sheldon Bush—father and grandfather of U.S. presidents—was stationed at Fort Sill in 1918, during World War I, he stole Geronimo's skull from the tomb to be used in initiation rites of Skull and Bones, the secret society he belonged to at Yale.

There is no conclusive evidence of the deed, but according to Harlyn, when the council members of Arizona's San Carlos reservation requested the return of the warrior's remains from Fort Sill for burial near his birthplace, they received instead a letter from the membership of Skull and Bones expressing the society's willingness to return Geronimo's skull, which they kept in a glass case in the fraternity's inner sanctum. Enclosed was a photograph of the skull. When the president of the reservation's tribal council traveled to New Haven to receive the remains, however, he was presented with a glass case that held the skull of a child. He refused it. The group of lawyers present at this charade, among them Jonathan Bush, brother and uncle of presidents, tried to make him sign a document stating that the secret society didn't have Geronimo's skull. When he refused, they took back the photograph they had sent him in the mail.

Harlyn Geronimo notes that while the story of the photograph doesn't actually prove anything, a 1918 letter—in Yale's Sterling Memorial Library archives—from one Skull and Bones member to another repeats the account of Prescott Bush desecrating Geronimo's tomb and depositing his skull (and two femurs besides) in the secret society's inner sanctum.

Skull and Bones's subsequent response to Geronimo's great-grandson and the many journalists who've chased the story has been that the rumor of desecration is simply that. (The Bushes have ignored requests for comment entirely.) Thus far there has been no move to take legal action, as it isn't easy to litigate against an association whose ranks include sitting senators, an ex–secretary of state, judges, and three presidents, one living and two dead (George H. W. Bush and William Howard Taft, whose tombs surely haven't been desecrated by some young Apache so that his fraternity buddies can pretend they're members of the Water Buffalo Lodge).

SHE WAS WOKEN BY THE SOUND of the cattle brushing against one another. She heard no other movement, so she went back to sleep, curled up in the calfskin and blanket.

Something was different. It wasn't just the feeling of being herself in her own body after having truly eaten and drunk, after being covered. It took her a while to realize that what was missing was the sound of the horses and the camp. They had left her alone. She shook herself out of her daze and confirmed that the warriors were gone. With luck, there might be some scrap of meat stuck to one of the stones from the fire last night. She got up, thinking about digging in the ashes, and a bundle rolled to the ground. She bent down to pick it up and undid it. It was clothes: short pants and a coarse shirt. Men's clothes, obviously, much too big for her. She was about to put them on when she heard a sharp voice. She covered herself with a piece of clothing, as if for days she hadn't been the world's most naked person. She saw the boy coming, his raised index finger intended to convey an authority he decidedly lacked. She smiled at him and turned her back. She was just pulling the shirt over her shoulders when she felt the boy tug at her. He took the pants from her hands, shouting and pointing to something beyond the cattle. She stood still, undecided whether to give him the slap he deserved. He grabbed her by the forearm and yanked, but not roughly, pulling her toward a bend in the creek where a pool had formed. He pointed to it and she understood that she should wash before she got dressed. She was so far gone that she hadn't even noticed she still had calf's blood on her from days ago, crusted vomit, grease from the feast the night before. As she was taking off her shirt the boy retreated to the hill, granting her a privacy that verged on comedy. She got in the water. It was no more than knee-deep, but she could wash sitting down.

As she sat there, something happened to her that hadn't happened since Chihuahua: she felt the need to move her bowels. She found a spot in the acacia bushes and felt a liberation that was almost a return to normality. With her foot she covered up the leavings and went back to the pool, lying back just to feel the water on her ears. She could have stayed there all day, but the thought of getting dressed made her rise from the water. She put on the pants and shirt, then sat to wait for what came next.

BY THE TIME THE SUN WENT DOWN, Pisago Cabezón had saved the nacionales. Though to say that Cabezón saved them is perhaps to cloak his impenetrable inner thoughts in motive. He'd led them westward out of the Valley of the Moon and brought them to a watering hole covered with branches so that it didn't gleam from a distance, without once turning to look at them. He set such a quick pace that they had to follow his tracks.

Like every evening, the nacionales lit a fire to cook while it was still light. Cabezón didn't join in the group's dinner, nor did he spread his blanket near them. He got some food out of his saddlebags and ate it cold. The only way he interacted at all with the Mexicans was by allowing his horse to drink alongside theirs, which were taller and less sturdy, infinitely more skittish and beat. When night had fallen and the camp was preparing to spend it in peace—the last few days had taken a crushing toll on the bodies of humans and horses—the Apache moved a little farther away to sing to his god.

To the surprise of all the nacionales, Márquez sat up on his own blanket and sang along with him on several of the songs. Doña Elvira shot a look at the lieutenant. I told you he spoke Apache, she whispered. Cabezón kept singing imperturbably, though he must have noticed he had accompaniment. The twins were furious. I always knew that faggot was a pinche fucking traitor, said one of them. Elvira had her revolver out and in his mouth in an instant. I told you, if you don't know what you're talking about, don't say anything. The Yaqui mumbled something incomprehensible; it was actually quite a long sentence for someone with the barrel of a Colt tickling his uvula. His brother reported that he was saying it was true, he didn't know anything, and La Elvis was right.

DURING THEIR CAPTIVITY IN FORT SILL, the Chiricahuas had a baseball team, on which the youngest—taken prisoner as children or born in captivity—played beneath what must have been the bored gaze of the chiefs, against teams of soldiers stationed at the fort. There are photographs of the boys with their arms around each other, in baseball caps, under the merciless Oklahoma sun. The name of their team was printed on their jerseys in the familiar cursive script of the king of sports. Predictably, they were called the Apaches.

IT WAS THE BEST THING that could possibly have happened: the warriors had left Camila and the boy part of the skin of the calf, with scraps of meat still clinging to it. Without speaking or even glancing at each other, they roasted it in the embers on three sticks and ate it. Afterward, they walked together down to the water to wash their faces and hands, and then he went back to tending the cattle and gathering mesquite beans and izote hearts. She returned to waiting in the shade of the cottonwoods for something to happen.

That evening they roasted what the boy had picked and ate it. Nothing else happened. Back in her spot under the cottonwoods, Camila began to think that what she needed was a horse to get back to Chihuahua. Also that if she could steal the boy's moccasins she could follow the creek south and maybe it would take her somewhere. Or north: they couldn't be far from the Santa Rita mine, where she knew there was a detachment of Mexican soldiers. At some point she walked a short distance even though she was barefoot: she wanted to climb a hill to see if she could see smoke from a fire, or find a hiding place, anything. She headed off like someone out for a stroll.

When she felt that she had left the boy's sphere of vigilance, she leaned against a cottonwood to enjoy air that she didn't have to share with anyone else. She heard a buzzing and felt a tug. She shook herself, thinking she was being attacked by an insect, and discovered that she was pinned to the tree; an arrow had passed through the tail of her shirt just a fraction of an inch from her stomach. She pulled out the arrow, walked back, and returned it to the boy, who put it away in his quiver, stony-faced.

Nothing happened the next day or the next, except that the beans and flowers dwindled. The boy didn't stray from camp. She considered bashing in the head of one of the calves when the boy wasn't looking. She even chose the beast and the stone, but she didn't have the stomach to go through with it.

Around the fourth or fifth day, the boy returned with his skin bag full of live pack rats. He made an incision between their legs with his knife and pulled off their skins like someone peeling prickly pears. While they were still kicking, he packed them into balls of mud and threw them into the fire. Camila thought there must be less cruel ways of cooking them until he handed her the first one. She ate the tender flesh and threw the rest away, scandalizing her guard, who retrieved the carcass and ate it, even the bones. Realizing that there would be nothing else, she ate every bit of the next one except the eyes, which were hard as marbles. She couldn't chew the skull, either, but she had no qualms about sucking out its contents.

She didn't regret it: for the next two days they had nothing to eat. On the third day without food, as she was picking a scab off her knee so it would close over again, she noticed that the boy, busy torturing a tarantula with tiny drops of boiling water, had sensed something in the air. He got up to sniff around, like a bear. Then he gestured imperiously for her to be still. She obeyed, excited by the prospect of something happening at last. Then the boy fell on her and bound her hand and foot in a single move, as if they were at a rodeo and she were a steer. He tied the end of the rope to a cottonwood. When he had gone, she realized that he'd left enough rope for her to be able to reach the water if she dragged herself on the ground. She inched like a worm toward the shade under the tree, praying there was no wasp's nest in its branches.

The boy returned relatively quickly, with a corncob grin on his face and two dead hares over his shoulder. He cleaned them before he untied her. She was stiff, but she could have endured much worse without deeming herself utterly miserable. Her threshold of discomfort had changed: she was clothed, she had no blisters, she hadn't been beaten or kicked. He pushed her to eat the raw entrails of the hares, and she decided they weren't bad. Then he made a fire and roasted the flesh on a spit.

That night they lay down together under the sky. She took her first long look at him. He really was very short, with an enormous square head, a permanent scowl, and the smoothest skin in the world. Ugly as he was, there was something endearing and sad about the adult way he carried himself. When he returned her gaze, she touched her chest and said: "Camila." Then she touched his chest. "Goyahkla," he replied, and pretended to yawn. She guessed he meant he was tired, or that she could sleep without fear.

WE DROVE THROUGH TEXAS ACROSS the Panhandle, the narrowest part, so we didn't have to stop or get gas. Texas is both the most Mexican and the most shockingly and even embarrassingly anti-Mexican state in the country. Until the nearly sixteen million non-Hispanic people who live there get therapy to resolve their flagrant father hatred, we refuse to spend a dollar on Texan soil.

THE SCENT OF CORREDOR'S RAISE-THE-DEAD coffee opened Lieutenant Colonel Zuloaga's eyes. They had agreed that as long as they had Pisago Cabezón around, they could make a fire before dawn without putting themselves in danger. He lay there for a moment, which was something he never did, trained as he was in Chihuahua's regular battalions at the end of the War of Independence. He rubbed his eyes and folded his arms behind his head, savoring the smell from the Raramuri's rekindled fire. The stars looked like rips in a black ceiling, with uncontainable light spilling through.

When he finally approached the embers, he found one of the Yaquis already sitting cross-legged by the fire with a pewter mug in his hand. He didn't know what time the twins got up—sometimes he suspected they never actually slept—but one of the unspoken rules of the expedition was that no one would come near the fire until Corredor and Zuloaga had had their first coffee of the day, talking about whatever they talked about, and the lieutenant had had a smoke. Any earlier and there was no dealing with them.

Now what? the lieutenant asked, irritation evident in his voice. The Yaqui raised the index and middle fingers of his right hand in a V, tapping his face under his eyes. The lieutenant snorted. He rearranged the blanket over his shoulders and sat by the fire, waiting in silence for Corredor to hand him a mug. He blew on the coffee and then he said: I don't remember ordering anyone to stand guard. But we must, the Yaqui replied. The lieutenant raised an eyebrow. Why? he muttered. The other man rolled his eyes, then pointed toward the spot a short distance from camp where Pisago Cabezón was already up, gathering his things and strapping them onto his horse.

Zuloaga fingered the tobacco in the pocket of his Comanche jacket. You think you have to watch him because of that fool idea about ancestral enemies? he asked the Yaqui. He's an Indian like any other: one day he's at war with one group, another day with another group, just like the rest of you. The twin raised his eyebrows. Are your people any different? he asked. Take your pretty Comanche jacket. Yesterday the Comanches were Mexico City's bosom friends, and today they're a plague on the Republic. The lieutenant rubbed his eyes with one hand and said: Let me finish my coffee and smoke a cigarette, and then we'll talk. The Yaqui narrowed his eyes and frowned. He kept quiet, but he didn't budge.

Zuloaga knew himself well, which was maybe why he'd made it this far in a world where things didn't always go according to plan. He would end up insulting the Yaqui unnecessarily if he didn't give himself some space, so he got up and went to sit some distance away, his back to the fire. He rolled a cigarette, lit it. He had taken two or three drags when he heard the Yaqui approach. He took another drag. If he'd thought God existed, he would have prayed for strength. Turning without getting up, he indicated an imaginary spot in front of him with the end of his cigarette. Sit and tell me what you want, he said. The Yaqui shook his head, gesturing to a point farther away from the camp. The lieutenant rose and walked with him toward the brush, far from Pisago, not that he was paying them the slightest attention. The sun was about to crack the sky, pushing up behind the jagged mountains. It had already swallowed up the starry rips and stained the sky green.

The twin stepped closer to the lieutenant. Those are the Chiricahuee mountains, he said with a reverence that struck the lieutenant as out of place. So? The pinche cabrón's leading us to the slaughterhouse. He brought us to water, which is what we asked him to do, said the lieutenant colonel. And added: Sure, he got us out of the way so his brother-in-law could ride on to sell the cows he stole in Sonora to the gringos of Santa Fé, but he kept his word: he brought us to water. We're deep in Apashee country here, said the Yaqui, and going north it'll only get worse. Pisago is Coyotero, said Zuloaga, he has

Mexican children, property in Santa Rita, he won't risk getting killed by the mountain Gileños or me shooting him in the fray as a traitor. The Yaqui rolled his eyes. And the dancing master, he asked, what about him? How do you mean? You saw him start to sing with Cabezón. El Márquez sings every night, he knows all the songs, even the Apache ones. Once fighting breaks out they'll turn on us; two is too many for a troop this small. Pisago isn't part of the troop, said Zuloaga, and there's more hatred between him and the Gileños than there'll ever be between us and them. You're Mexican, but we're Yaqui, mi teniente, and that boy making your coffee is Raramuri; Pisago hates us more than he hates the Gileños. Since our grandparents' day we've been at each other's throats. The lieutenant raised his hat and wiped his face with his hand. I understand what you're saying, he said, and I give you my word I won't make any decision that will put you or Corredor at risk.

The twin bared his teeth in a smile and gave Zuloaga a complicit look. Or there's another way, he said. What? Just do the deed. What's that? You know what I mean. I don't. Why head up to the Gila River when we could be killing Apashees right here in the Chiricahuee? The Yaqui went on: There's no getting revenge on the Gileños of Nueva México, they're tough bastards and the lady you're looking for is turned Apashee by now and there'll be no way to bring her back: who'd want to cuddle with a criollito once she's had a taste of the mountain? Who'd want to go back to kitchens and petticoats and bonnets and church pews and chasing kiddies all day and all the pinche shit you make your women do when she can run around raising hell? Better we take care of Pisago, head into the mountains right here, avenge the ranchers you wanted to avenge, and home we go, everybody safe and sound. Zuloaga laughed. You don't get it, he said to the Yaqui, I'm the law, and the Mexican Republic is this bone-tired body you see in front of you. Those Indians took some cattle and a woman and I'm the one who turns things back the way they were; it's my duty to go and punish the guilty party if possible, and if not, make it known that there are consequences, that if they come back down to Janos we'll lock them up.

The Yaqui shrugged his shoulders. You're the ones who don't get it, he said. If there's a war, you're going to lose it because there's fewer of you and you don't know how to fight; the place to get our revenge is right here, where there's just one camp and we can surprise them when they aren't expecting it, because over there in their hideout on the Gila we'll be wiped clean off the map. He shook his head without losing his smile entirely. If you hit them here, you hit them there, too, see? If you kill one, you're hurting the captain of them all, their leader, you're telling them what you want them to know, and they'll understand; anything else just ain't sense and they'll kill us like the idiots we are, because aiming to get into a shootout at the Gila with the gang you've got is dumb as a donkey's ass. Trust me, he said, and he gestured toward the others, who were still asleep even now that the light was strong. The lieutenant shrugged. I'm going to talk to Cabezón, he said to the Yaqui, and he went over to the fire to pour himself a second mug of coffee and take one to the Apache.

THE ARTIST ELBRIDGE AYER BURBANK, who painted several portraits of Geronimo during his captivity at Fort Sill, wrote in his memoirs that the war shaman's defining characteristic was his vanity.

One day in 1905, as they were talking during a session in Burbank's studio, Geronimo boasted that Ussen—father of all—had revealed to him that he wouldn't die in combat, so he was convinced he would die of old age: no one could kill him. The artist kidded him that he must have survived because he kept his distance from the action during gunfights.

The shaman raised his eyebrows and took off the shirt he had always refused to remove to pose. His chest was pocked with the scars of more than fifty bullet holes, some so big you could fit a pebble in them.

ZULOAGA STRODE TO THE SPOT where Pisago Cabezón was saddling his horse. Good morning, he said, and held out the mug. It was the first time that Zuloaga had broken protocol to speak to him directly since they were introduced by the cowboy from Virginia. When Pisago was done with his horse he accepted the coffee. Zuloaga scratched his beard, grown out now after days on the trail. Will you ride ahead of us again? he asked. You won't be able to follow my tracks, said Pisago, but tell your Yaquis that if I run into any trouble I'll leave them a bent branch and a stone, they'll know what it means. Zuloaga snorted. I'm a tracker, too, he said. Just because I'm Mexican doesn't mean you have to treat me like an idiot. The Apache looked up into the lieutenant's face. His eyes were tiny, and they looked even smaller under the enormous brim of his ten-gallon hat, which the lieutenant still couldn't get used to. He even cracked a smile. My wife is Mexican, too, he replied, don't get me wrong—do you have tobacco? Zuloaga took his little leather pouch out of his bag. Pisago rolled a cigarette, and the lieutenant followed suit. The Mexican lit his own cigarette, then offered the flame to the Apache. They sat thigh to thigh on a rock and smoked in silence.

When they had only two or three puffs left, Cabezón spoke. Someone must have come to you by now with the gossip that there's a Gileño camp in the Chiricahuas, he said. Zuloaga nodded. It's true, but they won't give you trouble if they don't think you're headed to Nueva México. If you follow me, when they see you pass they'll think you're chasing me and they'll let you go, unless any of your men has unfinished business with them. You aren't coming with us? the lieutenant asked nervously. I shouldn't be here, said Pisago, the Gileños are sworn enemies of the Coyoteros and I can't let them get a glimpse of me. What they'll see when they send people to spy on you is nacionales tracking a ghost. Is that so, said Zuloaga. The Apache went on, having missed or perhaps purposely overlooked the lieutenant's ungracious lack of trust: Just don't do anything stupid and you'll be all right; tell your nun no more shooting in the air. He glanced at the mountain and went on: So long as no Mexican has done anything to any Chiricahua Apache, they'll have no reason to seek revenge, and they'll let you pass. How can we know that? asked Zuloaga. You can't; the Apaches around here are as crazy as they come. Cabezón went on without a pause, obviously eager to get moving: You'll have to go on alone to the Sierra del Piloncillo. If you stay on the path, you'll find water at the end of the day, right outside an abandoned village called Portal. Your Yaquis will remember it, their people used it when they came from Sonora, in the days before Cuchillo Negro. Aren't we in Sonora anymore? There's no Sonora or Chihuahua here, just Apachería, said the Coyotero.

He gestured toward the Chiricahuas, without naming them. We have to get past them today—today and tomorrow—and then it'll be easier, he said. He adjusted his hat, and from under the vast brim he said, Don't try to hide, because you can't. Let them see you always moving, and don't stop except to piss. When you reach the watering hole let the horses drink first. If you have to fill your canteens, only one of you should dismount. Don't wash, and ride on well into the night. Don't make a fire or anything when you stop to sleep: make sure that whenever they can see you, you're moving. He took a last drag on the cigarette and put it out with the heel of his boot. Then he scraped a hole with the toe, ground out the butt in it, and covered it with soil. Like all Apaches, he left no trace. He handed the empty mug to Zuloaga, bowed his head slightly, and walked to his horse without looking back. He mounted it Apache-style, as Zuloaga watched enviously: in a single bound, his arms around the horse's neck.

The lieutenant colonel approached the animal and stroked its mane, which was much shorter and coarser than the manes of his Spanish horses. He looked Cabezón in the eye and asked: Can I trust you'll take us all the way? Only as far as Santa Rita in the Mogollones, said the Coyotero; I can't set foot in Mangas Coloradas's territory. Mangas Coloradas? He's the Gileño you're looking for, everybody knows he took the Mexican lady. Zuloaga raised his hand from the horse's mane. We'll see you in the foothills of the Piloncillos in two days, he said. Pisago touched his hat.

Zuloaga smoked another cigarette, then headed back to camp. He found El Márquez and El Gringo having coffee with the rest of the nacionales—Corredor rushing around, surely irritated because for once they had all gotten up at the same time. Everyone looked somber, so Zuloaga, irked by the gloomy mood, played the humor card. Now that we've come this far, what are your names anyway? he asked the twins: you never introduced yourselves. They looked unamused by the change in topic. How could I introduce myself when the minute you freed me you stuck the muzzle of your gun in my mouth? said one of the brothers. But now we're friends, said Zuloaga. Friends with the Apashees, replied the other twin. What do you mean? Friends smoke together, said one twin, and the other went on: And nobody yet's offered us tobacco when we parleyed. The criollo took the little leather pouch from his pocket and tossed it to him. Be my guest. The Yaqui began to roll a cigarette. I'm Guadalupe, and he's Victoria, he said, nodding at his brother. What? asked Zuloaga. Intent on his cigarette, the Yaqui glanced sideways at him. What d'you mean what? he asked, Guadalupe and Victoria, what's funny about that? The lieutenant colonel was surprised no one had laughed: it was a good joke. Like President Guadalupe Victoria? That's the man, said the other twin, the one who granted citizenship to all Indians. Zuloaga scratched his neck. Then you do want to be Mexican? Sometimes, said one, who might have been Guadalupe. I don't believe you, said the lieutenant, it's like if Corredor and I called ourselves Vicente and Guerrero. Nice names, said Victoria. And General Vicente Guerrero gave us our independence, said his brother. He frowned. Zuloaga and Corredor, he said, silly pinche little names when you could have been Vicente and Guerrero. The Raramuri, who was standing behind the boss, said: I would take Guerrero.

The lieutenant colonel looked around and saw that the other nacionales were watching him impatiently. They had little interest in the matter of names. He cleared his throat and said: We're going to give Cabezón a head start, so that the warriors in the Chiricahuas think we're hunting him. He met the Yaquis' eyes before he went on: We're going to ride along the edge of the mountains to a town called Portal, where there's a watering hole. Victoria interrupted him: We can't be stopping in Portal by day, he said, that watering hole is theirs, it'll only rile them. The animals will drink; we won't dismount, so they see we're showing respect. The twins exchanged glances. One of them—who knew which?—said to the other: He's been schooled. What if we get thirsty? asked the other. The lieutenant looked him in the eye. Come on, he said, and asked: Do they have a quarrel with any of you? They all shook their heads in unison. No quarrel, the twins said together, with such conviction that the lieutenant colonel felt somewhat easier. The idea is that they'll think we're on Pisago's trail, Zuloaga went on. He's going to move as fast as he can through the mountains. If they think we have a chance of catching him, we'll make it through without a fight. Who are *they*? asked El Gringo. El Márquez cuffed his head. The dancing master spoke seriously for the first time since the expedition had begun. There are names that should never be uttered, he said. The poor Gringo, who never spoke up on his own and who approached each task with touching zeal, lapsed back into silence, crestfallen.

Soon after they set out, Zuloaga noticed that Cabezón had turned east following the rocky bed of a dry river that led out of the valley, so that it was impossible to follow him without knowing beforehand where he was going. He guessed that after a while he must have climbed into the mass of hills that rose in the distance, disappearing the way Apaches always disappeared: into thin air, in front of your nose, just like that. The lieutenant colonel pulled up his horse. Should we follow to play it safe? he asked the Yaquis, or should we ride through the valley? Guadalupe said: He went through the Pilones; it's slow and hot that way, I think he was scared. Should we follow him? the lieutenant asked again. El Márquez chimed in from behind: Do we trust him? The Yaquis and Zuloaga all answered at once, the twins saying no and the lieutenant saying yes. What then? asked the nun. Zuloaga veered off toward the east and the riverbed. They all felt relieved to be riding away from the ominous mountains.

LATE ON THE SNOWY, ICY NIGHT of February 13, 1909, Geronimo fell from his horse on the banks of Turkey Creek. He was inside Fort Sill, close to the prisoner of war camp, but not close enough for another Apache on his way back to the barracks to find his body lying on the ground. He was nearly eighty. I've read almost everything written about him, and there isn't a single mention of another occasion when he lost control of his horse. That may be why the idea has spread that he was drunk. No one can say for sure, though it's a known fact that he was on his way home from a poker game.

It's a fact, too, that by then he had almost completely lost his sight. In the last photographs, his eyeballs are glassy. He could hardly hear, either; he shouted when he talked. For some time, he had expressed himself in a mix of Athabaskan and Spanish—only his last wife, Azul, and his nephew, Asa Daklugie, could understand him—and he swore to whoever came near that he had converted to Christianity: the clearest sign, as I see it, that his mind was in the grips of a cruel, senile dementia. It's true that in 1903 he had been baptized by the pastor of the Dutch Reformed Church who ministered to the soldiers stationed at Fort Sill, but he had been expelled from the congregation shortly thereafter, for gambling and disorderly conduct.

When Geronimo's horse returned alone to the prisoner camp barracks, Azul raised an alarm, and a group of young men (not warriors anymore, having grown up in U.S. Army prisons in Florida and Oklahoma) went out to look for him. They found him unconscious in a ditch, caked with snow. They wrapped him in a blanket and brought him back to the barracks.

Asa Daklugie, who spoke not only Spanish and Athabaskan but also perfect English, called the doctor, the one Geronimo had always refused to see when he was in command of his body: he was a war shaman, he would get better on his own. The doctor diagnosed a mammoth case of pneumonia. There was nothing to do but tend to him until Ussen summoned him to the special heaven for motherfuckers who turn rage into insufferable performance as an act of self-defense. He was unconscious for hours at a time, so they were able to take him to the military base hospital without protest.

He was delirious for three days, during which he plodded turtle-like along the tunnel of light that the nervous system apparently conjures up in brains near death. He regretted many things he saw in the tunnel, things that brought back the years of butchery and combat. Even so, his last words, spoken to Asa Daklugie just before he fell into a final coma, were: "I should never have surrendered. I should have stayed in Mexico and fought till the end."

IT WAS MIDAFTERNOON WHEN VICTORIA alerted Zuloaga that Pisago had taken a new turn. He's going deeper into the Pilones, he said. For the first time, the lieutenant doubted the Coyotero: Could he have ridden off to Santa Rita alone? Victoria clicked his tongue and pointed toward what in the distance looked like a fold in the Chiricahuas. The lieutenant noticed that his lips were white as he said: The Guadalupe Pass is coming, that's why; he's afraid to cross it, so he took to the mountains.

Like everybody, Zuloaga had heard talk of the pass. It was a canyon that bisected the mass of the Chiricahuas and Pilones, forging a passage along which riders could exit Chihuahua and enter Nueva México at a gallop. The trip from the San Bernardino Valley to the high prairie of Nueva México, which usually took a full day, could be done this way in under half the time, if the traveler dared. Any northerner with military training knew you didn't go there unless you had a company big enough to scare off whoever might choose to mount an ambush from above. The pass belonged to the Apaches and the outlaws who traded with them; setting foot between those walls was lethal for anyone else.

Zuloaga reined in his horse. But we'll keep going, won't we? he said to the twins. We'll just cross the pass. It's not so easy, replied Victoria, and he dismounted in a single leap, followed by the chief. The others approached. Come here, Elvis, said Victoria, and tell the lieutenant colonel whether I'm right or not. The nun got off her horse, and El Gringo and El Márquez followed suit; they all gathered in a circle around the Yaqui to hear what he had to say. Only Corredor, who was measuring the distance with a clinical eye, stayed mounted. Look, said Victoria, picking up a stick from the ground and kneeling so that the others bent in, heads together. He drew two triangles on the ground that came together at their vertices. These are the Chiricahuee, he said, pointing to the triangle on the left, and this is the Pilones, pointing to the other. He lifted his gaze and motioned toward the mountains in the distance, sheltering the relatively safe path they were on. The two ranges, he continued, make a funnel. Then he drew a line through the center point, where the triangles met. This is the Guadalupe Pass, he went on; the Chiricahuee belong to Cuchillo Negro, and the Pilones belong to Mangas; Cuchillo Negro is crazy and all he's got is the Chiricahuee, Mangas ain't crazy and he's got land enough, so the real worry'll be Cuchillo and his mountains to the left, but if anybody wants to fuck us, they'll come out from either side of the canyon on horseback and we won't know it until they're on top of us. If they're working together, they'll come from both sides and we'll have no place to run.

They all looked up, as if expecting a magic solution from the lieutenant. Let's go the way Cabezón went, said El Gringo, driven by pure fear to make a suggestion. One little problem with that is we're slow, said Victoria. If we go through the mountains, by the time we reach water, half the horses'll have died on us; Pisago can do it 'cause he's got a mountain pony. The nun put her hand to her pistol grip.

Are we men or clowns? she asked. Zuloaga looked at the others. You heard the boss, he said, we're going to take that pass balls out.

They proceeded at the same pace until they were close enough to the geologic formation the Yaquis had described for Corredor to see whether anyone was watching them from above. How are we doing? the lieutenant colonel asked every so often. Nobody, the boy replied. When the funnel was right before them, Zuloaga pulled up his horse and said to Corredor: Fix your God-given eagle eye on those slopes and tell me whether you see anything. The Raramuri took his time. There's nothing, he said again.

The twins got out their rifles and held them high, the way the Gileños would if they attacked; El Gringo followed their example. Zuloaga drew his revolver and shortened his reins so he could handle his horse with one hand. Elvira gathered her reins in her right hand and drew her Colt, but held it low: true killers keep it simple. So confident was she of her control of the firearm that she cocked the hammer. Zuloaga, who heard the click, thought: Pinche goddamn cabrona. Corredor took his rifle and held it high Apache-style, too, though the truth is there was no way he'd be able to shoot like that: he'd never tried such a thing. Ready? asked Zuloaga. El Márquez was still sitting on his horse like a gentleman out for a trot. When Zuloaga suggested with raised eyebrow that this was perhaps imprudent, the dancing master lifted his eyes to the deep blue desert sky and said: Not a bad place to watch the last minute in the world go by. The nun turned to the boss to explain: If he's unarmed he'll be shot in the head, killed like a child; as for the rest of us, our legs will be riddled with bullets and we'll be taken to their camp to be tortured for sport. You don't say, said Zuloaga, then he turned toward the Raramuri. Sorry, Corredor, you'll have the honor of leading the way with your eyes peeled: kindly inform Saint Peter that the rest of us are on our way. The others let him pass. To everyone's surprise, El Gringo was the next to snap his reins, heading at a gallop toward what was to come. They flew toward the pass in formation.

Seen from afar, the junction of the two mountain ranges looked as stark as a stone quarry, but once at the mouth of the Guadalupe Pass, the landscape became intensely green, almost tropical: there must have been underground springs. The pass itself was a volcanic valley with something uterine about it. Along the sides of the path rose the stone walls of the ravine that split the Chiricahuas and the Pilones. Yeehaw, cabrones, you're entering the vagina of Sonora, shouted Elvira.

The pass was wider than Zuloaga had imagined. Despite his nerves, or maybe because of them, he could feel the rhetorical genius of it. The slopes of black stone, imprisoned by the branching roots of the cedars growing atop them. The open sky like a dome. The tall grass scorched by the first frosts of winter. A hawk soared overhead in the opposite direction of their advance. Good omen, shouted Márquez, who was watching the hills with the curiosity of a speleologist, holding tight to his hat while the others sweated the triggers of their weapons and spurred their horses on. Bad omen, said the Yaquis simultaneously. Guadalupe completed the thought: Out of luck again—no fight today.

When the northern mouth of the valley was in sight, Zuloaga sensed that they'd make it across. If they were going to ambush us, he thought, it would've been here. He didn't say anything, nor did he slow his horse, maybe out of respect for the sacred lapse of time his nacionales seemed to be traversing, dangling from the sky by the handhold of their lofted guns. Glancing at Corredor, he gestured toward the walls at the end of the valley. The Raramuri shook his head.

CAMILA WOKE EARLY, DESPERATE FOR the boy to go out and get more rabbits. She went to him and picked up the rope from the ground. She said: "Camila," and pointed to a tree. "Cottonwood." He laughed and went to dig up a hunk of cornbread from where he'd hidden it. He handed her some. As they ate, he said: "Camila." She couldn't remember his name. The boy laughed. "Goyahkla," he said, again pretending to yawn. The woman repeated the sound until the boy found it acceptable. "Yawn," she said. He repeated the sound. "Yawn, Goyahkla," he said, and pointed to himself.

THE APACHES REALLY KNEW HOW to live, says Cosme from the hot springs tub on the hotel room patio, where we're spending the afternoon taking baths labeled curative by his mother. She's an optimist.

We're staying in modest lodgings. Everything is modest in Truth or Consequences, a town with a magnificent name of embarrassing provenance. It was called Warm Springs until the 1950s, when the mayor entered it in a contest sponsored by a radio station. The first town to take the name of the station's top show would get a visit from the show's host. The people voted in favor of abandoning descriptive, historic Warm Springs—a sad translation of the wonderful original name, Ojocaliente—for the awesome Truth or Consequences. The townspeople made a smart decision for the wrong reasons. In their defense, it must be said that it's usually the other way around: idiotic decisions made in the name of reason.

The hotel is an old ranch house built around a big courtyard. The rooms are the house's former parlors and bedrooms. Behind each is an enclosed patio, furnished and decorated with desert plants. The hot springs feed private baths constructed from feed tubs covered with tile so intensely Mexican it could only be found in New Mexico. The tub alone would make this an expensive hotel anywhere but Truth or Consequences, where no one ever comes.

I don't know whether it's right to say, like Cosme while soaking in the steaming waters of our private spring, that the Apaches knew how to live. For them life was a passage through hardship, a stretch of adversity between more comfortable eternities, a period as parched as the landscape of peaks and thorns surrounding the town: a beautiful wasteland.

There's nothing anywhere near Truth or Consequences, and there never has been, so one has to wonder why the U.S. Army was so determined not to let the Mimbreños have a reservation here, in a spot no one wanted. There's something tragic about the place, and the reason may be this: Victorio, the Mimbreño chief of chiefs—even Nana was demoted to captain when he fought by his side—gave his life to remain here.

Victorio had good reason. The mineral baths were as sacred as New Mexico's other big hot spring, located twenty-five miles north of Taos and shared peacefully by the Navajo and the Chiricahua, mortal enemies everywhere else. And there's the proximity of the Rio Grande, which in El Paso turns north, away from the border, burying itself in the desert. It runs just a mile or so east of Truth or Consequences. During the nineteenth century, what is today Elephant Butte Reservoir was a fertile valley, thanks to the regular flooding of the river. It was a small valley that could feed just a few families, but there were never many Mimbreños anyway.

The area, reservoir and all, is truly wild, desperately arid. Blindingly hot by day and icy by night. The springs are sulfurous—

nothing can be irrigated with their waters. The question persists: why didn't the gringos let Victorio and his Mimbreños stay in Ojocaliente, even if just to spare themselves a few deaths?

Relocation was always the cornerstone of Washington, DC's extermination policies for the original peoples of the northern part of the continent, so the capital's Bureau of Indian Affairs would not let the Mimbreños live on their land, instead forcing them to shuttle through reservations occupied by other Apache groups, usually their enemies. If all the clans that ultimately joined forces with the Chiricahua were famous for being recalcitrant and disobedient, Victorio and Nana's followers were always known as the most insubordinate, warlike, impatient—the biggest cabrones of them all.

AFTER THE INTENSE CROSSING OF the Guadalupe Pass the ride had become humdrum, dull, leached of meaning. They continued skirting the Chiricahuas, emboldened by the lack of action, and though it turned out that this decision gained them at least a league on Cabezón, the sun sank lower in the sky and they still had not reached Portal.

When it seemed clear they wouldn't make it to the town before dark, Zuloaga gave the order to halt and empty canteens into hats so the horses could drink. Sorry about tomorrow's coffee, he said to Corredor. S'all right, the boy replied, we won't be able to light a fire anyway: now they really are following us in the hills.

Zuloaga didn't share the news with the troop, but he made them ride until night was fully upon them. Once they stopped, Guadalupe came over to ask why they had ridden so late. The horses'll break a leg if they can't see the ground, he said. The lieutenant was unsaddling his horse. I wanted to see if we could make it to Portal, he said. Or could it be that the boy sensed we were being followed? asked the Yaqui. Go on with you, said Zuloaga.

He woke as the last edge of the Milky Way pierced the horizon and before the first light had broken. From where he lay on the ground, he sat up a little and leaned back on his saddle. He thought about the cleft in his wife's buttocks when she bent down for something and her petticoats fell around her. This has been a long expedition, he said to himself, rubbing his face with one hand, the other on the grip of the revolver that had slid from his chest to his lap when he sat up.

For a while he listened to the night, beyond the nacionales' snoring. He didn't hear anything, so he got up, tucked the pistol into the holster on his belt, and rolled up his blanket. He saddled his horse, thinking about the cup of coffee he wouldn't be having that morning. It wasn't until he strapped the blanket to his saddle that he realized the twins' mules were missing. Chingada mother of fucking God, he said, and he hurried to wake what was left of the troop. If he'd planned to set out while it was still night anyway, to throw off the Chiricahuas who'd been following them, the absence of Guadalupe and Victoria demanded an even quicker departure: the Yaquis, he thought, had gone to pick a fight with the Apaches in the hills, and when day arrived, it would bring bullets. The expedition was fucked.

Being shaken awake by the boss unnerved Corredor: he was always the first to rise. What is it? he asked. The Yaquis are gone, said Zuloaga. The boy stretched. They must be out scouting, he replied, they'll be back in a little while. Help me wake the others and let's go, ordered the lieutenant. And by way of excuse, mostly directed at himself: Believing they could stay out of a fight in Apache territory after five years in a shithole jail cell was like trusting a sailor to order coffee and a newspaper at a brothel in port; I fucked up. Corredor was sitting now. Let's go then, he said.

As everyone was saddling up—hair matted, eyes crusty, mustaches stiff with drool—Zuloaga kept adding and subtracting. Without his star gunmen, the expedition could no longer pretend to be anything but a parleying outfit. What kind of threat could a nun, a dancing master, a child, and a tenderfoot gringo pose to an Apache chief? He tried to rally the troop, mostly as a way of rallying himself. I promise in Portal we'll make coffee under cover, he said, it's close now. How do you know? asked Corredor, unable to hide his ill humor. Per my calculations, said Zuloaga, eliciting raised eyebrows among his crew. Elvira concurred. Maybe four hours, give or take, she said distractedly as she hoisted her Colt and prepared to mount; it would be three if the animals weren't so thirsty. How do you know? the lieutenant asked, drumming his fingers impatiently on the pommel of his saddle. They loved zarzuela in Portal, she replied, but when the Apaches set up camp in the mountains, everybody had to leave. What I don't know, she went on, is where the watering hole is. El Márquez said it was ten minutes from town, no more. Have you been there, too? asked the chief, in growing disbelief; apparently everyone except him knew everything there was to know about Apachería. This was a land of great dancers, replied the master, looking at Corredor, who nodded from his mule by the boss's side. It was a small town, said the kid, but cultured; people got so bored they taught themselves. So everybody but me has been up this way before? said the lieutenant. Not me, said El Gringo.

Zuloaga thought it best to change the subject. The Yaquis told me something about Cuchillo Negro being strong here, he said. Corredor, his caffeine-deprived fury finding a target in the authority figure, replied: They have names, you know. Who? The two Mexican citizens you call "the Yaquis"; they're people just like you. Am I just "the Raramuri" to you? Or worse, "the Tarahumara"? The nun stepped in to smooth things over: They're Mexican citizens, she said, but they don't have full rights anymore; they're murderers after all, aren't they? That's their Mexican side, not their Indian side, said Corredor. Ay, sighed El Márquez, how I wish I could say that wasn't true. What do you know about Cuchillo Negro? Zuloaga asked again. A renegade Coyotero, said El Márquez, who had his boot tangled in his stirrup. Mounting, he continued: Kin to Mangas, but he has his own band. He cocked an eyebrow at Corredor and added: Real upstanding gentlemen, Mexican citizens to the core. Corredor didn't laugh. The nun weighed in: Cuchillo grew up in the goteras, he's baptized, but they say he hates Mexicans so much he doesn't even speak Spanish anymore, he thinks indios de razón are traitors, that's why Pisago went his own way. The lieutenant puffed out his cheeks and exhaled. What about his band? he asked. All renegades, said Elvira; the very worst of the clans. The chief snorted. El Márquez said: Haven't you heard that Cochise joined Cuchillo Negro and they're together now? The nun crossed herself: Never speak that name, she said. Cochise? asked Zuloaga. Never speak it, I say, repeated Elvira, the man is the very devil. From his mule, Corredor said: But don't lose heart, mi teniente. What do you mean? asked Zuloaga, now desperate to get going; El Gringo was still strapping on his bedroll. Cuchillo Negro isn't winning by much, said the boy. How is that? asked the lieutenant. Corredor replied: Have you seen a Sonoran since we left Janos? El Márquez could tell that Corredor wouldn't stop taking jabs at the lieutenant until he'd had some coffee, and Zuloaga was about to explode. He corkscrewed his body with the vainglorious flexibility of a dancer, searching in his saddlebags.

He pulled out two prickly pears. Have some breakfast, he said to the kid, hoping that food would help.

Lieutenant Colonel Zuloaga was a reasonable man. His father had been a child of empire and a soldier for the king. But in the Mexican War of Independence, when it became clear that the insurgents had decency and imagination on their side, he had changed allegiance in the most gentlemanly fashion, and he was loyal to the new Republic like a true son of Chihuahua, the state that was the muscle behind that too-big, jumbled thing trying to call itself Mexico. The Zuloagas were people who knew how to reconsider, and how to do an about-face when necessary. Both father and son had wept with joy when news arrived in Buenaventura of the surrender of the king of Spain, in a lusterless ten-minute ceremony in some undistinguished Veracruz manor house. They were less enamored of the central government's subsequent treatment of the northern territories, but when Zuloaga's father retired from the army—now called the national army—Zuloaga had enlisted, and he hadn't taken part in any lootings, coup attempts, or mass desertions. When the Indian Wars began, he'd dealt harshly with groups that didn't want to be part of the new republic, but only because he believed in it. He was generous with the captains who wanted to assimilate: he didn't believe the authors of the constitution were idiots; they'd made everyone born within national bounds Mexicans for a reason.

The lieutenant knew how to change course, but since he'd set foot in Casas Grandes and begun this expedition he'd found himself in new situations again and again. He'd never been wrong about absolutely everything. Worse, it had been a long time since he was the most ignorant member of a company. It was hard for him to believe that his troop would still listen to him when that was so obvious.

He'd been wrong about Guadalupe and Victoria, too, as he realized when dawn broke and the sun rose and they didn't hear the dry crackle of bullets echoing in the hills. They're not off killing Apaches, he said to Elvira, half whispering. Of course not, she replied, they heard something and went to find out what it was; Corredor is right when he says you're the only one here who thinks the worst of everyone. Not true. Of course it is, you think El Márquez isn't man enough for your adventures, but he understands what's going on in the desert better than any of us, no matter who he sleeps with. I don't care who my men sleep with so long as they behave like men when the moment comes, said Zuloaga. What about me? I have great respect for you. If that's so, then treat me like an equal. She went on: And then there's Corredor: his senses are the sharpest I've ever seen, yet you have him making coffee, you treat him like a child. He is a child. Look who's coming, said the nun, pointing to the chaparral as the twins emerged from it. Two upstanding Mexican citizens, said the lieutenant colonel.

The twins joined them as if there were no question about where they'd been. Good thing you're up nice and early, was all Guadalupe said in acknowledgment of the separate paths they'd taken. Pleased to be of service, replied Zuloaga; what did you find? Victoria said: Turns out we aren't the only ones following Pisago. Cuchillo's people, in the hills, said the lieutenant, pretending to be in the know: we've got a bead on them. That's news to us, said Guadalupe. Victoria went on: Somebody else is following us, too. How's that? Three men on ranch horses, good ones. The lieutenant pointed to the Chiricahua Mountains: Well they're following us from up there, too. He caught Elvira's hard look and went on: Citizen Corredor says so. The twins exchanged glances. Guadalupe shrugged and murmured: Citizen? Isn't he just a kid? Doesn't matter what's going on up there, he added; if Cuchillo was going to attack, it would've been in the Guadalupe Pass; if he gave up already, running into him now would be a waste of ammunition. Must be lookouts making sure we're following Pisago, said his brother. Zuloaga turned his gaze in the direction the twins had indicated. Are they vaqueros? Eyup. How many did you say there are? Three. Mexican? For sure. Bandits? They shrugged in unison. The leader's on a fancy horse, ain't he? Guadalupe asked his brother. That's the worst kind, said Zuloaga, should I worry? We'll take them with one hand twiddlin' our balls, said Victoria. Begging pardon, Elvis, said Guadalupe. The nun grabbed her crotch in response.

CHIEF VICTORIO TOLERATED BEING SHUFFLED around by the bureaucrats in Washington because the moment the soldiers running the reservations were distracted, he would retreat deep into the impenetrable Montañas del Diablo, today's Black Range. There he would wait for things to calm down before returning to the barrens of Ojocaliente, erecting wickiups, and making camp until the army came back. It usually took a while. It was common knowledge in the United States and Mexico: better not mess with Victorio.

In *Once They Moved Like the Wind*, historian David Roberts writes that in the summer of 1879 Victorio and all his people—some thirty-five families—were sent to a reservation of Mescalero Apaches at Fort Stanton. Just after Victorio arrived, he was warned that Ojocaliente and the passes of the Montañas del Diablo had been occupied by the army, so he had nowhere to return to.

The Mimbreños settled where they were told—they had good relations with the Mescaleros—and tried to make a life for themselves in their new surroundings. The land was worthless and there was no hunting. Soon after they arrived, Victorio himself went to the reservation store, which was manned by the reservation agent, a corrupt man who happened to speak good Apache.

Roberts is a historian, so he has to stick to the documentary evidence. I'm a writer, so I can shave the facts with Occam's razor. The chief must have explained that his people needed food, because the land was nothing but sand and stone. The agent likely never lifted his gaze from the papers on his desk. Roberts writes that he asked for Victorio's ration card, and Victorio said he didn't have one, he'd just arrived. I can't give you rations without the card, the gringo must have replied. The Mimbreño asked where he could pick up the card, and the agent explained that he couldn't pick it up, it had to be requested from Washington and would take a month to arrive. But we have nothing to eat, the chief must have said. The other man likely replied: Too bad, because I have no ration cards.

Victorio, who had spent time only in passing on the reservations of other Apache groups and therefore didn't know the ways of white men, must not have understood, as I do, that corrupt deeds begin with an irrational denial, that bureaucrats who expect a bribe first ask for something the petitioner can't give, then allow the discussion to shift to the possibility of some other arrangement. Based on what happened next, it's conceivable that the agent said something that infuriated Victorio—maybe that the Mimbreños were famous for their endurance, so they should stick it out. Victorio must have made some retort, because it's reported that the gringo raised his eyes from his papers only to discover too late that he had made a mistake: Victorio, eyes filled with rage, was upon him. It's reported that he grabbed the agent by the beard and said something to him before leaving the office and slamming the door.

The agent knew the Mimbreño chief's reputation, so he barricaded himself in the office and spent the night there. Victorio, meanwhile, walked to the wickiups and informed his warriors that he was leaving that night, and if they wanted to come they should call a council, alerting the Mescalero chiefs.

When the agent opened the door to his office the next morning, the reservation was empty, and he was at war. And in a fix: Victorio, his warriors, and the Mescaleros had stolen the regiment's horses.

JUST AS ELVIRA AND EL MÁRQUEZ had predicted, Portal was slightly less than four hours away. They arrived before the horses collapsed. It was a tiny town, even smaller than Janos, but it had once had a solid footing in the world, with a church and a town hall. You could tell it had been founded by the conquistadors who followed Coronado by the size of the windows in the houses, built by people with Andalucian notions of how to fight the heat. Once burnished with grace, the town was now falling into ruin from abandonment. No one had yet gone to the trouble to break down the doors of the houses to steal whatever was inside, but the church had been ransacked. There must have been gold there, said the nun. Catching the glances exchanged by the twins, Zuloaga imagined the houses wouldn't remain untouched much longer, perhaps only until the end of the nacionales' expedition. A moment later, Guadalupe turned to him: There's no one here to offer us a nice cup of coffee; we'll have to make camp so our child citizen Corredor cheers up. The chief felt ashamed.

They crossed the town from east to west, strolling as if the place wasn't a ghost of its former self. The nun and El Márquez pointed out where things used to be in the years before the latest round of the Apache Wars. When they were on the far side of the plaza, she said: This was where they put the stage. El Márquez pointed to a house.

The Manceras' dances. And very fine they were, said the nun. What about you? Zuloaga asked El Gringo. Have you never been to this highfalutin town? No, he said, I'm ranch bred, not city bred. This is no city, the lieutenant replied, though he'd found it intimidating that both the main street and its cross streets were paved, a luxury in his mind reserved for his native Buenaventura. There was money here, he said. Like you wouldn't believe, said El Márquez. He continued: I was a teacher in one of these towns, but in the mountains, before the fighting started, and no one, not even the Apaches, was lacking a thing; I can't understand what happened. Was that where you learned to sing in Apache? asked the boss. That's a longer story, El Márquez said, looking up at the sky, a smile lingering on his lips.

As they reached the end of the street and the town, Guadalupe and Victoria swung around in unison to stare at Zuloaga. The lieutenant nodded almost imperceptibly. The three had noticed that a stone was missing from the pavement and unlike other holes in the street, this one was recent. They found the stone farther on, where Pisago had left it when the road became a dirt path again, not far from the last houses. It was half hidden under some dry brush that they recognized immediately as an Apache blind concealing the watering hole. Corredor had to hurry to move the dead branches, because the horses, who sensed water, would have impaled themselves on thorns in their rush to get to it. Under the brush was a well-trodden path along which the animals nearly bolted.

Zuloaga was surprised not to see the crowns of cottonwoods in the distance. They should have been visible if water was so near that the horses could smell it, but once they arrived he saw that all the trees around the pool had been cut down, the brush burned, and the benches that the residents of Portal had once upon a time set there to enjoy the fresh air were overturned. Pinche fucking war, what good does it do anyone? said El Márquez, from the back of the group. It's your fault, said Guadalupe. Whose? asked Elvira. Yours, said Guadalupe. Since the criollos didn't seem to understand, his brother continued: The Apashees always had their nice little desert and hid their watering holes, but that was all they had and the rest of us kept them in line; then the Comanches got fucked, we were forced into the mountains, and the Pueblo and the Navajos were sent north, and now Apachería is swallowing everything up because you people know how to work the land but you don't know how to defend it. Zuloaga turned to look at Corredor: The Apaches are good citizens, too? The nun scolded: Don't tease him, can't you see he's a child? Citizen or child? replied the lieutenant. Elvira noticed that although he'd taken her shot in good humor and fired back, he turned red as he spoke. He was learning.

The lieutenant ordered everyone to stay mounted while they let the horses drink. We're surely being watched, he said. At least let us fill the skins and canteens, begged El Márquez, pretty please. And what about a nice little bath? added Victoria, surely just to fuck with him. Yes to refilling, but hell no to baths, Zuloaga said, and there were whistles. Just let us get our feet wet, insisted El Márquez. Zuloaga said no again, but as he dismounted and unstrapped his canteen he felt the urge for a smoke. Water and some coffee, he said. Can you build a quick fire, Citizen Corredor?

They didn't unsaddle the animals, but they let them graze the new grass on the banks of the pool so that they could rest: there wouldn't be another stop until nightfall, and there was no telling what conditions would be like then. They stretched out by the fire that Corredor had lit to boil water. Victoria gazed up at the sky as the Raramuri put the kettle on. He said to Zuloaga: I'd better go see if the rancheritos from this morning are still following us. Were they that close? asked the nun, putting her hand to her Colt, just to feel it. They didn't look dangerous, said the twin. Go ahead, said Zuloaga, as if his people did what he ordered and not whatever they felt like doing.

The coffee was ready when Victoria came back. He said: They're getting pretty close. Zuloaga, who was rolling a cigarette, turned to look at him: Are you sure they come in peace? he asked. Get the boy to tell you that; all I can see are shapes in the distance. Are you willing, Corredor? asked the boss. His eyes on his fresh mug of coffee, the boy reddened angrily. He asked Victoria where he'd seen them from. The Yaqui pointed to a path: There's a little rise over the way, he said. Corredor took his mug with him. Let's hope they really do come in peace, said El Márquez, watching the boy amble along sipping his coffee.

Zuloaga was rolling a second cigarette when the news came back. Two Mexican ranchers, said the Raramuri, and somebody who might be a gringo or a Frenchman. Armed? asked the boss. Rifles and revolvers, but holstered. How close? We have time for more coffee. All right, then, said Zuloaga, but we'll wait for them on horseback when they get close. The troop stretched out on the ground again, in a show of support for the plan.

It took them a little longer to arrive than Corredor had predicted, which eased the lieutenant's mind: they might simply be passing through. Just in case, he ordered his people to wait for them in a defensive position. They arranged themselves in semicircles to each side of the path, to cut off the riders if they tried to go by without parleying, or to chase them if they turned tail. Desert courtesy required that they wait with their pistols on their hips and their rifles in scabbards on the animals' hindquarters, but they kept one hand on the reins and the other resting on a thigh, near the grip.

The new arrivals were as peaceable as could be. Their horses were skittish: they must have been thirsty, too. Good day, said their leader, taking off a strange hat with a flat, symmetrical brim and an almost conical crown, like a bell tower, encircled by a silver ribbon. It was obviously a fine hat. Its wearer was white, but not like a gringo or a Mexican criollo: a blond and ringleted white man with hair on his arms and chest. He was wearing a loose-fitting, light-colored shirt under a black vest draped with a serape, also black, like everything else he had on. Instead of trousers and chaps, he was wearing what looked to the nacionales like a wool skirt, fastened at the waist with a very wide leather belt trimmed with coins and little silver chains. Beneath it were tall boots with an improbable heel for men's footwear: angled and higher than normal. Still, he looked less like a bandit than a gentleman—a gentleman of other deserts, perhaps. Good day to you, replied Zuloaga. The two ranchers riding behind the stranger touched their hats. And to you, they replied in broad Sonoran accents. The man in black dismounted. He stroked his horse's mane before handing the reins to the Sonorans, who carried on toward the watering hole, leaving the strange gentleman behind.

He eyed the nacionales, then addressed Zuloaga, the only other white male. We must all be after the same person, he said. His accent was very strange. He was squinting, because the sun was high and blazing now, though the chill in the air made it a pleasant day. No one replied at first; they were still taken aback by his attire. How's that? asked Zuloaga after a moment. A savage, replied the other, a cattle thief.

The lieutenant got off his horse as lazily as ever and removed his right glove to shake the newcomer's hand. White as the stranger's skin was, it was weathered and almost leathery. He had light-colored eyes, hair streaked with gray, and three or four days' beard, which was how long Zuloaga calculated they must have been traveling. I'm

Detective Läufer, he said in a soft voice, shaking the lieutenant's hand. How'd you say? Melitón Läufer, detective. Come again? I find stolen things. What makes you talk so strange? I'm Argentine; my last name is impossible to pronounce because I'm Jewish, so don't feel bad; my father was a rabbi. Of all these words, the only one the lieutenant colonel understood was *Jewish*. Don't tell my boys, he said into the stranger's ear, and he took him by the shoulder to introduce him.

This is Detective Läufer, said Zuloaga to the others, who had dismounted by now, too. He's Argentine. What's that? asked El Márquez. The nun put her hand to the grip of her Colt. She didn't draw it, but the lieutenant colonel saw how her index finger stroked the trigger through the holster. He signaled with his eyebrows for her to be polite, but she didn't see him: she was scrutinizing the detective's very light eyes. I remember you, she said, you were a theater impresario before you became what you say you are now. The Argentine reached for his own revolver, but he was so slow that Corredor had time to put his arms around Elvira in an attempt to hold her back, and Zuloaga to put the muzzle of his own pistol to the detective's head. Don't even think it, he said. Läufer raised his right hand, as if in surrender, and Zuloaga holstered his gun again, the nun still in Corredor's embrace. That was my brother, Läufer said; he was killed in a brothel in Paso del Norte. The ranchers with him were standing calmly by their horses at the watering hole, talking. They hadn't even noticed what was happening. They're decent people, thought the lieutenant colonel, poor bastards. With a look, he directed El Márquez and El Gringo to go and talk to them, in case it became necessary to subdue them. So why are you following us? asked Victoria. It was out of line for him to ask questions that Zuloaga himself should be asking, but the lieutenant's admirable self-possession was in part the result of a remarkable natural sense of resignation, so he just raised his eyebrows at the detective. I've already told the lieutenant here that I'm chasing the same savage you are. Cabezón is Coyotero, said Zuloaga; the Coyoteros are hardworking, peace-loving Apaches. Nevertheless, he stole some cattle, and their owner has paid me to get them back. Corredor was also offended to hear Pisago Cabezón referred to as a savage, but he'd had his coffee now, so he didn't say anything. He just scraped some crusted food off his pants with the nail of his index finger, letting go of Elvira, whose breathing seemed to have returned to normal. The twins had turned to look at each other. Ultimately any hunter of Apaches was their friend, even if he insulted Cabezón.

Zuloaga scratched his mustache. Cabezón didn't steal the cattle, he said, it was the thieving Virginian he works with, they're family. The Argentine said: Robert McKnight, yes I know. And you're headed in the opposite direction of the cattle, which are being driven to Santa Fé. I know that, too, said Läufer, I am a detective, after all. So then? The Sonora government is paying one hundred pesos for Apache scalps, and he's alone; I'll have time to take care of him and catch up with McKnight before the cattle are sold. Zuloaga snorted. And you think you can get the best of a warrior like Pisago Cabezón and a professional gunslinger like McKnight with those pretty little ivory hands? he asked. The detective glanced at his hands. If you let me get a word in, I can explain, he said. Cabezón is brother-in-law to a gringo, he's assimilated, you can't scalp him, said Zuloaga. He was party to a theft, replied the Argentine, and he has long hair; the rest is for the authorities to decide. Pisago was a tracker, the gringo is the thief, said Corredor, seething but never lifting his gaze from his trousers. He who drinks from the bucket is as guilty as he who fills it with stolen milk, replied the other man. Elvira, who hadn't stopped scrutinizing his eyes, bent her head, as if in agreement. Maybe so, she muttered, and then she said: All the world's a stage. The Argentine responded automatically: And all the men and women merely players. The Sister shot him so fast that by the time Corredor turned to look at her the revolver was back in its holster. With no fuss or drama, the Argentine fell flat on his face. It was as if he had fainted.

When he realized that the inevitable had happened, Zuloaga shouted to El Gringo and El Márquez to seize the two ranchers; the twins were halfway to them already. Confident they would pose no problem, he turned back to the detective's body. A thread of blood trickled from the very center of his forehead. The nun said: He really was a theater impresario. Zuloaga shrugged. Fine, he said, I won't ask what he owed you, but that shot is going to make the Indians in the hills nervous; we need to get going right away. I'm sorry, said the Sister; we should leave him here so they see he's not one of theirs, but mostly so they feed his body to the dogs and so he finds no rest. What in god's name *did* he owe you, then? asked the lieutenant. She said only: It's a woman's affair.

GOYAHKLA'S BAND WAS GONE FOR so long that by the time they came back, Camila had learned that the stream was called Bear Creek and she could say it in Apache, and a good deal more. She was newly repelled by the blood and rennet of a fawn killed by the boy, but she understood that for some mysterious reason her survival depended on her eating it and so she did, without vomiting. She almost relished the moderately hallucinatory act of sinking her hand into the sliced-open belly, grabbing a lump of fermented milk and stomach acids, and putting it into her mouth. She had even acquired a taste for raw entrails, and she had learned how to hunt hares. If she wanted to eat them, she had to catch them herself, since the boy preferred pack rats.

Some of the sounds of the language of the Jicarilla children from the goteras of Casas Grandes had lingered on her tongue. By then she had also learned that the captain of the group had one name that couldn't be spoken and a war name, Kan-da-zis Tlishishen, which meant Red Shirt; that Goyahkla's grandfather had been a big chief and that Kan-da-zis Tlishishen had adopted the boy when he was orphaned. She knew that in the future, when Goyahkla had taken his war name and was no longer an apprentice and the chief had died, he himself would be chief of all the Bedonkohe, which was the name of the country or the people or the band or whatever Kan-da-zis Tlishishen and Goyahkla belonged to while still being Apaches.

The rest of the group returned in general good humor. Camila had by now lost count of the days she'd spent alone with the boy, and she faced her new circumstances with the spartan fortitude she'd learned as the wife of an old man. She helped with the cattle and made more traps for hares, entering a cycle in which she could be entertained and even enriched by watching the progress of her own shadow over the ground. She knew all the stars by heart, and she could predict which stones the sun would rise between. She greeted the chief in acceptable Apache when Goyahkla took the reins of his horse as he dismounted.

The warriors had returned with what seemed a fortune, by the look on the boy's face: pots, several crates of ammunition, six or seven desperately thirsty horses that happily mingled with the cattle to drink the creek dry and munch on thorns. That night they killed a calf and had a feast: they had also brought two bottles of sotol.

There was a respectful silence when she approached to drink the animal's blood, and frank approval when she swallowed a fistful of rennet. Upon being offered the raw heart of the calf, she ate it with genuine pleasure.

The meal went on, with Camila eating her share discreetly to one side. Then came the surrender to the sotol, which she watched from a more than prudent distance. She slept hidden between two boulders, lulled by the laughter and shouting, which amid such vast loneliness sounded like a debate in the Tepic Atheneum.

BETWEEN AUGUST 1879 AND OCTOBER 1880, Victorio fought what was perhaps the most successful Apache campaign since the U.S. occupation of New Mexico and Arizona. When he escaped the reservation of Fort Stanton, he had forty-seven Mimbreño and Mescalero warriors with him, and at his peak he came to lead a cavalry of more than one hundred, gathered from all over the region. Among them were Nana and Loco, the legendary Kaetennae and Sánchez, Cochise and all his Arizona Chiricahuas, Geronimo, who by then had fled the San Carlos reservation, and Chief Juh, leader of the free Chiricahuas in the Sonoran part of the Sierra Madre (Asa Daklugie, to whom Geronimo dictated his memoirs and who was with him up until the very last second of his life, was the son of Juh and Ishton, Geronimo's sister).

During Victorio's campaign, which lasted thirteen months, the chief was hunted by three U.S. cavalry regiments, plus uncounted Mexican troops stationed in Sonora and Chihuahua. He won all his battles and, according to rumor, killed more than one thousand soldiers from both sides of the border—ten per warrior.

By September 1880, after a year of steady fighting against half the world, Victorio acknowledged that his people were exhausted and his stores of ammunition on the U.S. side of the border gone, so he accepted when Chief Juh invited him to the Sierra Madre to rest and rethink a campaign that, though successful, didn't seem to be leading to a recovery of the lands of Ojocaliente.

High up in the blue mountains—as the Apaches called the Sierra Madre—there was little food, but Victorio's people would have freedom of movement and could recuperate from wear and constant strain. In addition to his warriors, the Mimbreño chief moved a group of some three hundred children and elderly noncombatants across Apachería.

EL MÁRQUEZ AND EL GRINGO stood with their rifles aimed at the ranchers. One of the men asked El Gringo to go ahead and disarm him, so that he could search the Argentine's body, because the detective had something that belonged to him. El Gringo turned to Zuloaga, who agreed. Disarm them both, he said.

The vaquero ambled over to the detective's body. Pulling the serape aside, he dug under Läufer's belt until he found a little cloth sack full of bills from the Bank of Sonora, which he counted officiously. Nearly complete, he shouted to his mate, who explained that they had been the producers of the expedition. The backers, the nun corrected him. Laüfer was a theater man, said the vaquero. Didn't I tell you? said Elvira.

Does anyone want the serape? the lieutenant colonel asked. One of the Sonorans corrected him: It's a poncho, not a serape; the man was a gaucho. Zuloaga turned to Elvira. What's a gaucho? he asked. A vaquero, she said, and a poncho is a serape without the color or the flair. El Márquez fingered an end of his serape, rolled behind his saddle. Not sure flair is the word for it, he said. It was Corredor who decided to keep the garment, still intact thanks to the nun's surgical gunshot. But what I really like, added the Raramuri, is the belt. Go ahead and take it, said the lieutenant.

The rest watched with something like patience and tenderness as Corredor puzzled out the mystery of the buckles on the Southern belt. When he managed to unfasten it, he stood up to put it on, focused on his task in a way that reminded them all he was still a child. Then he draped the poncho around himself though the sun was blazing overhead. It looks elegant, doesn't it? he said. He was walking away from the body when Zuloaga asked: Aren't you going to keep the other belt, too? The Raramuri turned to look at him in surprise. Can I? he asked. Elvira has the right to it, responded Zuloaga, but I don't think she'll want those toy pistols when she has her elephant-killer of a Colt. A warrior can't wander around Apachería without a revolver, she said. The Yaquis lowered their rifles, resting them between their legs to offer the hearty applause the occasion merited. The Sonorans joined in the clapping since they had their hands up anyway. Zuloaga thought that if Cuchillo Negro's people had been following them with any concern at all, at this point they must have realized that his nacionales didn't present the slightest threat to anyone but themselves.

The ranchers added some clout to the nacionales, if only in number. They were from Bavispe, in the heart of the Sierra Madre, which meant they were easygoing but tough. They had come out to hunt Apaches and they didn't care whether they did it under the command of an Argentine detective or a lieutenant of rurales. They were brothers-in-law, and one was godfather to the other's son. Neither of them was originally from the mountains: they were desert-town criollos and they had come to the mountains following rumors of gold.

The darker one was Vilchis. He had eyeglasses and a beard, a vest with watch chain, a charming way of conversing, and a gentleman's manners. The other was Eneas. He had been born in Pitic to Italian parents who had come to Mexico and failed spectacularly in a series of enterprises that should have succeeded. Neither man had found what he was looking for in the mountains, but in Bavispe there was still work to be had back then. Vilchis, married to Eneas's sister, had been lucky to buy some hillside land for a song, setting up a livestock operation. Though he was a good man, he knew very well that life wasn't easy on the fringes of Apache territory. Eneas took things as they came, moving to the music of the world in the most delightful way.

Zuloaga didn't even have to threaten to conscript them, because heading into the heart of the Gila and tangling with Mangas Coloradas himself was far more interesting to them than hunting a Coyotero and then negotiating the return of a herd of cattle with a gringo. Of course, the lieutenant colonel didn't explain that their only earnings at the end of the expedition would be time stolen from boredom: the Chihuahuan government didn't yet pay for scalps.

They set off. El Vilchis and Eneas hit it off right away with El Gringo. It turned out that they knew a family from Tesorababi with whom El Márquez had been associated in a previous life, years ago when the band he'd drummed and sung with had dissolved.

Turning away from the edge of the Chiricahuas was a relief for them all. They sailed through the Piloncillos—more a series of ridges than really steep terrain, with long strips of pasture and narrow arroyos—as if on a cloud of bliss. Back in the thin, grassy mountain air, Zuloaga felt that he was finally on the epic swell he had foreseen when he left Buenaventura. When two days later they met Pisago Cabezón at a bend in the San Simon River, the ranchers didn't show any signs of coveting his scalp. By then they knew how to dance the perro.

The death of the detective had an added benefit. After Pisago

Cabezón heard from El Márquez, in the language of his ancestors, how the nun had killed the man who wanted to kill him, he adjusted a little better to life in the company. He still ate and slept alone, but he showed Zuloaga how to chart their way by counting peaks, and how to calculate trajectories based on watering holes, their positions memorized by the numbering of mountains. The lieutenant learned that the route leading up to Santa Rita was an actual path, though no part of it looked trodden. The desert is full of trails, the Coyotero said; you have to learn to see them.

The horses, the hats, the guns, the setting sun: Zuloaga watched his troop on the move, feeling satisfied. Pisago in front on his short, sinewy pony, sitting with the world's straightest back on his Apache saddle. Shiny hair, sharp eyes, moccasins, and buckskin jacket meshing with the landscape. Elvira and El Márquez rode silently a few yards behind. She: rotund, the Colt on her hip in stark contrast to her veil. He: bolt upright, reins slack over his saddle where both hands rested. After them came the Sonorans and El Gringo: grime, beards, and boots. Close behind, Guadalupe and Victoria, nervous and alert, their gray-flecked hair at odds with the steel of their bare chests. They rode gripping their horses with their knees, reins slung over pommels and hands on hips, glancing all around them. Behind came Corredor, looking more solid in his gaucho costume. Seeing how long their shadows stretched in the orange late afternoon sun, Zuloaga felt free, a vaquero at last.

He spurred on his horse to catch up with Cabezón. Following an afternoon spent scaling the moderate but persistent slopes of the Peloncillos, the stretches of sand and stony land had given way to more fertile ground. Not prairie but meadows and pines, the soil black rather than red. It was cold. I didn't know northern Apachería was so pretty, he said to the Coyotero; this is almost as sweet as the lower valleys of the Sierra Madre. Pah, replied Pisago, wait till we get to the Mogollones.

They spent the night in the heights, delighted to make camp under the pines with a real fire.

AT THE BREAK OF DAY, Goyahkla woke Camila roughly. They went down to the camp together and he showed her which horse was hers. She mounted, covering its back only with the skin she was still using to sleep on and the blanket she wrapped herself in at night to ward off the cold.

They headed north along the bed of Bear Creek with no urgency, grazing the animals as they went, her captors nursing what must have been a warrior-grade hangover; they were meek as kittens.

The group went on like that nearly all day, unspeaking, until they reached the valley of the Gila River, where Camila finally understood that the Bedonkohe were not the masters of stony ground and sandy wastes, but people of paradise. Goyahkla went galloping ahead.

VICTORIO TOOK HIS TIME REACHING the Sierra Madre, attacking Chihuahuan ranches and towns before moving to high ground. The governor of Chihuahua at the time was Luis Terrazas, vulture-in-chief, master of corruption, first in the line of satraps who since his day have held Mexico in their grasp, the man who realized that businessman, politician, and banker were complementary occupations. In Victorio's time, Luis Terrazas was amassing the land that would become the Hacienda de la Encinilla, which, when the Mexican Revolution broke out—Don Luis was still alive—covered nearly five million acres.

If Governor Terrazas was good at anything, it was uniting forces around the allure of money. He treated the campaign against Victorio as a joint venture and offered a reward system irresistible to the combatants: fifty gold pesos for each warrior's scalp—a fortune even today—and two thousand for whoever could kill Victorio, which was more than twenty years of retirement pay for a government minister on full pension. He recruited a troop of two hundred and sixty elite soldiers, all fresh, under the command of his cousin Joaquín Terrazas. Nepotism notwithstanding, it must be said that Captain Joaquín Terrazas was a virtuoso of battlefield strategy. He lost a few fights, but never a war, and was the most implacable Apache hunter produced by the Republic in the nearly sixty-year battle that it fought against the bands united under the flag-name of the Chiricahua Mountains.

Captain Joaquín Terrazas had accepted his cousin's commission, provided that the governor pay a good wage to the thirty Raramuri trackers who were the secret of his success in the field. In this case, the monetary compensation was a fringe benefit. Any member of the Raramuri nation would have joined an expedition to kill Apaches for the sheer joy of it. The captain himself traveled to Casas Grandes to convince Mauricio Corredor—also a Raramuri but an assimilated one, and by this time a well-to-do rancher of about fifty—to accompany him as adviser and good luck charm. Corredor had served in his youth alongside the legendary lieutenant colonel José María Zuloaga—Joaquín Terrazas's role model and idol—and it was said that in addition to being an eagle-eyed shot, he could predict the Apaches' moves better than anyone. He was perhaps the last living Mexican soldier to have laid eyes on the giant Mangas Coloradas—a chief of majestic grandeur, maybe the only Apache greater than Victorio himself.

Until they faced each other, Victorio didn't know that the man hunting him now in Mexico was Joaquín Terrazas, so he made a bad decision, perhaps the result of overconfidence after he had defeated every military and civilian force to come up against him for more than a year. As he neared the blue mountains in early October 1880, an ill-fated month for the entire Apache nation, he knew that the old people and children couldn't go much farther without a rest. He decided to camp in the Valley of Tres Castillos, sure that no one would look for Apache warriors in the place where they were most vulnerable: the plain. While his people recovered their strength, he sent two of his men—Blanco and Kaetennae, both Mimbreños—to bring back ammunition so that they could safely embark on the last stage of their journey into the refuge of the mountains.

Not only did Blanco and Kaetennae take a long time to carry out their task, but their faith in Victorio's invincibility was so great that they were apparently careless on their way out of Tres Castillos: they left tracks that Terrazas's Raramuris found and were able to follow.

On the morning of October 15, 1880, the Mexican army trackers came upon the Tres Castillos camp. Their captain, confident in his numbers, knowing that the Mimbreños were on open ground and had nowhere to run, divided his men into two forces and sent half to trap the enemy's rear guard and the other half to charge at them head-on.

No late-nineteenth-century band of warriors could have withstood such an attack in like circumstances: no ammunition, no cover, nowhere to flee. Victorio's men knew they could not win, but for the first day they battled tooth and nail, to make sure they would die in combat. "During the night," Terrazas reported, surprisingly lyrical for a man who prided himself on his efficiency, "the Apaches ceaselessly performed the dance of their own death."

The battle resumed at first light. The Mimbreños no longer put up much of a fight, maybe having acquiesced to what was foreordained and even overdue. Mauricio Corredor found a vantage point where he could stand and calmly watch Victorio's maneuvers. Though he was a soldier and a Raramuri, he dressed for expeditions in the garb of a criollo civilian: heavy twill trousers, checkered shirt, canvas duster, needle-toe boots, and fedora. When at last he was able to get Victorio in his sights he put a bullet in his neck, killing him almost instantly.

Terrazas's report says that at ten in the morning on October 16, 1880, he brought the campaign to a close, counting sixty-eight warriors, five women, and three children among the Apache dead. He took one hundred and twenty noncombatant Mimbreños captive, their fate undivulged. He had lost only three soldiers, and he returned to Chihuahua City with ten wounded men.

A week later, in a solemn ceremony in the state capital, Governor Terrazas presented Mauricio Corredor with two thousand gold pesos and a nickel-plated rifle that he would never use in action; his battle days were over. He knew the Apache rebels wouldn't recover from Victorio's death, though Geronimo and Juh were still alive and free. To replace the sixty-eight dead warriors, the Apaches would need twenty years of peace and prosperity that they would get from neither Mexico nor the United States.

ZULOAGA UNDERSTOOD WHY PISAGO SPOKE so reverently about the Mogollones. They had the humiliating majesty of real mountains: as you approached, all you could think about was how incredibly fucking ominous they were. Are we in Nueva México yet? asked Eneas distractedly at some point. Since yesterday, the lieutenant replied. In the evening, when the climb was imminent, Pisago announced that the canyon bottoms were out of the question and they would go the Apache way—that is, along the ridge. It will be cold, he said. According to his calculations, they would reach snow by the next day.

The path was so steep and narrow that there was no room to maneuver: a succession of sheer walls and precipices, continental America's igneous orgy in all its splendor. For the plains cowboys, the ascent was slow and shaky; for the first time, they envied the Yaquis and Corredor on their mules. Once they were deep into the mountains, when the only way out was forward, the Raramuri slowed for a moment to whisper to the boss that there were lookouts on the peaks. Real warriors, he said, warriors like Guadalupe and Victoria, shirtless cabrones with American rifles. The lieutenant colonel took a deep breath and spurred his horse a little, moving carefully to the front of the line, behind Pisago.

The moment he felt the nose of the chief's horse on his knee, the Coyotero turned to speak in the low tones used everywhere on the continent by the original people when they want to be heard by a single person: Corredor told you. What? Sentinels. Are they yours? If only they were, but they're Mangas's, here to lick into us if need be. What do we do? They're a message, said Pisago. If we see them, it's because they want to be seen; the idea is to intimidate us so we stay on the path to Santa Rita and don't get near the Gila. Are you sure? Fifty percent hopeful, fifty percent sure. What are our options if they attack us? Your pinche fucking Yaquis will take two each, Corredor and Elvis another two per—or maybe three or four for her, there are six bullets in that Colt and she's a crack shot—you and I one each, and the rest are cannon fodder, but they won't last long anyway, except the professor, who could jaw his way into heaven; if it comes to hand-to-hand we lose the advantage with Elvis, but I wouldn't fuck with the Yaquis, and El Gringo is a big fellow—we just have to make sure he isn't killed in the first skirmish; send him to the back. So what are our odds? I say we're all right; this is just a welcome.

The boss scanned the landscape: he didn't see anything, but he had gotten this far by listening to Pisago, and for better or worse they were in Mangas's territory now. Just a little bit farther and he felt they would get a scent of the captive. He shouted at the top of his lungs: We have company, boys, guns out but don't break rank, and he heard behind him the sounds that weapons make as they come alive. He arranged his troops, too: Guadalupe and Victoria directly behind Pisago, then the Sonorans and the dancing master. El Gringo was between Elvis and Corredor, and he himself brought up the rear, everybody nose to tail.

The first leg of the ascent ended at a high, forested pass that struck them all as an impossibility considering that they had been in Nueva México since the previous day: endless pine groves over banks of emerald green, patches of fog drifting out of the trees. There were new, unexpected threats: to begin with, genuine cold, which was starting to make their fingers go numb. They didn't put away their rifles even after Corredor declared them alone again, because Pisago said there were wolves that must have scented them by now. A little farther, he added, they would find a French fur traders' camp where they could make a good fire and sleep behind barred doors.

And Mangas's people? asked El Vilchis. Pisago shrugged. The Bedonkohe don't fight at night. Who are the Bedonkohe? asked Eneas. Same as the Gileños, replied Elvira. Down there on the plain around Janos, said Zuloaga, I was told they're not called Gileños or Janeros or Mimbres anymore; now they're all Chiricahua. Pisago considered this. It's because of the young warriors who went off with

Cuchillo Negro; the oath they swear is hatred of Mexicans, not loyalty to any band, but they're almost all Bedonkohe, and they're called Chiricahua, too, because they have their camp in the mountains. He scratched his temple and concluded: Same thing but different. Eneas shook his head in disapproval, as if his opinion mattered to anyone. Zuloaga gave him a warning look as El Márquez, with exquisite courtesy, took the trouble to ask Pisago for an explanation in Apache. After listening carefully to the response, he turned to the lieutenant colonel, ostentatiously ignoring the Sonoran. He's right, he said: same thing but different. Let's go on to the fur traders' camp, said Zuloaga, noticing with a start that patches of fog were gathering in the tops of the pines. As they got close they had to hurry: the veil of damp was turning into a curtain behind which Corredor could hear the wolves running. They aren't singing, noted Pisago, that's bad.

The mood was grim when they reached the fur traders' camp. The place was completely abandoned. There was a hole in the roof and it smelled of den: only animals had lived there for who knows how long. But it had a chimney, and nothing would bite them if they spent the night inside. There was also a stable, or the ruins of a stable, with a door that could be closed. After examining it alongside Corredor, Zuloaga said that someone would have to sleep with the animals. I'm not sleeping alone here, the Raramuri replied, this isn't a camp, it's a rat trap. The chief nodded, and ordered him to go make a fire on the hearth. Then he went out, shouting that there was shelter for the horses and they could stay.

Spirits improved when the scent of Corredor's coffee infiltrated the cabin, relieving the smell of damp and mouse droppings. The smoke and crackle of the fire had driven off the flies, too. The lieutenant colonel gathered his people at the door of the cabin. We're going to set watches, he said. El Gringo, Vilchis, and Eneas will bed down with the horses; you'll sleep one at a time, in shifts of any length you like. Corredor and I will sit up in the cabin until midnight, and we'll wake Pisago and El Márquez to take the second watch. What about Elvis? asked El Márquez. Can't you see I'm a lady? she replied. There you have it, said the lieutenant. And a word of warning to those of you in the stables, he said, looking at the Sonorans and El Gringo: that's where the wolves will gather, so there must always be two men armed and awake by the door, barred from inside. The company scattered.

IN TRUTH OR CONSEQUENCES we had dinner one night at the only more or less cosmopolitan restaurant in town. Eating Asian fusion at a table that owed more to a sense of design than pure necessity was a relief and a respite. We made a party of it.

Tongues loosened by the wine, my wife and I chatted with the waiter, and I went so far as to ask him whether there were still descendants of Victorio or Nana in town. He was a tall, blond, broad-chested kid, and he declared himself part Apache, which I wouldn't have guessed at first. There aren't any Mimbreños left in New Mexico, he said, but there are Chiricahuas: I'm descended from Geronimo's sister.

The children were speechless, and they treated him with respect and reverence; he was royalty to them. They even ate all of their food.

PISAGO WOKE THE BOSS AS NIGHT was ending but before first light. The fog has cleared, he said, and the path is easy here; the horses will be able to follow it by the light of the moon; let's go now, so we can get past the snow without having to camp again. Zuloaga rubbed his eyes, aware of a noise that had been raising his hackles maybe even as he slept. Listen to the wolves, he said, they aren't far off. We have rifles, said the Coyotero. The lieutenant shook Corredor, who was snoring next to him. Put on the coffee, he said.

Once outside, smoking, Zuloaga was better able to articulate what he meant: If the wolves attack and we have to blast away at them, Mangas's sentinels will get even jumpier than they are already. Pisago shrugged. They're in the same fix, he said, and if we have to fight it out, we will: there aren't many of them, and if we're lucky they'll kill one or two of those numbskulls in the stable. Zuloaga told him to go and prepare the tack. As soon as he was done smoking he would give the order to leave.

The Apache went ahead to search out potential obstacles along the path. Zuloaga, Corredor, the nun, and the twins, saddling their horses in the dark, discussed the safest order in which to ride, considering that they would be followed by wolves from below and Mangas's warriors from above. The boss dug in his ear, sniffed the wax, and wiped his finger on his trousers, which were stiff with grime by now. Don't be a pig, said Elvira. Judge me by my deeds, not my hygiene on the trail, he replied. Then he asked: So how are you at tracking? Terrible, she said, I'm blind, I'm fat, and I don't give a damn about nature. What about you, Corredor, could you follow Pisago's trail? I've never done it, he said. Guadalupe was about to speak, but Zuloaga cut him off: The two of you can forget it. Why? asked Victoria. If there was ever a risk of a fight it's now, and with all the time we've spent on the trail it would be a shame not to reach the captive. I see, said Guadalupe. He narrowed his eyes. And you think we're itching to kill someone because we're Yaquis. He looked at his brother, who put his hands on his hips and said: Maybe the lieutenant colonel here is right, and that's not even accounting for the tickle we feel inside, not having done the deed in so long. You mean fucking? asked his twin. That's right: what do you say? Should we rape every one of our friends here—except the nun, who's a woman of God—and then kill them, or should we kill them and then give them a taste of the one-eyed snake? Depends what your animal instinct tells you, replied Guadalupe. Zuloaga rolled his eyes. Fine, you do the tracking.

The rosy light of dawn glanced off the new-fallen snow. The cliffs, the titanic rocks, the pines perched on slopes, the babble of creeks at the bottom of ravines, this whole world seemed freshly hatched.

Though it wasn't as risky as the route they'd taken up the mountain, the path high in the eaves of the Mogollones was narrow, so they continued to ride single file, wrapped in blankets with hats pulled down to their eyebrows. The Yaquis in the lead, then the Sonorans, El Gringo, El Márquez, Elvira, and Corredor. Zuloaga brought up the rear of the convoy, as always. It was a dry year, so there was just a dusting of snow; it was no trouble for the animals, but it gave the air an edge. And the sun was coming on strong: the snow would melt soon. Zuloaga looked ahead and upward. Except up there it won't, he thought.

It was afternoon by the time they reached the summit. At that height the snow was only up to the horses' knees: they were lucky. They ate lunch without dismounting, everyone for themselves, gnawing chunks of cured beef marinated in lime, salt, and chile that Corredor had distributed before they set out. El Gringo had finished his share before ten, so he was hungry for the rest of the day. Zuloaga was thinking of finding an excuse to halt the convoy in order to smoke a cigarette that he had already rolled when there was a commotion at the head of the line. Everyone had stopped in their tracks and Victoria was riding back toward them. The lieutenant put his right hand to his revolver instinctively.

What's wrong? he asked when the Yaqui reached him. We need to parley, let's move away a little, was the reply. Are we in danger? asked the boss. Not just now. Zuloaga turned his horse and they went a few steps and stopped. Seeing his chance, he dismounted and lit his cigarette. He asked again: What's wrong? The Apache's gone. What do you mean, gone? Like that, boom, he disappeared. He can't have disappeared, especially with snow on the ground. The Yaqui rolled his eyes. As if you don't know what they're like, he said. Gone, just like that? All of a sudden the tracks end. Zuloaga moved to the front of the line, leading his horse and followed by Victoria. Nobody move, not a single step, he shouted. When they reached Corredor, Zuloaga handed him the reins. The Yaqui dismounted, giving his reins to Guadalupe.

The trackers walked on along the edge of the path. What's happening? asked Elvira. Nothing, said the boss, but nobody move. El Márquez frowned and waited for them to pass before dramatically mouthing *Pisago Cabezón*. Then he opened the fingers of his hand suddenly, as if performing a magic trick, and made a sound: *Fffpt!* The nun looked distraught. She gave him a questioning glance and drew her index finger across her neck. The dancing master shook his head and opened and closed his hand, as if waving goodbye. The nun nodded. He hung on a long time, she said.

It troubled Zuloaga a little that his guide had vanished, but his excitement at the prospect of getting an up-close look at the most famous Apache trick was greater than his distress. He and Victoria stepped completely off the path so as not to miss any tracks in the snow.

Pisago's horse, its small hooves unshod—as Zuloaga had noted some time ago—had trotted along one side of the path. In the middle of the path were the deeper tracks of the twins' mules, which had come this far following the Apache's trail. At a certain point, the pony's prints simply stopped. Zuloaga dismounted and removed his gloves to touch the last hoofprints. Nice and fresh, he said. He looked forward and back, smelled the snow. Pinche fucking Apaches, he said, they're motherfucking geniuses. He got back to his feet and joined the Yaquis. What now? asked Guadalupe. Learn to do it ourselves? asked Zuloaga. All right, said the Yaqui after thinking it over for a moment; for once, he was at a loss to respond. But he quickly recovered. And how does that help us get to the captive? Zuloaga said: We'll continue along the only path there is, the one we know leads to Chief Mangas's winter camp. He pointed to a pine branch bent in the direction they were headed and concluded: All we have to do is follow the instructions our guide left before he disappeared. Victoria chimed in: I saw that, but I was so mad it was like I didn't.

They checked the path ahead and behind, several times. There was nothing of note, except that in a gully to the left there was a puddle with lumps of dirty snow floating in it. He could have turned off here, said Victoria. So how do you explain the hoofprints farther ahead? asked Zuloaga. Maybe he has a pair of special little shoes, with little hoofs, said Victoria. Next to the puddle was some brush that, when nudged, scattered on the ground. Then came a stretch of dense forest, the snow marked with fresh prints of the Coyotero's horse. There you have it, said Victoria. Santa Rita must lie along that ridge; the tricky bastard went home. Should we follow him? asked Guadalupe. The lieutenant shook his head: He took us as far as he could; we must be close.

They went on without offering explanation. Evening fell upon them when they had left the pine thickets and foggy mountain passages behind. By the time darkness brought them to a halt, they were surrounded by desert flora announcing the Nueva México lowlands, though they were still high on the trail. They spent the night in the ruins of a mission attached to a building with several rooms. On the wall was an inscription: "Colegio Casitas." The wolves had been left behind, though perhaps not far enough. Mangas's sentinels were still nearby, docile and easier to spot. Even Zuloaga had noticed them and taken off his hat in greeting when he glimpsed them among the rocks in the distance: the expedition felt more shepherded than threatened. Still, they took turns keeping watch.

It wasn't until they were eating supper around a banked fire that Corredor asked tactfully whether they weren't in trouble now that they had no guide. Zuloaga said no. Pisago had gone home to his family the way normal people do, leaving them very clear instructions. They must only be two or three nights from Mangas's camp. Corredor had noticed the disappearance of the Apache's horse's tracks. I think they snatched him, horse and all, he said; otherwise he would have said goodbye. The question is how they did it so that his horse seemed to vanish into thin air. El Márquez, who was stirring the ashes with a small stick, said it was one of the tricks the Apaches learned as kids. It's easy if you know how to do it, he said. They make the horse stand still and they sit backward on its hindquarters. They hang over the horse's haunches, gripping with their moccasins, then they step it backward hoof by hoof in its tracks; all Apache horses are trained to do it. Zuloaga and the Yaquis looked at each other. This time it was the boss who resorted to the ancient wisdom of Americans: It feels like I get it, he said, but I don't get it.

At dawn the twins brought juicy news: a short way ahead, the path plunged down into a canyon, at the bottom of which ran a creek they could just barely hear. Though they hadn't been able to see to the bottom, it seemed the Apache path did go down that way—Pisago had sent them in the right direction. What was troubling was how steeply the trail descended into the canyon. Across the creek bed, there was a wall, so there would be nowhere to run except north or south, a death trap. It's another funnel, said Victoria. His brother went on: If Mangas's sentinels want to have some fun with us, that's where it'll be, so let's think on how to get down there without getting slaughtered. What if we go back along the path Pisago took and enter the canyon from the other side? asked Zuloaga. The brothers gave him a scornful look. Are we men or clowns? they asked at the same time. Men, said Elvira.

WHEN GOYAHKLA BROKE AWAY FROM the group at full gallop, Camila noticed that the rest of the warriors were tugging at their horses' bits so they didn't bolt in longing. They were getting close to the place the animals called home. It wasn't easy to balance the horses' urgency and the cattle's desire to settle down in the fields to graze. The cows would have lingered forever if they hadn't been herded and driven on. As they moved, they clipped the tallest grasses nervously. Maybe they were spooked by the horses' skittishness, or maybe—being creatures of the desert like Camila herself—they didn't know there were places where life is not a perpetual coin toss between death and salvation.

For some time they wandered aimlessly through the Gila Valley, or so it seemed, on a trek so long it felt like a lifetime to Camila. Or more precisely, it was as if her whole life had been a journey leading to this other life, so brimming with fear and novelty that everything else seemed blurred and prefatory. Goyahkla soon returned at a good clip, accompanied by an old woman wearing a cotton skirt and a geometric-patterned vest. The woman's hair was streaked with gray, her eyes buried in wrinkles. She might have been sixty years old, or ten thousand.

The contingent stopped when it reached her. Kan-da-zis Tlishishen and the two old men got off their horses to greet her, the older men joking among themselves but the chief slightly fearful, overcome by something that made him seem younger than he was. The old woman rode past them without a word, examining their plunder from her saddle with a look somewhere between arrogant and interplanetary. She was talking to herself, as if scolding an imaginary friend. Once she had made a more or less clear accounting of the goods strapped on the horses, she cast a glinting eye on the cattle, counting them. She returned to where the warriors stood waiting for her, and only then did she descend from her horse, taking such care that Camila was inclined to think she was closer to ten thousand than sixty. Once she was on the ground, it was plain that she was well shy of four feet: she was tiny. Without coming too close to Kan-da-zis Tlishishen, she gave him a toothless smile, and he slumped a little in apparent relief, bowing his head. Sich'iné, Goyahkla whispered to Camila. Su madre? she asked in turn. La madre de su madre, replied the adolescent, who by now could perhaps be considered a speaker of Spanish. The old woman approached the chief; she came up to his midsection, at best. She said something that made the old men laugh. He bent down. She pinched his cheeks and he turned red.

Camila had no time to contemplate what seemed the first sign of humanity she'd seen in her captor, because just then both he and the old woman turned to look at her. The old woman pressed the chief's hand, then advanced determinedly in Camila's direction. Goyahkla took a step backward. Respect, he said before retreating to stand with the other warriors, she is diyin, war shaman, much respect.

The old woman planted herself in front of Camila, who got off her horse as reverently as she could. The war shaman examined her from head to toe, like a jealous goddess. She took her by the left shoulder and turned her around, felt her hips with both hands, turned her around again and pried her mouth open, ran her fingers over her molars, pulled down the skin over her cheekbones to check the whites of her eyes, turned her around once more and gave her a shove. Camila understood that she was supposed to walk in the direction she'd been pushed.

They walked together, the old woman talking ceaselessly, to a gully. Here she moved a few steps ahead, urging Camila on. They stopped behind some brush, where the old woman made her understand that she should strip. Though she proceeded to undress without shame—she'd lost any trace of modesty in her first days of captivity—the shaman had the delicacy to give her some privacy, continuing to talk aloud as she walked down the slope.

Camila left her man's shirt and trousers hanging from a branch and caught up to the Apache woman, who cast an approving glance at her hard legs and workingwoman's shoulders. Hand in hand, they crossed a shallow creek with a stony bottom. Then came a reed bed, the old woman parting the reeds with fingers of steel so that the blades wouldn't scratch the younger woman, though Camila's skin had grown tough enough to withstand a rain of fire. Before Camila sank into the wide Gila River—deep waters at last—the old woman was moved to squeeze her buttocks and breasts, stroking the almost masculine curves of her belly with satisfaction, grabbing the thatch of her sex and touching her vagina with the flat of her palm in an evaluatory, gauging kind of way, feeling her hips again, smiling. They're big even though I'm skinny, said Camila in her precarious

Apache, and the old woman answered with more gibberish in her own tongue.

When she came out of the water, the shaman was taking a fringed buckskin shirt and a feather-patterned skirt from her bag. She handed the garments to Camila, who put them on. The diyin pointed to her bare feet, scolding her. Then she stood on tiptoes and tugged at her shoulders. Camila understood that she should get down on her knees. Even so, she was taller than the old woman. The shaman took a little pouch out of her bag and emptied its contents on her head, spreading it with a bone comb. A little trickled onto Camila's face, and she saw that it was pollen. Finally, the old woman braided her hair, untied a strip of red cloth from around her waist, and wrapped it like a band around her forehead, tying it at the back of her head. The old woman asked her to get up, signing to her that it was time to return.

CHIEF NANA SURVIVED THE DEFEAT of Tres Castillos despite being past seventy. It was he who gathered the survivors of the massacre, who'd scattered before they could be arrested by Joaquín Terrazas. He led them through the mountains into New Mexico. There were forty-six altogether: male warriors and female warriors, boy children and girl children, the old and the very old, fighters and camp followers. He sent Sánchez, a Mimbreño who had been kidnapped as a child by the Mexican army and had rejoined his people after living the life of a vaquero for nearly thirty years, to count prisoners in the Chihuahua City market, where the captives were being sold as slaves. Sánchez counted one hundred and thirty-one in total, eleven more than the number accounted for in Terrazas's war report. The Terrazas cousins had a little hustle going, of course they fucking did:

otherwise what was the point of running a business called the Chihuahua State Government?

IT WAS SOMEHOW DELIGHTFUL, the lieutenant thought, that the brothers judged it ridiculous to retreat in order to avoid a lopsided encounter at the end of the Apache road through the Mogollones. He was about to light a cigarette. Pisago had insisted they could handle a shoot-out with Mangas's people no matter their position, and Guadalupe's and Victoria's faith cemented the notion. Ta bueno, he said, striking a match on the sole of his battered boot. He gazed with something like tenderness at the huddled shapes of his sleeping nacionales and added: Let's just let them sleep a bit more; if the climb down is as steep as you say, better wait till it's light.

They set out as dawn broke and reached the cliff before the sun was hot. They were still in the shelter of the mountain trees—their leaves dusty now, since what came next were the barren lands. As the twins had forecast, the path continued downward, so sharply the nun said she felt her horse was on tiptoes. You all better draw, called the chief, trying to sound commanding while willing his voice not to shake: he knew that once the first stage of the descent was completed, they would face the even steeper track to the bottom of the canyon. Corredor reported that he didn't see lookouts to either side, which added a ladleful of worry to the boss's troubles: it meant they were waiting ahead.

Soon everyone noticed what Zuloaga and the Yaquis already knew: the last stretch of the descent ended in a ravine where the path was barely a thread. The bottom of the canyon was narrow, and across the creek was the wall where anyone posted would have them in their sights. No one said anything, but the commander watched them turn pale as this understanding took hold. So ashen were they, it was as if they were dead already, he thought.

They rode slowly, once again in single file, like droplets squeezed from the mountain. Like nine targets. The boss noted that there was a crook in the path before it reached the ravine. How many Apaches up above? he asked Corredor in a low voice. Now at least six, came the reply. Wearing shirts? No shirts. War bands? Neatly tied. Zuloaga raised his revolver so that the barrel was aimed vaguely at the mountain. He shouted to the others: Trot down making sure they can see your guns, and when you reach the bend in the trail, stop and dismount; take cover behind the horses.

Of them all, only the Yaquis, as usual, understood exactly what the lieutenant was ordering. They reached the bend in an instant and occupied its most exposed flanks, leaping to the ground with rifles in hand and crouching behind their horses' hindquarters. You're covered! shouted one of them. Split up, called the other.

The boss shouted to the nun: You take the middle, Doña Elvira, and she rode forward gallantly. The horse almost lost its footing as she scanned the ridgeline, Colt in hand. Though they were still in a precarious position, each horse would cost an enemy marksman a bullet, and, more important, any head popping up to shoot a horse would become a target.

The remaining nacionales settled in behind, taking cover as they came to the bend. The lieutenant brought up his horse behind all the others and dismounted in a leap, kneeling and aiming at the heights. The others surrounded him, rifles at the ready, prepared to fire a second volley if necessary. They waited. When they heard no movement in the canyon—and Corredor reported that all was quiet—the boss gave instructions.

He told them they would break into three groups. The first would be El Gringo, El Vilchis, Eneas, and El Márquez. They would descend on foot, in tight formation, shielded by their horses' backs, rifles aimed at the enemy. The horse gives you a one-shot advantage, so never take your eyes off the Apache position, he said. Be decisive, be quick, be as efficient as soldiers. This is a matter of numbers: how many shots per head, how many of them we kill before they kill one of us. He looked at El Márquez. You're in charge, he said. You see those boulders? He pointed to the creek at the bottom of the canyon. Yes, sir. You get your people settled there and yell when they're under cover; you're responsible for everybody's lives, and if one of your men goes down, you turn around and bag me a dead enemy for each head of ours. He motioned toward the nun and the Yaquis: These fiends will be covering you, so there's nothing to worry about. Is that clear? Clear as water, sir.

He looked at Corredor. You and I will go next. We'll be heading to the big cottonwoods by the river, he said, indicating a thicket of trees on the banks of the arroyo, where a shooter in the upper reaches of the canyon wouldn't be able to get a bead on them without exposing his entire body. He looked at El Márquez: Meanwhile, you're going to be covering us from below. Once Corredor and I are safe, I'll give the order for the three of you to come down, he said, pointing to the nun and the Yaquis. Elvis, you'll be the officer in charge if I'm out of commission, so I expect Guadalupe and Victoria to die protecting you. Boss or not, we'd do it, said one of the twins without turning to look at them, scanning the mountain with narrowed eyes, ready to let a bullet fly as soon as the first head appeared. The twins and Elvis will make for the cottonwoods, too, and once they're safe, you—he looked at Márquez—will meet us there.

Ready? asked the chief. The dancing master met his eyes. Today is a great day to die.

Everything is always a matter of perspective. To the Sonorans it seemed but a split second that they were running alongside their horses, nearly plunging down a path with no room to move abreast. To Zuloaga, who, rifle in hand, had found a spot for himself beside the nun, the first group's descent seemed slow, labored, agonizing. When they reached the canyon bottom, the stretch to cross without cover looked so long to El Márquez that he pulled a stunt that made his watching comrades' eyes bug out. He got up on his horse Apache-style and rode slung along its rib cage, shielded from gunfire—it turned out that this, too, was something he knew how to do. He pulled ahead of his men and rode to the boulders, where he leapt off his horse, landing with spectacular dexterity, his rifle aimed at the cliffs above. Well done, shouted the boss, and, addressing the Sonorans, who were somewhat nonplussed: Keep cover behind the horses, rifles up; you're fine. They made it.

The lieutenant turned to Corredor. What do you say? he asked. The boy smiled. How about we ride down on horseback, six-shooters in hand. Are you out of your mind? Zuloaga asked. The Raramuri replied: Mangas's people didn't think we'd make it this far, and they're scared; either they left or they aren't going to fire. Without taking his eyes off the ridge he was watching unblinkingly, Victoria said: Chingada madre, the words of an honorary Yaqui. Yessir, proclaimed his twin. Buck up, mi teniente. Zuloaga stuck his rifle in the scabbard across his horse's haunches and pulled the pistol from his belt. He licked the barrel, and once he was in the saddle he jammed down his hat with the thumb he'd used to uncock the revolver. He spurred the animal on, wide open. The boy couldn't let himself be bested, so he rode clinging to the horse with his thighs, holding the reins in his mouth and brandishing the revolvers he'd taken from the Argentine detective.

Seeing Corredor cavorting like a bandit, Elvira adjusted her veil, never shifting her gaze from the edge of the cliff. Ta loco, she said. No one heard her, because the Yaquis were raising a din that must have made a shiver descend the spines of the Apaches above. The Sonorans, who were covering the riders from below, didn't join in the racket. They were perhaps too stunned to open their mouths. Only Eneas managed to say something, once the Raramuri had reached the bottom of the cliff: Olé. The nun watched them cross the arroyo and ride into the cottonwoods. She said to the twins: We'll have to ride down now, boys, or we'll make fools of ourselves.

Their descent was outrageously bold, but no one cheered this time, partly because they were all taking their covering duties seriously—these big guns had to be protected at all costs—but mostly because Corredor had already carried the day.

The cottonwood thicket gave them shelter. Zuloaga yelled to El Márquez: Stay covered while we figure out what to do next. In reply, the dancing master rode out from the boulders at a saunter. Are you crazy? called the lieutenant. Not a bit, boss; they're gone: we had a good view of them from here. The nun stuck the Colt in her belt and said: Well played. If I know Mangas, we're safe now until the Gila Valley. The chief gave her a look. You know Mangas? He's a very handsome man, said the nun, adjusting her veil.

Zuloaga had enough experience fighting Apaches to be persuaded that his scheme for exiting the Mogollones would have won the respect of any chief, and the right to parley. They could carry on north through the canyon at their ease. They couldn't be very far from the camp.

Still, he took precautions: he kept the twins at the rear and sent Eneas and El Vilchis on ahead. The arroyo soon sank into the earth, and the canyon became much less dramatic.

NANA KNEW THE MOUNTAINS of Chihuahua and New Mexico like no one else. He was the most experienced of the chiefs, and the best rider of them all. He was still sound of mind and agile despite his age—he would live to be nearly one hundred. He had fought as a captain with Mangas Coloradas and as a chief with Cochise, had been right-hand man to Victorio during his last military campaign. He had seen it all and kept his composure.

Many years later, one of the survivors of the massacre said that when Kaetennae and Blanco, the Mimbreños sent by Victorio for ammunition, returned to Tres Castillos, they found the trail that Nana had left for them to follow. The chief was waiting for them by an arroyo, his people's spirits broken and himself on foot. When Kaetennae and Blanco presented him with the boxes of ammunition they had stolen, Kaetennae said: "Too late, Chief." Nana replied: "It is never too late so long as one Apache lives." And he made a speech, as reported by more than one informant. "Victorio," he said, "died as he would have wished, fighting alongside his people. He died as he lived: free and unconquerable."

After skirting the Montañas del Diablo on their way to the Mescalero reservation where they knew they could surrender without fear that the U.S. Army would hand them over to the New Mexico authorities, Nana's forces passed the springs of Ojocaliente. The warriors who had gone ahead as scouts reported that the squad of U.S. soldiers stationed to guard the place had decamped.

Nana must have weighed the situation carefully before he decided to give his people a respite, allowing them to bathe in the sacred waters of the mineral springs. Kaywaykla, one of the children who lived to tell of this march, would say to Eve Ball many years later: "How wonderful it was to step into those waters. In the desert we washed by scraping ourselves with sand, and suddenly we were at those clean, life-giving springs."

Yesterday I watched my own children bathe in the same waters: just another tourist attraction on a road trip through the U.S. Southwest, an unearned interlude paid for with cash. I watched them in the hot springs pool, red from the heat and mineral salts, and I couldn't help but think of Kaywaykla, the Apache boy washing away the exhaustion, hunger, horror, and orphanhood that must have clung to him during the flight north with Nana. Being a criollo in America—no matter how innocent we are—is to be born an entitled pig.

NATURALLY, EL VILCHIS AND ENEAS rode straight past the watering hole where Camila and Goyahkla had settled down to wait while Mangas and his warriors were trading some of the cattle taken from the Ezguerra ranch. The Yaquis pulled up their horses the moment they noted something different about the distribution of plants by the side of the road. There's water here, said Victoria, and he got off his mule to search in the brush. Soon he was looking up from the ground, calling to Zuloaga: Come and see all the pretty tracks they left for us.

Zuloaga dismounted and ordered the nun to go after El Vilchis and Eneas. He asked the others to find shade for the animals and handed his reins to Corredor. Hands on hips, he scanned the full perimeter of the hideaway, this time with a tracker's attention to detail. Here we go, he said to the Yaquis, pointing to what looked like a pile of branches and dried grass by the canyon wall. It's a watering hole, he said. Guadalupe added: With a chingo of cows drinking from it for days. They advanced on the terrain, as eager as children.

The cattle had been in the gully long enough to make a wallow. There had been no rain, so most of the cow pies were intact and the ground was vigorously trampled. They were here for at least a week, said one of the twins. After carefully examining the ground and touching the hoofprints, he added: One animal is missing. A calf; they'll've eaten it along the way. His brother concluded: They were taking their time, sure no one was following.

Guadalupe came across another uneven patch of ground, and he knelt down to brush away layers of soil. Soon he found the first bone: the tibia of a fawn. His brother snatched it away and began to dig with it. A considerable quantity of bones piled up, mostly of small animals. It isn't much food for a week, said the chief, something doesn't add up. Yes it does, said Guadalupe, if a single warrior'd stayed behind to keep watch over the cattle. Or the captive? asked the chief. They wouldn't've left her alone, replied Victoria, who had bent over to get a closer look at what his brother had dug up.

Zuloaga watched them, intrigued. Each time they found a bone, they put it in a pile according to the animal it had come from. After a while, they realized that in addition to the fawn, some pack rats had been eaten, but the remains were mostly of hares. Guadalupe began to pick out only the hare bones, while Victoria laid them one after the other: seven ribs, six heads, eleven or twelve femurs. When enough long bones had been dug up, the lieutenant colonel understood at last what they were doing and asked permission to take two and compare them.

Three of the five bones had been put in the ashes to roast and pierced by teeth to extract the marrow. The other two had been stripped of meat and discarded. He smiled and looked up, meeting the brothers' grins, more open and expressive than ever. Victoria held up a femur in each hand and said: This one was eaten by a young Apache, apprentice to the warriors who attacked the Janos ranch. Then he held up the other. This one, he said, was eaten by your captive.

The three of them rose, as happy as if they had rescued her already. Zuloaga returned to the path to take the reins of his horse, which Corredor had been holding for him. The Raramuri had been watching them curiously. Why so happy? he asked. Because Señora Camila is alive, said the chief. He led his horse to the watering hole and unsaddled it. With the tip of his boot he brushed away the grasses with which the Apaches had covered it. He stroked the animal's mane as it bent to drink. Turning to look at the others, he said: Come over here. And to Corredor: Once the horses are finished drinking, you boil water, because I have a feeling this little arroyo won't make another appearance until we reach Mangas's valley.

El Márquez and El Gringo were the first in the water. Zuloaga watched them with an oddly tender smile before retreating to the shade of the cliff wall to roll a cigarette. Then the Yaquis were taking off their boots, too, and the lieutenant sat on a stone and basked in the pleasure of a peaceful smoke, no longer beset by the responsibility of leading a group who, it seemed, had ultimately shown themselves to be not only competent but capable of scaring off a band of actual warriors.

The sun caught something on a stone, and he went to see what it was. Pushing aside the brush, he saw that Camila had left a bone arrow pointing north. He scratched his beard, grown out mightily by now, and smiled again, in the unguarded way of the unwatched. He turned toward his nacionales as they splashed at their ease, thinking that he should bathe, too, maybe wash his clothes: it was early enough in the day for them to dry. It would do his people good to rest, he thought.

He rolled another cigarette, sat on his stone to smoke it, and returned to the watering hole, which the Sonorans and Corredor had gotten into, too. Elvira was sprawled on the ground, propped on her saddle; she had hiked up her habit to get some sun on her bare legs. Today we rest, shouted the lieutenant colonel at the top of his lungs, as if anyone had been awaiting his orders to loaf, or was even listening to him. He sat on a stump and took off his boots. The smell of his feet reminded him that he hadn't taken them off since the long-distant night when El Márquez taught them to dance the dog.

THE WARRIORS DIDN'T TURN TO LOOK at Camila when she returned, now in Apache dress, and—to her mind—quite fetching. Goyahkla's expression was openly mocking, as if a friend of his had appeared one day in lady's garb. When they all got back on their horses, Camila tried to mount hers Apache-style, but she overshot and fell on the other side. No one laughed at her, and she shook off the dirt and tried again, this time successfully. When everyone set off, she waited for Goyahkla and rode beside him, watching the cattle graze to calm her nerves.

At some point Kan-da-zis Tlishishen and the old woman drew away from the group. Goyahkla approached Camila and instructed her to follow; she was to ride directly behind the chief.

She rode ahead and caught up with the pair. The war diyin slowed her horse and fell in next to her. They crossed a parched valley and an unexpected field of crops, sheltered by a wall of trees of a size that Camila, used to the stunted scrub of Janos and Casas Grandes, hadn't thought could exist anywhere but Guadalajara.

A woman kneeling in one of the fields got up to watch them from a distance. The shaman rode closer to Camila, as if to protect her from the woman's gaze. She took the reins of her horse so that they wouldn't be separated. The woman in the field raised a sharp, undulating, predatory cry. This is the beginning of what comes next, thought Camila, and she held her head very high, in case what came next was death.

The contingent slowed even more. The chief raised his right hand. Goyahkla rode up from behind at a gallop and handed him a spear. Then Camila heard the war cry of Kan-da-zis Tlishishen. It halted the cattle, bent the trees, broke the stones on the mountainside. She thought: Let me live, dear God, even if it's only so that he plows me once, like a tilled field; then let thy will be done.

I IMAGINE THAT WHAT SEEMED a haven to the Apache boy Kaywaykla, a place where he could bathe and recover his strength, must have been a metaphysical ordeal to Chief Nana. If ever there was a desperate man in the desert, it was Nana after the battle of Tres Castillos. He must have sung all night, who knows how many nights.

He had sixteen warriors and thirty-two noncombatants, all exhausted, starving, their minds shattered by images of the dead but also and especially by visions of the living. The forty-eight Chiricahuas saved by Nana were a motley group. They were Gilas, Mimbreños, Coyoteros. Children who had seen their fathers run through with bayonets and whose mothers would be scrubbing shit in the latrines of wealthy Chihuahuans for the rest of their lives; fathers who had seen their children torn apart by bullets; mothers whose daughters would be annihilated by rape in the brothels that served the presidios lining the border. Who would grow up to forget they were Chiricahua.

Even if, like Sánchez, all of these Chiricahuas growing up as prisoners of the Mexicans kept the secret of where they belonged until they managed to escape, they would have nowhere to go, because Apachería really was being eradicated now. The little piece of the vast earth that Ussen had deeded to his people, who for three hundred years had withstood the onslaughts of Navajos, Pueblos, and Comanches, the Empire, and the Republic, was finally being stolen by the armies of Mexico and the United States. The armies were closing in on them, crushing them, splintering them on all sides.

Ussen was a generous god. He must have heard Nana's pleas, must have spoken to him, offered him some guarantee, because the son of a bitch lived thirty more years. He went to Oklahoma to die—we saw his grave a few days ago.

After those nights of songs and incantations in Ojocaliente, the chief changed his plans. He entrenched himself in the Montañas del Diablo and sent Kaytennae north to lead the noncombatants to the reservation and appeal for reinforcements, in case other warriors had survived the battle of Tres Castillos and had found their own way there. Then he launched a revenge attack so vigorous, masterful, and savage that there are still towns in Chihuahua and Sonora where, when things are about to get ugly, people say it will be like la noche de Nana.

Just as the chief was leaving the Montañas del Diablo, close to the border with Mexico, a gift was bestowed on him from out of the blue, a bounty that could only have come from Ussen. Nana ordered an attack on a wagon well-guarded by Mexicans. The plunder would have been a blessing had it been guns, as the chief believed, but it so happened that there were silver ingots in the wagon bed instead, under a tight canvas cover. Kaywaykla, allowed by Nana to join the expedition as a novice, later described how the chief, who never lost his sense of humor, asked whether he thought they should exchange the silver for bullets or for sotol, to forget the battle of Tres Castillos.

Nana gave each warrior three ingots to exchange for ammunition as best they could, and he set a meeting place at a refuge in the Sierra Madre, going on ahead with Kaywaykla and the rest of the silver. There he buried it, and no one ever found it again. Not everyone returned to the meeting place, and no one can say exactly what happened in the Sierra Madre—Kaywaykla only reported that they lived for a while as the Apaches had lived in the old days—but in June 1881, Nana came down from the mountain with fifteen warriors, determined to spare no one.

For two months, always chased but never harried by the armies of Mexico and the United States, Nana covered three thousand miles, carrying out attacks with implausible swiftness. Sometimes he set fire on consecutive days to ranches so far apart that his pursuers imagined there must be more than one band of rebels. When by some miracle the cavalry of either country stumbled into him, Chief Nana, who remembered the glory days of Mangas's gunfights on horseback, didn't shrink from pitched battle. He won every skirmish with just his fifteen warriors and Kaywaykla.

For almost two thousand years, Julius Caesar was judged history's greatest general because his legions could cover fifty miles a day. It wasn't until the nineteenth century that Napoleon equaled the feat, until then believed to be mythical. Nana could move seventy miles a day, battles and all. Motorized units had to be invented to beat his record.

When, toward the end of August, the last group of rebel Mimbres had used up their ammunition, Nana returned to the Sierra Madre to rest, satisfied. There he joined forces permanently with Geronimo, to whom he grew very close: they returned together to San Carlos after surrendering at the Cañón de los Embudos. There is no log of Mexican losses during the two wild months of Nana's attacks, but the U.S. 4th and 5th Cavalry Regiments recorded thirty-nine dead between them, plus an uncalculated but very high number of civilians killed on both sides of the border. In those two months, Nana didn't lose a single warrior.

IT WAS BECAUSE THEY HAD CHOSEN the shady side of the canyon, riding along like idiots, that they lost perspective, Zuloaga thought later. Corredor, hugging the cliff wall like everyone else, couldn't see that they were being hunted from above. The Yaquis didn't see it either: they had fallen behind, joking with the boss and the nun and leaving the inexperienced Sonorans to head the convoy. What happened was bound to happen, thought Zuloaga. How could he not have seen it coming? When exactly had he decided that he was a better hunter than Mangas's Gileños?

At a bend in the trail, just as one might be met all of a sudden by a boulder or a big-bellied cottonwood, they were greeted by the lethal little eyes of the Springfields, gringo-supplied, of a band of Apaches perched on a steep, rocky slope. Now we're fucked, said Guadalupe and Victoria together when the Gileños rose as one. The nacionales had come around a corner of the canyon exposed and daydreaming, with their pistols in their belts and their rifles in their scabbards.

Zuloaga put his hands up, the right one a tiny bit lower than the left, ready for the moment they'd have to resort to guns. Nobody move, he said to his people, and put your hands up nice and slow. A strange, grating voice called in Spanish from the canyon wall: Put your pistol hand up higher, ándele. He obeyed, his eyes alone moving as he calculated any possible advantages of their hopeless position: they would be unable to turn around and return to cover without suffering losses; ahead there wasn't a single hiding place, just the dry riverbed under a blazing sun, which meant they couldn't count on marksman's error. He thought: The bastards have known for days that they'd get us here.

He counted the Apaches. Eighteen in sight, all aiming at them. The odds were two to one. There was no way to win. Nobody move, he said again.

He raised his eyes without lifting his face and saw a buzzard hanging in the air. A breeze stirred the branches of a sweet acacia so slowly that he could see the leaves quiver before the branch moved. One leaf fell. It seemed to fall so slowly that he imagined he could get off his horse, walk to the shrub, and catch it before it touched the ground. He looked at the twins: he could see the sweat beading on the backs of their necks, pearls suddenly swelling, catching the sun, and rolling down. He eyed the line of their shoulders: the Yaquis were the surprise factor. Everything was riding on them. He could see their tensed muscles under skin bronzed from days of riding in the sun. The fact that they were shirtless must have been a provocation from the start; he shouldn't have allowed it. That had been another mistake. He rewound the whole trip in his mind. He saw that the Yaquis should always have been riding half a day ahead, but they were crazy after being in jail for so long, how *could* they be sane after being stuck in that presidio hellhole, stewing in their own shit. He saw that Corredor and the nun, his best marksmen, should have been deployed on their flanks behind the advance party, always; that he should have sent them high up the canyon; that he had two gifted people and he had wasted them simply because he didn't entirely trust them or anyone but himself, or because he thought he was so smart, and circumstances were showing him now that he wasn't. He saw that he had been a trifler, a fool, an incompetent. He saw that Guadalupe and Victoria were waving the tips of their fingers like spider's legs and he saw that the Apaches could see it, too. He could hear the precise drumming of their finger bones, like drops falling into a barrel of water. Don't try it, he shouted, and he could see his voice shuddering in the air, warping the air, stamping the air before working its way into their ears and proceeding to bounce off the canyon walls. He saw them turning ever so slowly, barely glancing at him out of the corner of their eyes, their gaze telling him they could do it, telling him to release them, let them raise holy Christ-loving hell. He saw them beg him to give the order, this was why they had come, but he also saw the scattered line of the Sonorans, El Márquez, and El Gringo in the middle of it all and it filled him with sorrow to imagine them killed the way they would be killed if a single shot issued from a single rifle. No, he said, don't do it, and he turned back toward the mountain because the echo of his words was tangling with that sharp, arrogant, grating voice, harsh as a motherfucker. It was saying something. He swiveled his ears as if they were hands, as if his ears had elbows. He listened carefully. The voice had a question and the question was: Chihuahua or Sonora? He calculated. He bellowed: Chihuahua and Sonora. His voice was so booming, so deep that he watched it bounce off the walls like a ball, feeling as if he were riding along an endless canyon, reaching the pine forests and snows of the farthest north. Who Chihuahua? came the voice from above. He raised his hand and said softly: Boys. He watched his people's fingertips piercing the air, very slowly. First Corredor and the nun, then El Gringo and he himself. Who Sonora? asked the voice, but it didn't give anybody time to raise a finger. He saw Vilchis's and Eneas's heads snapping back, he heard the slight crunch that their skulls made as they burst, the fatty sound of their brains absorbing the lead, he watched them succumb to gravity. He shouted, *No*, but it was too late. He shouted, get down, take cover behind your horses, but nobody heard him because now smoke was trailing from the Apaches' Springfields, they had thundered, and if he hadn't panicked he would have seen the buckshot parting the air.

I'm motherfucking fucked, he said to himself, bringing his hand to his revolver. And he saw the Yaquis leaping off their mules and he saw their fingers at the buckles of their scabbards and he saw the buckles release and he saw the impossible, because before they dropped to the ground behind their horses they somersaulted in the air, balls of muscle, sinew, brilliance, balls of light and rage, and he saw them lying on a cushion of air, yanking out their rifles, and he saw them aim and fire as if floating, one two three shots each maybe, and he saw them shitting themselves laughing because now they really were fucked but each was taking a few Apaches with him: the ancestral enemy. Stunned as he was, he counted the fallen on the other side: one, two, three, four, five. Fuck, he said to himself, Pisago was right: we could have handled the shooting if I hadn't been such a coward.

He drew his revolver, leapt to the ground shooting, and took cover behind his horse. He heard bodies falling, and he concentrated on the firepower he could unleash to cover El Márquez, who fell wounded despite his efforts. He saw the nun run to El Márquez's aid and he scanned the field again. Rather than hitting the ground, the twins had melted into it, as if the earth had been content to receive them.

The unbearable voice said: You can come out now, we have no quarrel with Chihuahua.

Zuloaga closed his eyes. They stung. He had sweated so much

that the brim of his hat could no longer contain his juices. He began to calculate again: without the Yaquis the expedition was lost. He shouted to gain time: We'll come out if you put your rifles down. He wiped his forehead with the sleeve of his jacket and scratched his ear with the muzzle of his pistol. He licked the muzzle. He could never match the Yaquis, but there he was behind his horse, revolver in hand. He could take out two or three, and Corredor as many more; Doña Elvira, though distracted by El Márquez's wounded body, might spring into action. Against all odds, the voice shouted: Ta bueno, no rifles.

He closed his eyes and could clearly hear that they really were setting down their guns on the mountainside. He heard Corredor, who had taken cover behind his own horse, calling, and he turned to look at him. Corredor, too, was pressed close to his animal, back turned to the shooters, the Argentine's two revolvers clasped in his hands. The lieutenant raised his eyebrows and the Raramuri shouted that there had been twenty Apaches; the twins had killed five, but even so, only twelve had set down their guns. Zuloaga didn't quite understand. There are still three of them aiming at us, the boy said. The lieutenant colonel took a breath and shouted: Drop the other three guns or we'll open fire, and, mingling with the echo of his own voice, he heard El Márquez's, even deeper and more gravelly than usual. He was translating into Apache. There was a silence and then the voice from the mountain said again: Ta bueno. He heard another rustle. He glanced at Corredor, and the Raramuri nodded, confirming that they could come out now. He stuck his revolver in his belt and stepped forward.

Pulling his handkerchief from the back pocket of his trousers, he wiped his face, put the cloth back, and stuck his hands in his belt, to show that he, too, was unarmed but ready to draw in an instant. He looked up into the heights. The warriors he'd seen with perfect clarity when he'd realized they were being ambushed had disappeared, camouflaged on the mountainside. He walked over to the bodies of Guadalupe and Victoria. Most of the fire had been aimed at them, and their faces and chests were blown to bits. Look at them, just look what they've done to them, he said, and everyone heard him in the profound silence. He turned toward the nun and El Márquez. How's the dancing master? he asked. Give me a minute and I'll be doing push-ups and sit-ups, El Márquez himself replied. The nun said nothing, which struck the boss as eloquent.

Then there was movement on the mountainside. He raised his eyes. A boy was climbing down the rocky slope.

BOOK II

ALBUM

AUGUST 8

Westerns are the fairy tales gringos tell themselves to assure the triumph of bureaucratic reason over the excesses of individual will; they are the most effective vehicle for the dissemination of productivity culture in a country whose other founding myth is respect for individual freedoms.

Most of the classic westerns—the ones from the fifties and sixties—are about more or less the same thing: the arrival of moral principles intended to foster economic progress in a community of outlaws. Sometimes (in *El Dorado*, for example) the frontier town is beset by bandits and there's a hero who vanquishes them in a hail of bullets and then renounces violence, settling in the mountains. Sometimes (in *Unforgiven*, for example) the agent of the law is himself a despot who must be sacrificed so that the written word—and its sublime emanation, the Law—can be spread among the unwashed frontiersmen.

There is always, of course, a trace of nostalgia for the lost world: in *Mackenna's Gold*, a gang of outlaws—Apaches, Mexicans, a sheriff who is a decent man though his morals are clearly loose (he takes an Indian woman as a lover)—make a final bid to get rich without adhering to the Puritan precepts of work and thrift and are punished for it. In one of the best westerns ever made, John Ford's *The Man Who Shot Liberty Valance*, a senator returns to the town where he began his political career and tells the near-mythic tale of how, armed only with his lawbooks—and, admittedly, John Wayne's friendship and six-shooter—he propelled a whole region of the American Southwest into the cycles of productive democratic life.

All of this is only confirmed and reinforced by the absence of this formula from spaghetti westerns, which were conceived, written, directed, and filmed by Italians, plus a few gringo actors so that at least one or two of the cowboys wouldn't speak atrocious English. In a western conceived in the non-U.S. mind, what happens is what always happens in the real world: chaos rules, the bad guys win, things stay the way they are or get worse. A spaghetti western is the mirror image of a classic western. All its values are inverted, and that makes them cornerstones in the construction of the mythology of cool: alienation, indifference, detachment. An Italian cowboy movie is an ode to the failure of any civilizing effort, and Sergio Leone is an existentialist. The original westerns work the other way around: they tell us that the North American soul is optimistic and liberal, not tragic; that progress is not only possible but inevitable, so long as you make an effort—or at least close your eyes and wish as hard as you can.

Ultimately, the story that westerns tell is about the conquest of emptiness. In cowboy movies, what was once a chaotic no-place—nature, banditry, violence—is sanctified by the ritual imposition of the written word, a path out of nothingness.

The information that's always missing—and it's information that explains so much about the relationship between the U.S. and Latin America—is that the wild nothingness rescued from chaos by lawyers in cowboy hats and boots was actually something: Mexico. What we are told by westerns is that democracy and hard work tamed the space of Mexicanness, won by the signing of a treaty, not a war of conquest. First there was nothing, then there was a chaotic mix—Mexicans, Indians, dissolute whites—and in the end there was democratic and productive order.

Westerns are the final chapter in the anthology of the conquest of America. They promise us that gringos are from Europe, not America.

PHOENIX JOHNSTON MCMILLAN

Redhead from San Antonio, TX

Amyntor Blair McMillan rode the brand-new streetcar from San Antonio's Broadway to Fort Sam Houston, which in those days was quite a distance from the city. It was a Sunday, so he was with his family: his Texan wife, Helen Howard, and their son, Phoenix Johnston. Like everybody back then, the McMillans believed the slow, green spirit of the river winding its way through the city sapped vitality and took a toll on the body, so on Sundays after church they went for long walks far from San Antonio's muddy streets. Proximity to the desert does that to people: they think the sun hammering them on the head and the dust blossoming in their lungs is healthy.

And they aren't entirely mistaken: though by the end of the nineteenth century the waterway that bisected San Antonio had already been walled off into a more or less hygienic canal, the riverbanks on the edge of town were pestilential, if not worse. The McMillans, like all inhabitants of San Antonio, had always viewed the river with mistrust, but when they became parents, they deemed it indispensable to spend as much time as possible in the scrubland outside city limits, strengthening their child's constitution and their own.

They were a young family living in an old house they had inherited in the city's downtown. It was the house that enabled Amyntor Blair to live in a manner befitting the dignity of a white man with a university degree, despite his modest salary at the criminal law office where he was a junior attorney.

The morning of Sunday, September 9, 1886, had announced itself blazingly hot even before church, so the McMillans boarded the streetcar at the corner of Broadway and Commerce dressed as lightly as one could in those days: he in a gray cotton suit and cravat instead of a tie, with a narrow-brimmed Mexican straw hat. Like all genuine lawyers in that time and place, Amyntor Blair didn't carry a gun: his weapon was the law. His wife was wearing a light-colored skirt with muslin petticoats and a single-hooped crinoline, a sky-blue blouse with no corset, a white shawl over her shoulders, and a cotton bonnet on her head. Both were wearing boots: his were riding boots, and hers were calf-high lace-up boots, because for all the city airs they put on, nineteenth-century Texas was still too rough for any other kind of footwear. The boy was gussied up like a posset in a frilly white gown that must have made him itch terribly. He was wearing a little white bonnet that kept off the sun and contained the unruly mop of red hair that made him the most recognizable baby of his generation in San Antonio.

According to what we know about Amyntor Blair McMillan—one of his grandchildren was city historian—he was an easygoing, sophisticated, good-humored man, with a condescending attitude toward what he considered the volubility of the female persuasion. Though he was a Texan by birth and so was his daddy, he was proud of being descended from an Alabama gentleman who had left the South, never to return, when it was discovered that one of his sisters was accepting visits from an officer who had fought with the North in the Civil War. His Irish genes were particularly marked in his physiognomy: he was red of face and hair, though the Texan diet of meat and more meat had made him as tall as an Englishman. His wife, Helen, must have had Mexican blood, or Mediterranean at least, whether she admitted it or not: she passed for white, but in the sun her skin turned toasty brown rather than mottled purple like her husband's; she had jet-black hair as glossy as a show horse's, and big honey-colored eyes that she claimed as evidence of her Caucasian origins. She plucked her eyebrows so they wouldn't grow together over her nose.

If he'd still been a bachelor, Amyntor Blair would have spent his Sunday at a ranch or taking a stroll around some exceptional geological site—there were plenty of them in Texas—but he understood that his wife was dying to get an up-close look at the prisoners who were the talk of the town and he wanted to surprise her by handing her a small social victory. After an exchange of telegrams with a Captain Lawton stationed until very recently in Mexico, he had obtained a safe-conduct that would afford Helen a closer look than anyone at the U.S.'s most famous detainees. Due to a disagreement between President Cleveland and the War Department's commander of the territories of New Mexico and Arizona, the prisoners were being held in limbo at Fort Sam Houston, and depending which side of the coin landed face up, they would either be sent to the fort-turned-jail in Florida where their family members awaited them or to the gallows in Tucson, Arizona.

McMillan was nervous and excited when they boarded the streetcar to Fort Sam Houston, though he never would have admitted that he, too, was dying to look into the eyes of Geronimo. And Chapo, son of Geronimo. And Naiche, son of Cochise, chief of the Chiricahuas in the United States. And Lozen, lethal woman warrior and master of survival like her brother, Mimbreño Chief Victorio. And Chief Nana, probably the person who had claimed the most lives in a part of the country where at this point almost no male had clean hands. Amyntor Blair sat on the front bench of the streetcar, conscious that of all the passengers, his family was the best turned out and the most up-and-coming, and that when the time came to peer through the bars offering the people of San Antonio a view of the prisoners, the gate would open so that he, his wife, and his son could get even closer. It never would have occurred to McMillan that in order to talk to the Apaches he would have to speak Spanish.

AUGUST 8: LATER

Today we reached the Bolas de la Peñascosa. In English the name is less lyrical and lacking in patina, but it does have a powerful ring to it: Cochise Stronghold.

We arrived late, though we were coming from relatively nearby in New Mexico, because we drove to the Tucson airport first, barreling down a horrible, dreary highway, to pick up my eldest son, Cruz. We tossed his things in the back of the station wagon and headed into the city to eat. The children were thrilled to be in their brother's company. Coming to pick him up, touching him, hearing his voice, smelling him: this is the point of our trip, and also notice that it's ending. We'll be spending the last week of summer vacation in the Peñascosas, and then we'll return Cruz to the airport and his own life. And we'll drive back to New York in a straight shot, only stopping at motels to sleep.

The place we're renting was once the main house on a ranch, a historic stone-and-log cabin in the middle of nowhere. It was abandoned by its inhabitants toward the end of the Apache Wars and stood empty until the Peñascosas were incorporated into Coronado National Forest, when it was rebuilt to house the park rangers. Now it's rented out to tourists desperate for quiet: there's no Wi-Fi, no television, no phone, and you have to walk a long way to get a cell signal. The email we got when we rented the house stressed that it was twenty-five minutes by car to Sunsites, the nearest town, where there was only a gas station convenience store, and almost an hour to Willcox.

So on our way to Bolas de la Peñascosa, the final stop on our trip, we stocked up on provisions: a cooler full of meat and chicken to grill, and grocery sacks of vegetables, fruit, cereal, milk, toiletries, wine, and beer. The plan is not, of course, to reenact the life of the pioneers who settled in this wilderness—a vain effort—but to end the trip in style and share a moment of peace and perhaps recalibration with Cruz.

Nobody calls the mountains along the western edge of Sulphur Springs Valley the Sierra de la Peñascosa anymore. U.S. army cartographers rechristened them the Dragoon Mountains in the nineteenth century, and the name was so evocative that it stuck. It's a remote, unpopulated mountain range, modest in size—25 miles long, its highest peak just under 7,500 feet. It would be just another string of peaks if it weren't for the mountain at its center, blown to pieces by some presumably magnificent cataclysm. The scar left by the explosion is a succession of giant red domes and crags, so rare that when Zúñiga, the conquistador, made the first mention of it in a European language, he couldn't find a better word for it than *bolas*. And that's what it is: a random pile of massive stone balls, a mountain kicked to pieces by a boy so big he could yank down the moon. Standing at the summit and looking east, you see a cascade of giant slabs that form a cliff like something on another planet; hostile. The passage was called Cañón de Tejas, or Slab Canyon, after those flat stones. The Spanish colonists who forged their way into Comanche territory in the New Philippines ended up calling it Tejas because that was the way they had come. The road to El Paso del Norte still runs nearby, a secondary route now. If you follow the slabs west, you reach the town of Tombstone. The murderer Wyatt Earp, obsessed with avenging the death of his brothers, used to bring his victims to the wilderness of Slab Canyon to torture and kill them. By then the Republic of Tejas had been annexed by the United States and was spelled with an *x*, like Mexico—in both words the *x* stands for a sound that doesn't exist in English, the rough Semitic *j* that stands as a living reminder of the eight hundred years during which Spain was part of the Muslim world.

We arrived when the sun had set behind the range, the detail of its stony convolutions mostly lost in the dusk rising swiftly from the earth. The rhythms of Apachería are more like those south of the border than anyplace else in the country that ultimately swallowed it up in its furious race to the Pacific. Night doesn't creep in with a golden hue, like in New York or Chicago; it comes all of a sudden, like in Mexico City.

We inspected the kitchen, and unpacked the groceries. The children chose their beds and dressers, dumping out their clothes and separating them into clean and dirty piles. I swept the porch—which was covered in dead bugs and live bugs, mouse shit and bat shit—and the kids pulled out the furniture and wiped it down, one of their favorite activities. Cruz—a little taken aback by the military precision of the occupation system developed by the other four members of the family over the course of the trip—opened a beer and went outside. When I joined him with my own beer, he was sitting in a chair he'd taken from the porch, watching the colossal spectacle of the Milky Way: God's vagina. I sat on the ground, about to lie back and enjoy it. You'd better get up, he said; something will bite you. And he went to the porch to get me a chair.

I asked how his mother was doing, and he said she was fine, he hadn't seen her since she visited soon after his move to Guadalajara, but she was happy with her new husband and his children, she treated them like her own kids. What about you? I asked. Same as here, he said, I have to make space for myself, but they're nice to me. I put my hand on his shoulder and gave him an affectionate manly pat. We're always missing you here, I said. When you leave, there's a hole we can't fill, a void in the middle of the living room. He didn't answer. A little later I went into the cabin to make dinner, something light. I sent him Cosme, who had been complaining he'd never seen the Milky Way. It's all right there outside, I said. He asked, joking, Cruz or the Milky Way? Cruz, I said; the Milky Way, Apachería, all of it.

During dinner, a field mouse made an appearance, big-eared, tiny, more curious than frightened at our presence. The children gave it a name: the Neighbor. As we were cleaning up, Cruz asked: So why are we here? Maybe we had all been slightly too enthusiastic when we told him about the wonders of the U.S. Southwest at the supermarket in Tucson. For us, Apachería and Cruz himself had been the destination; for him, this was a few days far from everything before classes began again. Amelia rushed to say that we were here because I was writing a book about Apaches and we had come to see the places where the book goes (as if it were a car or a train), and also, we were here to play Apaches. She ran to the drawer of her belongings in her room to get the plastic bow and arrows we'd bought her who knows where. Cruz expelled air from his nose, as he does when he's a little uncomfortable. I think you came because it reminds you of Mexico, he said. It used to be Mexico, said Cosme, proud of the knowledge he'd acquired on the trip. Of course, replied Cruz with gentle condescension, but it's just like Tepoztlán, an abandoned Tepoztlán.

Now I'm writing and everyone else is in bed: we've promised the children that tomorrow we'll take them on the ghost town route ending in Tombstone. Since it's August there will probably be tourists everywhere, so we want to leave as soon as the sun is up, to beat the hordes and sustain for as long as possible the illusion of solitude bequeathed to us by this house in the middle of nowhere.

GROVER CLEVELAND

President of the United States
At Home in New York State

Grover Cleveland stuck his little finger in his left ear and sniffed the wax that he dug out with his fingernail, which was a smidgen longer than the other nails. He wasn't the most brilliant chief executive the U.S. had ever had, but his morals were bulletproof: his political success had always rested on a steely regard for the word of the law rather than on his vision or administrative abilities. He was, above all, a decent, pulchritudinous man, who equated perfect cleanliness with a pure heart.

He took his handkerchief from the breast pocket of his jacket—he was never seen without a jacket, even at very informal meetings in the study of his private home in upstate New York—and wiped his fingernail with it. Only then did he realize that his secretary of war, who had risen from the desk a moment ago, was still standing by the door. What are you doing there, Mr. Endicott? he asked, impatient and uncomfortable at having been caught out. Forgive me, Mr. President, replied the minister, there's just one more thing. Cleveland folded the handkerchief quickly and stuck it in his trouser pocket, as if to hide the evidence. What is it? he asked. It's a last-minute bit of business that wasn't included in the agenda. The president raised his eyebrows. Sit down again, please, he said.

In the week leading up to this meeting with his secretary of war, Cleveland had been on a tight campaign schedule, crisscrossing the state where he had been sheriff, mayor, assistant district attorney, and governor, and upon which his majority in the Senate might ride in the coming elections. This Sunday he was at home with his wife, not because he needed a day of rest, but out of respect for his voters' beliefs. He had spent the day meeting with his cabinet members, who were handling most government affairs in the capital without the benefit of his presence as the elections approached and the outlook grew ever darker for the remaining two years of his term.

It's nothing critical, said the minister, a minor detail, but you should be aware of it. Speak up, then. A dispatch has arrived from Arizona Territory. The president threw up his hands and snorted, visibly annoyed. The minister went on: General Miles says he has the Indian chief Geronimo in the palm of his hand; he'll be surrendering any moment now. The president pursed his lips, expelling air loudly through his nose: Again? he asked. How many times have we received the same dispatch from Arizona? He must be arrested and tried; we can't wait for him to surrender. The minister looked down, taking the scolding. It isn't as easy as all that, he said; they have him cornered in Mexico, and he has to be gotten out. Miles is asking what conditions we can offer him. Cleveland didn't give it a second thought. None, he said, he's a criminal; he must be arrested and tried. The secretary risked a bold suggestion: We could lie to him, offer him something, and then simply turn him over to the sheriff in Tucson. The president fixed him with the cold stare that had earned him his reputation as an implacable prosecutor. We've been lying to them for one hundred years and we haven't made an inch of progress; they have to be treated as citizens, and that's all there is to it. The secretary made a face that the president knew well, heralding the imminent delivery of some uncomfortable truth: But they aren't citizens. The president said: If I win the Senate, I swear to you I'll raise it with Congress; in the meantime, bring him in and put him on trial.

The minister stood there without a word. What is it? asked his boss. If he's tried in Tucson, he'll surely be hanged; he knows that, and he'll escape from us again. Do we have him or don't we? He's close to turning himself in. Can't we just capture him? It's never been done before. Our army is the biggest in the hemisphere. The secretary shrugged: Not in the southwest territories, and our boys there are a bunch of kids. Anyway, Geronimo is in Mexico: we need to offer him a deal. The president raised his right hand to his jowls. What part of your orders don't you understand, Mr. Endicott? The minister sighed: If we brought him in, it would be good news for your campaign, sir, but we'd have to lie to him, promise him something and then send him to trial and let the people of Arizona handle it. My administration doesn't lie, and you needn't concern yourself about my campaign: if I win, I win, and if I lose, so be it. They'll hang him. How many people has he killed? A great many. So let him hang. What should I tell General Miles? Tell him that General Crook, who preceded him in his post, made a pact with Geronimo and today he's at the ass end of Montana chasing goats; that I want Geronimo to be tried.

The minister was impatient, too: it made him uncomfortable not to be able to smoke in the rooms where the president did business, and where he had already spent the afternoon waiting his turn to get his marching orders. If that's what the law decrees in Arizona, so be it, said Cleveland, bringing the conversation to an end. The secretary nodded, made another attempt. With all due respect, Mr. President, the savage wants to turn himself in because the Mexican army has him cornered and he thinks we'll treat him better; if he knows we'll turn him over to a sheriff in Arizona, he'll run. Can't we chase him? the president asked. In Mexico our hands are tied, and the Mexicans will end up arresting him themselves and President Díaz will get all the credit; we can still bring him back, but we have to make a pact, offer him something the Mexicans can't: promise to let him live. The president shook his head. We'll give him a fair trial, won't we? And that's guarantee enough; the Mexicans won't give him that. The secretary held firm: Neither will the people of Arizona, and they have no vote anyway, so what does it matter to us? The president replied: If we respect the law down there we'll do well here on the coast. The appearance in the conversation of the common enemy—the voters of the Southwest, stubborn bastards—softened them both, perhaps reminded them that they were working together. The president made a gesture of resignation, which told Endicott he didn't like the decision he was making either. On one thing they agreed: it was a disgrace to try an Indian as a citizen if he didn't have a citizen's rights, and to try him in hostile territory. Shall I tell General Miles the surrender must be unconditional? You know I don't like to kill Indians and I respect our agreements with them, but if what he's done merits hanging, he should be hanged. Are you sure? Cleveland nodded. The secretary said: It will be on your conscience, not mine. Cleveland closed his eyes. The decision is mine, he said.

The secretary hurried out, already savoring the cigar he was going to smoke on the porch with the other cabinet secretaries before boarding the train to brand-new Penn Station, and then on to Washington.

The president was heavy-hearted when he sat down for dinner that night with his wife—Frances Folsom Cleveland, cultivated, brilliant, a model of discretion; it was said she had won the presidency for rough-edged Cleveland. Now she asked: What is it? I may have condemned a hounded man to death simply because Endicott's impertinence made me angry, he replied. Who? she asked, handing him a plate of lamb chops and green beans. The secretary of war. I know Endicott is the secretary of war; who's to be killed? she asked again. A brigand by the name of Geronimo. The Apache? she asked, her eyes wide. You know who he is? He's more famous than you are. The president looked up from his plate to see whether his wife was joking. She said: Invite him to Washington instead and introduce him to me, let us have a photograph of the three of us together, and we'll win the Senate. Cleveland took off his spectacles, pressing his right thumb and index finger to his eyes. Jesus, he said.

AUGUST 9

You can take Interstate 10 west from the Dragoon Mountains to Tombstone, but the old road is in fine condition, even if it goes nowhere recognizable and no one ever uses it. It's a dirt track that begins a mile and a half from Sunsites on the way to Douglas, on the border between Arizona and Sonora. It takes about forty minutes, maybe an hour or a little longer if you stop at the ghost towns—more ghost than towns—left there to attract hypothetical tourists: the only cars we saw on the drive were Border Patrol pickups, raising dust on the trail of undocumented immigrants, also hypothetical.

We had forgotten to buy soap at the supermarket in Tucson, so we stopped in the town of Pearce (ten or twelve houses), following arrows to a farm selling artisanal goat's milk soap. We turned in and there was the owner, who approached the car to explain that she was closed on Sundays and had only come to feed the goats; we'd better come back tomorrow. I said we needed soap, and since we were here and she was here, we might as well buy some. She repeated that it was Sunday. But if we see a drugstore, we'll end up buying it there, I said. It's Sunday, she said again. This exchange may explain better than any history or sociology book why there are so many ghost towns in Apachería.

Arizona's abandoned towns, unlike New Mexico's, which we'd just seen, are really ghost farms, marketed as something they're not by somebody looking to make a buck. And then there's Tombstone, so asphyxiatingly ridiculous it's hardly worth recording what we saw there, though I think the kids enjoyed it. It's basically a sweaty town staged by misguided entrepreneurs aiming to inform us that southern Arizona was never anything but towns built by white people so that other white people could prosper.

According to this narrative, Tombstone is the basis, origin, and foundation of something. But in fact it's the end product of a tremendously untidy historical process in which the latecomers took all after three hundred years of trade, intercultural sex, and violence.

In Tombstone, designer ruins—looking more like a stage set than like any of the sand-scoured towns of the era—are built on top of real ruins: Mogollon Indian ruins, inhabited until the arrival of the Comanches in the fifteenth century and then overrun again by Athabaskan nomads from Canada, who pushed the Comanches toward Texas over the ruins of the Spanish empire; the Spanish dubbed the Athabaskan speakers Apaches and took their side in the war against the Comanches. Ruins of the first Mexican Republic, which was never able to take back the territory of northern Sonora. Chiricahua ruins, left by a nation that traded guns and won a space of independence in the 1830s and 1840s. Ruins of the outposts of Union soldiers and buffalo soldiers, who occupied the land after the retreat of Mexicans perhaps relieved at no longer having to battle Apaches now that the gringos were handling those unshakable inhabitants of the land.

The myth of the frontier town, of which Tombstone is the prime specimen, dramatizes the arrival of pioneers in a world ruled by natural law and their successful introduction of legal standards and productive habits. It's as if a bunch of Uruguayans had stormed Wall Street and built a South American town out of the stone and steel of the skyscrapers, complete with town hall, central bank, promenade, and butcher shop, and then claimed that what they'd made was the original New York City. And that *Moby Dick* was a Uruguayan classic because its first scenes were set there.

Strangest of all, the few tourists who visit are modern-day gringos, as real as the original occupants of the town must have been: people of different races and backgrounds, the usual mix. There are white tourists, of course, but many are Mexican American, Black, the descendants of southern Europeans, Native Americans, Asian Americans from the East Coast. The only places where everybody is white are the fake historic reenactment sites. It's odd that a country of such abundance, with such enviably rich genetic stock, should try so hard to represent itself (in popular self-dramatizations and on the political stage) as a place as boring as Scandinavia, a land of people who all look alike.

GENERAL JAMES "EL GORDO" PARKER

Reliving the Good Old Days
At Fort Sam Houston

On March 31, 1917, Division General James Parker was on his way to Fort Sam Houston, outside of San Antonio. By then no one called him Gordo, gray-haired and medal-festooned as he was.

He had come a long way by train from his home in Portsmouth, Rhode Island, where he lived in retirement. He was returning to the haunts of his youth, persuaded to take up active duty again because President Woodrow Wilson had ordered an incursion into Mexico in pursuit of revolutionary general Francisco Villa, who for reasons unexplained had successfully attacked the border outpost at Columbus, New Mexico. Everybody knew the expedition to find and arrest Villa was only a pretext to test the capacity of the new motorized troops and air units set to depart for Europe when Congress eventually declared war on Germany.

Sitting in the rear of the olive-green Ford bringing him from the station to headquarters, General Parker noted that the people of San Antonio were dressed formally, like him. He smiled, his expression tender and melancholic. He was wearing his blue general's jacket, stiff and braid-trimmed, because he understood it was necessary to comply with the rituals of assuming a new command, though with the Texas sun beating savagely down and the damp rising from the river and its swampy environs, it was as hot as it could be for a man recently arrived from the East Coast. The combination of heat, humidity, and uniform stirred the embers of memory that had been sparked by the telegram requesting his return.

The heat, he said to the driver, who was nervous about transporting a general. Excuse me? asked the driver. The goddamn heat, he repeated, once again tasting the bitterness of his scorched-earth sallies in Cuba and the Philippines in command of New York's 12th Infantry battalion, waging wars to wipe out the final vestiges of the Spanish empire, on whose farthest borders he had fought all his life. To us, this is cool, said the driver; get through July and August and you'll understand why the cadets call the Sam Houston base hell. The general laughed. I know, he said, I was here for a few weeks years ago, but it felt like civilization: I was coming from Fort Bowie, in Arizona. Gee, said the driver, they shut that one down for being inhumane, right? The general closed his eyes, took off his cap, scratched his head. It had its advantages, he said. Apache Pass is the most beautiful place in the world, and it built character; the missions they sent us on were so tough that when we got back, Fort Bowie seemed nice and refreshing.

The Ford stopped in the outer courtyard of Fort Sam Houston, where the young man assigned to be the general's secretary was standing at attention. He opened the car door with a military salute. The general gave a half-hearted salute back and got out of the car, replacing his officer's cap and tugging gently at the lapels of his blue jacket. He patted the young man on the arm, encouraging him to relax while also brushing him aside as he headed for his office, which he entered with the assurance of someone on home ground.

The secretary hurried in after him and found him already circling what was to be his desk: old, solid, and wooden, not steel like all the desks now on the other side of the country. General, said the young man. Parker removed his cap and hung it on a hat stand. It smells the same, he said. His subordinate eyed him anxiously, not daring to ask what exactly he meant. The general took off his jacket. He was sixty-three, so his movements were a little clumsy; his secretary, still unsure how to behave in his presence, neglected to leap to assist him. It smells like all the forts in Arizona and New Mexico, repeated the old man, now rolling up his sleeves. The young man nodded, afraid to smile. I hear you know the Southwest, he said. Every inch of it, replied the general. The young man nodded toward the door. Should I have your trunks delivered to the house where you'll be staying? The general shrugged, uninterested. I'll go and tell the driver, said the boy. How far is it to Mexico in the Ford? the general asked before he left. I don't know, I've never been. The old man rolled his eyes. Before they take my things, get my hat and bring it to me; it's in the hat box, you'll see it there.

When the young man returned a moment later with a tan Mexican fedora—the brim so wide it looked almost like a cowboy hat—the old man was gazing out the window overlooking an inner courtyard where an officer was shouting hideous things in a strong Southern accent at the first group of volunteers. They're hopeless, he said to his secretary, but they'll improve as soon as the Senate approves the pursuit of General Villa and more poor bastards enlist in the belief that there's honor in invading Mexico again to practice for the invasion of Europe. He made a broad gesture, encompassing all Texans of fighting age. Then he glanced down at his considerable belly, freed now that he was in shirtsleeves. He smiled: I looked better when I was campaign fodder, he said, and even then they called me El Gordo Parker. He took the hat from his secretary's hands. We're going to the quadrangle. Don't you want to meet your officers first? the young man asked. They're waiting for you. The old man adjusted his hat and looked directly at him for the first time. Though his gaze was severe, deep in his eyes, which drooped at the corners, was the vague stare of the young officer who'd cut a swathe through the stone fields of Chihuahua and Arizona during the final stages of the Indian Wars. The boy felt compelled to explain: I thought you might prefer to meet your men before you see the stables. The old man stroked his gray mustache with the thumb and index finger of his left hand and asked: Were you taught to obey or to ask questions? To obey, general. Then move your ass, said the old man, because I don't know if I remember the way.

General James Parker hadn't been back to Fort Sam Houston for over thirty years, when he'd spent twenty days stationed there as a lieutenant in the 4th Cavalry, accompanying his direct superior, Captain Elpenor Ware Lawton. They had come on the train carrying Geronimo and the other last Chiricahua warriors to Fort Marion, Florida, as prisoners of war.

The quadrangle gate was closer to the administrative offices than he remembered. This is where we kept them, he said to his secretary, looking out over the pens of cattle; in his day, it had been a vast lot with good grazing and decent shade, stocked with deer, quail, pheasants, and peacocks. Who? asked the young man. The Apaches, he replied without further explanation.

They made the rounds, the young man pointing proudly to the space that had been turned into a production facility for all the milk and meat consumed in the fort. At some point the general rested his elbows on the top bar of one of the pens, not to catch his breath but to reminisce. You wouldn't believe how hard it was for us to get here, he said. He puffed out his cheeks and expelled the air, smiling faintly and rather sadly. We were on our way to Florida when we received orders from the War Department to halt until President Cleveland decided the warriors' fate. They wanted us to send them back to Tucson to be tried. The secretary, who must have been twenty-four or twenty-five, didn't quite follow what the old man was saying. The general clicked his tongue: It would've been less cruel if they'd ordered us to line them up on their knees in the yard and shoot them.

Now the young man looked with interest at his commander, who was pressing his temples under his hatband, eyes half-closed: They were the most innocent men of courage I've seen in a life full of innocent dead. Which is strange, he said, because they were all goddamn killers. He pointed to the barracks. That's where they lived, he said. And he ordered: Come.

They walked along the corridor bordered with pens, the smell of manure rising as the afternoon sun began to really heat up the plain. He stopped in front of a storeroom and took off his hat. The secretary wasn't sure whether he was raising his hat just to wipe the sweat from his brow with his forearm or as a sign of respect. The general put his hat back on again and said: It was impossible not to be on their side, impossible. He fingered his mustache again, eyes glassy with all he'd given up to become a general, the dead tugging constantly at his trouser cuffs. Dead Apaches, but also Cubans and Filipinos. Geronimo slept here, he said.

AUGUST 10

Standing in contrast to the irritating ideological ruin of Tombstone is the silent, genuine ruin of Fort Bowie in the canyons of Puerto del Dado, its English name resonating so strongly in the North American psyche that everybody knows it: Apache Pass.

You don't visit Apache Pass, you make a pilgrimage to it. It was the very heart of Apachería and the center around which the old world of the Chiricahua nation turned. Funnel of all trade, setting of the only battles between the U.S. Cavalry and an Apache cavalry of comparable size and force, led on the field by Cochise, the greatest, bravest, deadliest, most unyielding and elusive Chiricahua chief of them all. Cochise was the last chief capable of mustering an army to face the invaders on equal terms. Geronimo was his war shaman.

It was here at Puerto del Dado—the Spanish name, which can be translated as Dice Pass, is perhaps too cryptic to compete with the powerfully graphic Apache Pass—that a spring became the point of discord destined to destroy the more or less harmonious relations between Apaches and Anglo-Americans after the U.S. occupation of northern Sonora and the establishment of Arizona Territory. I don't know how many books I've read on the Mexican and U.S. wars against the Chiricahua, how many hundreds of times I've read about that spring, which was the only place in the northern Sonora desert where mail and mule trains plying the route between Santa Fe and California could be watered. Maybe Apachería would still be a small state, like Rhode Island, if it hadn't been for that spring; it was its existence that set the U.S. Army against them, and the war between the two sides played out in the valley around it.

Apache Spring—as it's called in English—is the site of the making and unmaking of a culture. Seeing it was a surprise: it's just a trickle, an earth-child's thin stream of pee, a transparent thread most visible from the distance amid the vastness of cliffs and valleys, overgrown as it is with the only true greenery in the area: creosote bushes so flourishing they look like trees. When one stands over the spring, which falls into a modest stone basin and flows for a few yards before going underground again, the trickle of water becomes the saliva of a god who lets worlds topple with a toss of the dice at Puerto del Dado.

A rather sober internet page devoted to Arizona hydrology reports that the Apache Pass spring is a trickle today because the farms of San Simon and Sulphur Springs, the two valleys connected by the pass, siphon off the region's groundwater supply. The spring, it claims, used to be a gusher. This is to some extent borne out by the topography of Puerto del Dado, which is crossed by a good-size creek bed that now fills only during summer storms. Upon visiting the spring, the information that seemed so plausible on the internet becomes less so: though Apache Pass lies in a hollow between the Chiricahua Mountains and the Dos Cabezas Mountains, the spring is still on high ground; much higher than the two valleys into which it descends. The water that falls on the Chiricahuas and Dos Cabezas runs together and bubbles up from Apache Spring long before it reaches the aquifers below. The experts surely know how water pressure works in the artesian basins of the high desert, but if I were allowed to choose the theory that best fits my understanding of the place, I'd choose to believe that this oasis was always as modest as it is today, its small size an inverted metaphor for its historical implications: the forced withdrawal of the Chiricahuas as human cataclysm and as an event that changed nothing, depending how you look at it.

The Apaches, like all members of the Athabaskan family, never settled in a single place. Like Alaska's Tananas and northern Canada's Yukon peoples, as well as their own forebearers as they made their way down the West Coast, the Athabaskans known as Apaches settled over a vast territory, moving along set routes from one seasonal camp to the next, following the natural cycles of the earth and the path of big game. They never built anything intended to last more than a season. Even so, if they had anything that might have been defined as a metropolis, the place where most of them got together for the most time, it would have been their winter camp at Apache Pass.

All that's left on the mountainside today are the ruins of a fort, a cemetery, and the subterranean phallus of an impotent god. Accounts in European languages written between the seventeenth century and the beginning of the nineteenth describe lands scattered with wickiups and small campfires. A place where the various clans basked in an abundance that later they would have to scrounge from mountains covered in dark forests in summer or from dry valleys in spring. Their love for the place goes some way toward explaining how Cochise was able to muster cavalry forces willing to engage in open battle in its defense, an extremely rare thing in the military history of his nation. What the many Apache bands of New Mexico and Arizona had in common was the watering hole at Puerto del Dado; any chief who governed it was, in some sense, the natural commander of all the others, and if they were called upon to defend it, even warriors from the farthest-flung bands—sometimes enemies of the summoning chief—were generally prepared to enlist and put guns, horses, and bodies in service of the place.

Apache Pass cost the Apaches and the Americans oceans of blood. The Spanish and the Mexicans, who knew their enemy much better, never tried to plant a flag there. They had a practical understanding, peacefully exchanging goods at Puerto del Dado while a few miles away they were firing madly at each other. The Spanish-speakers brought in illegal supplies of flour, ammunition, and liquor, and the Apaches provided firewood, skins, baskets—and, of course, access to water.

The gringos understood that to subdue the Apaches of eastern Arizona and western New Mexico (who by this time thought of themselves as Chiricahua) they had to seize the mountain pass. They built a stone stagecoach station—most unusual: these were usually frame structures—and a fort to defend it. I don't know whether this was a purely commercial decision to safeguard the flow of riches from California to the Atlantic coast and back again, a naive move by recent arrivals, or a strategic strike for which the gringos were prepared to pay any price.

In any case, when Arizona Territory first came under Washington's governance, the citizens of the U.S. kept their truce with the Apaches, who were delighted by their arrival because the white-eyes had kicked the Mexicans off their land and in exchange for water and firewood were giving them guns better than any soldiers' guns south of the border.

Those first years of coexistence with the gringos were the last years of abundance for the Chiricahuas: they had a safe refuge protected by the white-eyes on the U.S. side of the border and superior firepower when they attacked Mexican ranches. It was their victorious period, and it was ruled by Cochise, severe and implacable chief of chiefs shadowed by his war shaman as strategic genius, venerated and feared by all the other Apache nations. When he was young, Geronimo had heard from Ussen himself that he wouldn't die in combat, so he took every risk, bringing along anyone who dared to follow him.

Though the ruins of Fort Bowie at Apache Pass are a historic site cared for by the U.S. government, they are lonely. The only way to reach them is along a somewhat harrowing dirt road from the town of Bowie, off the highway leading to Chiricahua National Park and then on to the border, where Douglas sits across from Agua Prieta. It's a short drive, but not an easy one. In the rainy season it can be dangerous, requiring the navigation of hairpin turns that might unexpectedly turn into rushing streams cascading from higher ground. At a crest in the road there is a public restroom, a picnic table under a tidy corrugated tin roof, and an arrow pointing to a path: "Fort Bowie, 2.5 miles." The last stretch is on foot along a well-marked but difficult path. We set out.

We hadn't gone more than half a mile when the children were clamoring for us to turn around: the temperature was nearing 110, the brush was spiky, and the ground was carpeted with insects bearing a close resemblance to their prehistoric ancestors. Along the channels where water rushed during downpours we had to clamber over loose, tumbled boulders. My wife—relieved, I think—returned to the shade with Amelia and Cosme and the jugs of water we kept in the trunk of the station wagon. But so ravishing was the silence and so powerful the meeting of mountains at the pass that Cruz said to me: The two of us will go on, won't we?

A little more than a mile in, a valley opened unexpectedly before us. There stood the remains of the station where the mail stage halted on its way to California—nothing but stone foundations. Then came a cemetery, the spring, the ruins of the original makeshift adobe fort and a second fort, more solidly built of brick. To reach the ruins you have to climb down into a dip—the Puerto del Dado itself, which is where the wrinkles in the earth's crust that we call the Dos Cabezas and the Chiricahuas really collide—and scale a hill from which the U.S. troops could keep watch over the slopes filled with Apaches in winter.

Before these landmarks, just past the dry riverbed where my wife and the kids turned back to the picnic table in the shade, there is an almost bucolic slope. In Apachería, nothing is bucolic and everything is brutal, but sometimes the razor-sharp grass looks nice from a certain distance. A marker here memorializes the start of the ten bloodiest years of war between the U.S. Army and the Chiricahua nation, with Chief Cochise solidly at the helm. The incident occurred in February 1861. The gringos called it the Bascom Affair. Apaches of every stripe still remember it as Cut the Tent, a name so redolent of the American West it would be a shame not to use it.

On January 27, 1861, a group of Apaches attacked the ranch of an Irishman and naturalized Mexican citizen by the name of John Ward, who had become a U.S. landowner despite himself. He belonged to the generation that, as Mexican popular wisdom has it, turned gringo not by crossing the border but by being crossed by it. His ranch, once in Sonora, ended up in Arizona Territory when the Mexican Congress ratified the sale of La Mesilla in June 1856, shifting the border from the Gila River to the line that today runs between Agua Prieta and Nogales.

In his Sonoran past, Ward had married a Mexican widow and adopted a son from her previous marriage, who, after his adoption, was called Felix Ward. On January 27, 1861, the boy—later to become one of the most sinister figures in the history of the American West under the pseudonym Mickey Free—was kidnapped along with twenty head of cattle by a group of Apaches during a raid on his adoptive father's ranch.

Since La Mesilla was now part of the United States, it fell to the U.S. cavalry to find the boy and attempt to rescue him, despite its lack of experience, strategy, or existing channels of communication in the struggle with America's prickliest Indigenous nation. The man in charge of the search was 2nd Lieutenant George N. Bascom, recently arrived in Arizona. Following a false tip and apparently more eager to carry out orders quickly than to do his job well, he concluded that the boy and the livestock had been stolen by the Apache band living in the Chiricahua Mountains under the command of Chief Cochise.

After conducting his investigations, Bascom returned to Fort Buchanan, where he was stationed, and was given a cavalry unit and instructions to rescue Felix Ward come hell or high water. His company was a bunch of soldiers on mules, as inexperienced in the field as he was. It also included a group of civilians led by John Ward and, later, the men commanded by a Sergeant Robinson they met along the way.

They all reached the stagecoach station at Apache Pass on the afternoon of February 3, where to their relief they discovered that the station employees had an easy, cooperative relationship with Cochise and his people. The chief was nowhere nearby, but they could send for him in the San Bernardino Valley, where he spent the depths of winter with his people. Some Mexican women, probably housekeepers for the stagecoach office employees, were sent to speak to the chief, with the assurance that everything would be resolved quickly. Cochise never stole cattle on the U.S. side of the border—his perpetual war with the Mexicans was a broad enough front. Also, as everybody knew except the poor blond nineteen-year-olds dressed up as soldiers, Cochise didn't kidnap children, whether Mexican, American, or of any nation: he was a fierce nativist who would never have adopted children of other races to turn them into Apaches and warriors, as other chiefs did. By then Cochise was a man of about fifty, already more famed than Cuchillo Negro, who had preceded him in the Chiricahua region, and nearly as renowned as Mangas Coloradas, his father-in-law: he had never lost a battle, never signed a treaty, and never been expelled from the territory he defended with a warrior's honor. With Dos-Teh-Seh, a Gileño Apache and the eldest daughter of Mangas Coloradas, he had two healthy, determined sons who could assume command if he fell in battle. Everything was so clear-cut and unthreatening that the Mexican women, on their way to Cochise's camp, led Bascom to a likely campsite.

Siphon Canyon is where Apache Pass opens toward the valleys of San Simon and San Bernardino: no spot is more visible from anywhere in that formidable ring of mountains, or less sheltered. Standing in that exact place, it was evident to me that everyone involved was expecting a peaceful conversation the next day: a parley between a seasoned warrior, unbeaten and incorruptible, and a moron in a blue coat, who had probably made the trip to Puerto del Dado just to meet him.

It was two days before the chief appeared. This was no show of arrogance. He had sent scouts to learn who had kidnapped Felix

Ward and to ask what they would accept in exchange for him. When he had the information in his power—the kidnappers had been a band of Coyoteros—he climbed up to Apache Pass, accompanied by Dos-Teh-Seh and his brother Coyuntura, greatly feared in Arizona and Sonora and greatly beloved in Chihuahua, along with another couple of warriors. Considering the company, it seems he had no intention of wiping out the white-eyes treading his territory. He had simply come with his people to introduce himself to the army that had been occupying the country since the Mexicans left. He was likely bringing good news: instructed by Cochise to return a child, the Coyoteros would almost certainly have chosen to comply rather than make an enemy of the Chiricahua chief. He must have been disappointed that the gringos had sent him a low-ranking officer rather than a general, but even so he dutifully accepted the summons, agreeing to drink coffee and smoke—not that this was surprising: no Apache would refuse such an invitation—in Bascom's tent.

The gringos poured coffee, passed it around, and then, instead of offering tobacco, they drew their guns without even listening to what Cochise had to say. They told the Apaches they would be held prisoner until the boy was returned. This wasn't the first time the chief and his warriors had faced such a situation: Cochise had been arrested a few years earlier, in similar circumstances, in Fronteras, Chihuahua. The chief must have kept a cool head. In any case, he wasn't one to take fright at the sight of a gun pointed at him: sooner or later, every gun in the southwestern U.S. and northeastern Mexico pointed at Cochise. He explained to Bascom through whoever served as translator—Cochise was never heard to speak a word in Spanish or English—that he didn't have the Ward boy, but given a few days, he'd bring him in with any cattle that hadn't been butchered, along with an apology from the Coyoteros. The lieutenant said no. The chief would have to send someone else, and meanwhile he would continue to be held prisoner.

In a split second, Cochise must have made the decision that freed him to die of stomach cancer as an old man after a life in combat. He understood that there was no talking to the fool Bascom, so he took his knife, cut the canvas of the tent, and fled into his mountains. Only a single bullet hit him as he ran, even though the tent was surrounded by Bascom and Robinson's men, their guns drawn and cocked.

Before the military tribunal reviewing the affair, a witness declared that during the chief's escape Bascom's soldiers had shot at least fifty rounds. The story goes that when Cochise, wounded in the leg, reached a hill where there was no way he could be caught, he was still carrying his coffee cup. By then the soldiers had closed in on the rest of his entourage and there was no escape for them. During this first skirmish, one of the Chiricahua warriors was killed in the 2nd lieutenant's tent in what has to be called an act of betrayal, no matter how you look at it.

Cochise, as I've said (probably advised by Geronimo, who at the time still saw the gringos as allies against the Mexicans), would have preferred not to open a front against the U.S. Army: it was enough to be the most wanted and hated Apache in Mexico. He tried to take the high ground and make the white-eyes see reason, and Bascom, like a child throwing a tantrum, said what gringos always say: he didn't negotiate with bad guys—as if there were any guarantee that his people were the good guys. Before Cochise vanished into the stony folds of the Chiricahua Mountains, he shouted that they would regret what they had done.

The stagecoach company men, who must have heard the gunfire and come to the windows, and who were well aware what kind of chief Cochise was, were surely peeing themselves from the moment Bascom made his jackass move. The soldiers, in their perilously exposed tents, must have been hugely proud of their great accomplishment. By evening, Cochise had returned to the highest reaches of Siphon Canyon and sent down a warrior with a white flag. The Americans accepted the truce and everyone shouted back and forth for the last time: Bascom from outside his tent and Cochise from high up in the mountains. The Apache chief insisted he didn't have the boy but could find him; the white-eyes replied that they wouldn't return Cochise's friends and family until the Irishman's son appeared.

The stagecoach men, who were gringos but also friends of the Apaches, came out now to mediate in a conflict that they, like everyone except Bascom, found absurd. There were five of them. A group of Apaches came galloping down and tried to take them hostage. Another gun battle commenced and everyone scattered in all directions. Three of the mail employees managed to escape. One reached the stables and was killed there by U.S. soldiers who took him for an Apache. Another, by the name of Wallace, fell into Cochise's hands. And no one gave another thought to the Irishman's son, because both sides were out now to see who had the biggest dick: prisoners had been taken.

The Chiricahua chief paraded Wallace once more, before nightfall. His hands were tied behind his back and he was dragged along by a rope around his neck. Bascom insisted they wouldn't exchange him for Coyuntura, the other two Apache warriors, and Cochise's wife. That night, the gringos broke camp and crowded into the stagecoach station, which had stone walls. In subsequent reports, it was recorded that the muffled rumble of a war dance began to be heard on the mountain.

Nothing happened the next day, or the next. Cochise was waiting for a more comfortable negotiating position to present itself, and it arrived when his scouts alerted him that a freight wagon was climbing up toward Apache Pass from the San Bernardino Valley. The wagon belonged to a Mexican trader by the name of Señor Montoya, to whom the Apaches had offered protection in exchange for modest quantities of flour. This time he was bringing several mules to sell along the way. And he was well-guarded: he had an escort of seven Mexicans and three gringos. Eleven men in total.

When Montoya saw the Apaches coming, he halted the convoy and climbed into the wagon bed to retrieve the rations for the Chiricahuas. He didn't realize that he was under attack until the shooting began, and he had no way to defend himself. The warriors seized them all, took the three Americans aside, and chained the Mexicans to the wheels of the overturned wagon. They beat them, stoned them, and ran them through with lances, setting fire to the wagon while they were still alive. This deed was documented in the Mexican press, which identified Geronimo as commander; he was already a familiar figure in Mexico. The U.S. press also recorded the deed, but didn't identify the leader of the group: it had yet to learn his name.

The gringos were bound and taken up the mountain. That night Cochise ordered Wallace to write a message explaining that the Chiricahuas had three new prisoners now, and they were prepared to exchange them all for Cochise's family and friends. The message was posted on a cottonwood near the stagecoach station. When an investigation into the affair was launched, Bascom declared that he'd only seen it, not read it, and if he'd known there were four U.S. hostages he would have negotiated. His superiors didn't believe him but they didn't punish him either.

He wasn't the kind to talk about himself, she said. She had her eyes closed, so she couldn't see the güero, could only hear him scraping at the ground, the crunch of the stick stabbing into the soil to loosen it for removal with a tin plate, which was all she'd been able to find to perform a task she believed was deserving of more dignity. There was nothing ordinary about him, she went on. Trust me, you got to know him as well as anybody could. His heart was like diamond—unbreakable, unknowable. I never met a soul with the money to buy it. Who the hell can say what he was like inside.

He had a name, though nobody used it. Not even me, except when we indulged in our little tipples. His name was Damián and he was the son of a choirmaster from the city of Puebla de los Ángeles, in the very heart of the country, where they say people are more civilized but they're just folks burdened by all manner of things they don't understand, things that weigh on their backs and plug up their rear ends: good manners, fashion, the goddamn pinche government swallowing everything. He was older than he looked. Like all of us, he was sung the silly lullabies of empire back when we still thought we were part of something big. Can you imagine? We thought these lands were ruled by God and king, idiots that we were.

They had carried him into the shade while he was still breathing. She had given him water and all the comfort she could, until his eyes grew fixed and his mouth twisted into a grimace. It's over, she said to the güero, who had been kneeling beside her. He helped her lay the body out on the ground before it got stiff.

She kept talking about him, as if the güero needed to know who he'd been, maybe making a mental list because nobody else would remember once he was buried. He was lucky or unlucky enough to have had dozens of mothers instead of a single one, she said. One morning before playing the organ at the six o'clock mass, his father turned up in the visiting room of the Convento del Carmen carrying a baby in a crocheted gown. The mother superior took the child in because his father agreed to come for him each day after his last mass, or his last solfège class, or a late meeting of the penniless Symphonic Society of Puebla de los Ángeles.

According to Damián, the mother superior asked just one question before she accepted him: Wet nurse? And the musician replied: Can't you see he's just a few hours old? Likely more moved by the man than the infant, the nun must have reached out her arms for the child. Damián always insisted she said: We have plenty of serving girls with babies, I'll give him to one of them. This was the key detail for him. In his telling, the organist had offered to pay board and the mother superior had said there was no need just yet, not until he began to eat solid food, because she knew the musician didn't have a peso to his name. And that was how Damián lived, she said—stroking the dead man's hair—like money didn't exist, like there was no need to have a house, like a pinche fucking Apache, and she wiped the sweat from her forehead. Getting up, she inserted her index and middle finger under her wimple and pulled, freeing tangled masses of gray hair.

It's true his birth was wreathed in mystery, she said, but even good and explicable things were wreathed in mystery in the lean days at the end of empire. She passed her hand over his forehead, covering his face with the cloth she had just pulled from her hair. Not knowing where he came from—he loved that. Sometimes he said he was born to a thirteen-year-old saint, a solfège student who played the organist's beloved Viennese cantatas, not just well but better than anyone in Puebla. Other days he claimed he was actually his father's nephew, that the organist had gone to retrieve him from a convent in Tlaxcala, where his younger sister had lived cloistered ever since she tried to run away from Mexico City with a peddler of Cuban goods. And there was the sixteen-year-old daughter of the owner of the boardinghouse where they lived, who to me seemed the likeliest candidate. She ended up in a convent, too. They all ended up there, but I don't know whether it was Puebla's fault or the empire's, because I haven't been back to the middle of the country in years. I know about her because every so often Damián sent her money. I think he believed she was his mother, though he liked the other stories better.

She looked at the güero. We play dumb, she said, we make things up, we pretend we don't know, but the truth is that all stories end and begin in the same place. His father was happy to go and play at mass, give his solfège lessons, and compose cantatas no one would ever hear, after leaving the baby at the convent, thinking he would be nursed by a mulatta like the women he saw dancing in the street during carnival. Every morning little Damián was actually handed to one of the Indian women newly arrived from Sonora, one who'd had her children taken from her—or maybe killed, it was anybody's guess. The military government of the province of Nueva Vizcaya sent them to the convent with barely enough food to eat, threatening to stop paying the bills if the nuns didn't teach them everything from speaking Spanish to how to prepare chicken mole. Then they came back for them and sold them to well-to-do families in the city to recover losses from a war they'd been fighting for years, I think, only to get their hands on more Indian women to be peddled in the middle of the country, so they could go on fighting the same as they had been for years. Every afternoon, after lessons and masses, his father picked him up at the convent door. Poor he may be, said the organist, but he isn't an orphan.

It's not that things end where they begin. It's that we all keep scribbling like fools in the notebook of fate, as if anything will ever change.

There was no way he could have remembered the Apache wet nurse he lost early on, but there was always a shimmer of legend around her: even back then it was said the Apaches were fierce bastards, the toughest of the Indians who had risen up. They would never learn reason; they drank the blood of their enemies for breakfast. And you know those cloistered women: they believe everything, repeat everything. They said that as a babe he had drunk the savage milk of an Apache woman and they wouldn't let it go, so that as he grew up into a well-meaning whirlwind, the novices sang a song composed for him by one the convent's Black slaves: "What was in the milk he drank? Earth, stone, and Apache blood. And who lay with his father? Ay mamá, the Sierra Madre." She looked up and fixed her eyes on the güero, who was listening as best he could, jabbing the stick in the hole and bending down every so often to shovel out loose earth with the plate. She turned back toward Damián's body, laying her hand on the veil over his eyes. For the rest of us, the Sierra Madre is a jumble of mountains, but for him it shone like the true mother of all the women who mothered him.

The convent was always pure light to Damián, or that was how he talked about it. Like the mountains, once he got to know them. Not that his father was a bad man, not at all, but he remembered him as always busy, beset by the gnaw of poverty, his mind elsewhere: on configurations of notes, or candidates for players in the horrendous chamber groups he put together when he could, on masses, weddings, baptisms, the trail of humiliations that came with being a private teacher. The organist and the boy walked every day from the boardinghouse on Calle del Sardo, where they lived, to the Convento del Carmen, the seat of the kid's happiness. They always walked hand in hand. Father in the cape and bonnet of an academician and son in a red nursery smock, not because he went to school, but because his father thought that was how children dressed. Whenever he got a little drunk and talked about those days, Damián always insisted he remembered the length of their shadows on Puebla's everlasting walls as they passed the watchman's lantern; the heels of his father's buckled shoes echoing like cannon on the deserted cobblestones, before the stirring of slaves and widows who for three hundred years were the clockwork of what I always thought was the most Spanish and most Catholic of cities, the ass-kissingest city of the vast, flabby kingdom of New Spain.

She looked up at the sky. He was probably horribly spoiled by the sisters. He grew up happy, self-confident, and, truthfully, much better educated than he would have been at the school, because the nuns taught him to read, write, and do basic sums, but they also wore themselves out keeping him entertained, teaching him to mend, cook, and cure ailments with garden herbs. She laughed a madwoman's laugh, so intense that it distracted the güero from his labors. One day one of the older nuns discovered that his pink button of a penis was turning into a pit viper. Shortly after his thirteenth birthday, the organist came for him upon leaving the six o'clock mass at the cathedral and found him starved and bored after eleven hours in the antechamber, the door to the refectory barred to him by the mother superior. His pouting mouth already sported a pitiful little mustache.

She half closed her eyes and sat like that for a while, then she leaned over the dead man. She took one of his hands. She noticed that his fingers had grown stiff and she began to blow on them to soften them so they would lie smooth, as if he had died peacefully. The güero knew what was happening was important, so he muttered, wait a second, stop, and hurried to the spot where they'd tied the horses to see whether there were any better tools for the job, which otherwise would never be finished.

She waited for him to return. Among the possessions of all the dead bodies to be buried, the güero found nothing to help him dig, but he did come across a flat stone, better than the stick for scraping at the soil. She paid no attention to the purely technical part of his troubles: all that mattered was his presence. The güero didn't have to ask her to continue; she went on as if she had never been interrupted. Other than a long and lanky lad spoiled by a whole convent full of nuns, his father bequeathed to the world a bountiful host of offertories, pastorelas, and masses that no one would ever play, mostly because they were terrible. Luckily for the people soon to be known by the strange name of Mexicans, none of those pieces was ever published, either. But he was a competent organist and a hardworking choirmaster, and he could get together a passable group of musicians, though it was always too full of gaps to be called an orchestra. He was generous enough not to play his own compositions, at least, instead energetically abusing scores from European printers—parts that invariably sounded better in his head than when he copied them and put them in the merciless hands of his park bench violinists and his trumpeters from the city's military band.

The güero stopped digging for a second. He rubbed his forehead, brown with dirt. When are we talking about? he asked. She shrugged. He must have been born around '99, she said, ten years after me. I can remember the year 1800—imagine that. It was dull as can be. No one dreamed we were dancing on the brink, that we would soon be plunged into a decade-long war, that we would come out the other side as something different. If anybody had told a Spaniard in 1809 that by 1821 New Spain would be called Mexico and governed by Mexicans alone, he would have died laughing.

According to my calculations, they kicked him out of the convent around 1811, which was a fateful year in the middle of the country. After that, the choirmaster dragged him here and there, sometimes to help haul and tune instruments, sometimes to sit in with a group that was short a musician. Puebla was always on Spain's side even if people claimed otherwise, so despite the war it remained more or less what it had always been, whether it was in the hands of the royalists or the insurgents; and it was a big city, a mighty city. You could go about your daily business without interruption, just hearing from time to time about this or that town that had fallen or been retaken, this or that person who had been shot or risen up the ranks.

But there wasn't much work back then for musicians or anybody else, and as he told it, little by little his father's players were drawn to the battlefields, almost always playing the drums on the royalist Catholic side. So it went until one day an impresario from Saltillo turned up at the boardinghouse from the neighboring but none too friendly realm of Nueva Vizcaya, where for reasons unknown there was an opera company desperate for a director who had some idea how to bully a choir. The organist didn't hesitate and packed up his belongings and his son, who by then was about fifteen, and headed north, like all Mexicans with half a brain.

CHARLES B. GATEWOOD

Lame Knight of Apachería

Lieutenant Gatewood was a tall, thin man, with bushy eyebrows and a banker's mustache, which he combed carefully into two symmetrical wings. The Chiricahua, who truly respected him, had accorded Gatewood the rare honor of a not-too-mocking Apache name: Bay-chen-daysen, or Long Nose (another soldier, who imagined himself handsome, was dubbed Turkey Snot). His eyes were dark and sunk in oily mahogany rings, probably another symptom of the raging rheumatism that had wasted his body ever since he graduated from the military academy and prevented him from walking or sitting in a chair without pain. He spent most of the time either on horseback or lying down because any other position was excruciating. He wore broad-brimmed hats for protection from the sun, and he dressed in civilian clothes when he was on missions away from headquarters. He was a slow, orderly, melancholic man, in the habit of establishing excellent relations with the enemy and terrible ones with his superior officers. He obeyed orders, but his methods were irritating at best. His superiors tended to hate him just a little bit less than they needed him.

Despite having received very clear orders to bring along a troop of twenty-five soldiers from the 1st Cavalry stationed at Fort Bowie, Lieutenant Gatewood left for Carretas, Chihuahua, accompanied by just two Apache trackers and three pack mules that he led himself. He didn't trust the American mule drivers, who were no good at traversing the ravines that always figured into his missions, so he usually took charge of the gear himself until he crossed the border into Mexico, where he had someone trustworthy waiting for him, though how he managed to get word all that way is a mystery.

General Nelson Miles, charged by President Grover Cleveland to end the Apache Wars, had sent for Gatewood from the remote outpost in Navajo territory where he had been exiled. Gatewood was the only officer in the region who got along with the Chiricahua, even if he got along with them so well that he was reputed to be if not a turncoat, then at least a renegade. General Miles knew that the lieutenant, though recalcitrant and sickly, was the only member of the U.S. Army Geronimo trusted, and Gatewood understood that his best bet to be promoted out of the purgatory of the Indian Wars and the barren lands of the Southwest was to arrest the Chiricahua leader. There was a risk in sending for Gatewood: if, at the moment of the arrest, the Apache leader had to be killed, the lieutenant would almost certainly intercede, but it was a risk worth taking. Worst case, a stray bullet could solve the problem by embedding itself in the back of the Virginian's head, and no one in the army would miss him if Geronimo wasn't around anymore to make him needed.

It was getting on toward midnight when Gatewood left Fort Bowie. Night departures were one of his idiosyncrasies. He had received orders that morning to deploy to Mexico, because word was that the Chiricahua under Geronimo and Naiche had sent two women to the fort in the Chihuahua town of Carretas, to negotiate a truce with the authorities. According to the dispatch intercepted from a Mexican army runner, the warriors were exhausted and low on supplies: if surrounded, they could be eliminated. General Miles sent an urgent message to the governor of Chihuahua asking permission to move another column into Mexican territory. This was Gatewood's column, a one-man column: the ghost column. The governor of Chihuahua instantly extended an expedited permit. To this day, the governments of Mexico and the United States get along best when they're focused on screwing somebody else.

By the summer of 1886, Miles already had three 4th Cavalry units in Mexico. And yet he knew that the presence of seventy-five soldiers with tack and provisions in the vicinity of Carretas would set the Apaches in motion, so he assigned Gatewood the task of drawing the warriors north and keeping himself and the enemy out of the newspapers until the arrival of the 4th Cavalry.

The lieutenant's mission—ordered by General Miles without consulting the War Department—contradicted the U.S. government's general strategy. The 4th Cavalry, under the command of Captain Elpenor Ware Lawton, had direct orders from President Cleveland to find Geronimo and arrest him to face trial in Tucson. At the least sign of resistance or any attempt to parley, he and his followers were to be shot. It was expected that Geronimo would put up a fight, which meant that it was really a mission to kill. If Miles had sent for Gatewood from his exile on the Navajo reservation, he must have been desperate enough to need a backup plan. As a precaution, he ordered Gatewood to bring along a heliograph so he could be monitored from afar. General Miles ordered the lieutenant to report daily at eight a.m., and Gatewood responded in his usual idiosyncratic way: he didn't know how to use the machine and he couldn't take along an operator on an expedition requiring uncommon speed and precision. The general replied that Captain Lawton, commander of the 4th Cavalry's operations in Mexico, had a communications officer, and Gatewood should hand the machine over to him as soon as they met.

Gatewood and his Apache scouts made the trip in leisurely fashion, the hallmark of their missions. Not only did they follow Indian paths, but if they saw something that tempted them, they pursued it. When they came to a pool, they watered the horses and filled their canteens, and if the pool was full, they took baths, not caring whether they wasted half a day. It's good for my rheumatism, Gatewood would say, spending hours in the water. They crossed the border two days later than expected—a mystery, given that Fort Bowie was a stone's throw from the line—and there they met the mule driver who would accompany them. This time he was waiting for them with his son, both of them named Doroteo.

The two women Geronimo had sent as envoys to Carretas had seen that it was full of soldiers. They returned with the news, and the shaman and Chief Naiche decided it was better to go hungry in the mountains than to risk betrayal. By the time Gatewood reached the presidio the Apaches had already retreated up into the mountains, leaving no trace, as ever.

What the lieutenant's scouts did find on the ground was evidence of the presence of twenty-five U.S. cavalry soldiers, probably part of the 4th Cavalry stationed in Mexico, surely responding to the same news they were.

It's Parker, said one of the trackers, whose name was Martino. And he went on: This is his horse. Gatewood shook his head, without bothering to dismount. They're very faint hoofprints, he said, hardly deep enough for an animal as big as El Gordo Parker's. They were famished, wasting away, replied Martino. He went on. Look at the other hoofprints, those aren't clumps of grass and mud; that's shit; the horses had diarrhea because they'd had no feed in who knows how long, and they were given it in town, probably to make them go faster. Gatewood shrugged. I tell you it can't be Parker, he repeated, those aren't the hoofprints of a horse carrying a fat man.

They followed the trail with little hope it would lead to Geronimo: the Chiricahua shaman's strategies for eluding pursuit worked too well for a troop of twenty-five sunstruck gringos to find them anywhere, let alone in Mexico. Still, they thought that if they found the 4th Cavalry, they might learn something new about the real state of the campaign. The people of Carretas, like all Mexicans, were evasive when a gringo soldier asked for information, especially if he was accompanied by Apache scouts. It was a bewildering phenomenon to them: savages dressed as savages who were also soldiers in the U.S. Army. It didn't bother Gatewood much. He could always send the mule driver and his son for information or food or tobacco, if necessary.

They found the column six days later—on June 27, according to Gatewood's diary—outside Huachinera. The lieutenant and his scouts were riding swiftly along the Apache path above the Bavispe River—the Doroteos were in town buying food—when, far in the distance, they spotted the cloud of dust raised by their quarry. They won't find anyone that way, said Martino to the lieutenant, who was chewing on a jojoba twig. They rode faster to catch up with the column, the scouts out ahead cutting across the mountainside along safe paths and the lieutenant following close behind.

Gatewood registered the precise instant when the commander of the horsemen riding along the Bavispe River noticed a threat on the slopes and pulled his troops up short. As he watched, the commander ordered his men to take cover, so Gatewood rode faster and passed the scouts before the soldiers could open fire. They were already scattering for shelter among the stones, Springfields in hand, when Gatewood shouted: Fort Bowie 1st Cavalry, watching with relief as the troop's commander gave a piercing but hardly military whistle, signaling his men to abandon the positions they were just settling into. It was only then, as he watched them emerge from the rocks, that Gatewood saw they were in tatters: their trousers torn, their shirts sleeveless and ragged, their boots cracked. The only one wearing a regulation shirt was the troop commander, but it was too big on him and so dirty you couldn't even see the insignias.

There was something leaden about the soldiers turning their horses back onto the path, a prisoner-like slowness in the sad, resigned way they returned their rifles to the slings in their tack and mounted again, as if they were being punished for terrible sins committed in the past. They didn't fall in line to await the new arrivals, as U.S. cavalry would normally do. They stood scattered where they were, some of them watching the riders approaching from the mountainside and others looking straight ahead in an aimless way. The horses were skin and bones, the men worse.

Gatewood felt a little ashamed to be so tidy in his clean hat and shirt and short Southern riding jacket with the buttons done up, his cap-toed boots dirty but in good repair, his spurs shiny. He approached the commander flanked by his scouts, as was proper. The officer in the filthy shirt was a bearded man, thin enough that the cloak of hair falling over his face couldn't hide his hollow cheeks. The skin of his forehead was tight under his tattered cowboy hat, his brow like varnished bone.

Gatewood was so shaken as this grotesque sight came into focus that it took him a moment to pay attention to Martino, who kept trying to tell him something. He halted his horse and asked the Apache to repeat what he had said, because he never did anything without getting his scouts' opinion. You were right, Martino said; it looked like the prints of El Gordo's horse, and I've never been wrong before. You weren't wrong, replied Gatewood. The next moment he gave a military salute, saying: Lieutenant Parker, at your orders; Lieutenant Gatewood, Fort Bowie 1st Cavalry.

The specter gave a gap-toothed grimace, vestige of a welcoming smile. What are you doing here in hell, Charles? he asked. General Miles sent me; I've been looking for you. Parker wiped the sweat from the back of his neck. I don't even know what we're looking for anymore, the Chiricahuas or Captain Lawton, who sent us into the mountains. How long have you been lost? Just us, or counting the time we were lost with Lawton? It doesn't matter, replied Gatewood, and he gestured toward the path they'd come down: You'll be seeing my mule driver come that way soon with tortillas and beans, coffee; we're going to eat. Got tobacco? asked Parker. That we have. Parker smiled again.

Though on the day they met near Huachinera, Gatewood and Parker were more or less the same age—the former thirty-three and the latter thirty-two—Parker looked much older. He also had a more commanding presence: he was used to wielding power over raw recruits because he'd been sent directly from West Point to the Indian Wars and had always shown excellence in the field. Gatewood, on the other hand, had been an extraordinary officer in training, but his health problems, the countless leaves he'd taken to visit his wife in Virginia, and his tendency to learn the enemy's ways rather than fighting unquestioningly had kept him from becoming a troop commander. He put himself immediately under Parker's orders, though they were of the same rank—I have no column of my own, so I'm not in command, he told his colleague—and suggested that since neither of them had any idea of Geronimo's whereabouts, they had better search for Captain Lawton's battalion on the way back—Lawton being the highest-ranking officer in Mexico—and join forces. How will we find him? asked El Gordo Parker with an ironic smile as he filled his pipe with tobacco. His men were making a fire to heat the tortillas and beans the Doroteos would be bringing from La Huachinera. He pointed toward the mountains, which vanished into the distance all around, infinite and massive. Gatewood shooed a fly. Martino and his cousin will find them for us, don't worry.

Over the six days it took them to track Lawton, the Southern gentleman had time to convince Parker that finding Geronimo and killing him was essentially impossible: in Geronimo's fifty or perhaps sixty years of fighting, neither the Spanish imperial army nor the Mexican army nor the gringo army had managed to do it. There was no reason why they should succeed. Better to convince him to return to the U.S., deport him.

AUGUST 11

On the morning of February 8, 1861, after five days of intermittent clashes, it snowed in Apache Pass. The Apaches had been dancing and making noise all night, but they hadn't come down to the pass itself. When Sergeant Robinson led his horses to the watering hole, guarded by half his men, there were no tracks of unshod hooves or moccasins in the snow. He didn't know, couldn't have known, that the giant hullaballoo the Indians had raised the night before marked the arrival of the legendary Mangas Coloradas. He had come to the Chiricahua Mountain refuge bringing two hundred warriors on horseback to join Cochise's one hundred and twenty or so loyal fighters.

A soldier with more experience fighting Apaches would have guessed that if they hadn't shown themselves it was because they weren't in the habit of attacking well-defended positions. He would have sent the horses to drink one by one, accompanied by just a few men to avoid exposing his forces to the warriors waiting for their chance on the mountainside.

Cochise sent a small party of his men to attack Robinson so Bascom would take the bait and lead all the others out into the open. He didn't count on Bascom being a coward: when the 2nd lieutenant heard that the Apache riders were coming down the mountain, he locked himself in the mail depot.

Robinson's men fell back and defended the depot gallantly from outside. They lost their horses but few men, and Bascom finally let them into the improvised base. Cochise and Mangas had already played their best card, exposing their full strength, but they kept attacking in waves, and the Americans did a good job holding them off.

By the end of the afternoon Cochise calculated that his family and friends must be dead, and he ordered a retreat into the mountains and on to Fronteras, in Sonora: too many of his men were wounded to keep fighting, and the Americans never came out into the open, nor would they let the warriors get close enough to set their stronghold alight, barraging the Apaches with constant gunfire. He hanged his gringo prisoners from a cottonwood at the foot of a mountain known today as Cochise Head, after they had been tortured and utterly disfigured.

Four days later, when Bascom's soldiers got up the nerve to leave their refuge to return to their forts, they came upon the dead men's remains; they identified Wallace by his golden molars, which he'd been very proud of in life. The lieutenant released the women and Apache boys he had taken, and ordered that the warriors be hanged from the same cottonwood as the tortured gringos. In his report to his superiors, Bascom said the two warriors had asked to be given whiskey and then shot. Both wishes were denied.

The Cut the Tent incident was a mouse that became a mastiff, a rhinoceros, a whale, an aircraft carrier. Cochise found out from Dos-Teh-Seh that Bascom had refused to grant his brother and Coyuntura their last wishes, and though he had tortured his own prisoners without mercy, he fell into a vengeful rage, which in turn demanded that more lessons be taught to the U.S. Army. Every so often he crossed into the United States from his stronghold near Janos and laid waste to everything he found, taking no prisoners. So swift were his strikes that the gringos simply couldn't respond.

Ten months after the events of Cut the Tent, the *Missouri Republican* reported that all of U.S. Apachería, once brimming with white settlers, was a wasteland. Around the same time, a miner named Sylvester Mowry wrote a letter to the secretary of war in Washington asking him to do something: all the ranches and farms in the area were abandoned, and Tucson and Tubac, the only towns still inhabited, were honest-to-goodness refugee camps.

In July 1862, Indian-killer James H. Carleton, stationed south of Tucson, was named governor of New Mexico Territory. His procession through the cactus groves of Desierto del Pinacate to the town of Albuquerque on the banks of the Bravo acquired the status of legend: the three-hundred-mile stretch of Apachería was left littered with rock-pile graves, charred ranches, bodies swinging from trees, and bones devoured by coyotes.

It was in Saltillo, a city riding out the war untouched in the shelter of tortured mountains more like the Carpathians than the prim and proper ranges in the middle of the country, where little Damián, good for absolutely nothing but tuning instruments for his father and being spoiled at the butter-greased and almond-oiled hands of the Carmelite sisters, had to make a life for himself.

The choirmaster, used to working with meticulous older folk like himself, or with mystical widows and virgins who spent hours every week rousing God with their caterwauling, didn't have the patience to train the clumsy hands of a boy who woke up each day with one finger longer than the next: the flower of youth. He soon got exasperated and left for the theater if something musical was on the bill, or the chapel if he'd been offered work that week, or the Symphonic Society he'd founded in imitation of the one he'd left behind in Puebla, even if this one was nothing but a group that met for coffee under the arches of the plaza because he had yet to collect enough music lovers who could play an instrument and actually owned one.

This was where Damián strayed from the path, or rather, where he chose the path that would drag him along by the ear to the place where a bullet was waiting with his name on it. He would head to the cantina and put to use the little bit of nothing his father had taught him, playing in a trio—accordion, guitar, and tololoche—begun by a German kid only slightly older than Damián himself and already well-established in Nueva Vizcaya. They would play an outlandish mash-up of local ballads and Austrian waltzes, and though their songs had a certain flair and even a name—people called them polkas because they thought they sounded like gypsy songs and they were sure that gypsies and Poles were more or less the same thing—no one imagined they'd have any future.

Damián's fumbling fingers exasperated his friends, too, but the leader of the band, with his Prussian upbringing, saw that though the kid tortured the accordion, he was good at keeping the beat, and he remade a drum for him that he'd gotten cheap at the presidio bodega. It wasn't a good drum: the screws were loose, so that no matter how tight the leather was stretched for the first song, it had already sagged by the second. There was something savage about its raspy, drawn-out sound, and it came into its own when Damián himself added a cowbell, lending brightness and zest.

It was the insistent beat of that abject drum and bell that truly taught the polka to the mob of liquored-up ranchers, uncomfortable Indians, Chinese laborers, and drifters who had ended up in Saltillo because anywhere else they would have been hanged. And they danced frenetically to it when, later in the night, the band left the cantina to play at one of the city's brothels. The move to a more public venue happened naturally: at some point the mayor of Saltillo was in the audience when the band played a number at the whorehouse, and, having had a few drinks too many, he invited them to take the stage on Sundays in the Plaza de Armas with the municipal band, a wretched children's choir trained by local priests, and an orator who made the multitudes weep even though he always recited the same poems.

Believe it or not, she went on, the group was a hit from the start, mostly because the poems weren't danceable and neither were the war marches or the halting Latin of the bullied children, and if there was anything the Saltillans were hungry for it was joy. The band began to win recognition and even to attract imitators, so its members decided to give it a name: the Northern Bavarians.

Then, around the year '22 or '23, when the middle of the country finally realized that Saltillo existed, a regiment of soldiers battle-hardened in the fighting down below arrived to manage an election featuring a single candidate for governor. Once he had won, he informed everyone—at a dance played by none other than the Northern Bavarians—that Nueva Vizcaya had stopped existing a year ago, and they were part of Coahuila, in the Northern Territory of the Mexican Republic. Now they would really see what it was like to be part of a republic.

The governor, reportedly suspicious of a region that had contributed few bodies to the insurgent armies, imposed a regime of fear that drove most of the city's youth of marrying age—the Northern Bavarians' most devoted followers—to the cities of Monterrey or Paso del Norte, better connected through San Antonio and Santa Fé with the middle of the country and also to the promising alliance of white millionaires who had founded a nameless country along the Atlantic coast, already stretching to the Missouri River and coming dangerously close to the Rio Bravo.

The güero raised his head from the grave he was digging. What do you mean a nameless country? he said, it's called the United States. That's a description, not a name, she said. With a name like that, they might as well call themselves Over Yonder or Decent Folks. All right then, he said, and went back to his digging.

Another wave of men went south, she went on, and it was as if instead of telling the story of the dead man lying there in front of her she was sipping anisette in her own parlor. Now anybody could take whatever government posts they wanted, because bribes and appointments didn't have to go through Spain to turn up a bone to gnaw. The slaves the governor freed went to new places—not better places, because America never got better in any way for Black people, but where they wouldn't run into anyone who had been their master. No one freed the Indians who were slaves—they still haven't—but nobody paid attention to them either. And the soldiers were never around anyway: when they weren't being sent to lose battles against the Lipan Apaches or the Comanches, they were snuffing out bids for independence in the Territory of Nuevo León, where they won, and in Texas, where sooner or later we're going to lose because there's no beating those wildcats.

It was after a series of bleak dances where girls in the guise of drapes sat watching the old criollos get grotesquely drunk (they had stayed because they'd always been there) that the Prussian suggested they turn the Northern Bavarians into a traveling company hosting shindigs that would reveal the true nature of their polka-and-drum creations: new music for a new country, though actually it was just incomprehensible music for a country no one could understand. Then the band changed its name to the New Mexicans and set out for the western territories.

ELPENOR WARE LAWTON

Hungry Captain in the Sierra Madre

Captain Elpenor Ware Lawton was on a hillside, tossing stones into the bed of the Aros River, when he spotted a series of moving dots on a distant mountaintop that could only be the column of twenty-five cavalry soldiers he had lost six weeks back. The horsemen were riding one by one down a slope so steep that in addition to having lost their way he thought they must have gone mad. Jesus, he said to himself, imagining that Lieutenant Parker, commander of the lost column, had died, and his inexperienced men were wandering the mountain alone. They looked like wild goats.

He felt his pocket to see if by chance he had put the spyglass there when he left camp. He hadn't. He had lost so much weight since they sent him to Mexico with orders to bring Geronimo back dead or alive that when he put things in his pockets, his pants fell down.

There is a record of Captain Lawton's physical appearance worth consulting as evidence of the damage wrought by the expedition to the Sierra Madre. Lawton had a portrait taken shortly before leaving for Mexico in pursuit of the rebel Chiricahuas, and he appears in a group photograph at the end of the mission, back in the United States. In the portrait, shot at a studio, he wears a buttoned-up military jacket. He wasn't a handsome man, but he seems to have been charismatic: his eyes have the squint that comes from peering at things with a curious smile; a droopy walrus mustache spills down both sides of his face. His unruly hair is cut short enough to disguise the inability of any comb to tame it. In the portrait he isn't looking at the camera, but at a point beyond the photographer. He has a pleasant, interested gaze. He isn't fat or thin. He's strong, of sound body.

The second photograph was taken outside of San Antonio, at the foot of the train carrying the Chiricahuas into exile in Florida, defeated at last and escorted by the 4th Cavalry. Lawton's mustache has grown so much that it makes him look like a prospector. Or maybe it's the same size it was at the beginning of the expedition, but it looks disproportionately large because his face is all cheekbones and sunken eyes. He's wearing a clean uniform, but it's comically large on him. His hat, on the other hand, seems to be the very one he wore on the mission that won him a reputation as a tenacious, trustworthy officer, willing to do what it took to carry out orders. It's a felt hat, dusty and so battered it looks as if a goat tried to eat it. The impression the viewer gets is that during the four months he spent in the Sierra Madre he never once ate or slept. This must have been how he looked when he spotted what might be Parker's lost column, though at that point the clothes he was wearing were rags.

He returned to his tent to look for the spyglass. He'd had the camp pitched two days earlier in a hollow in the hills, about a thousand feet from the descent to the river. The spot had been chosen more to protect horses and men from the savage midday sun and the icy winds that came down from the mountains at night than from an unlikely Apache attack. Rummaging in his campaign rucksack, he reckoned that the column he'd spotted had to be Parker's: the soldiers perched on the mountainside definitely weren't wearing the white uniform of the Mexican army's desert troops, and no one but El Gordo could have ridden so far into the Sierra Madre at this date. But it was odd to see Parker and his men show such aplomb scaling heights the Northern cavalry usually reached only by mistake.

He emerged from his tent, spyglass in hand, squinting—the sunlight was already unbearable though it was just past nine—as he surveyed the shameful state of his camp, hands on hips. Patched tents were scattered every which way, as if they'd tumbled down the mountain into the valley; the few men who hadn't gone out to hunt or procure food from some improbable Mexican town were paring their nails, shaving with a knife, or cleaning rifles unlikely to be used that day or week or month, because by now everyone was sure they would never find the Chiricahuas.

His own mind ran in ever tighter and more repetitive circles the more weeks they were stuck in the sierra. His chief scout was in the worst shape of all: he was sitting on a stone, just staring into space. He was a mystical man, like all those of his trade: scouts spent too much time alone, too many nights listening to the locals' strange stories. Of the whole company, Lawton knew he felt the absurdity of his position most keenly, since from the moment General Miles assumed command of army operations in the Southwest, it was forbidden to use Apache scouts on official missions, so Lawton's scouts were gringos like him who could track warriors on horseback through the mountains of Arizona but could never follow a band on foot through the colossal Mexican sierra.

Lawton walked over and asked what he was doing. The scout didn't even have the courtesy to rise and give a regulation military salute—for weeks the 4th Cavalry had been operating like just another ragtag mountain band. He answered that he was staring straight ahead. That's plain enough, said the captain. If you look far enough into the distance, said the chief scout, you can see the future: the day we get back to regular beds and meals at headquarters, with time off to write to the family. Lawton felt the bite of sarcasm and remembered what another of his lieutenants had told him, maybe to convince him to send a telegram declaring the mission officially failed: the troops were saying the expedition couldn't last much longer because any time now Geronimo might die of old age. That's not much of a joke, Lawton had said to the soldier. The reply: Who said it was a joke?

Why don't we leave it up to the Mexicans, captain? the chief scout asked from his stone. They know the territory, and when they get to the towns the people actually give them food. What towns? Lawton asked; the war has gone on so long they're deserted. The scout shook his head. There are people somewhere. Otherwise, how is it that every time we come across a Mexican column they're well-fed and well-dressed? The captain looked up at the sky. It didn't matter to him what his people said. He understood that circumstances were dire, but he had orders and he wasn't going to give up. And then there's the fool idea of arresting Geronimo, the chief scout went on. We don't work for some sheriff; we don't make arrests. Lawton took off his hat and ran his hand through his hair, which by now had overrun his skull in a manner unbecoming a soldier, and said: I think we'll be down here until President Grover wins or loses the elections. Are you saying you think it's impossible to catch Geronimo? Lawton clapped his hat back on. How long has it been since you picked up a trail? The scout smiled, turning his attention to the imagined day when his captain would receive orders to head north.

The captain was already starting back toward the river, spyglass in hand, when he turned and said to the chief scout, maybe just to fuck with him: Get dressed and come with me. I am dressed, captain. You're in your underwear. It's all I have left. The captain glanced down at himself. He was in his undershirt, too, because his flannel shirt had fallen into tatters during the longest haul across the mountains, though he still had his trousers—ripped, but a regulation pair. He gestured with the closed spyglass toward a vague point in the heights, where no one wanted to look anymore because the mountains seemed to fence them in, as if in a nightmare. I saw Parker coming that way, he said, maybe he's got spare uniforms. The chief scout raised his eyebrows. He's probably in worse shape than we are, he said, but he got up with a hint of enthusiasm. In their situation, any news, good or bad, would be good because at least it was news. And maybe Parker wasn't coming this way because he was looking for them, but because he'd picked up Geronimo's trail and needed backup.

Once they reached the river, the captain and chief scout confirmed that the man riding down the mountain was Parker. They had proof of it almost as soon as they raised the spyglass. The men high up on the mountain spotted the gleam of sun on the lens and signaled back with a mirror, identifying themselves. The scout grinned: That's Fort Bowie cavalry's mirror trick. And he ventured: Gatewood must have found Parker and led him to us. Gatewood? asked the captain. Nobody else would've come through the heights. The captain shook his head: It can't be. Gatewood is being punished. The chief scout smiled again: General Miles must be desperate. He let Lawton peer for a long time at the men riding down.

When the captain recognized the man riding Southern-style at the head of the column, dressed like a dandified lord of cliffs and gullies, he said: Why yes, Gatewood is with him. He counted the men in the group. There were twenty-six and two mule drivers, which meant that Gatewood had come alone: he had no troops under his command. He smiled, closed the spyglass, and gave orders to the chief scout. Call the officers, tell them to gather the men and break camp; I want everything packed by the time Parker and Gatewood get down here. The chief scout paid no attention; he was gazing attentively at the boulders and pines nearby. That's where they are, he said, pointing to his immediate surroundings. Who? Gatewood's Apache scouts. Apache scouts are forbidden, said the captain. I tell you, the chief scout said, Miles must be desperate; Gatewood's scouts are listening to our conversation right now. He shouted: Martino! A hand rose from the brush and waved.

The last stage of the Apache Wars had an almost homey feel to it: it went on so long and so few men fought in it that ultimately everybody knew everything about everybody. At their meeting on the Aros River, Parker and Gatewood settled firmly on a posture of negotiation with Geronimo. Lawton reiterated his instructions. We have to arrest him or kill him, he said, after hearing Parker's case, made rather informally; Parker had yet to fully recover his sanity, though he was now eating again with some regularity. Geronimo must be arrested or killed, the captain insisted; maybe not Chief Naiche—we can deport him with the others—but my orders are absolutely clear: the president wants Geronimo arrested or killed, and that's what I plan to do. Parker and Lawton were standing: El Gordo (he'd kept his nickname even in the grips of malnutrition) with his madman's stare, the captain stroking his mustache and tracing circles in the sand with the toe of his holey boot, his stubborn, sheeplike gaze fixed on the ground. Gatewood was sitting on the folding chair he always carried by pack mule because his rheumatism was so painful he couldn't stand. Next to him was the son of his Mexican mule driver, ready to help him up and down.

Why are we playing dumb, captain? El Gordo asked his superior, as the three of them talked and smoked, ringed by the commotion of the reunited columns of the 4th Cavalry. The sickly señorito carried regulation tobacco in sacks for the troops and for negotiation with the Apaches, but he always brought along a wooden box of cigars rolled in Virginia for occasions demanding a conversation among gentlemen. Parker went on: The lieutenant here may have a personal interest in saving Geronimo because they're friends, but I don't; I just want this to be over, and it won't be until we offer the Chiricahuas a way out. Maybe that was true yesterday, Lawton said, but now that we have Gatewood and his Apache scouts we should at least try it. And, with a glance at the Virginian, he added: Because there's no question you're under my command, is that right? I'm under your command, certainly, said Gatewood, and I'm no rebel. With a nod at Gatewood so Parker would understand that even the lieutenant agreed with him, Lawton concluded his argument in conciliatory fashion: If the Indians escape us again, we can rethink it. Gatewood raised his cigar. His hands shook a little with pain, tolerable in the freedom of the mountains but terrible when he entered the realm of military discipline. He said, as if to himself: You're right, but the problem isn't my friendship with Geronimo. It's a waste of time trying to kill him because he isn't going to die in combat: it's a matter of conserving resources. What do you mean he won't die in combat? asked Lawton. It won't happen; don't ask me why, but it won't. The captain gave him a look, at once intrigued and ironic. Parker, who had known Gatewood longer, explained that the lieutenant had been a chief scout and knew strange things about Indians. Like what? asked the captain. Gatewood waved his cigar in the air again. It doesn't matter, he said, what's important is that we won't be able to kill Geronimo. Lawton rolled his eyes. If you don't tell me why, I won't listen to you any longer. The Virginian gazed up at the sky. His god told him so, he said; superstition or not, he believes he won't die in combat, and so he won't. That's no way to talk, said the captain, raising his cigar to his mouth. He drew in smoke and blew it out. He said: I'm in command of this expedition and I can either follow orders from the president of the United States or defy them because a lieutenant under my orders, with nobody but two Apaches and two Mexicans under his command, believes what the Indians tell him. He pointed his cigar at his officers. Put yourselves in my place and obey, he said. What you're suggesting isn't a plan I could even present to the general: how do I explain that you think Geronimo talks to his god and that's why we have to do this or that? Trying to kill him will do no good, that's all, said Parker. Lawton shook his head. Break ranks and muster your men, he ordered. Neither of the lieutenants moved. He repeated: This conversation is over, that's an order. And, with a glance at Gatewood: Prepare your scouts. Parker scratched at his prospector's beard. Using Apache scouts is an act of insubordination, too, he noted; it's forbidden. Lawton fixed him with a stare. Shut up, he said. El Gordo shrugged, saluted, and turned to call his men. Gatewood nodded as if to say he understood the circumstances. He stubbed out the cigar on his bootheel with some regret and tucked the remaining half into the pocket of his fancy coat. Don't you have a uniform in your tack? the captain asked. Yes. Put it on. The lieutenant beckoned for the younger Doroteo's help getting up from his chair, and, leaning on him, asked Lawton: Can I at least see the battalion's surgeon before we leave? Of course, said the captain. The mule driver's son handed Gatewood his cane, and the two of them shuffled toward what was left of the camp. By the way, Gatewood added cordially, there's a gadget on one of the mules that I was asked to bring for you, a heliograph. Lawton rolled his eyes. The lieutenant smiled: It's to keep you on a short leash, he said, but think about it this way: you can request uniforms for the boys and raise their morale.

The captain didn't move. He watched Gatewood greet the surgeon, who had finished taking down his tent and was loading his meager gear onto his horse. He watched them exchange a few words, and he watched the surgeon take the lieutenant by the elbow and walk him over to some cots that were still standing, though there was no tent over them anymore. Lawton spat on the ground, grinding the saliva in with his bootheel. He turned to his own affairs.

The mustering was complete. Lawton and Parker sat mounted at the head of their troops, waiting for Gatewood with a courtesy befitting the battalion's new sense of purpose, when the surgeon approached the captain, still on foot. It was he who gave orders when Lawton was indisposed. He knew Lawton well, so he could sense when he had to tread with caution. I'm sorry, captain, he said, but the lieutenant can't go on with us. Lawton's face fell. He's utterly incapacitated, continued the doctor. But he's made it this far, replied the captain; he can't be in such bad shape if he got himself here and brought Parker with him. The doctor shrugged and said: If he chooses, he can march with us at his own risk, but I'm duty-bound to discharge him indefinitely. What if I issue a counter-order? asked Lawton, though he already knew what the doctor's response would be. You risk being court-martialed if you retain him.

The captain took off his hat and scratched his matted hair violently. He asked the doctor: Where is he? He's on his way into the mountains; he requested the discharge in writing so he could deliver it to Fort Bowie. The captain went galloping after Gatewood. Parker, his sanity perhaps returning, had the delicacy to wait until he was gone to dismount.

Lawton caught up with Gatewood as he was trotting toward the mountain, flanked by his Apache scouts and followed by the mule driver and his son, the mules loaded with food and tobacco urgently needed by Lawton's troops. Lawton closed his eyes, screwing up his face and breathing in and out deeply several times to dredge up a gesture of friendship and patience instead of drawing his revolver and shooting the man, which was what he would have liked to do. Then he rode up to him and said: You win, lieutenant, I'm open to every prospect when we find Geronimo. It's the wisest course, said Gatewood, good luck: I don't know whether the doctor told you that I've been discharged. The captain restrained himself with difficulty. Yes, he told me, he said, but I'd like you to accompany us; Geronimo is more likely to survive an encounter with the battalion if you're with us. Gatewood asked Martino something in Apache and got a few words in reply. My scout says that if we want to find Geronimo, we must find the Mexicans first; he's heard from the people of the sierra that they know where he is. What people? asked Lawton, letting an edge of rage show; the problem is precisely that there are no people in the sierra. To them there are, said Gatewood, shrugging in a conciliatory way.

AUGUST 12

We'd planned to have a lazy day. The idea was to go for barbecue in Safford. What we have this summer is time: intense, charged days, but easy days, too.

We ate breakfast early in the yard. Once the sun is high in the sky there's no sitting outside at the cabin, partly because the sun bakes your brain, but also because there are so many creatures out and about—many of them poisonous—that you can't relax: wasps the size of coffee spoons; praying mantises as big and fat as rats; black widows; wind scorpions (they don't sting, but they're terrifying); ants so big you can see the hairs on their backs. They land on the tablecloth and stroll around the plates and food, confident of their odds in hand-to-hand combat with humans.

After clearing the table and doing the dishes, the kids played cowboys and Indians. The little ones love to run and play with their big brother, who is still close enough to childhood to get caught up in chasing them in a cowboy hat with plastic pistols as they run ahead shirtless with their plastic bows and arrows, squealing. They were having so much fun that we could actually read for a while. When the heat became unbearable even on the porch, we stocked the cooler and got going.

We took the Willcox road, and since it was the first time we'd driven through town without any big plans, we stopped in the downtown. We saw the historic train station—it didn't amount to much—and some antique shops that were more like secondhand stores. The town historical society's Chiricahua Museum was an adorable little house containing not a single memorable object aside from a display of photographs featuring a great-granddaughter of Chief Cochise, who, at least according to the explanatory text, was the last person in town to speak the Chiricahua variant of the Apache language. She gave lessons to Tommy Lee Jones for the movie *The Missing*, in which he played a white man gone native. The photographs were mostly of Tommy Lee Jones in Willcox, and there were none of her without him. The purported last representative of a way of describing the world is only remembered in the county that bears her great-grandfather's name because she taught an actor to pronounce a few words. Clearly, we've fucked things up.

A language is the fullest expression of humanity, and therefore it says nothing good about us that a Hollywood movie stands as the tombstone of a language. And yet it's also true that because *The Missing* features a relatively well-known actor, anyone can still hear the Athabaskan language spoken by Geronimo, Cochise, and Mangas Coloradas. We may have wiped out the Apache speakers of the Chiricahua Mountains, but at least we put some of their words on ice. It should come as no surprise. Among many other things, westerns are graveyards dotting the mantle of the Southwest, the embellished memory of a profoundly unwashed founding moment: marble and roses on top, and a generation of genocidal killers and their rotting victims beneath a layer of dirt. So that was all, America.

High and deep in Apache Pass is a cemetery where no one has been buried since the nineteenth century. Like the world where it was established, it is a segregated, multiracial space. There are two separate groups of gringos—one white and one black, I imagine, though I have no way of knowing for sure. In another section, all the Mexicans are buried together. They are just as many as the gringos, though they are erased from the official histories of the region. In the back corner are the Apaches: only three of them—once the Americans arrived they were fewer in number—and all children. One is Little Robe, a son of Geronimo, who perished at the age of two, in September 1885. Because these three graves are at the back, they're framed by the majesty of the Chiricahuas, which makes them look bleak and grand. They're the only ones with flowers on them. Plastic, of course, but still flowers. I don't know whether the bouquets are here because the dead are children or because their bones are a memorial to freeborn Chiricahuas in this place, never to be removed from their land. But someone leaves the flowers, someone wipes them clean when storms speckle them with mud and replaces them when the desert sun bleaches away their color.

Mangas Coloradas has no grave. His decapitated body was buried in the potter's field at Fort McLane, where he was betrayed and killed after a night of torture, his hands and feet bound and his body burned with red-hot bayonets when he was past seventy. His killer, Joseph Rodman West, commander of the fort, had summoned Mangas, promising a truce. West took his scalp as a trophy and cut off his head to boil it and preserve his massive skull. It can't be hard to find what was left of the chief. His son Mangus and his grandson Naiche lie in the Apache Cemetery on the military base in Lawton, Oklahoma. A genetic sample could be taken and matched with the bones in the potter's field at Fort McLane, where Mangas's decapitated body was surely buried. Then the body could be returned to the Gila Valley to find the peace it never had in life.

Cochise's grave is impossible to profane. He was the only one of the Chiricahua chiefs who never lost or surrendered, who set his own conditions for peace, and who died like the undefeated: among his own people and leaving not even a photograph behind for us to sully with our systems of mechanical reproduction.

There was something about Cochise's impossible defiance that intimidated even the usual bullies. He fought until the age of sixty-five, when he passed into history as perhaps the most successful Native American chief of all time. In the fall of 1872, he negotiated a peace treaty so advantageous for himself and his people that it reads as if it's the U.S. that's surrendering. General Oliver Otis Howard, Arizona representative of Washington's secretary of the interior, allowed Cochise to establish a reservation wherever he chose—in the Chiricahua Mountains, of course—to be run by Tom Jeffords, Cochise's only white friend, without any type of U.S. Army presence. Since it lay on the Mexican border and wasn't under the supervision of any military body, Cochise's warriors were able to continue their attacks on Sonoran ranches, selling stolen cattle and horses in Chihuahua and returning to Arizona, where the Sonoran troops only rarely ventured despite an agreement that permitted close pursuits between the two countries.

Many chiefs of many nations signed treaties as advantageous as Cochise's, but none was ever respected; no chief was able to make the U.S. Army relinquish its rights and privileges in a territory and leave them in peace. Cochise's pact was honored until the day the chief died, despite pressure by local military leaders, the incipient political class of the gringo towns springing up in Apachería, and the Tucson press. The only possible explanation for such an unprecedented and singular achievement is that, of all his contemporaries, Cochise had amassed the greatest capital of fear. The government in Washington was prepared to give him whatever he wanted if he would stop fighting. And it must be said that he kept his part of the deal faithfully: he never again left the reservation to carry out attacks on U.S. territory.

There is an air of abnormality about the events of Cochise's final years. He had fought all his life and he must have been tired, disheartened, spent by all the violence; he knew his people didn't have the numbers to continue much longer on a war footing, and he was aware that his time was short: he had a gnawing stomach cancer that for years had made it hard for him to ride out on the warpath.

On July 7, 1874, Cochise and Tom Jeffords saw each other for the last time. For ten years they had been fierce enemies on the battlefield and great friends in the realm of conversation. During the chief's final two years of life they had also been successful business partners: whatever Cochise's warriors didn't sell in Chihuahua was passed on to New Mexican traders through the reservation agency headed by Jeffords. They were linked not only by love and hate—after a breakup, everybody knows you miss the dark moments as much as the bright ones—but also by a truly lifelong bond forged by complicity in massive corruption schemes.

Jeffords, who lived until 1914, described his last encounter with Cochise in an interview. The chief's legendary body was so ravaged by the illness wasting him and the sotol he drank ceaselessly to forget that it was plain he couldn't hold on much longer. Do you think we'll meet again on the other side? Cochise asked Jeffords. The agent, who had seen and inflicted every imaginable horror as witness to and participant in the Apache Wars, could not have believed in God; death could only mean deliverance if it was final. He said he didn't really know; he greatly doubted it. Cochise, whose famously grim expression never softened, smiled a little, maybe because he could count the hours remaining to him in the world with the fingers on two hands. He said: I think we will, because good friends always meet again.

Cochise died that same night, June 8, 1874. This must be myth, but it was said that the terrifying howling of his people was heard all the way to Fort Bowie.

Cochise was a war machine. Having battled the greatest empire of the day in his youth and the two richest, most populous and powerful nations in North America in his adulthood, he managed to survive only two years of peace. He was a man of blood and struggle, a whirlwind of destruction, a weapon, pure force in motion, the glorious essence of the unproductive and untamable.

Chief Victorio—who was Mimbreño, not Chiricahua, but just as lethal and vengeful as Cochise—died shot in the neck by the Raramuri Mauricio Corredor. Mangas Coloradas died on his knees, bound hand and foot. Geronimo died of old age, brought low as a prisoner of war in a concentration camp. Cochise refused to give his enemies the satisfaction of witnessing the hour of his death.

On June 9, the Chiricahuas prepared the body of their chief as if even this final voyage would not be a peaceful one. They took off his shirt, put on his warrior's headband, painted his face with pollen, and laid him across his horse in his buckskin trousers and moccasins. Around his waist they once again strapped his bullet-lined cartridge belt, tucking in the silver-handled Mexican pistols he could fire while hanging sideways on his saddle, shielded from enemy fire. They wrapped him in the splendid New England quilt that General Howard had given him two years before, when they negotiated the peace that led to the warrior's death. They set off into the mountains and canyons of the sierra that belonged to them. His dog trotted behind him as if he were still alive.

No Apache has ever spoken another word about that day. An oral history of it was hard to compile because of the taboos around death; it wasn't until a somewhat Americanized generation of Chiricahuas grew up in Oklahoma that anyone was even allowed to speak the names of the departed. Tom Jeffords was present, and it was he who eventually told the story. With Cochise's whole band, the agent climbed up to what must have been the warrior's seat of power. Here, in a place never revealed to anyone, Cochise's body with all its trappings was dropped into a ravine, his horse and his dog let fall there as well, to speed his journey to the other side. His body has never been found.

I told my children this story as we were having a mostly vegetarian supper at the table outside the house in the Peñascosas. We had eaten half a cow at the barbecue joint in Safford. Unlike Bowie, no Mexicans had ever lived there, and so it seemed a little more developed. In Arizona, public funds are as unevenly distributed as water: they go to just a few, and those few are white. The children agreed that tomorrow—our second-to-last day in Apachería—we should get up early and make a trip to the Chiricahuas, that vast cemetery for a single body, to honor the memory of the greatest of all Apache chiefs. Seeing those mountains might be the reason we made the whole trip.

She glanced at the güero, who was making more progress digging the grave with the flat rock, but also working harder—he looked like a ghost, with dirty rivulets of sweat running down his cheeks, so pink just that morning. Imagine little Damián's joy, free spirit that he was, finding himself liberated from the choirmaster's teachings. His few years with the New Mexicans would've been the happiest of the bastard's life if he weren't already the type to be happy no matter what: five minutes alone with a rock and he could find the fun in it.

You should've seen how tickled he was telling me about those days. Soon after the New Mexicans set out into the mountains in search of towns with appreciative audiences, little Damián discovered that the ranch folk would go wild if he left the drum in the middle of concerts, hurling himself into the crowd to show people how to dance to this cutting-edge music, revealing them to themselves as navigators of a strange world in which everything was new, though nothing had actually changed. He loved the moment in each town when he stepped clapping into the circle of chairs filled with timid dance-goers, picked a girl who looked willing, and set her spinning to the strains of a Viennese waltz, usually so stuffy. Once a few people had ventured to shake off the dust, he loved returning to the drum; he loved the trancelike moment when his cowbell clanged in unison with the accordion and the tololoche, and the New Mexicans attained a higher level of harmony, driving those who'd been brave enough to take the floor into a frenzy and moving the others to join them there. Then the music rose, clamored, reached fever pitch. In that moment he would shout, transported to a world where everything is equal and belongs to all of us: What was in the milk he drank? And the band would cry: Earth, stone, and Apache blood. He would shout back: And who lay with his father? And again the band would reply: Ay mamá, the Sierra Madre. And he would bang the cowbell as if to shatter it.

He loved being the center of attention, the heart of the madness, passing as a musician though he was really just a master of ceremonies raised to greatness by the cowbell; but what he liked most of all, more than anything, was the last part of it, the quiet moment when they loaded their instruments into a cart pulled by two mules and set off to see what they could see. That was what really thrilled him: the hour of departure when they took their cartridge belts and pistols from the traveling trunk and fastened them around their hips, the moment when he set his hat on his head, reloading his revolver and stowing his shotgun in the sling across his saddle. The cart was driven by the Prussian, the tololoche player perched beside him with his gun on his knees, though he never used it. And then the silence, the stars, the men sitting around the fire in the cold of night. Lying and looking up at the sky, while on the edge of camp another musician played a song on the guitar composed when Mexico had yet to exist, when the immense desert moon was the modest, watery moon of a feeble empire where a hundred mothers watched over him, and his father—stubborn, silent, and distracted though he was—always came back for him.

Far from it all as they were, the roads were always quiet, but there was news everywhere, which the New Mexicans weren't sure whether to believe or laugh at, because of course this desert and the towns in it weren't just a different country from the one that was being violently born farther south, but another fucking world. Sometimes they had the feeling that if they stopped for a moment on the road, the waves of chaos would sweep over them. He had a story that he told with great success at all the parties, his charm on full display. After a dance in El Caballo, the New Mexicans learned that the Spaniards had made a desperate attempt to retake the country, but General Santa Anna had corralled the Spanish troops in the Sierra Mojada, brought them to the island of San Juan de Ulúa, had their throats cut, and hurled them into the sea, where they were a banquet for the sharks and many were eaten alive. In Santa Bárbara, the New Mexicans heard that the English were coming, and in Huajatlán they heard that they had withdrawn, but either way there was no money left in the public coffers and there had been another coup. Next came his favorite part of the story. As the New Mexicans moved west though Chihuahua, they learned that there had been two different presidents between back-to-back dances hosted in Yoquivo and La Bufa, and by the time they reached Samachic, over a little hill, there had already been another, who held power for an hour and a half—shorter than the dance itself.

The güero didn't laugh, so she addressed him directly. You'd have no call to remember any of this, you were too little, but you've heard your parents talk about it, haven't you? she asked. Maybe, he said, knee-deep in the hole by now. How well do you know Chihuahua? she asked. Out of breath, he replied that he didn't know it well. Those towns are all right next to each other, she said, that's why it was funny. And she went on: In Delicias they realized that if they wanted to carry on west—they were traveling through lands ever more open to the sky, as if ruled by a stone giant—they would have to abandon the cart and proceed with their instruments on muleback because ahead lay the mountains. Imagine what that meant to Damián: the mountains, his chingada madre.

She turned back toward the body and gazed at it tenderly. She tried to fold the dead man's arms across his chest to give him a saintly look he definitely hadn't earned, but to do that she realized she would have to break his elbows, so she laid them across his belt instead. Then she thought a little and hooked his fingers under the leather as if he were dancing one of his polkas or simply talking to friends up in the mountains.

AUGUST 13

Today, as promised, I took the kids to Cochise's grave: the Chiricahua Mountains—intricate, severe, frankly eerie, their unearthly monolithic outcroppings shaped by the brutal weather of the Arizona highlands. The canyons brimming with stone towers may be familiar from countless movies filmed here, but even so they look like vestiges of structures built by engineers from some pre-Sumerian civilization. It was just the little ones, their big brother, and me. Inés decided to stay at the Peñascosas cabin.

After a long ramble through the Chiricahua canyons by car and on foot, we drove up to see the grottoes high on the mountain, where the air is different, crystal clear. When we parked we noticed that the other tourists were all leaving, even though it would be a good four hours before the park closed. The edge of a major storm had appeared on the horizon, as a father from one of the departing families pointed out to us.

With typical Mexican cockiness, Cruz and I imagined the gringos were leaving because of some safety obsession—after all, the man who advised us to leave the park was wearing a safari hat with a mosquito net over his face. We knew how fast storms move in Arizona, but we calculated we could reach at least one of the grottoes and hurry back to the car before it hit. Our resolve was strengthened by the knowledge that this would be our last afternoon in the area, and we'd never be back here together again.

We had no problem reaching the first and most spectacular grotto, the sun still shining radiantly. It was a kind of hole bored through the top of the mountain by millennia of running water. A natural drainpipe, big as everything else in this land.

We were inside it when the sky turned black and hostile. We made an attempt to run back to the car—not easy with Amelia still so little and the terrain so steep—but the sudden violence of rain and lightning forced us back into the grotto.

Under cover and relatively dry, we congratulated ourselves: watching a storm from inside a cave on top of a mountain was a wonderful way to spend our last afternoon out in the elements of Arizona.

In our moment of happiness, we didn't realize we were still only on the brink of the storm, though this was already the most violent weather we'd ever seen. Suddenly the sky got really dark, as if night had fallen with a thud, and the entrance to the cave was veiled by a curtain of water. Lightning bolts began to strike, one after the other. They lit up our whole refuge, shaking the ground. We endured the tremors in tense silence, me telling myself these grottoes were thousands of years old; there was no way they could collapse. Then the grotto began to work the way it was intended: as a drainpipe. A whole river came gushing at us.

Cruz and I clung as best we could to the stone ridges of the wall, with water rushing up to our knees and Amelia and Cosme pressed between our bodies and the rock. If a tangled branch or a drowned animal had come along it would have swept us away with it, and we would have been carried over the edge into the abyss.

At some point the downpour ended as abruptly as it had begun, and the waterfall over the entrance cleared a little; lightning struck more sporadically. We crouched down to wait for the thunder to grow distant so we could run back to the station wagon. I sat Amelia between my legs and put my arms around her to keep her warm: her lips were blue. Cosme, instead of huddling with us, sought the embrace of his big brother, who whispered in his ear, making him relax and even laugh. Cruz was his giant, his brother bear, his hero.

When we reached the station wagon at last, a park service van was waiting. A ranger got out of the van as soon as she saw us emerge from the pines, soaked and shivering. We were looking for you, she said without reproach. She handed the kids astronaut blankets and poured each of us a cup of hot chocolate from a thermos. She gave me precise instructions: Turn on the station wagon and run the heater until you're warm and the clothes on your upper body are dry; you can't drive while you're shivering because the roads are slippery and full of debris; then head down carefully, hugging the side of the mountain; the park has been closed for two and a half hours, so you won't run into anyone. Two and a half hours? I asked. She nodded. Cruz turned to look at me. I thought it was more like twenty minutes, he said. I'd thought so, too.

I started the car, and Cosme asked Cruz to sit in the back with them, saying they needed him urgently. Their elder brother gave me a look, impatient and apologetic: he would rather sit up front, but he didn't want to disappoint the kids. He moved into the back. His brother nestled under his arm and fell asleep.

How I would have liked to be there the day little Damián finally met her, his guiding light. The Sierra Madre, what a fucking name. She closed her eyes as if to imagine it, as if the mountains could fit inside a person's head. Have you been there? she asked, but she didn't turn to look at him because she guessed he would say no again. Hard and yielding, intricate and clear as day, merciless and giving, solid as his own sierra madre.

They rode up into the mountains, scared to death, to the rallying cry of earth, stone, and Apache blood, led tirelessly by Damián with his cowbell, at the risk of spooking the horse and ending up at the bottom of one of those absurdly tall and beautiful cliffs. It was like exploring Saturn, and in the end there would only be more Saturn.

I don't know how many days later it was that they crossed back over the Sonora line and came to Basaraca, a place that is both past and future, a world suspended. Those who choose to live in the upper reaches of the Sierra Madre make their home at the ass-end of the world, the craggiest, most remote place on earth. I've been there. I went as a girl, when I worked selling soap made by a man in Pitic. It isn't easy to get there, to leave, or to stay. It's a shitty town, but it was the closest thing to a town the New Mexicans had seen in days, so they thought they might as well hold a dance. A ludicrous idea. Let me see if I can explain. Basaraca's mission church is so poor it never had the money to build a tower, so the bell is in the church atrium, hanging from a wooden beam, and to be rung it has to be pushed like a swing. It's always cold, even when the sun shines, and it can snow in May, so people almost never leave their houses, and when they do they're so bundled up they might as well be in their shrouds already, about to be nailed up in their coffins. She touched the dead man's hands and said: Ay Damiancito, forgive me, there'll be no coffin for you.

She went on: Anyway, they stayed the night, and the next day they agreed to hold a dance at the church, not because a walk around town had made it seem a good bet for a party, or because people had the money to pay for it, but because their provisions were running low and a bag of beans would make all the difference in their diet until they made it down through the mountains on the Sonoran side.

The way Damián told it, the New Mexicans were tuning their instruments, starving to death and freezing cold, when a lady walked into the church, dressed for a day in the English countryside, accompanied by nine of the most beautiful girls the musicians had seen in weeks. What's this? asked the Prussian. The lady raised her veil, gave a little curtsy, and waved her hand as if to say they shouldn't pay them any attention, as if that were possible. She instructed her daughters to start setting out chairs for the townspeople when they arrived. Then she asked the musicians whether they were hungry, and their answers ranged from very to extremely; they weren't entirely sure whether under the circumstances they should adopt the manners of city gentlemen, which deep down they were, or of the badlands players they had been masquerading as for months. I brought a cook and a man with a brazier in case a little refreshment might be in order, said the lady. They're outside if you like.

The Prussian, suspicious of such generosity, asked the lady what she was doing there and where she was from. Why, we come from nearby, she said, just a little way down the river on the other side of the peak; my girls and I live on a hacienda where there are never any dances, so we came to have a look; but go on, eat, and then we'll see. Waiting for them outside the mission were tacos of carne asada so tender it made their teeth grate, and the dazzling treat—so rare in the mountains—of hot chocolate made with boiling water. I also brought aguardiente for these poor people so that they enjoy the dance, said the lady when they came back inside, sated as boa constrictors.

The dance was not a success. There was no way it could have been in that town, no matter how well-oiled the throats of the attendees, male or female, by the doña's sotol, and no matter that her nine daughters were in the audience. But it wasn't bad either, considering that brio and dancing spirit were not the forte of the Basaracans. At the end of the show—because it was hardly a dance in the usual sense of the word—the lady approached little Damián and asked to have a word with him outside the mission.

When the band set out west the next day, down to the desert and across to Rancho Nuevo, little Damián gave the Prussian a long hug, saying: Why would I go on when I've found my Sierra Madre at last? The lady had offered him a job as music instructor and a house on the hacienda at Tesorababi, twenty miles down the mountain from Basaraca. He had accepted because of something she mentioned in the middle of their conversation: the reason their chocolate was so good was because it was sweetened with mosquito honey. Mosquito honey? asked Damián. Yes indeed, confirmed the lady, harvested by our Apache neighbors.

DOROTEO THE YOUNGER

In the Caves of Tres Montañas
After Achieving Immortality

Right here at Tres Montañas is where I met Geronimo, said Doroteo the Younger. He was lying on a mat by the fire, rolled in his serape. Stretched out there unsmiling, his face permanently furrowed with worry—narrow-eyed, stiff-haired, blunt-nosed—he resembled a puma. By winter's end, the sierra had taken its toll. He breathed laboriously, like a locomotive. These weren't happy times: back in the barrens, living hand to mouth again, nearly alone, spending days perched on cliffs and nights in caves; this was defeat and also an exercise of memory. How to track the enemy so they think they're after you but you're really after them—we learned that from him, he went on. Who? asked one of the men lying around the fire. Geronimo, or not from him, exactly, but from his Chiricahuas; Geronimo was a ghost, when he was in the mountains no one ever saw him, but a couple of his warriors were always just over the hill from us. Doroteo the Younger took a hand out from under his blanket and rubbed his face, unspooling more recollections that no one had inquired about, not because his men weren't curious about his life, but because no one dared to speak to him if he didn't speak first:

There they are, my señor padre would say, and point to the mountain; he could smell 'em.

Doroteo the Elder had been dead for so long that the Younger couldn't remember his face at all, though since he had returned to the mountains he thought of him every day. He remembered what he'd been taught about plying the gorges, but especially the drunken binges, the beatings, the day when, still a boy, he had to take a machete and step between his mother and his father, who was raving with aguardiente and misery as always when he spent too long on the ranch. He remembered fleeing with his mother and sister, the trip south to the mountains of Durango, where they started over.

I think my señor padre didn't want the gringos to catch Geronimo because he knew he'd be out of work; that's why I was the only one he told when he spied 'em. He would whisper in my ear: Look sharp, Doroteo, they're nearby, don't budge from the convoy.

By now no one would have called him Doroteo the Younger, as Gatewood and Parker had done on the Sierra Madre campaign. No one would even have dared to call him by his name. By now he was thirty-nine and could lay claim to a truly countless number of dead, though neither his age nor his bloody past showed. He was still friendly, playful, sometimes even jovial, though when he was in a rage no one wanted to be near him. At the height of his career, he would make hideous decisions with a shrug of the shoulders: Sorry, amiguitos, he would say to his prisoners, be there a hundred of you or not we have to shoot you.

Toward the end of his last flight into the sierra, during the inhospitable October of 1916, he didn't have much left but his fame. Lying under his serape by the fire in a cave in Tres Montañas, he had only four men with him, two of them his cousins, the other two related by marriage. He had sent the rest away when he learned that President

Wilson, in a show of disproportionate force verging on madness, had assigned Black Jack Pershing a body of five thousand U.S. cavalry soldiers to chase him over the border.

Life had steamrolled him as ferociously as it does everyone, but also with the special violence that forced a whole generation of Mexicans to live with jaws clenched and pistols on hips. From the moment the Revolution began in '10, Doroteo the Younger couldn't remember a night when he was able to sleep unarmed, or an evening when he could sit down to eat carne asada with friends, drink a few beers, and weave quietly home, lying down to sleep it off without a care until morning. He couldn't remember falling in love with a woman who wasn't capable of waving a pistol and hijacking a train. He belonged to the class of men and women who, whenever they paused to take a piss, had to ask somebody to watch their backs. People from the end of one world and the beginning of another. In this he resembled Geronimo, who had also gone through life under a name not his own.

Now only his wife, sitting out this campaign at a ranch loaned to them in Parral, dared to call him Doroteo. Everybody else called him mi general, always with a ballooning of terror between tongue and upper palate. The day he told his wife he was leaving on campaign again, they were on the military train that had been their home on wheels for years. He said he would leave a few men to take her to the ranch and help her with the children while he was gone; none of them could go anywhere without an escort. She tried to argue with him—nobody else could. What's the point of fighting, Doroteo Arango? she asked, the Constitutionalists have already defeated you on all sides and you have no army or weapons. He replied nonchalantly: I'm just going underground for a few days, a small operation with a few men and guns, I'll be back soon. She squinted her eyes.

What are you planning, Doroteo Arango? He smiled: I'm going to invade the United States of America.

Then he strode into the night with his last Dorados, who were now so few—about eighty—that they might have been a band of Apache warriors. From the Apaches, after all, he had learned to vanish on stony ground, to cure a whole cow to eat on the trail, to shoot from a running horse. They crossed the border and attacked Columbus, New Mexico, and President Wilson sent Pershing after them as practice for the now imminent invasion of Europe, and General Parker received orders at Fort Sam Houston in San Antonio to ready the troops to invade Mexico. General Parker could never have guessed that when he was just a boy, he had met the fearsome revolutionary general his men would be pursuing: that Doroteo the Younger and Pancho Villa were the same person. If he had known, he would have sent a note of unsolicited advice to the War Department: You'll never catch him, best not to try.

Doroteo the Younger raised his head to ask one of his cousins for a cup of the coffee he was drinking. You won't be able to sleep, mi general, the cousin said. You know I never sleep anyway, he replied. He propped his elbow on his bedroll and his head in his hand. When we met him right here on this very spot, I think Geronimo already knew his good days were numbered: not once did my señor padre get a glimpse of his braves, and Don Carlitos's Apaches only found 'em because the federales already had 'em surrounded. One of the Dorados emerged from sleep or what had seemed like it to ask: Don Carlitos? Apaches? Federales? With all due respect, mi general, I have no idea what you're talking about.

Don Carlitos was a gringo, friend of Geronimo, said Doroteo; he was a soldier, but he wore a three-piece suit on campaign, don't ask me why; big mustache, big nose, always sickly, but the perfect gentleman. Of all the gringo officers who hired my señor padre a thousand times to come and hunt Apaches in Mexico, Don Carlitos was the only one who wasn't completely lost, because he had two scouts who could have found a ladybug in a thicket. One was Apache Apache, I can't remember his name, but he was quiet, faraway, the way those bastards always were until they double-crossed you. The other one talked to us more because he'd been adopted as a boy by a Mexican family, and though one day he decided to return to the mountains, he didn't lose his Mexican side, and he was devoted to my señor padre. His name was Martín. He was the one who told Don Carlitos and the gringos that the only way to catch Geronimo was to track the federales, because if the gringos hadn't run into either of 'em for days, it was because they were at each other's throats somewhere else. Martín and Don Carlitos persuaded the captain of the whole troop gathered there at the bend of the Aros River, and they rode north, into the part of the sierra where Geronimo liked to go to regroup, as everybody knew except the pinches gringos, who were always lost.

Pancho Villa and his men had invaded New Mexico and attacked the garrison in Columbus because the U.S. government had cut off their supply of arms and chosen to back the Constitutionalist leader Venustiano Carranza as president of the new revolutionary Mexico. No one expected that he would make a bold move never attempted before or since: invading the United States.

He attacked the military outpost of Camp Furlong and set fire to the buildings that the townspeople had taken up arms to protect after the Mexicans overcame the battalion charged with their defense. He took all of the outpost's horses, guns, and munitions. This was an act of lunacy, never mind Doroteo the Younger's failure to calculate that it was an election year in the U.S. A military campaign that looked easy to win was like manna from heaven for President Wilson; it would buy him four more years in power, allowing him to plunge fully into the war in Europe.

Who knows what Villa was thinking when he decided on this plan, but he surely didn't imagine that the U.S. would respond with a show of force that eventually brought some ten thousand men to Mexico along with the deployment of new technology that no one, not even the Americans, knew very well what to do with. There was a hint of imperial adolescence to Pershing's Punitive Expedition: it saw both the last U.S. cavalry charges and the first combat action using gasoline-fueled vehicles and planes.

I thought Geronimo was dead, said the other man. Doroteo the Younger laughed. Of course he must be dead, he said; when I knew him, more than thirty years ago, he was probably sixty, though he could have been a thousand; the war had worn him down: he was thin, tense as a wire, gnarled. The general squinted, rubbing his eyes. He went on: He had that Yaqui broad chest but he was all shriveled up. The most impressive part of him was his legs: brown, sturdy, the son of a bitch might as well've been walking on two tree trunks. And his eyes: he would look at you, not even intending to hurt you, and you'd wet yourself, you'd be so scared. They were small, sunken, slanted, one pupil bigger than the other and both pupils ringed with yellowish whites. He was sun-wizened, his skin tough and dark. He had a nose like the beak of a turkey buzzard, and he was always so pissing mad that his mouth was turned down and his lips drawn in, invisible. When I met him, who knows how long it had been since he laughed? I think he already knew it would be his last day of freedom because it took him a while to make up his mind, but in the end he handed his soul to the gringos. And they fucked him in that cheery, cruel way of theirs, like the shitty things they do aren't their fault, they're the fault of the people getting fucked. They pardoned him, let him live, let him die of old age, humiliated and pickled in drink. They didn't even grant him the privilege of simple, righteous, eternal death, which is what he would have gotten from the federales: a death like the life he'd lived. They paraded him around like a trophy, showing him off at fairs like an animal, humiliating him every fucking second of his life until he ended up humiliating himself.

Doroteo the Younger had been thinking of his father almost every day since he'd taken to the sierra some eight months ago, according to his calculations, but Geronimo's face, the grimace of rage he never forgot after a lifetime of witnessing flesh quivering with fury, came rushing back to him when news reached him that the 5th Cavalry had succeeded in killing one of the men who had fought longest by his side. Candelario Cervantes? How can that be? asked General Villa. Did they take him prisoner? Everyone scattered, replied the messenger; including the one man who was wounded, but they recognized Candelario by his sword and the gold star on his hat. How could he let himself be caught when those gringo machines can be heard miles away? The messenger explained that the 5th Cavalry didn't have trucks because they were crossing the sierra. One night Candelario Cervantes's people had stolen horses from the gringos because they'd had to eat their own, but they hadn't counted on the gringo captain bringing along Apache scouts. General Villa took off his hat, tracing a circle with the tip of his boot on the stony ground. Tell me, my friend, he said, do you mean the 5th Cavalry has got Apaches? They caught us late at night, said the messenger, after we had already ridden a long way; Candelario didn't expect it. Did they take back the horses? We killed them before we scattered. All right, said the general, go and sit with my men and have 'em give you something to eat. He put his hat back on. Before he ate his own first taco, of dried beef with sauce so hot it stung, he announced that they had to break camp. They would go up to the caves for a while.

He draped his serape over his shoulders and sat cross-legged, fixing his cousin with a stare: Are you going to pour me some coffee or not? he asked. The other man raised his palms in a gesture of peace and made a show of serving him. When we were with Don Carlitos we were clueless for something like two weeks, said Villa, reaching for the pewter mug. Until some mule drivers who were unloading corn at a mine told Martín they'd seen Geronimo near Fronteras, that he was trying to make a deal with the city prefect because his people were out of their minds with hunger. He took a swallow of coffee, narrowing his eyes even more: it was reheated, bitter. He went on: Don Carlitos felt that it was now or never and requested permission for us to separate from the convoy. We set out late at night, at forced marches with him, his scouts, two interpreters for the official talks, and another couple of soldiers; the regiment followed at its own pace.

We were going so fast that for the first time in my life my señor padre worried about the mules, though we had taken only two with us, leaving the rest with the cavalry corps' mule train. By morning we were already outside Fronteras, the municipal seat, where Don Carlitos was to meet with the prefect of the whole region, who had been told that Geronimo wanted to parley. Before we rode into town, Don Carlitos had ordered Martín's cousin to stay back, to head into the mountains in search of Geronimo's trail, just in case. I heard from Martín, who was seen in Fronteras as Mexican, not Apache, that the federales had been coming into town a few at a time all night and were hiding everywhere, and the prefect had collected all the sotol in town to give to the Apaches during the talks so they could up and kill 'em when they'd had a skinful. The prefect told Don Carlitos that he would arrest him if he interfered, and the gringo said he certainly had no plan to do so; he was happy to let 'em finish the job. He came back to us and told us to rest for a while; as soon as the sun went down we would return to the regiment.

And that's what we did. We rode calmly south, still by daylight, so that the prefect and the federales he had planted on the mountainside to cut off Geronimo's retreat would see us leaving. We met up with Don Carlitos's scout when it was full dark: he had found a trail, and we followed it back into the mountains. We were all scared to death, moving slowly to keep under cover, with a white flour sack on a dry stalk of flor de maguey at the front of the convoy, so that Geronimo's people would see that we came in peace if they found us before we found 'em, as was usually the case. The scouts went first, Don Carlitos and the translators in the middle, and my señor padre and me a little way behind, driving the mules. What I remember best about that trip was how terrifying it was to cross a canyon where someone had left a pair of breeches hanging, who knows why. Martín and his cousin shrank back. Don Carlitos said he would take the lead so that he would have the glory of dying in the field if the Apaches ambushed us from the cliffs. The scouts said no, they wanted that honor for themselves. In the end the three of 'em went ahead together, Don Carlitos holding the white flag high.

Nothing happened in the canyon, luckily; we thought it was empty. Then we found out it wasn't. The braves were following us from above, and Geronimo did want to talk to Don Carlitos. It took us all day to reach the bend in the river where we were the other day; that's why I recognized it. We camped there so Martín and his cousin could climb up here, to the caves, to tell Geronimo we had come for peace talks and he shouldn't be afraid, the regiment would stay back. Then the next day at dawn, they arrived.

The general paused to take another swallow from his cup: if he'd been successful as a military man, it was because he'd known to surround himself with brilliant strategists and because he had so much charisma the very stones would follow him, but also because he was gifted with the sense of drama that distinguishes remarkable people. His three men sat around the embers, as intent on him as three cats. He shook his head, his expression somewhere between mocking and angry.

If you could've seen 'em, he said, rubbing his chin. They emerged from the rocky ground as if they'd been sleeping beneath it, just like that. They didn't arrive; they sprouted, the sons of bitches. They were tough bastards, through and through. All of 'em, even the women, were carrying rifles and pistols. He took a swallow of coffee. I was watching 'em sidelong because my señor padre had taught me never to look 'em in the face, and it seemed to me I saw a whole cemetery trailing behind 'em. The first to spring up was Lozen, Victorio's sister; we knew her. We also recognized Fun, who had been raised Mexican, like many of 'em, and Chapo, Geronimo's son. Don Carlitos knew all their names and greeted them one by one, asking after their families. Then Geronimo came out of nowhere, his pistol with its mother-of-pearl grip tucked under his belly and his rifle pointing at the ground. He asked the gringo in Spanish why he hadn't come up to say hello when we arrived; it offended him a little that the lieutenant had thought they'd do him harm in such company.

Don Carlitos was green with fear: he knew Geronimo well, but that was on the reservation in peacetime. After months on the warpath and in the sierra, he was somebody else. Tightly wound, pure prowess. He was wearing the usual knee-high moccasins, short breeches, and a muslin shirt. He wore his red war bandanna around his neck, like a cravat, and a heavy wool jacket with round patches on the shoulders. No matter how friendly he tried to seem, his face was pure rage. He sat down on a stump, leaning the Springfield up against it. He asked Don Carlitos to sit with him and the lieutenant obeyed—he asked in Apache, but the way he beckoned was clear to everybody. The lieutenant was scared enough that he forgot his rheumatism. He sat down. They were so close that their thighs touched. Then Geronimo asked in Spanish, in a voice loud enough for all of us to hear—peace talks were parleys, and also vaudeville acts—whether we'd brought sotol. The lieutenant shook his head. Tobacco? My señor padre handed the soldier a sack, never once looking at Geronimo's face: he knew that whenever Geronimo met a Mexican, he would shoot before he asked questions.

The warrior weighed the bag with a smile as Don Carlitos handed him rolling papers. Geronimo gestured his thanks and took a pipe out of the inner pocket of his jacket. Tell them to go, he said without looking up, pointing at my señor padre still holding the sack of tobacco. The lieutenant nodded and asked him to guarantee our safe return: El Doroteo is a man of trust, he said, and his son is a child. He stared up at me with his eyes like two stones. You have my word, he replied. My father hadn't lowered his eyes, because he'd never raised 'em: no Mexican, unarmed as a mule driver had to be when he was on a job with a military convoy, would have dared to look him in the face.

I held his gaze. I'm not bragging: I was a foolish kid and I couldn't take my eyes off him, the way you can't look away from a dead body. This was Geronimo, after all. The bastard waved his pipe, motioning for me to come close. I started to obey as children obey, without thinking, but I felt my father holding me back by the shoulder, so I didn't move, but I kept my eyes on his. Come, he said, in his cracked, deadly voice; I won't do anything to you. My father wouldn't let me go until Don Carlitos insisted there was no need to fear, he was there to protect me—I really was scared, and not just a little, but I've always had a taste for deep holes, and for throwing myself in.

The other warriors were sitting around 'em in a circle, like us. There must have been twelve or thirteen of 'em. I advanced like a man on his way to the gallows and planted myself in front of him, two palms away, in the middle of the circle, which now included the gringos, who had moved in to listen. He beckoned me closer again. When I was right in front of him I could smell his buzzard breath, the yeasty fragrance of his jacket, the horse-sweat scent of his legs, the sun and the dust, but also the flower perfume the Apaches washed their hair with when they were on campaign; his hair was still very black. In an instant, fast as a rattlesnake, he grabbed me by the ribs and pulled me to his chest, which felt warm to me, almost gentle, taking me by the hair and lifting my face. He stuck a finger in my mouth to feel my teeth, looked in my ears. Then he let me go, giving me a few genuinely friendly slaps on the belly. He's a good one, he said to his people, we should take him with us. Looking at me, unsmiling but relaxed now, he asked in a joking tone: Are you coming with us? My señor padre ordered me to return to his side with a look that I knew very well, and so I did.

Later, when we were almost done unloading the mules so we could go back to where the regiment was supposed to be waiting for us, Chief Naiche appeared. Naiche was Cochise's son. I never met Cochise, but back then it was said he was the bravest Indian who'd ever lived. Naiche was young. He had very dark skin, like his face was made of clay. Geronimo wasn't a chief, he was a captain. His job was to keep the band strong, attack, run. Naiche was different: he was the chief—more like a politician. He passed us as if we weren't there and went to shake hands with Don Carlitos, eking out a smile. I don't know what happened next because we left, and when we caught up with the regiment the captain just paid us, thanked us, and gave us back our mules: he'd been sent his own mule drivers from the United States.

The general lay down again and pulled the serape over himself, saying with his eyes half-closed: Who's on first watch? The cousin who had distributed cups of coffee said he was. So what else happened? he asked. When? When you met Geronimo. The general shrugged: Before we left Don Carlitos and Geronimo behind, we stopped at the river; my señor padre noticed I had pissed myself. Of course, said one of the Dorados. It wasn't fear, said the general, it happened after we left; it was fury, because I wished I'd gone with 'em.

LATER

The storm in the Chiricahuas filled our night somehow. When we got back we took long, steaming baths, though it was hot in the Peñascosas cabin. During dinner the children kept interrupting each other to tell their mother about the water, the lightning, the astronaut blankets they would probably keep forever, and what they were convinced was the best hot chocolate in the world. Even Cruz reverted to childhood, making the occasional interjection and retreating again, serious and a little aloof, the way he always is around Inés.

I wonder whether he's imagining how things would be if his own mother were here to play the role of watcher and worrier, secretly proud of her children's toughness. Whether he's remembering the years I spent with her—hard years for me—as a world we shattered without consulting him. But I think he's mostly happy, excited, like all of us: in our minds, we looked into the jaws of catastrophe and we survived. Maybe he sees himself as part of the family, just as we see him, rather than as the visitor I think he imagines himself to be.

We sat around the table until late, in part because we were trying to finish the wine we'd bought for our stay in the cabin.

By the time we'd done the dishes, we were falling asleep, so we decided to go to bed and wake up early to pack and break camp. We said good night happily, replete, none of us thinking much about the fact that by ten o'clock the next morning we would be going our separate ways, Cruz on a plane back to Mexico, the rest of us back to the Northeast, with no concrete plans to meet again.

I've been to Tesorababi, too, and it's nice, but Damiancito might've exaggerated. Who's to say, though? Times had changed when I was there. I've heard from more than one person that those were its glory days, and it hasn't been the same since. When he got there, he said, it was like the station where the best people get off when they die. Though one day he turned up in Janos to start his dancing school, so it couldn't have been perfect, but what do I know? He never told me why he left.

Tesorababi grew up around the manor house of the señora's hacienda, she went on, putting a hand on the dead man's shoulder. The hacienda had been bought by her husband's grandfather, a Sonoran of long standing, who built it into something fine. Since it's at the very bottom of the canyons, it's an otherworldly green there, which explains why it filled up with people. A grain shed was cleaned out for Damiancito to make room for a stove, a bed, and a table; a piano, too, which was a real calvary to carry along the twisting trails of the sierra and which he didn't really know how to play.

Life in town must have been good, because the scoundrel spent seven years there. The mistress of the hacienda took care of absolutely everything for him, and in exchange all he had to do was give imaginary piano lessons to the boss's daughters. It took him a while to make contact with the Apaches the lady had talked about the day she convinced him to move to the hacienda. He asked about them soon after he arrived, and though no one hid anything from him, no one could tell him much either, because they didn't know exactly where they lived: they came down from the mountain with no warning, bringing little jars of honey tied up with the string their women made from maguey fibers. They didn't set up a stand in the plaza to sell them, like the other Indians. They went straight to talk to the hacienda overseer on the terraces where the cattle were kept, and he sent for a heap of corn from the hacienda manor house for them, and gave them suckling calves to be raised in the mountains.

Your Apaches came down again this morning, Don Damián, the foreman said one day, and Damiancito asked why he hadn't been sent for so he could meet them. The man answered that they were wary of strangers. Damiancito loved to recall this conversation. He would imitate himself as the curious outsider: hand on chin, standing tall, eyebrows waggling; when he played the rancher, he was cagey and closemouthed. How did it go? he'd ask, and then, replying as the foreman, exaggerating his mountain accent, he'd say it had gone very well: I had to give them three calves. The señora told me they were given jerky, Damián would say he'd said, to which the other man replied that the señora had no idea. This surprised Damián, but he forged on nonetheless. The foreman told him they didn't exchange guns or horses with the Apaches, though every season the Indians would insist they had enough cows, and what they needed were rifles and mounts to be able to hunt farther afield and bring skins down to Tesorababi for the winter. Are they really so dangerous? asked you-know-who, who had quickly grasped what the cattleman was insinuating. They're good people when they want to be, replied the foreman, but it's better to be out of their way when they lose their heads. And is it really mosquito honey? Mosquitoes don't make honey; it tastes different because it's from wasps. Wasps? The Apaches are such tough bastards they milk the critters. The señora says it's the best honey in Sonora. The foreman thought a little and said: The federal army shakes us down even harder when its people come through, and they don't leave us any pinche honey.

This story didn't make the güero laugh either, so she shrugged apologetically. After all, she had been a dramatic actress and singer; she'd never been good at comedy. I'm sure I'm telling it wrong, she said, to ward off criticism, and she went on with a glance at her dead man, as if he were just sleeping. He really was a talented actor; people would roll on the floor laughing when he told the story I've just told. What he stopped saying at parties was that when he asked the foreman how to find the Apaches, the man answered that they didn't live anywhere, they had their jacales and they shifted them depending on the weather and the hunting, and he could only find them if they wanted him to, which they wouldn't. Damiancito insisted on being told when they came down to the hacienda, and the foreman said: What do you want me to tell you, if I knew when they were coming I'd be waiting for them with my gun along with every cowboy on this ranch.

The güero interrupted her and she turned to look at him with the eyes of a sleepwalker, bent on tormenting the waking. Ma'am, he said, but she was quiet. Ma'am, he said again, wiping the rivulets of sweat and dirt from his forehead. She was clearly somewhere else, her body emptied of the present. Ma'am, he said for the third time, and only then did she respond. What is it, child? she asked, as if they were two strangers at a stagecoach stop. Is this good enough, do you think? he asked, pointing to the hole he'd dug. He was a little more than knee-deep. She got up, inspecting the pit as if she didn't quite know what she was doing. A little deeper, she said, I know it's hard, but make it a little deeper for me; we owe it to Damiancito. If you want, we'll just scatter stones on top of the others so the coyotes don't eat them, but Damiancito should have a real grave. The güero went back to scraping at the dirt.

She returned to her dead man, sitting cross-legged like a girl. She went on talking, maybe for her own sake. It wasn't only the foreman who considered the Apaches a ghost nation better left in peace, she said, and you've seen yourself it's best not to summon them. One day an Irish miner was passing through town and Damiancito asked him about the moccasins he was wearing. The miner said he'd traded for them at an Apache ranchería up in the mountains, on the Chihuahua side. Damiancito said his wet nurse had been Apache, and the nuns who raised him had convinced him he'd grown up strong-willed because of their powers. They don't have powers, the miner replied; they're just more cussed than anybody else. He'd asked how to find them, and the other man said it didn't work that way, but if one day he happened to be passing by and they needed something of his, they would show themselves and propose a trade; but he shouldn't wish for it, because if he refused they would take what they wanted and kill him, fast or slow, depending on their mood; and it was strange he wanted to meet a people who everyone else, the miner included, would rather didn't exist. He'd asked the miner what he'd gotten for his boots, and the miner didn't answer: he just walked off.

A few days later he met the miner again. The man was on his way out of Tesorababi, gloomy because he'd come down to find a wife and had had no luck. He had a terrible hangover, but even so he said he'd thought of the musician, and he had an idea for him: he should go to Chihuahua, where the Apaches hung around the presidios and the government gave them free food so they wouldn't go out on raids. Does it work? he'd asked. No, they ride out just the same. Why do they give them food, then? So they'll raid Sonora instead of Chihuahua. Then I should just go and talk to them? If they don't kill you, sure. Why would they kill me? Because they're Apaches. There was a strange moment then. They stood for a second staring at each other, and then Damiancito had a thought. He asked: Do they like music? The Irishman nodded, with the same sad look on his face. They have their own kind of celebrations, he said, and then he left, as if they'd never spoken.

GENERAL ESTRADA

Hero of the Battle of El Carrizal
Returns to Fort Sam Houston, Too

It was scarcely seven one morning in June 1916 when the two men met again, thirty years after they'd last seen each other. General Parker was going over pending business with his secretary as they walked the corridors of Fort Sam Houston to the meeting room where the envoys of both countries were gathered for the peace talks between Mexico and the U.S., when someone tugged his arm. Don't you remember me? It took him a moment to place the smiling face. Of course I do. He handed his assistant the notebook he was carrying and ordered him to handle everything as he saw fit, then he embraced Estrada. In English, he said he'd seen his name on the guest list and he'd wanted to stop by the rooms where the Mexicans were staying to greet him, but the minister left him no time for anything. Then he stepped back and said in a Spanish that had seen better days: Veo que no soy el único que tiene progreso aquí, general. Estrada laughed: he had just been promoted to brigadier general; both of them had been lieutenants when they had parted all those years ago, just after the internment of Geronimo and the rest of the Chiricahuas. Así mero, General Parker, the Mexican replied. But you haven't put on as much weight as I have, Parker said. Es que enviudé, I lost my wife and I married a younger woman, me trae en chinga. Parker smiled broadly: it had been years since he'd heard this particular variant of the verb *chingar*, which for a while he had used with abandon, since no other word works so well to say so many things—in this case: "she keeps me in line." Parker looked at his watch and said: We're both required to attend the official dinner tonight. Why don't we have a drink in my quarters after that? You must try the bourbon a general can get around here.

They had met on the brutal morning of August 29, 1886, on a piece of open ground in the heart of the Sierra Madre, near Nacozari, Sonora. The peace talks, first between Geronimo and Gatewood and later between Chief Naiche and Captain Lawton, had led to a relatively favorable outcome for both parties. Lawton had agreed not to hand Geronimo or any of his warriors over to the law in Arizona, and Geronimo had pledged to return with all his people to the United States in the captain's custody. It was a bare-bones agreement that would last only until Naiche and Geronimo could speak directly with General Nelson Miles. Gringos and Apaches alike all knew that the conversation would end with them agreeing to be sent to Fort Marion, in Florida, where the U.S. Army was already escorting the Chiricahuas who hadn't fled to the Sierra Madre during the final breakout from the San Carlos reservation. Azul, Geronimo's last wife, was even then on her way there with her infant daughter in her arms.

Lieutenant Estrada hadn't taken part in these initial negotiations between Apaches and gringos. At the time he was billeted with a force of two hundred well-armed, uniformed men in the city of Fronteras. Having gone to school for a few years in the United States, he served as secretary and translator for Colonel Francisco Aguirre, prefect of the district of Arizpe and head military and civilian authority in the area. The prefect didn't speak English, so Estrada's presence was indispensable.

Part soldier and part politician, Aguirre was a fat, pink little man. His pockmarked cheeks thrust up a red, repugnant mouth from which issued a nasal, always mocking voice. He had blue eyes that he felt gave him the right to anything he liked; they were sunk in the upper part of his face, an eyebrowless lump of lard. He set out from Fronteras with his infantrymen and his secretary when his informants alerted him that Captain Elpenor Ware Lawton's 4th Calvary was near Nacozari, about to return to the United States with the captives.

Though Aguirre knew he wouldn't be able to take Geronimo by force, given that the gringos were in Mexico with the authorization of the governor of Sonora, he believed his honor would be tarnished if he didn't try to get him back. If nothing else, he could get hold of Naiche and shoot him, or intimidate the gringo soldiers, who were in a bad spot just then, and kidnap Geronimo, shoot him quick, and send him off to Mexico City in a pine box.

Before he left for Nacozari, Prefect Aguirre had sent a message to Captain Henry W. Lawton informing him that though the U.S. Army's presence in Sonora was legal, under no circumstances was he prepared to let them carry Mexico's most wanted fugitive into the United States. The message noted that Aguirre had done all the intelligence work leading to his capture, and the 4th Cavalry had turned up at the last minute to steal Mexico's prey. Friends and good neighbors and gentlemen simply didn't behave that way.

On this point he was right, though his argument failed to consider that the fugitive had turned himself in to the gringos after days of talks, a manner of proceeding that would never have occurred to the Mexicans, accustomed as they were to more brutal practices: plying the Apaches with cheap liquor and massacring them once they were drunk. In these talks, the captive had bargained with lichen-like persistence for the right, once he was back in U.S. territory, to negotiate with the top military commander in the U.S. Southwest.

There was polite and persuasive language in the prefect's message, but its tone was threatening. The dispatch announced that Aguirre had more men than Lawton, and they were better armed, better rested, and better fed. It insinuated that Aguirre could cut off Lawton's passage north if the prisoners weren't returned to those who had trapped them in the first place.

Lawton received the message with concern, though it wasn't entirely unexpected. He knew he had been tugging too hard on the perpetually frayed ties of border relations, but it was thanks precisely to the prefect's encircling of the fugitive that he had achieved what no other U.S. soldier could: capturing Geronimo for real and returning him to the United States, not to a reservation from which he would simply escape again, but as a prisoner of war. He was already imagining his name and picture printed in the American papers accompanied by laudatory comments, so young and innocent was he.

Parker, meanwhile, had watched the Chiricahuas come and go night after night to discuss the terms of the agreement, had seen them preparing the medicine required to read the draft of their fate spread by Ussen like a survival map in the desert, had seen Lawton sweating—he would have lost weight if he'd had any fat to burn—as he made promises that he knew ran counter to direct orders from the president of the United States. He had smoked and smoked and smoked with the warriors; he had breakfasted, lunched, and dined with them. Like many U.S. soldiers who were curious or lucky enough to be forced to acquire the patience to understand the Chiricahuas' way of doing things, he had ended up sympathizing with them.

While Lieutenant Estrada did his best to manage Aguirre's tantrums—killing Geronimo would have meant a promotion for the prefect, and, more important, the chance to get out of the desert—Lieutenant Parker played with the Chiricahua children, giving the chiefs time to repeat the same conversations over and over, advancing by a hair each round. He had gotten to know the women, learned everyone's names, and played cards or ball and joked with warriors he had spent his entire adult life fighting. It wasn't exactly hard to learn their names: the formidable Apache army that had kept Sonora, Chihuahua, Arizona, and New Mexico on a war footing for months consisted of twenty-seven Chiricahuas.

For Lieutenant Parker, who hadn't witnessed the U.S. cavalry and Chief Cochise's horsemen engaged in pitched battles in Arizona, and who had only taken part in a few skirmishes and pursuits amid the boulders, the Chiricahuas were shadowy shirtless figures with Springfields who vanished after getting off a single, often unerring shot at a soldier's head. Like the other members of the 4th Cavalry expedition, he was surprised to find so few of them, and to discover that though the band was as battered as the U.S. troops by the physical strain of months of playing cat and mouse in the mountains, they were a group of clean, strong, good-looking people, dazzlingly attired. Maybe what impressed him most was their ability to enjoy themselves in the most wretched circumstances, because that's what these were: everyone knew that in the end Naiche, backed by Geronimo, would surrender for the last time after a war that had gone on for so long no one knew anymore why it had started.

When he saw them sitting in the canyon or the shadow of the cottonwoods, talking among themselves, playing with the children, often elegantly dressed in white with buckskin vests or woolen jackets, feet sheathed in moccasins with invisible seams, their long black hair held back with red cotton bands—more than anything else, the Apaches seemed explicable. They weren't a mystery or a force or something beyond redemption. They were a nomadic village, a few families, a group of friends who kept their wits about them and preserved their way of life despite knowing that they were on the ropes.

Of all his soldiers, Lawton trusted the surgeon most, and like every gringo doctor, the man spoke perfect Spanish. Lawton sent him to Aguirre, with a message begging the prefect to come and visit him at his camp at Nacozari so they could talk in peace, as friends. He explained there was no way he could turn over either the fugitive or his accomplices without authorization from the presidents of Mexico and the United States, but he could guarantee that no Chiricahua would ever again set foot on Mexican soil; they would be confined to a fort in faraway Florida with no way to return.

Aguirre accepted, and around one o'clock in the afternoon on August 29, the prefect and the captain sat down with pewter mugs of coffee in the shade of a cottonwood. Both were professional military men, well-educated and well-trained. Both had studied the law and knew what they were doing. Both had at this point survived the internal wars that lashed Mexico and the United States in the second half of the nineteenth century, so not only were they skilled soldiers, they were adept at political fencing.

Aguirre quickly understood that if he wanted to take the fugitive it would mean a gunfight, and he was aware that enmeshing himself in unauthorized combat with the 4th Cavalry would ruin his career. In the end, he knew that the government of the Republic would order him to let the gringos take their captive and go if they guaranteed he would never return, so he swallowed his rage and asked simply to talk to Geronimo: he wanted to hear him say that he accepted the will of the U.S. Army even though he was Mexican by birth and citizenship. Lawton understood that the prefect felt slighted more than anything else, so he accepted his terms and arranged for the two men to meet on the same field at six o'clock the next morning. Aguirre and the fugitive would each bring seven armed men, and Lawton and his officers would keep the peace. The Mexican infantry retreated to a camp ten miles away, and the prefect returned with his seven men at six on the dot the following day. He sat under the same cottonwood, where Lawton was waiting for him.

Then Geronimo appeared. Though he was wearing his muslin shirt and his famous jacket with the two suns stitched to the breast, his red band also circled his head, signaling that he was at war. As always, he came out of nowhere, followed by seven shirtless warriors armed to the teeth. His Springfield was in his left hand, dangling from his trigger finger. On his belt, slung low, was his six-shot revolver with its mother-of-pearl grip. His seven warriors, weather-beaten and sturdy as trees, closed ranks behind him when the prefect stood up to greet him. The seven Mexican soldiers followed suit, clutching their rifles and huddling together. Lawton and his men must have noticed the brilliant irony that all those present were armed with U.S. rifles: then as now, politics may change direction, but money has only ever flowed one way.

Aguirre held out his hand and Geronimo shook it, but instead of then letting it fall to his side, the shaman rested his on the grip of his pistol. Aguirre laid hold of his own pistol, which had been hanging at his right side, and shifted it to the middle of his belt without letting go. Geronimo looked at the Mexican and drew his pistol just far enough to reach the trigger if he had to shoot. The whole world froze until Gatewood, who was unarmed, approached the group. He stepped between them, his back to the Apache and his eyes on Aguirre's. The prefect mustered the courage to let go of his gun. He put his hands behind his back. Geronimo set his on his hips. The prefect asked the Apache in Spanish whether he was going with the Americans of his own free will. The renegade replied that in Mexico they would shoot him, and in the United States he would only be a prisoner. The prefect nodded and without another word he walked toward Lawton. Gatewood gripped Geronimo's right hand to make sure he wouldn't shoot Aguirre in the back: he could have done it, even though the seven Mexican soldiers would have had their pistols trained on him in an instant. Which might have been what Geronimo wanted: to die a clean death.

Through the surgeon, Aguirre told Lawton that it went without saying but he was grateful to him for keeping his word. The captain thanked him sincerely for his restraint. I'm going to ask you just one favor, said Aguirre; I don't want to be held responsible for Geronimo escaping again—after all, he has spent twenty-some years escaping from you—so I beg you to take one of my lieutenants with you. His English is good, and he can return to Mexico with proof that you have the pinche Indian in lockup in Florida where you gave me your word he will rot. The captain replied that this seemed a reasonable request. Estrada, shouted the prefect.

In 1909, when General Parker learned that Geronimo had died a prisoner of war in a concentration camp recently renamed Lawton in honor of the captain who had officially declared victory over him, what he felt most of all was rage. Now he and Estrada had finally met again, at the peace talks intended to put an end to Pershing's Punitive Expedition. Parker was only present at the meetings as the head of the military base lying exactly midway between DC and Mexico City; his role was strictly ceremonial. And Estrada's presence was decorative: he was there because he had just beat the gringos at the Battle of Carrizal, not fighting for Pancho Villa, but for the Republic that had given him some rights, a name, an education, and the means to live a regular life.

A few months before the meeting in Fort Sam Houston, down in northern Mexico, the 10th Cavalry soldiers had overstepped and opened fire on federal army troops who were blocking their pursuit of a group of Pancho Villa's men. The fighting turned serious, with much loss of life on both sides: all the officers in the field were killed—gringo and Mexican alike—except Estrada, who was a colonel by then, and on the verge of retirement. He took command, and he and his men managed not only to repel the Americans but to take enough prisoners to be able to exchange them for the Mexican soldiers who had been captured.

So it happened that Estrada was promoted to brigadier general at an age when he should have been looking after his grandchildren; the newspapers turned him into a hero of the resistance against the United States. And so it was that he'd made his first appearance as part of President Venustiano Carranza's war cabinet a few days before his reunion with General Parker. Covered head to toe in medals, he had done more listening than contributing to the discussion.

The brigadier listened carefully to the talk among the president, the minister of war, the division generals, and the secretary of foreign affairs, reading through the folder of documents he'd found at his seat with his name on it when he sat down nervously at the table in the Palacio's Salón Juárez. At the end of the meeting, once the president had left, he discreetly approached the minister of war, who had decorated him just two days ago. He said that in looking over the list of U.S. participants in the Fort Sam Houston meeting he had noticed that one of them was his good friend General James Parker; perhaps if he accompanied the Mexican diplomatic mission he might be of some use. When the war minister requested authorization to include him, President Carranza said yes of course. The hero of the Battle of Carrizal should be flaunted; bring him along and if you can rub the gringos' noses in it, all the better.

Despite their promotions, neither Estrada nor Parker had sufficient rank or influence to take official part in the talks, or to prevent the Pershing expedition from escalating. No one wanted war, but when a scorpion is angry, it stings itself in the head. President Wilson had entered Mexico to win an election, and he couldn't leave until Francisco Villa was caught or the elections were won.

By then, however, it was clear that Villa was like Geronimo: he could invade the United States, set Columbus ablaze, humiliate the biggest army in the Americas, and emerge unscathed: there was no way to catch him. Perhaps under other circumstances Wilson might have chanced an all-out fight south of the border, but now, as he was about to enter a European war of obscene scale, opening a real front in Mexico would have been folly. The verdict of the peace talks, then, was that General Pershing would remain south of the border, but with the unique provision that he could engage in close pursuit of groups of Villistas if they came near his encampment, which meant that ten thousand soldiers would be stationed on a plain, waiting for November to come and the elections to be over so they could quietly retreat.

Without any real role to play at the talks, the two generals were free to sit down to a dose of nostalgia more potent than the bourbon they enjoyed in the gringo's office after the official delegates' dinner. You and I, said Parker, were there when General Miles promised Geronimo that his reclusion would be temporary. But he was never allowed to return to Arizona.

The Mexican slowly swirled the bourbon in his glass, three ounces so dense it looked like chocolate. Twenty-three years as a prisoner of war, he said, with a sympathetic wince. In a few weeks exactly three decades will have gone by, he continued, and nothing has changed: there your people go again, mucking around like goddamn swine in the Sierra Madre. And Mexican bandits still attacking us, said Parker. Everybody knows Villa is no bandit, replied Estrada. Nor was Geronimo, said Parker. Neither Parker nor Estrada liked the shape of things. Nobody does, but it all keeps happening over and over and over again.

You know, said Parker, we all had to write very extensive reports about that day, and I discovered recently that the whole file is here. General Nelson Miles had to give a full accounting of his reasons for not killing Geronimo as President Cleveland had ordered, and the event was preserved in writing from multiple points of view and in every official and personal document available. There is one that haunts me, said the general. In a letter to his wife, Lieutenant Gatewood wrote that when Aguirre shifted the revolver to the middle of his waistband, the whites of Geronimo's eyes flushed black with blood, his eyeballs as opaque as billiard balls.

After this revelation, Damiancito began to make forays on muleback into the mountains, carrying an accordion. He would ride up to the rancherías, sit a prudent distance away, and sing the songs of the New Mexicans in versions I imagine were heartbreaking. Mostly he was left to himself, sometimes for days, so the Indians could be sure there was no group of nacionales following after him to slaughter them. When the sun went down, he would make a fire, cook something, and sleep under the stars.

He would go unarmed on these excursions—yes, he was crazy. If the Indians had wanted to kill him, they could have. Sooner or later some old woman would approach him, inviting him to dine with her people. He would accept. Getting to this point could take several nights out in the open. But it was hard not to feel kindly toward him. When he was invited to join them he would take off his hat and walk toward the fire with that grin of his that always won people over. They would ask him to sing, watching stone-faced as he played his tunes, then they would play theirs for him. Afterward, he would go to sleep next to his mule and leave early for Tesorababi, though sometimes he stayed a day or two. He knew that the next time he met one of those Indians in the sierra, they would tip their hats in greeting, though when they came down to sell in town they acted as if they'd never met him.

GENERAL NELSON A. MILES

Slave to Social Media Avant la Lettre
Commanding Officer of the U.S. Army of the Southwest

General Nelson A. Miles took off his hat and jacket. The sun was already hellish, though it wasn't yet eight a.m. He unbuttoned his collar: he was red as a lobster and sweating. Is it ready? he asked the engineer, who was having a harder time than usual setting up the heliograph because he wasn't used to doing it while his superior was watching. Five minutes, general, came the reply. The engineer was sweating heavily, too, because he didn't dare take off his jacket in the presence of Miles, who had been appointed commanding officer of the regular U.S. Army in Arizona and New Mexico so recently that no one knew yet how to behave around him. The engineer had worked until recently with General Crook, who was an old-fashioned soldier first and foremost, with needs so basic it was almost galling: he went out on campaign on a mule, and he sent telegrams only in exceptional cases—most of his instructions were handwritten and hand-delivered. Miles, by contrast, was all about urgency, glamour, and confidence in new technology. The heliograph system that he'd had sent from England worked well but was demanding. The gadget had to be carried up the mountain every day and set up in a hurry, because at eight on the dot all the officers in the general's service lined up their devices for a long-distance review.

Miles was a good-looking man, charismatic and vain; all determination and recklessness. He was a war hero many times over, and his ambition had a fixed trajectory: the White House. He knew that his blue eyes, the virile slant of his eyebrows, his luxuriant mustache with turned-up tips, and the sheer height and mass of him, almost always greater than anybody else's, would land him on top no matter what.

Is it ready yet? he asked again, glancing at his watch with his proverbial impatience. Even though he only opened his mouth to demand things, he had the kind of voice that made people feel that obeying him would lead to greater things; everyone on his team would always come out ahead. It will be ready on time, said the engineer, taking a sighting with his theodolite to calculate the location of the next plate of silvered metal, on a mountaintop ten miles away. I'm lining it up now, he added, as he calculated the proper degree of tilt for the mirror. The general scratched his chin, perfectly shaven at that hour. We don't have all day, engineer. It's not eight yet, the other man replied nervously. The general flapped his shirt by the buttons to move air in through the neck. As soon as the signal comes, announce me and order the men over there to connect us to Captain Lawton, wherever he is in Mexico. He glanced around and sat on a rock, but some sinister ants, half-black and half-red, began to crawl up his boots. He stood up and shook them off. He was fanning himself with his cap when the operator said they were getting a signal. Did you announce me? They're looking for Lawton.

Establishing contact with the camp in the Sierra Madre took the engineer another three or four minutes, which seemed an eternity to the general. When a reply came at last, he stood by the heliograph to decipher it himself. It wasn't a matter of trust, but of haste. Ask them to confirm they still have Geronimo and all the other prisoners. If you'll just stand to the side, the engineer said, and he began to send a message in Morse code, manipulating the lever, which opened and closed the shutters controlling the pulses of sunlight. The replies from Mexico took a while to arrive. Lawton says he has all of them; they're twenty or twenty-five miles from the border, on their way to Apache Pass. Confirm to them I won't be there as requested yesterday; I don't want to meet with Geronimo. Both men saw the response as it came in. It was what they'd expected, since they'd been receiving the same message every day since Gatewood had managed to drag the Chiricahuas out from under who knows what rock. Geronimo will run if he can't speak directly to you, the message said; the agreement we made with him is provisional until you confirm it. The general replied: Shoot him if you've got him there with you. Lawton: I gave him my word. Miles dictated: When have we ever kept our word in dealings with Indians? Lawton's reply was a little longer in coming than usual. It radiated the heat of mutiny: I had instructions from President Cleveland to kill him and you sent Gatewood. Miles didn't reply. The Morse code flashed again: And if we hadn't had Gatewood, we wouldn't have caught him. The general thought for a moment. He put on his cap. Tell him to head to Skeleton Canyon, he ordered. The reply from the Sierra Madre came as fast as if Lawton were around the corner. Shall I tell Geronimo we'll be meeting you there? You can tell Geronimo that, but I probably won't be coming; I'm going to send you a few cavalry units for reinforcement.

Lawton made no reply. I'm going back to the office, the general said to the engineer, send signals to Fort Bowie, to the detachment at San Bernardino, to that incompetent at the head of the San Carlos reservation; let all of them dispatch as many men as they can to Skeleton Canyon. He put on his jacket. He had already turned away when the engineer said: It's Lawton again. The general sighed. He's begging you to talk to Geronimo; he says the Chiricahuas have got something. Miles thought about Sitting Bull: he'd had something, too, better than anything the Apaches could possibly have, and he'd been betrayed anyway. He thought: Sitting Bull wasn't the chief of some tribe, he was the prince of a vast nation that fought as an equal with the United States and lost a proud, terrible war. Tell him that's exactly why I don't want to go, he said; I can't look an Indian in the eye anymore without feeling like a snake. Is that what you want me to tell him, general? Yes—precisely that.

Just past eight thirty, the general made an appearance in the telegraph operator's office. The operator couldn't bring himself to inform his superior that a shred of the scrambled egg he'd just eaten—probably standing up—was snagged in his illustrious mustache. The general must have been preoccupied if he hadn't made his usual stop at the pump before sitting down to handle his morning correspondence with Washington. General, the operator said, with a salute that was perhaps too crisp for the headquarters' communications manager. His superior, usually so formal, simply patted him on the back. His jacket was open and the thumb of his left hand was stuck between belt and waistband. His eyebrows and mustache quivered as if he were already engaged in a complicated conversation with a ghost. He collapsed more than sat in the chair beside the telegraph operator, his thumb still stuck in his belt. Exhaling, he began to dictate:

>   attention stop secretary william c endicott comma
>   department of war stop g stop nelson miles comma
>   regular army commander department of arizona stop

> mr secretary stop confirmation received from field
> stop geronimo and all in his party under army
> custody in mexico stop expected to cross border
> today stop

The general let out a sigh when the operator had finished sending, as if he'd been holding his breath. Both stared fixedly at the reels, which were as still as the grave. In Washington they weren't sitting around waiting for his report, which was always good news. Miles relaxed in his chair, removing his thumb from his belt and running it over his mustache. He felt the piece of egg, seized it between thumb and index finger, and glanced at it with momentary disgust. The silent machine put him in such a good mood that he jovially upbraided the operator: Why didn't you say something? Isn't that what friends are for? Yes, sir, replied the operator, which pleased Miles. What's your name? he asked. Warner. Next time you let me know, Walter. Yes, sir.

Miles smoothed his mustache again, smiling. Good, he said slapping his thighs loudly. Just then, the telegraph came to life. He made a face. Not so good, he said as the machine's reels spit out a new message at maddening speed. Perhaps it's not the secretary's office? he asked. The operator lifted the ribbon of paper as carefully as another man might stroke his wife's hair. It is, general. Are you sure? The operator read:

> attention stop g stop miles a comma arizona
> territory stop from secretary endicott comma war
> department stop

Here we go, said Miles. The operator gave him a look of commiseration and solidarity, not because he fully understood what was going through his superior's mind, but because he could recognize a troubled soul. As the communications middleman for the officers at headquarters, he was a kind of priest: he heard everything and kept it all to himself. Go on, Miles said.

```
general stop kindly indicate exact entry point of
prisoners into united states territory comma in
order to alert tucson sheriff stop
```

Based on the time it had taken the response to arrive, Miles was sure the secretary of war was standing next to his telegraph operator, just as he was himself. He had no time to come up with a strategy. He dictated:

```
entry point unknown comma mr secretary stop
coming through mountains stop seeking cover
because of possible mexican army cutoff stop
communications via heliograph easy to intercept
stop my boys in the field not sending sensitive
information stop
```

The reply was quick:

```
order complete halt once across border stop report
crossing point immediately so department can alert
tucson authorities stop
```

The general twitched his mustache and rubbed his hands. He gazed upward for a moment before turning his attention back to the telegraph operator's hand, ready to begin tapping the key. He dictated:

```
with all due respect comma mr secretary comma
prisoners highly dangerous and hard to manage stop
```

> strongly recommend they remain in army custody
> until final destination stop

The response was immediate:

> fail to understand stop do you not have them
> shackled question mark

The general exhaled.

> this is a tribe not an army stop most are women
> children elderly stop

The reels leapt into motion almost without a pause:

> but geronimo is shackled question mark

Miles kneaded his eyebrows with his left hand. He was aware that the return of the Chiricahuas to U.S. territory bore more resemblance to the conciliatory stroll of a married couple after a quarrel than a military march. Warriors and soldiers might be great enemies, but they were linked by a deeper hatred of the Mexicans. He replied:

> of course stop and all his braves stop

The reels were still for so long that General Miles began to think that Washington was getting information from another source contradicting him. As he waited for the response, he ran his index finger around the collar of his shirt, which he hadn't buttoned since his heliograph session. The reels began to turn.

> sending direct orders from president cleveland
> stop

Miles closed his eyes, taking a deep breath. The reel went on:

```
but your recommendation should be heeded since it
comes from the field comma a place unfamiliar to
me stop president still in new york stop await
confirmation or new instructions this afternoon
stop
```

I think that's all for now, don't you? he asked the operator. Up to you, general, came the reply; I know nothing about anything. But you've been receiving messages from Secretary Endicott for a while now. I believe that's all, general; if a new message comes I'll send someone for you.

General Miles spent the rest of the morning at work: he signed dispatches, went over plans to build more barracks at Warm Springs, and received a committee of army surgeons concerned about the problem of supply shortages in regiments all over the New Mexico and Arizona territories.

The doctors had begun an independent report on why it had been impossible to contain an outbreak of malaria affecting the regiments posted near the San Carlos River, and as they gathered information they had discovered that none of them had the materials or medicine necessary to do their jobs. While one of the surgeons was reading the report, the general began to mentally compose the letter he would write that night to his wife, who had stayed behind with the children in Westminster, Massachusetts.

Dear Molly, he thought, as one of the doctors presented a detailed list of the postings where the sick had no access to quinine pills, it gives me great happiness to hear how well you and the children found my mother. It would seem things will be easier than last year. Please give her my love and remind her I plan to come to see her myself as soon as I settle the Geronimo affair. I must spend a few days in Boston on business and I have a mind to stay with her this time, so as to spend a few hours each day with her even if she has trouble recognizing me: she is always good company. I'm pleased that she recognized the children: there's still something there inside. He hesitated a moment: it wasn't the most diplomatic way to put it, even if it was accurate. He thought: There's still something in her of the world she cultivated all her life, flowering like a garden of impatiens at the foot of an oak tree.

He nodded at some emphatic remark by a doctor who thus far hadn't opened his mouth, thinking it was just as well he'd chosen a military career over a literary one. He registered that the doctor was saying he couldn't condone such an outrage, and his nod turned into a sympathetic waggle followed by an emphatic shake of the head. After that, you and the children can come and settle here with me, like the good old days in the Dakotas, he went on composing in his head. The poor things were accustomed to moving wherever his command sent him and they likely thought crossing the country every two years was part of the American way of life. Another doctor began to speak. Miles gathered that he was talking about problems of the Black battalions, and he ratcheted up the expression of commiseration on his face, raising his eyebrows as high as he could. It's a very big country, he continued in his head, too big; and those on the other side of it simply haven't the faintest idea what's on this side. The letter carried on: This afternoon I received some doctors who operate with knives and saws, and rather than demanding lancets and scalpels, they're asking for buckets and mops to keep their operating rooms clean. There's no way to make anyone over there understand, there simply isn't. We must teach the children to understand the whole of the nation we are called to lead.

Nelson noticed that the circle of doctors was watching him attentively, perhaps patiently. I need documentation, he said. You have it in front of you, replied the Black surgeon, who, lacking most things, had ended up taking a leading role in the discussion, which was clearly making more than one of the other doctors uncomfortable. The general picked up the file lying in front of him. He flipped through the pages like a fan. This is a report, he said. No one in Washington will read it—I don't know whether there's anyone left in the War Department who knows how to read. The doctors laughed politely, maybe condescendingly. I need brief, to-the-point requests that I can telegraph to the department so they can work out a budget with Treasury and Congress. We can make that list here and now, said another doctor, and you can send a telegram tomorrow, or whenever you've next agreed with the secretary. The general smiled, pointing his index finger at the doctor: I like men of action. Another surgeon, who might have imagined himself the most distinguished—though he was simply white and old—lowered his glasses to the tip of his nose disbelievingly. Do you mean what you say? he asked the general. Or do you take us for voters? Miles replied with a melodramatic shrug, a plea for their trust. Very well, said the doctor, turning to his colleagues to inquire where they should begin. To further reassure them, Miles added that he was about to make a trip east, and he could promise them that on his return he would pass through Washington, where he would personally follow up on the matter. When the doctors began to talk among themselves he allowed his mind to drift: there was nothing just now that required his attention.

Maybe this time we should take the northern route, he went on mentally drafting the letter he would later sit down to write. Spare ourselves the visit to Washington and Cumberland, travel along the top, through the great plains, so the children can get to know the part of the country where I fought in order that they might live where and how they do. If they could see the herds of buffalo grazing under the Black Hills, if they could see the blossoming of Rapid City or Deadwood, maybe they would understand why we have to live in this hard land, doing what we do, fighting to the death with a people who only want to live in peace, like us.

He watched the surgeons making their list, arguing over the details. I'm heartsick, Molly, he thought, wanting his letter to venture into the depths where his wife served as insuperable guide to his inner self; this Geronimo business has done me in.

A discreet knock on the door interrupted the general's train of thought. His private secretary looked in without waiting to be asked. Miles raised his eyebrows. From the War Department, said the assistant, not daring to cross the threshold. The general nodded and the secretary came in, handing him an envelope. Close the door, said Miles. The young man gave him a worried look. I'll wait outside, he said. Miles saw that the envelope wasn't sealed: the telegram had been transcribed in great haste. Inside was a card written in the meager and insufficient language of telegraphs. It said:

```
attention g miles comma department of arizona stop
from secretary endicott comma war department stop
you must receive apache prisoners in person the
moment they cross the border so that they remain
in regular army custody stop president cleveland
will not negotiate stop surrender must be
unconditional for subsequent delivery to civil
authority in tucson stop orders of the president
stop please stay put until confirmation received
that geronimo is on his way to tucson
```

The general put the card back in the envelope, calculating whether he could possibly pretend he hadn't received the telegram until the next day, when the Apaches would already be at Fort Bowie, ready to be transported to Florida, and it would be too late to follow orders. He murmured a vague *back soon* in the surgeons' direction and left the office. He found his assistant waiting for him in the hallway, standing at attention.

Miles took a deep breath, exhaling slowly and pressing his fingers to his temples. Is there any chance we can tell the secretary I'm not here? he asked. He looked up at his subordinate, who shook his head. The general raised his eyebrows inquisitively, perhaps ironically. The secretary knows you're here in the office and he requested immediate confirmation that you'll follow orders. I see, said Miles. He stroked his mustache. When would I have to leave to reach Skeleton Canyon by tomorrow? Right away, said the assistant. In a soft voice he said: I'm sorry, I know the meeting with the surgeons is important to you. The general gazed up at the ceiling, as if giving dictation: An escort of twenty men, good horses, full tack. He scratched his buttocks and went on: Ask someone to give the order and prepare my horse; you may go back and confirm to Endicott that I'll receive Geronimo as a ranking officer of the regular army. Make no mention of the words *prisoner of war*. Send clear coordinates of the meeting point. Then go up the mountain with the engineer and send word that I'll be at Skeleton Canyon tomorrow. Let the Bowie, Knoxville, Douglas, San Bernardino, and San Carlos regiments be waiting for me there, camped and neatly arrayed, in parade uniform and full regalia. The secretary nodded: he, too, had read his military classics and he understood that Miles wanted to march in like Julius Caesar to impress Geronimo. He thought: He must admire Caesar. The general did have imperial dreams, and everybody knew it, but this time he had requested a triumphal entrance out of pure habit: his mind was elsewhere. Molly, dear Molly, he mused as he returned to his office to make his apologies to the surgeons and ask them to leave their sheaf of requests with his secretary. Today, Molly dear, my job demands that I throw a brave man to the dogs: the sheriff of Tucson is a thief, a dimwit, and a fanatic who thinks all that Jesus and God business is true; a shirker who's never set foot on a battlefield, never seen an enemy become a brother after being shot full of lead. Geronimo is the best soldier I ever faced in a lifetime on this country's battlefields. What's happening here and what the president thinks is happening here have nothing to do with each other.

By the time he left the office, he had mentally crumpled up the imaginary letter and thrown it away.

On his wanderings one day he came across a group of mountain Apaches. They were just a few families, he said, who had prospered at the presidios on the other side of the sierra, but chose to return to live like their elders and the slightly forgetful god who created them. He claimed they were no different from other Indians, as people believed in Tesorababi. He waited it out, playing the accordion near their camp for a few nights, and in the end they invited him to sit down to eat with them. They didn't ask him for anything and he didn't feel threatened. They were so much like other Indians that the ass didn't realize they were Apaches until he talked to one of them, who spoke good Spanish.

How happy he must have been. He did say they were more playful; they almost wet themselves laughing when he solemnly told the story of his Apache wet nurse, which to him was a serious, life-changing thing and to them only a dirty joke. Mind you, he was careful not to tell them that the woman who had nursed him was a slave. You know how he was, he hated to hurt anyone's feelings, and I guess he was afraid they would be angry. When things go cock-eyed, they really do get madder than hornets: there's no way to talk them down once they're riled up.

I asked him lots of questions about that first encounter. I could hardly believe it never occurred to them that an Apache woman nursing him down there in the middle of the country must have been a captive. He said it never did, because if there was one way they really were different from other Indians, it was that they were so proud they were actually naive. If anything, they probably thought he was the captive—they laughed so hard they cried when he explained he'd grown up in a big house with nothing but women.

And it may be he was right. They have so little truck with others, and they're so confident their way of life is the only good way, believing they're the children of their god and the rest of us are cow dung, that they probably swore there were bands of Apaches down there, too. It's how they are. If you talk to an Opata or a Yaqui they'll talk your ear off about the government, or other Indians, or the city. Not the Apaches. They go to the presidio, get baptized, learn Spanish, and twenty years later they're back in the mountains like it was a Sunday jaunt. For the Yaquis there's no going back once they've left the ranchería; the Apaches are always there even when they've gone.

Damiancito said they had accepted him, and it must have been close to the truth because he learned a few scraps of their tongue. They spent only a few weeks a year at the camp on the Bavispe River and he couldn't be with them all the time. For better or worse, he had to give his classes at the hacienda. But he lived with them on and off over the years. He got to know them; he knew their songs. I wonder whether they learned his.

He said it wasn't that they were stubborn, the way everybody says; they just had a perfect little untouched world. They seem like madmen to us because they're the only ones who are like us. The güero looked up. How can that be? he asked. She gave him a motherly smile. Haven't I been telling you? she replied. She fixed him with her gaze. They're pushing us out, she said. You're like them, you think all of this belongs to us, but we're just passing through. We're a tribe like any other, but no one realizes it. It's us or them, and whoever wins, wins. Just look what they did to him, and he spoke to them in their language.

She paused and glanced at the güero, who was on his knees at the bottom of the pit. She thought he looked like the larva of a giant Indian woman grinding corn in the metate. It's time to rest, she thought. Just fire off that last broadside of dirt and we'll cover him up, she said. That'll do. She looked at the body. I couldn't have children, so I don't know, but maybe that's how it goes: fated to be shot full of lead by the one who suckled you.

INSOMNIA

There was a single pass linking New Mexico and Sonora through the sierra, and it was called the Paso de Guadalupe. After the Gadsden Purchase, the Chiricahua Mountains ended up on the U.S. side and northern Sonora was rebaptized Arizona. The Paso de Guadalupe was also renamed Skeleton Canyon. The change erases the Arabic past of the place name with the pure hardness of Latin, a military, legalistic language, the network of empire. In Mozarabic Spain, Guadalupe was the Virgin who appeared in a stony riverbed, and in Mexico, her Hispanic name was given to Tonantzin: our mother, the womb that nurtures and devours us before and after life. Guadalupe is the mother, giver and taker of life, and the skeleton is what remains when life is done wearing us down; when Ussen can no longer hear us. And then the pass and the canyon, but there's no need to elaborate even on that, or not much. First came the Europeans screwing over the Indians, then the children of the Europeans screwing over one another to name things with borrowed words. And that is all, America, whatever you call yourself.

DEPOSITION OF LIEUTENANT ESTRADA IN ARIZPE, SONORA

After Prefect Aguirre ordered me to go wherever the 4th Cavalry might take me, to report on the detention of Geronimo and his band of warriors, I put myself at the orders of Captain Elpenor Ware Lawton, a man who liked his drink but was very kind. He told me he appreciated my willingness to serve, saying that as an officer of the Mexican army I was there as his guest. My orders were those the prefect had given me, and I need follow no others.

Once I joined the unit, I realized that his gesture had been neither diplomatic nor deferential. The chain of command was clear, but I found the battalion lacking in discipline: apparently the Sierra Madre campaign had been so rough that they moved through the world more like a posse of cowboys than a military body. Don't misunderstand me: Lawton's men were some of the bravest and most loyal I've seen, but it took them a while to regain their dash, or so it seemed to me, maybe because by then they were so thin and ragged they looked less like a troop of soldiers than a line of sheets flapping in the wind. Nor did I realize at first that when the prefect and captain met, the gringos had just reestablished contact with headquarters, so their first rations were only then arriving on muleback from over the border. Until then, they had been living on whatever they could get in the mountain towns, where nobody trusted them.

We moved fast, not that Captain Lawton was in a hurry. The only thing driving him was the urge to stop and uncork a bottle of the barley sotol they drank, calling it bourbon. Really, it was the Indians who were hustling us along. I had never before seen for myself the speed at which the Apaches move on foot over treacherous ground, old people and children and all—faster than our mounted troops. And faster yet if there are Mexican soldiers after them, because their hatred and terror of us is matched only by ours of them. The gringos have a strange role to play in this game: they're onlookers to a fistfight between two cousins bound together since childhood.

I told Lieutenant Jaime Parker, who'd been assigned to me as travel companion, that there was no need to rush like mad, or to take this route through the mountains, because Prefect Aguirre was a man of his word and my presence in the party guaranteed no one would pursue Geronimo or try to block our path. The lieutenant said he and his superiors knew as much, and they'd already sent a messenger with a note conveying their gratitude to the governor of Sonora, but the Apaches didn't trust us after years of betrayals on both sides. It was at their bidding, not the captain's, that we were riding through the mountains at such a clip that the horses and sometimes even the mules were imperiled. Those weren't betrayals, I told him, this is an ongoing war, older than the Republic; it's been going for so long that there have been times in Mexico when civilians fought it alone, with whatever tools they had at hand. Getting Apaches drunk and killing them is no military strategy, he replied. I was there in a diplomatic capacity, albeit a minor one, so I did the best I could to follow my training and what I had learned of the law at military college. I said carefully that it was more complicated than that, explaining as judiciously as I could that sometimes gringos are full of opinions, especially about Indians, colored folk, and Mexicans, maybe because they feel slightly guilty about regularly screwing us so they can live in their little houses with their little yards, as if they're trying to blame us for what they do to us—because they're also very religious. Lieutenant Parker, as is always the way with gringos in the field, told me I was probably right but he was just obeying orders. Very diplomatic he was, too, to tell the truth.

The battalion followed the Apaches as closely as it could. As I've said, command of the unit was in the hands of Captain Lawton, though because he was frequently incapacitated—due to overindulgence, let us say—it was often passed off to a surgeon whose rank was never clear to me but who had the respect of the troops and could establish order so suddenly it was near miraculous. Beneath the captain and the doctor was Lieutenant Parker, known to everyone as "El Gordo," though he was skinny; and a very strange man I hardly got to know, another lieutenant by the name of Carlos Gatewood, who though he dressed like a city señorito, rode the roughest stretches of mountain highlands with Geronimo, each professing admiration for the other. The only men under Don Carlos Gatewood's command were two Apache scouts, and I realized at once that it was they who had really convinced Geronimo to surrender, or at least they had arranged the talks that made him decide to go with the Yankees. I should explain that everything I've described so far I learned on the first day's march. I never caught sight of Gatewood or the Apaches that day—that's how far ahead they were.

It wasn't until we made camp, half a day's journey from the border—stopping early, partly because the horses didn't like the stony ground and partly because the captain needed his liquor—that I came into contact with the Apaches. I asked Lieutenant Parker to take me to them. Some I had met before: Geronimo and his son Chapo, and also Naiche, youngest son of Cochise, the legendary chief (Coche, they call him in Mexico; he was baptized José, and the people from the sierra called him Coshee, as in Apashee). Naiche isn't short and stocky like Geronimo, but tall and muscular like his grandfather, the giant Mangas Coloradas. There was also the Mimbre warrior Lozen, who had fought alongside her brother Victorio since she was a girl; with her was La Niqui, equally fierce. Loco and Chief Nana were there, too. Both were well-known figures in Mexico, the former well-loved—he was in and out of the mestizo towns in the mountains, being half-Mexican and half-Apache—and the second bitterly reviled: he was Victorio's avenger, and the payment he exacted was harsh. There were others I didn't recognize, but these few alone could've taken Delicias. There were many children and two or three grannies, twenty-seven of them in all.

I had seen Geronimo in the newspapers, every day for years. Not counting President Díaz, he was the fiercest and most cutthroat man I've ever come across; they're tough in the same way, both being Indians who devoured the whites who tried to keep them down. The difference is that if Don Porfirio had been from New Mexico instead of Oaxaca, he would never have become president—he would have ended up dead, poor man. There are other differences, of course, and I mention them with all due respect for the supreme commander of the armed forces to which I belong and the Republic that gives me my daily bread. Mi general Díaz is watchful and wary, while Geronimo is all turbulence. He's like nitroglycerin: you touch him and he explodes. Naiche makes an impression, but he's very different: he has the same grace the old soldiers say his grandfather had, as if he's at peace with himself. And the bastard is handsome like Mangas

Coloradas, too—Mangas, who even took a Mexican wife. He's commanding, but not frightening. I did see him later that day, when he was in no mood for smiling. But even having surrendered his authority to a Yankee general, he was calmly making the rounds of his people, checking that they were comfortable and had what they needed. He sat down with the old folks, joked with his men.

And yet it wasn't either of them who impressed me most. That would be Lozen. I did get a good look at her that day. She was making dinner while the male warriors played with the children. Lieutenant Parker pointed her out to me, and she was so quiet that I had the guts to approach. I didn't intend to talk to her, I just wanted to see her from up close, because the way she looked, absorbed in her task and wrapped in her shawl, I couldn't believe she was what people made her out to be. I was still some ten feet away when she sensed a Mexican approaching and turned to look at me. That was all. She didn't do as the other warriors did when they spotted me nearby, putting a hand to the grip of her pistol, which she carried slung under her navel, too, though in a cotton sash rather than a holster. And she didn't need to: her eyes were so full of death that I backed right up without saying a word.

Honestly, I would have loved to see her in the heat of battle. Not galloping down on our soldiers but just before, at the whisper of *Danger!* from the Apache god, when she would rein in her horse in the middle of nowhere and dismount. People say the other warriors would stop and circle around to protect her, and then she would start to sing softly and spin and spin, her arms outstretched as if the wind would take her, until suddenly she came back to herself, her eyes funny, shaking her head like a cat. Then she would announce where the enemy was coming from, how many men and horses, with what weapons.

Don Carlos Gatewood, who had set up camp with them, came to me when he saw me wandering around. He's tall, but not as tall as Naiche, and he's thin as a reed. He walks with a cane, young as he is. He introduced himself to me properly, but he also said, with the sad smile of a consumptive child, that if I liked I could call him Long Nose, as the Apaches did. Seeing him, I thought they probably trusted him the way they did because if it came to a fight he could be trounced by an Apache child of six. He led me to a circle of grannies, where several warriors were sitting with their children. Chapo was the only famous one. He spoke to them in Spanish as a courtesy to me, introducing me very formally as el amigo mexicano and smiling a terrifying smile that showed his teeth, like a puma. Gatewood explained that I was traveling with them so I could return to Mexico with the news that the white-eyes had spared their lives, and that they had kept their agreement to go to Florida. Only the grannies gave the faintest hint they'd gotten the message. I took off my cap as a sign of respect. Other than Chapo, they didn't even turn to look at me. Gatewood said that while I was with them I would leave my weapons in the Yankee camp, and he hoped my offer of friendship and respect would be reciprocated. Chapo scratched his belly under his shirt to show me that he, for one, was carrying a revolver, then he turned his gaze elsewhere.

Away from the camp, I asked Gatewood whether it was true he was a friend of Geronimo. I asked him in English, so he would trust me more. He said in Spanish that he had the honor of knowing him a little better than average, but Geronimo didn't have friends in the gringo army—that's what he said, gringo, and I liked him for it. The last Chiricahua who made the mistake of being friendly with us, he said, was Mangas Coloradas, and look how we treated him. I said I would have liked to shake his hand, as a token of my respect. Don

Carlos shook his head. You saw him at the meeting on the Aros River, he said, and in the uniform of a Mexican soldier I think that's the closest you'll get to him. He touched his hat and walked away without exactly saying goodbye, in an absent-minded way. When he had gone a few feet, he turned. They're very uneasy right now, he said. Once we've crossed the border you'll be able to meet him, maybe.

What struck me most about that first encounter with the quelled Apaches—they didn't know it yet, but they were already prisoners of war—was its normality. It was like walking though a camp of Pápagos, or strolling around a mountain town, where Indian women are making tortillas and their husbands are horsing around with the kids. No bitter rage or clenched jaws, none of the things reported in newspapers or whispered in barracks and cantinas; just family folk. Indians dressed in their own fashion (though not all of them: Loco, for example, was in cowboy duds) going about their business in less than ideal circumstances. I mentioned it to Parker when I got back to our camp and he said that what surprised him most when he met them was how clean they were. The Yankees have been at war with them for forty years and we really haven't learned a thing; we're the only ones in these parts who don't wash whenever we get the chance. I did my best not to laugh, and seeing an opportunity to get a dig in, I asked: Are your people always so filthy and poorly dressed on campaign? There's a kind of American innocence that always wins me over in the end: he glanced at his grease-spotted shirt, his ripped trousers, and blushed. It's been a bad few months, he said: we're desperate to cross the border, too, even if only to change out of our uniforms. That's the gringuitos blancos for you: they've got their opinions, and they never once think they might not be the best at absolutely everything. But they're a straightforward people: they're so sure of themselves there's no resentment in them, while rancor is the engine driving perhaps ninety percent of what Mexicans do. But now I'm acting like a gringo, filling this deposition with opinions, *sorry*.

The next morning we headed north—later than a person might think the U.S. cavalry would set out, though whether that was a Yankee tradition or a bad habit of Captain Lawton's I did not know. I had gone to bed early even though Parker invited me to the captain's tent for a few swigs of his sotol de bourbon. I'd had half a glass, to be polite, and then I turned in. I'm no saint, but I get tired early: the prefect calls roll at five a.m., winter or summer, and punishment is unsparing if you oversleep. The few days I see my wife when I'm on leave in the city, she says I'm on country time.

I made myself the first coffee of the day when it was still dark, then took my mug up the mountain to sit on a stone and watch the Apaches packing up and moving out as the sky brightened above. They moved quickly and in absolute silence, like jets of air—the only things making a sound other than the birds and insects of the early desert morning were Don Carlos's and his guides' horses. I was sitting at a distance, for safety's sake, but I recognized the scouts—or coyotes, as they call them here—leading the way on foot. Then came Naiche, with his family: it was easy to recognize him, slender and tall. Behind him came the people, and then a circle of warriors bringing up the rear. Watching them go, it was easy to see why no one could catch them on the march. The group set off together but soon there was a kind of explosion, each person going his own way. They don't move in a straight line but on a slant, radiating out in a rough half-moon and then reuniting at the place where they've agreed to meet in the evening. Don Carlos Gatewood rode off last, nonchalantly, as if out for a stroll; he did ride in a straight line.

I was excited to see Naiche on the move, which made me imagine that Geronimo was among the warriors in the rearguard. Watching the long figure of the chief vanishing into the sky's pink rays, the blood of Mangas Coloradas and Cochise running through his veins—blood that had ruled these lands for who knows how many hundreds of years, blood whose war cry still makes half of Mexico start from sleep, dead afraid—I wondered whether this was how Europeans felt when they saw a king. Or better yet, whether it's how the Spanish felt when they finally saw Emperor Moctezuma: a king, but also something different, something that defied explanation.

As I said, we left much later, moving as fast as Captain Lawton's headache allowed. Watching him in the throes of his hangover, I finally understood why the 4th Cavalry, proud as it is, had spent so much time searching for the Chiricahuas in precisely the parts of the sierra where they weren't to be found.

We moved along, also scattered; not for strategic reasons like the Apaches, but because we were talking as we went. It was past three by the time we reached Agua Prieta. Rations were distributed before we crossed over to Douglas, heading for the property of a Mr. Kimbell, friend of Captain Lawton. We were in Arizona now. Homesickness is a genuine phenomenon: once they had crossed the border, my companions—thus far a raggle-taggle bunch—fell into line and stood up straighter, as if their mothers would be watching them pass by from the mountaintop. The mess of blond boys turned into what Parker had always said they were but I couldn't make out: "the finest group of young men you will ever see." They stopped looking like a starving band of hairy misfits and began to look the way they saw themselves: like returning heroes, even if there were no hurrahs to welcome them and our column was hardly on parade, there in the middle of nowhere.

The Chiricahuas were supposed to be waiting for us at the Kimbell ranch, liberated from the needling of the Mexican army. It was here I learned of the plan my friends from the 4th Cavalry had been guarding jealously from me, even as we'd spent the day telling each other our life stories: Geronimo's official surrender would take place after he'd spoken with the regional commander, a man by the name of Nelson Miles. This would happen at the Paso de Guadalupe, where the rest of the region's officials would be waiting for us, Apaches and Yankees alike.

All very friendly, all very friendly, I said to myself, but still they don't trust us. What news would I be able to send to Mexico of the official surrender? And with whom? I had no heliograph to keep Prefect Aguirre informed, nor would it have occurred to me to borrow theirs: I was present as a diplomat, not a spy, though I suppose that if one truly aspires to take possession of everything beneath one's horse's hooves, it is just as good to be an emissary as a spy.

At the ranch, Gatewood was waiting for us, and so was a mule train sent from the detachment at Fort Bowie with a load of clean, pressed uniforms. General Miles's secretary had sent them so that at the surrender the general's men would be attired in a form befitting the occasion. As I watched my travel companions opening sacks of clothing like children opening birthday presents, I realized something about gringos, something we Mexicans always realize too late: we're the suckers. The Yankees had put one over on us. This was a show, a vaudeville act. They would convince their people via the press that they had fought a war and won it. And meanwhile we, the ones who had actually won it, would be left picking our noses.

We rested no longer than it took to water and feed the horses, though the parched, pale look of the officers seemed to call for more. The captain, after putting on fresh trousers, shirt, and socks, sat on a rock to sew his stripes to the dress coat he had just unfolded. He had kept them safe with touching devotion in a corner of his rucksack.

He took a single swallow of spirits so as to make it steadily—if not soundly—through the last part of the trip.

We reached the entrance of the Paso de Guadalupe while it was still daylight. The group under Gatewood's command was waiting for us. They were like a swarm of bees; a blanket that folds and spreads on command. Just now they were tight as a dry sponge. Naiche, his height giving him an air of serenity, and Geronimo, short, square, and full of rage, were waiting for us at the head of the group. The others stood at full attention. They took our measure, aware of every sound we made and all that surrounded them.

Parker and I were at the front of our squad, the captain and the surgeon bringing up the rear—we were in strict marching order now. It wasn't until we came very close to the Apaches that I could see that what from a distance had seemed a knot of bodies was a strategic formation. Arrayed around the edge of the group were the warriors, Lozen and La Niqui included, their backs to the rest of the troops as if they were protecting the heart of something. Maybe they were. They were staring intently, the way the Indians of the north stare when they're on the defensive; it's a sight it would be better never to see, because it almost always means you're about to meet your maker. Inside the ring of warriors was another ring, formed by the women I'd seen cooking and washing the evening before. All the women had rifles in their hands; every index finger was on a trigger. The old men and women inside the circle were quiet and just as still. The children kicked restively at the ground, ready to take off running.

I had no duties, nor was I consumed by a desire for things to go smoothly, as my travel companions had been since we crossed the border, so I was able to watch the movements of the Apaches as we dismounted and waited for Lawton to reach us. As the warriors scanned the landscape, they stuck out the tips of their tongues and touched them to their upper lips, as if registering a change of temperature; they didn't wipe the sweat that ran from the bands around their heads, worn to show that we were still on a war footing and there would be no surrender until they had talked to the commander. Like the women, every man had his index finger on the trigger of his Winchester, his other hand resting on the grip of the pistol he wore in front, not on his hip like us.

Don Carlos approached Parker as soon as he had dismounted, followed impatiently by Naiche and Geronimo. There they were again, just steps from me. Naiche was a mystery, but Geronimo was easier to read, maybe because Mexico had been fighting him for so long. He was much older than I imagined. In those days, he was deeply tanned by the sun, big-boned but gaunt; battered all over, the poor man. He had no teeth left, and the hardships of the last campaign had left their mark: his skin was tight on his skull. He had the squarest jaw I'd ever seen, and a nose so long it appeared to brush his upper lip. He wore his hair shorter than the others. Despite his age, he moved with quickness and agility. As soon as you looked at him, he turned a gaze on you that none could withstand. There was something in it of the hatred so often cited in the newspapers of the north of Mexico, but the base ingredient was calculation: he saw through you, as if when he looked at you he could see what was going on inside your head.

The first to speak was Naiche—a man of few words, as they say his father, Cochise, was. He spoke in Apache, addressing Gatewood, who translated for the rest of the squad. He says half the U.S. Army is down below and his people are going back to Mexico, the lieutenant translated, his calm at odds with the drama of the circumstances.

Tell them they're coming with us; they have our word their lives will be spared, said Parker. I've told them already, replied Gatewood. Tell them to wait, said Parker, here comes Lawton.

They obeyed, nervously, as the full regiment came to a halt without dismounting. Don Carlos was greeting the soldiers when the captain and the surgeon appeared over a hill. The two Indians came forward quickly. I clearly saw Geronimo berate Gatewood for something; Naiche silenced him with an authoritative gesture. Then Don Carlos turned and came back toward me, moving faster than I thought possible for a man with a cane. He took me by the arm, saying: Let's go, and hurried me over to where the captain and the chiefs were meeting, using me as a crutch to speed his way. They'll speak to you in Spanish, he said, you translate into English and I'll testify to what you say, and then the other way around.

We all arrived at nearly the same time. The captain had dismounted in a hurry and was taking off his fresh pair of gloves while still holding the horse's reins. Gatewood said to Geronimo: Speak Spanish and we'll translate. Geronimo gestured with his chin at Naiche, all the while keeping an eye on me. The chief faced Lawton without the usual preamble. We sent scouts to the Paso de Guadalupe, he said, and there are more armies camped there than we've ever seen before. I translated, substituting "soldiers" for "armies," and Gatewood made a motion as if to say he finally understood something that had never been clear to him before. He confirmed that my translation was correct. The captain told the chief it was because General Miles was coming, and he was the chief of chiefs of all Apachería and of the lands of the Navajo, Pueblo, Pápagos, and Comanches in New Mexico. He said Miles was a friend of the Great Father in Washington, and wherever Miles went there were many armies—or "soldiers," as I translated it—but they had his word nothing would be done to them if they didn't try to escape.

Naiche asked: How can I trust that you speak for him? How can I trust that Geronimo speaks for you? Lawton countered, a barb that for the first time made me think he might actually be a brilliant man and not someone who by sheer luck had ended up victor of the Apache Wars. The chief nodded. We must move along, Lawton said to Naiche; the general may arrive any moment. I translated. Geronimo whispered something in the chief's ear and he repeated the request. We want to travel among you, he said, in case there are sharpshooters. I translated. Agreed, said the captain. Yes, I said. Geronimo touched the chief's shoulder. We must move swiftly, he said. Agreed. Another thing, said Naiche: We choose the camp, on high ground; it is a place known to us. The captain revealed some impatience when I informed him of this new request, but he assented. We camp alone, but you leave us hostages. No. Then we go back to Mexico now; you'll catch the children but not the warriors, as you well know. Gatewood grew tense as the dialogue turned prickly. He listened carefully and confirmed with a nod that I had translated correctly. We have you surrounded, said Lawton, we'd kill you before you could scatter. I looked at Don Carlos, and he indicated that I should translate exactly what was said. I did so. You won't kill us, replied Naiche, you're a good man. He made a counterproposal: two hostages and no more; your officers. I translated, though I imagine the Yankee already understood. Lawton thought for a moment. The lieutenants, he said. I translated; Gatewood confirmed. Naiche looked at Geronimo, who was in agreement. The lieutenants, he said aloud. There was no need to translate. Then Naiche said, looking at me with what I can only describe as loathing: You keep this one. I was quiet. Gatewood broke in, also in Spanish, and what he said may have offended me even more: This isn't one of our lieutenants, he's just a Mexican. The gringos are decent people until they're not. Are we in agreement? asked Lawton. I had been insulted, so I didn't translate. Instead I touched my cap and turned toward my horse. I heard Gatewood finishing the job with his moth-eaten Spanish, certainly greatly inferior to the English of your humble servant.

When the Apaches had returned to the shelter of their people, a bugle signaled the troops to assemble. It sounded a call unknown to me as the Apaches discussed among themselves the agreement their leaders had reached. The warriors weren't entirely content. They lined up two by two. Lawton remained in the rear: he was transporting prisoners, so he had to play the part of the responsible officer, not strut at the front of his unit. The two lieutenants took the lead. We waited a little while until the puzzle of the Chiricahuas was solved; in the end, they slipped like snakes among the horses, taking their places in the middle of the squad. I was directly behind Parker and Gatewood, so I got only a sidelong look at the Indians: they were agitated and in a very dark mood.

I understood them completely as soon as we crossed the mouth of the canyon, the Chiricahua Mountains to one side and the Peloncillos to the other. Waiting in the valley that opened up before us—the Paso de Guadalupe itself—was the full complement of regular U.S. Army detachments in the region, camped in geometric rows with tents, horses, and wagons, each unit under its own banner. It looked like the celebration of a Roman triumph.

We passed swiftly through the encampments. All credit to the Apaches: when they run it isn't easy to keep up with them, whether on foot or horseback. The poor things were scared to death, of course. Who knows what they had imagined was waiting for them on this side of the border, but it was not what we saw before us. The neatly arrayed tents; the brio of leather and steel; the elegant blue, gray, and yellow uniforms; the tall horses, their well-brushed coats gleaming in the sun: it couldn't help but impress.

I think the Chiricahuas' fear as they crossed the gringo-occupied part of the Paso de Guadalupe was reciprocated: the Yankees must have respected them greatly to mount such a display. It was only then that I understood why the Apaches, when forced to choose, always went with the Americans, even though our own ties with them are so strong and long-lasting that we're almost the same people.

To us, they were always just bandits to be stamped out, because we'd given them religion, land, and nation, and they'd rejected it all. We refused to understand that they had their own place in history, and that their history was also ours. To the gringos, these twenty-seven Chiricahuas were an enemy army. What we had to offer them was a fitting death for their warriors and assimilation for their children, absorption into the particular Mexican fabric of sorrows and joys. What the Americans had to offer was a life of humiliation, but one in which their difference would be recognized.

Geronimo knew perfectly well where he was going, and he dragged us all through the pass at lightning speed. The men who were camped along the slopes to either side came out of their tents and abandoned their duties to watch the Apaches—the mythical force that had kept this vast territory in a state of vigilance and fear for so many years—go by along the bottom of Guadalupe Canyon. Many applauded Lawton, who surely would have preferred to parade grandly through rather than holding his horse to a syncopated trot to keep it from breaking into a run as it would have liked. He touched the tattered hat he'd kept as evidence that he was returning from a difficult campaign.

Once we had reached the mesa that Geronimo was looking for, the Apaches broke away from the party and scaled it in loose formation, scattering like goats but not haphazardly—each grandmother taking a child and each back protected by the encircling presence of the warriors climbing with one eye on the mountain and the other on the valley. Parker and Gatewood broke away from the unit and followed them up the hill on horseback, very laboriously.

Lawton ordered that camp be set up at the foot of the hill, so the Indians would feel protected: as always with the Chiricahuas, he'd ended up on their side. He came to me and said I could sleep in his tent if I wanted, since Parker would be sleeping up above. He said it with a smile, whether superior or uncomfortable I wasn't sure, though it certainly wasn't straightforward. The mystery was solved when he looked down at the ground and said: Problem is, there will be no whiskey until Miles goes back to Albuquerque. He didn't want to be left alone. I thanked him for the offer and said sincerely that out of respect for his privacy and rank, I'd rather find another place to stay; this was an important night for him. In speaking I was cured of my resentment, so I let myself be carried away by the solemnity of the moment and told him something else he deserved to hear: Now it really can be said you've caught Geronimo, captain, and that's no small thing; when the general leaves, we'll drink a toast to you. He took off his battered hat, and for a second I think he felt that maybe we Mexicans weren't the garbage he'd always been told we were. It was your people who caught him, he said; I just brought him in.

General Nelson Miles arrived the next day in a hurricane of protocol more befitting the president of the Republic than the commanding officer of the lovely but desolate wastelands of Arizona and New Mexico. He came in as if parting the seas, galloping up full tilt in a cowboy hat at the head of an escort of dragoons, apparently to prove that he was a real frontiersman. His emissaries gave enough advance warning of his coming that I was able to climb a steep slope as the soldiers were being called to assemble, and I sat myself down to watch until I was summoned as a representative of the Mexican army—if indeed such a thing were to happen.

I like the gleam of rifles and the thunder of drums. I like the flying of flags, so I can't say I didn't enjoy my stolen glimpse of a very private ceremony that suddenly felt as if it were being performed just for me.

General Miles crossed the westernmost end of the Paso de Guadalupe, where his cavalry battalions were arrayed in squares for review. At the far end stood Lawton's company, target of his advance and prow of the muster. He moved toward it, saluting and reviewing his men along both sides of his path, his manner at once soldierly and politician-like. Lawton was waiting for him on foot at the head of his unit. His lieutenants had come down from the hill where they'd spent the night with the Indians and were standing just behind him. The Apaches themselves were watching nervously from the flat top of the mesa where they'd camped: they had balcony seats, too.

Miles reined in his horse, which capered a little, and leapt down with unexpected agility for a man of his age, crisply saluting the captain. Although the display was for the general's benefit, in the end all eyes were on the victorious officer and his troops. Seeing them there, neatly dressed and in parade formation, was to know a thing that can almost never be understood about war while it's underway: Lawton's men were a group of kids who had endured indescribable hardship to serve a country that had no notion of their service. One of the longest wars in the history of this corner of the world occupied by gringos and Mexicans was ending, and the final act was happening under wraps, in the belly of a canyon no one had ever heard of, with me as the only witness.

The parties met, and I saw that Miles had many words for Lawton, who nodded as he listened, his shredded hat under his arm. Then the general moved on to greet Gatewood and Parker, though I was surprised to see that he shook only Parker's hand. I guessed that by now the captain had told Miles it was the lieutenants who were the real heroes of the day; Lawton had done well to present this information the moment he received congratulations himself, I thought. The general moved a little farther on to speak a few words to the battalion, walking along the front row and saluting the boys, who must have been awestruck.

Once he had finished his remarks, the general removed his gloves and jacket in the delightful, easygoing way of gringos and ushered the captain toward the entrance of his own tent for a talk. Miles's staff, the surgeon, and Parker followed them in.

Gatewood parted discreetly from the group, in sad and telling fashion. He was the only one who could truly claim credit for the victory, and he leaned on his cane as he walked toward the Apaches' mesa, skirting it so no one could see where he was going. No one noticed when he left, because the companies were breaking ranks now. He was alone, utterly alone—his loyal scouts had vanished among the Chiricahuas up above. Shortly thereafter, Parker and two officers I hadn't seen before came out of the tent. My comrade climbed up to the mesa with one of the officers to bring down the Indians; the other officer came walking toward me, so I stood up.

It was the general's aide-de-camp, who had come to hand me a sealed letter—I later delivered it to the proper Mexican military authorities—in which Miles assumed responsibility for Geronimo's detention and promised that neither Geronimo nor Chief Naiche nor any of the warriors accompanying them would be set free again until the day they died. That was what the officer told me, anyway. The officials who read the letter, which I delivered sealed as it was when I received it, can confirm this if necessary. The aide-de-camp also informed me that if I wanted to stay in order to personally witness the conversations between the general and the Indians and their final surrender, I could do so at his invitation. I said yes because I felt it was my duty, but also because the story of the Chiricahuas' last march had become very important to me, and I wanted to be there to see how it ended.

Following the officer, I came to the spot where the Yankee and Apache leaders would be meeting: in the shade of the oldest cottonwood in the valley of the Paso de Guadalupe. Lawton and Parker were already there, with such long faces that even their dress uniforms looked lackluster. What's the matter now? I asked my erstwhile companion. He shrugged. We were scolded, he said. They blasted us for making a deal and not arresting the Indians unconditionally. Is that why Don Carlos left? I asked. He's been on medical leave since we were south of the sierra, he said, but he left because Miles doesn't want to see hide or hair of him; it was odd he called him back into service, but even stranger that he sent for him and won't speak a word to him; he thinks he's a traitor. We wouldn't be here without him, I said. Parker grimaced. It's Lawton who ultimately deserves credit for the arrest, he said, and Miles knows it, but the deal means there won't be medals or promotions for anyone, the general included. He thought for a moment. Apparently the secretary of war is going to dress him down.

They could still put a bullet in Geronimo's head when he arrives, I said; that's what we would do in Mexico. Parker shook his head.

Lawton suggested it when we were in the tent and Miles said no. The captain looked all around and once he was sure no one was watching, he pulled a flask from his back pocket and took a swallow. He offered it to me and I felt I had to do him the honor even though I was on duty. Miles really bawled us out, he said, but in the end he's no empty uniform; when he finally let the captain speak and Lawton offered to kill the warriors, I swear I saw the general search his conscience for a second before he said no. The captain repeated the offer, he was like a whipped dog, he said the newspapers would tear him to pieces if he didn't kill Geronimo, and he offered to shoot him though he didn't like the idea either. Miles put his hands in his pockets and shook his head, saying he preferred to make a quiet retreat and be able to look his children in the face, but he never wanted to see hide or hair of us again.

The general came out of the tent soon afterward with his retinue of aides. His shirtsleeves were rolled up now and he was breathing heavily: he was in a visibly bad mood, making it clear with every move that he had more important things to do than wrap up this stunted little epic—hundred-year struggle though it was—that had fallen to him to conclude. When he was introduced to me, the hand he extended was already somewhere else; I doubt he even understood what part I played in the events of the day. It must have struck him as odd to see a man in a buff-colored uniform among all those blue coats.

A little later the Apache warriors began to turn up, as if fallen from a tree. God knows how they manage to appear out of nowhere, even when you're waiting for them in the middle of a field, but it's a mystery we'll never solve now. First the scouts dropped in. According to what Martín told me later, they led the way because they wanted to get a close look at the general to whom they'd delivered their people, to be sure he wasn't going to betray them. Then came three or four young warriors, Chapo among them; Lozen, too. Last came Geronimo, looking more nervous than angry. He wasn't carrying a rifle or a pistol: here in Guadalupe, surrounded on all sides, guns were no good to him anymore. He shook hands with the general, who treated him very deferentially. Since this was the high-flying, high-expectations final meeting, it wasn't conducted in Spanish. There were four translators, English–Chiricahua and Chiricahua–English; two for each leader, one translating and the other testifying to what was said.

Geronimo was docile, even obliging. Many said General Miles had a gift, and he really was charismatic, but I believe history was weighing on the Apache: hundreds of years of war, done and gone. There was nothing left for him but to play the fool. He began by saying that Long Nose and the other boys in command of Miles's bluecoats had told him the general was a good man, and he, who had seen so much, could say the same; he hoped appearances weren't deceiving. The general was about to respond when Geronimo raised his hand. He made his authority felt, even though his expression was pleasant—or would have been, on a face less harsh and battered. He concluded by saying that he would do the talking; Naiche wasn't going to come down because he remembered what had been done to his grandfather in similar circumstances, so Geronimo himself would fetch and carry the words spoken in each stage of talks and then come down to report what Naiche and the other warriors had said.

The general replied courteously, saying first that it was an immense honor for him to speak to the greatest warrior he had ever faced. I think he meant it sincerely. True politicians have the ability to believe the words they speak. He said that he and the Great Father in Washington were ashamed of past betrayals, that the Great Father had chosen him to govern Apachería because in the big city it was known that he would treat the Apaches with dignity and respect. Speaking with gentle firmness and transparency, he told Geronimo that there wouldn't be multiple rounds of talks; he would inform the Indian of the conditions of his surrender, and Geronimo would go up and report to Naiche. Either they would accept the conditions or they would accept death, because in less than an hour he would be returning to Albuquerque and the Apaches would set off for Fort Bowie, where they would board the train to Florida.

Geronimo replied that General Miles was surely a good man and the Great Father must be a good man, too, if he had sent Miles to talk to them. He asked the general to sit with him on the ground, and he sat down cross-legged himself. From his seat he ordered Lawton to bring tobacco, so they could smoke as friends. The captain glanced at his superior, who replied simply that he didn't smoke. I haven't come to bargain, he repeated. I plan to sleep at my headquarters tonight. Then he made a single concession: he didn't sit on the ground, but he crouched down on his heels across from Geronimo. The Chiricahua didn't protest: he knew there was no way out anymore.

Miles said he would abide by the agreement Captain Lawton had made with Geronimo in Mexico, and the Apaches would remain in the custody of the regular army, which was the only body that wouldn't sentence them to death. He said: We can return you to Mexico, where they'll shoot you—and he turned to look at me, which meant the conniving devil knew perfectly well who I was; he had simply ignored me because I was mestizo and not lily-white like him—or we can turn you over to the Tucson sheriff, who will hang you. He crouched even lower, unexpectedly fit for a man of his age, and traced an arc in the red dirt with the tip of his finger. Then he took two black stones, setting one beside the arc and the other thirty or forty centimeters from it, in a blank space that represented very clearly what he thought of us desert dwellers. He pointed to the stone by the arc and said: This is Geronimo's family and the other Chiricahuas, already in Florida. Then he pointed to the stone sitting all by itself, and he said: This is Geronimo. He picked up the lone pebble and set it next to the other, declaring: I will unite all of the Chiricahuas.

Geronimo made as if to speak, but the general silenced him with a gesture of polite authority. He took a palmful of dirt and said, pointing with his other hand: These are all the grievances between Apaches and Americans. He scattered the dirt, brushing his hand clean, and said: If you agree to spend two years in a fort with your families in Florida, the Great Father will forget all grievances and bring you back to Arizona.

Miles's aide-de-camp had told me something different; according to him, Geronimo would never return. But I understood that this was a solemn ceremony, and I made no objection. It wasn't just anyone the general was negotiating with, and I could see that the situation was extremely delicate. I sought the aide-de-camp with my gaze, not moving a muscle, and I saw that he was staring determinedly at the ground. As usual, the gringos were pulling a graceful trick on somebody. What I had no way of knowing was whether it was us or the Apaches.

Geronimo thought about it for a moment. He gazed at the stones with narrowed eyes. I never thought I'd say this about the borderlands' most famous killer: I felt sorry for him. He was convincing himself that he could trust this man. He took a fistful of dirt and said that the general seemed good, honest. Blowing away the dirt, he asked: Two years? Two years, said Miles, rolling down his shirtsleeves to make it clear the conversation was coming to an end. The Indian made his calculation in the time it took the Yankee to dig in his pocket for studs to fasten his shirt cuffs. I'll go to Florida with my family, he said. The general requested his coat. I could tell by the urgency with which he motioned for it and the way he avoided the eyes of the aide holding it, that he was deathly ashamed. It was Geronimo he was fooling. I fingered the letter in the inner pocket of my coat as he put his on. A few warriors will come with me, said Geronimo, maybe aware now that the general wasn't even looking at him. Chapo, Lozen, Nana, those who are with me down here, he said. The general smoothed his mustache. And I will go up the hill to try to convince Naiche and the others to follow me, but I can't guarantee it. The general tugged the sleeves of his jacket down to meet his shirt cuffs. If they don't come with you, he replied, they won't live very long. He looked Geronimo in the eyes—a commendable thing; no one else dared to do it—and said: You're an intelligent man. Then, unexpectedly, he embraced him. He took Geronimo's right hand between his and called for his horse. It's been an honor, he said, and I could see clearly that he was relieved; all he wanted was not to have to kill him. He buttoned his jacket and touched his hat to Lawton. You're a hero, he said to the captain, though it will be a while before anyone acknowledges it.

Geronimo and his people returned to the mesa as all the battalions that had witnessed the surrender from afar began to break camp. The Apaches would sit in council, they would spend all night asking for advice from their god, whose name is Ussen, if he cared to give it, but it was very clear that Geronimo had already decided; there would be no need to send a guard to accompany him. He asked Lawton for a portion of tobacco for the council and said they would meet the next morning at sunrise to travel to Fort Bowie to board the iron horse and go where the general had told him their families were. I can't guarantee that everyone will go, he said again, and it was sad to see him so careful, showing such attachment to life when ten years before he would have pulled the revolver from his waistband and escaped with a cry, unscathed as ever. I have orders to kill anyone who doesn't come with us, said the captain.

Though I already had the document I'd come for in my coat pocket, I asked Lieutenant Parker whether I could go along to see them off on the train. To tell the truth—which is the point of a deposition, even a routine one like this—I should say that while I wanted to go with them to finish the job I had started, to be assured they were well-dispatched before returning to Arizpe to declare the mission accomplished, I also felt that something very big had ended too quickly.

AUGUST 15, LATE

Juh died young in the Sierra Madre. If he had lived longer, he would have gone down in history as the greatest rebel Chiricahua chief.

Geronimo left Juh on the outskirts of Nacozari after the defeat of Victorio, a few years before his unconditional surrender to General Miles. The decision to return to the United States with Chief Naiche must have been hard. Geronimo was Juh's cousin and brother-in-law, but also his war shaman, his strategist and his voice: Juh stuttered, so in war councils and negotiations with Mexicans or white-eyes he would whisper his opinions into his lieutenant's ear to be repeated.

It may be that Juh isn't remembered because his name never made it into his contemporaries' annals of fear. When he lost Geronimo, he stopped making raids that people remembered. Or he kept making them, but they were clumsier, less dazzling. He was a novice under Mangas; he belonged to the council of diehards who supported Cochise in all his war actions; and he joined Victorio's campaign early on, though he had respectfully hated Victorio since childhood. Like Cochise, he was an implacable warrior and an inscrutable chief. He was also a model father—he must have been. His son, Asa Daklugie, was closer to Geronimo than his own offspring, and when Geronimo died, he adopted Lenna and Eva Geronimo, the war shaman's daughters, who were still little girls; he was also the living memory of the Chiricahua universe. It's from his conversations with Eve Ball and his faithful translation of Geronimo's autobiography that we know what we do about the private life of the Chiricahuas in the last stretch of their story.

It was Juh, not Naiche, who inherited de facto command of all the Chiricahuas after Cochise and Victorio died. Unlike other chiefs, he was always free and always at war. If Naiche had issued a call to battle, he would have been followed by what remained of his Gileños; if Juh had, every last Apache would have joined him.

He had no time to test his command. Shortly after the surrender in 1886, he fell off his horse into a ravine during a storm; no one knows the exact date. Like Cochise, he rests alone. Unlike Cochise, there was no funeral for him and no town in Sonora named after him. His memory has not been reclaimed by Mexico, nor has the memory of any of the giants of his generation. Mangas, Cochise, Geronimo, Victorio, Nana, Cuchillo Negro, and Loco were all Mexican. The gringos may have been cruel to the Apaches, but we Mexicans were left motherless by what we did to them, and we remain motherless. We've forgotten them, and the hole in our memory diminishes us: they are the brother who went away. Juh is gone, America, and that is all.

With Juh dead and Naiche, Chihuahua, Loco, Nana, and Geronimo prisoners, the last free Chiricahuas turned to mountain dust. The final warrior of the line, Apache Juan, died near Bacanora in 1924. He was shot by some rurales who knew he was an indio de razón but wanted to collect a reward that had been promised to whoever found the person responsible for killing some sheep that everybody knew had been devoured by wolves.

Apache Juan, the last free Chiricahua, was killed by foul means: shot in the back from a distance, at the entrance to the cave where he lived peacefully with his family. His mother, wife, and two daughters heard the shots and came out to see what was going on. They, too, were slain.

When the rurales went into the cave to look for evidence pegging Apache Juan as a thief and sheep killer, all they found were little pots of honey, a stockpile of corn, and a rag doll that his daughters had played with. There was also a one- or two-year-old boy.

This child, Apache Juan's son, returned to Bacanora with the victors of the last grotesque battle ever fought against a free Chiricahua warrior. The twentieth century was so far advanced now that no one even remembered it had been only forty years since Apache captives were sold as slaves in the markets of Chihuahua and Sonora. The boy was adopted by a doctor and his wife, who gave him a good life. He learned Spanish and went to school. At seventeen he was sent to Mexico City to study at the Escuela Normal and became a junior high school teacher. He retired in Hermosillo, a beloved and respected figure. In 1957, President Adolfo Ruiz Cortines presented him with an award declaring him one of the country's best teachers.

I don't know whether the president realized that the copper-skinned, broad-chested man upon whom he bestowed a medal was the son of the last free Chiricahuas. I don't know whether the teacher himself knew it. By then Apachería was just a blank spot in the desert. There are still Chiricahua Apaches today, of course, their culture alive and vibrant even if their land was stolen. But they've had to adapt to life under the governments of Mexico and the U.S. in order to survive. America, that is all.

BOOK III

ARIA

Camila was sitting peeling a heart of agave in the metate when she saw a pair of sharp-toed boots before her. It had been months, maybe—she honestly had no clear idea how long she'd been at the ranchería—since she'd seen anything but moccasins. The boots were backlit because the sky was flooded with light, the sun about to slip behind the Mogollones. When the women with whom she was frantically preparing stores of food to survive the lean months of January and February fell silent, she should have known something serious was afoot. Above the boots she saw trousers of coarse twill, pale with dust. She remembered that in Chihuahua the cloth was called mezclilla, and the diminutive filled her with fondness: she loved the language she now spoke to almost no one. She saw the belt with its sash of bullets leading to the revolver, the Mexican eagle buckle, the buttoned fly hiding the timid little cock of a criollo, the checked shirt, the fringed buckskin jacket, the soiled hat that seemed to hold off all the bad weather in the world in the swoop of its brim. The man had a straw in his mouth and a serious look on his face; he hadn't shaved in weeks. She could see from the way he squinted that he wasn't at all sure the Apache woman before him was the widow he was looking for.

Camila wiped the blade of the knife on her skirt-covered thigh and rested it in her lap, still clutching the handle. I want you to know, she said, that no matter what you try, these hellcats will skin you alive before your thumb touches the safety of your pistol.

The man clasped his hands behind his head to demonstrate that he wasn't about to do anything, and if Camila wanted she could slash him in the gut with the knife. He eyed the other women carefully; they were watching him from behind her, tense as the strings of a flesh violin. He let the straw drop. I won't do anything against your wishes, señora, he said, but first I have to know what you want: I was sent by your family to find you. The woman narrowed her eyes: First tell me who you are. He touched his hat: Lieutenant Colonel José María Zuloaga, at your service. Now tell me what family of mine sent you, when they've all been killed. It was your aunt and uncle in Casas Grandes, said the lieutenant colonel; they informed me you'd been taken captive, and they asked me to bring you back.

Camila looked down at her lap, running a finger along the flat of the knife. How did you get here without being killed? she asked. The lieutenant twitched his overgrown mustache. God knows, he replied. She looked at him again calmly. Sit down with us, she replied, and be our friend. If I sit, said the soldier, I'll have to shift my pistol, and if I put my hand to it these ladies will butcher me. You do well to worry, said Camila. He said: If I help you return to Chihuahua, will you come? The woman touched her stomach. Here in my belly the son of the manliest man in the world is already kicking, and I want the boy to be like his father. If he's his father's son, he'll be like him, but he can grow up civilized, said the lieutenant colonel. That's exactly why I want him to be an Apache, so he'll be civilized. What if it's a girl?

Then she'll grow up happy, as I never was. Zuloaga unclasped his hands, rubbing the beard that grew up his cheeks and scratching his jowls. Is this the man they call Mangas Coloradas? That's right, the chief of chiefs; if you swear to me you come in peace and you'll go back the way you came and not tell anyone where we are, I'll bring you to him; if you're seen talking to him, you might live until nightfall. Nightfall is ten minutes from now. Exactly. He had me brought here, the lieutenant colonel said, if he wanted to do away with me he would have done it on the mountain. Did you come alone? When I parleyed with his warriors they told me I could bring one man and talk to you; we didn't have to leave our weapons if we came in peace. Where is the other man? He's not a man, he's a boy, and he stayed by the river; he didn't want to come because he's Tarahumara. Raramuri, said the señora, maybe he knew best. She nodded at the women around them. Do you think these hijas de la chingada will believe me if I tell them everything you've told me? Zuloaga shrugged. Didn't you say you're Apache now? She frowned. I'm Mexican, I'm the chief's new wife, they'd like nothing better than to find a reason to cut my throat and then make up some story. The lieutenant puffed out his cheeks and exhaled, massaging his earlobe. You and me both, he said. The rustle of skirts and shawls from the other women reminded him that this could all end very badly.

From her seat on the ground, Camila said: I'm going to get up and we're going to take a nice stroll while there's still light; these ladies' husbands are the most terrifying warriors in existence, and even they are terrified to death of their wives, if you know what I mean. They sound like Chihuahuans, said Zuloaga. Don't joke, she answered, and went on giving him instructions: I'm going to get up slowly, understand? Understood. You're going to walk ahead of me and I'm going to keep my knife out while we're talking, so the señoras can see I don't trust you. Do you trust me? I can see you're a good man, but you never know; we're going to stay within sight of everyone while you say what you need to say, and then you're going to get the hell away the minute you're done; it's a miracle you're here at all. Yes, ma'am, he said, resting his hands on his hips. Camila looked back at him and said: You'd better put your hands back behind your head, the way you had them before, so I can get up. He obeyed and she rose and shook out her skirt, saying something to the women, none of whom went back to what they'd been doing before the lieutenant arrived. She said: If Mangas sends for you, whatever you do don't ask him about the cattle from the ranch, because the cows were mine, too, and here they considered them a dowry; even mentioning their existence will land me in deep trouble. Did they eat them that fast? I told you I don't want to talk about it. Sorry. They walked a short distance away, far enough that their voices couldn't be heard inside the wickiups but still near enough that it was clear they weren't going anywhere. She kept smoothing her skirt, as if she'd been woken suddenly and was still in her underthings. She touched her hair, too, which she was wearing in heavy braids. She said: They cut them up as soon as they got here, dried the meat, packed it away in baskets somewhere on the mountain, but I don't know where; they hadn't accepted me yet. You'll have to tell me about that, too. Did you come all the way just with your Raramuri boy? He's not mine, he's a Mexican citizen, they killed my Sonorans, and even a jackass who thought he was Apache and raised his hand when they asked, though it was clear he was no Sonoran. She looked him in the eyes. It hurt you to lose him, she said. Like a motherfucker, but not just him, though his death was the worst. Who else? A couple of Yaquis. Never mind them, they walked into the wolf's den; they had it coming—but where were they killed? In the canyon that leads to the valley, less than a day's journey from here. Bear Creek, she said, if they ventured that far they were crazy. Maybe you knew them, he said; I let them out of prison in Janos to come help rescue you. The twins? The very ones. Well of course; they had been locked up for twenty years, they were killers once, but they've been out of their minds for a long time now. Not twenty years, he said. Probably longer, she said, they wouldn't have come here if they'd known what they were doing, believe me. They seemed to know. They must have been sixty years old, she said. He thought about it. Maybe they were. And everybody knew they had killed a rancher. They told me that much. So the one it hurt you to lose, was he from Janos, too? I have no idea where he was from; they called him El Márquez. She looked at the ground. He danced like an angel, she said, but the idiot believed he was from Tesorababi; he said when he met the Apaches there it was like being born again. I don't know, I hardly knew him, but he was truly good. Poor man.

She looked around. The women had returned to their hearts of maguey; no one was paying attention to them. I think we can sit down now, she said, and she sank to the ground with an ease that made Zuloaga think maybe she really did like being Apache better than Mexican. So what happened to your men from Chihuahua? He smiled a little. One was a woman, he said. Elvis, she replied immediately, and she went on: I'm starting to like you. She laughed: The nun had it bad for the pinche Yaquis: she must have convinced you to let them out. In her own sly way, but so she did. And what did you say your name is? Lieutenant Zuloaga. Is that your war name or what? You could say that. You did well to bring her along; she's worth five men. I've never seen anyone shoot like her, and she didn't get much chance to practice. Why didn't you bring her with you, so we could talk? She stayed behind to bury El Márquez, with another boy from Janos, they call him El Gringo. She shrugged. Will she come and see me when she's done? She'll be heading back through the canyon, they gave her safe conduct to the plains and told her she'll be fine if she goes straight back to Janos; they don't want her armed around here. She nodded: They'll make it back all right.

After a long silence she asked the lieutenant: And you say there's a Raramuri boy waiting for you? Yes, will he be all right? There's little quarrel with them here, but don't take him into the Chiricahuas: Cuchillo Negro hates them; where did you leave him? By the river. How young is he? Thirteen or fourteen, I guess. If you don't make it out they'll probably adopt him, so don't worry about him. He can take care of himself, replied the lieutenant; Elvis taught him to shoot. She laughed and looked at the sky. Did you say he's about thirteen? The lieutenant shrugged again. I think they would have him, she went on. That means you think I'm not going to make it out, said Zuloaga after a moment of silence. Then she asked: Does Mangas know you came to talk to me? That's what I told the novice he sent me, that I wanted to talk to you; the boy told me I was crazy, but he claimed the chief said Chihuahua was all right. Everybody in these parts has been crazy for a long time: your people and my people both. So you're on the other side now? Most of the time. How long has it been since you spoke a word to a Mexican? No one comes here; we go there when we need to trade, but they always leave me here. Will they kill me? I think so, but maybe Mangas likes your daring, and if he asks me I'll tell him you're a friend to the Apaches and you were sent by my aunt and uncle, and I'll make sure he knows you're from Chihuahua; if you talk to him, keep repeating that; he doesn't give a shit that to us it's all the same country. Ta bueno. Did El Márquez translate for you when you talked to them? No, the novice spoke Spanish; a strange kind of Spanish, but still. Camila smiled widely. Goyahkla, she said, I taught him. Does your husband speak Spanish?

Either he doesn't speak it or he pretends not to, but I think he doesn't speak it. The boy told me I should just come to the ranchería and find you, and you would bring me to the chief. Then that's what we'll do, she said, shrugging. Mangas is a good man when he's not at war, and he must have had reason to send for you. She got up and said, What we'll do is this: I'll introduce you in my feeble Apache and you'll say yes to everything, then I'll leave you alone with him and he'll call someone who speaks Spanish—there are several who grew up in the presidios and worked as vaqueros at ranches down below before they went back to being Apaches. What did you say your name was? José María Zuloaga. And are you a good man, José María Zuloaga?

HELEN "ELLIE" HOWARD MCMILLAN FIXED her gaze on the tram steps, warped, crooked, and inhumanly narrow even for a dainty foot like hers. Her lawyer husband, Amyntor Blair McMillan, had leapt out of the car to give her a hand down at the Fort Houston stop in San Antonio. It was no easy descent, perched as she was on high-heeled boots and carrying a baby swimming in crinoline. She lost her balance for a moment, reaching for the railing. McMillan caught her around the waist with one arm and took the baby with the other. She looked up, and her husband watched as the expression on her face shifted from laughter to chagrin. The whole city of San Antonio, it seemed, had come to the same conclusion about how to spend Sunday, such a long day once church was out. They were all here to see the Apache prisoners.

It was the year 1886 and there were no movies yet, so Ellie had no model for ladylike displays of disappointment. And she was Texan: skinny, strong, wiry. She narrowed her eyes and said: Filth, which was more or less her general opinion of most residents of San Antonio.

The people crowding before the bars were mostly immigrant day laborers: white, Black, Chinese, and Mexican. She wasn't sure whether they were recent arrivals or whether they only newly dared to be visible in public, emboldened by the revolutionary preaching of the Methodists and Quakers who had come from New York and Pennsylvania after the North's victory in the Civil War.

Though he hailed from a family with roots in Alabama, McMillan understood that times had changed, and that an opponent's political ideas were simply that: ideas. Now and again he could even be seen carrying on a cheerful conversation with a Black shop attendant or street cleaner, or with the Comanche chiefs who came to town to lodge complaints about agreements the authorities had neither kept nor ever planned to keep. With Mexicans it was a different story: he couldn't forgive them for the Alamo. He did have good relations with the old Spanish families in the city. And after too much whiskey he could be heard to say that Chinese food wasn't bad.

We won't be able to see anything, Ellie said to her husband, raising her palms to the sky in frustration at the crowd, though she was still standing on the rickety steps of the tram and there was a long line of passengers inside the car behind her, waiting for her to descend. He ignored her complaint and lifted her up without neglecting the baby on his other arm. He set her down on the ground, not with the airy gallantry his descendants would later learn from the movies, too, but in a brisk, practical way. Nor was she able to cling to him to keep her balance, because he was already busy putting the bonnet on the baby's head—those unruly red curls spilling everywhere, almost blinding under the torturous desert sun. He performed this whole operation with no thought for the other passengers who were still waiting. He was an easygoing man, but there was no doubt in his mind about who commanded and who obeyed.

He tucked in the child's last few curls. We should go up to the gate, he said to his wife. She was still in the same spot where he had set her down, adjusting her own bonnet. You go, she said, I'll wait for you here. He turned to look at her and only then did he seem to notice that they were in the way. He tugged her by the arm and she stumbled a few steps after him before pulling free, saying she'd better go and find some shade and asking him to hand over the baby; she wasn't going to make her way through all these people just to see a bunch of savages. Don't be a donkey, said McMillan, taking her by the elbow again, it's the chance of a lifetime: they're leaving for Florida, where I'm told they'll rot in jail, forever this time.

They walked toward the gate, McMillan striding along, never considering that the motion might be uncomfortable for the miniature neck supporting the baby's solid Irish head, and his wife hurrying, picking her way along the gravel road in her high-heeled boots and lifting her petticoats so the salt grass wouldn't cling to them. Up close, the mass of people crowding before Fort Sam Houston's quadrangle gate was not just tight but impenetrable. Men and women of all shapes, backgrounds, and colors sweated flank to flank, hands clutching hats so as not to lose them in the fray. At waist- and knee-height, throngs of ill-behaved children flowed around the adults' legs, trying to be first to reach the bars separating free people from prisoners. Not even McMillan, tall as he was, could see the Apaches yet. A sensitive man, he did note that the people clustered there were being as respectful as circumstances permitted. Barely a sound came from the back of the crowd, where no one could see anything, and the people in front were utterly silent, even the children. Whenever anyone, letting moral weakness or a sense of superiority get the better of them, yelled out something, people shushed them, not because a break in discipline could spoil anything—putting the Chiricahuas on display was part of the process of humiliation entailed by their defeat—but maybe because most saw in them what they themselves lacked: endurance, determination, a pair of mile-high balls.

McMillan passed—almost threw—the baby to Ellie and plunged into the crush with a *wait for me here*. He buried himself in the scrum, trusting to the currency of his height and the double authority of his fancy hat and his profession.

He squeezed past people, making himself skinny as a cat, inching sideways: he rested a hand on the sweaty backs of the people he was pushing aside, using his weight as leverage and muttering apologies, as if he really had something to do up ahead. Finally he reached the gate and could see the Chiricahuas. They were facing forward, lined up some thirty feet from the bars, talking among themselves, seemingly unaware that already they were a memento of the wild years of the American West.

There was nothing unusual about them as far as McMillan could see: they were just three dark-skinned gentlemen, not very tall, dressed in the local fashion. Every so often they glanced curiously at the crowd, their faces expressing something more like disbelief than mistrust or fear. He said to himself: The prisoners are us.

McMillan had learned from Captain Lawton's emissary the night before the name of the officer in command of the troops assigned to guard the prisoners, so he shouted: Lieutenant Parker. A cadaverous man with a bushy mustache, wearing a uniform three sizes too big for him, turned to look at him. I'm McMillan, the attorney shouted; Captain Lawton told you I was coming. The lieutenant, who seemed more afraid of the Texans than the warriors, touched his hat and came up to the gate. He didn't offer his hand, and McMillan was squeezed so tight he wouldn't have been able to extend his. He said: The captain said you were coming with a woman and a child. They're back there, the lawyer replied. The lieutenant nodded. Get them and come to the stable door, I'll give orders for you to be let in. The lawyer lifted his top hat to hide the slight disappointment he felt at the lieutenant's pragmatism: he had already imagined a scene in which a group of soldiers pushed the gate open, linking arms to allow his wife and child to ford the choppy waters of the throng like the children of Israel crossing the Red Sea.

Even so, the lieutenant's response seemed to embolden one of the crowd to shout: Geronimo. When none of the three reacted in the slightest, he called out again, louder this time. Others, encouraged, shouted the shaman's name, too. At last the oldest-looking of the Apaches turned to scrutinize the crowd. Once again it struck McMillan that the man was acting more like a prince in exile than a beast locked in a cage. He doesn't understand yet that he's a prisoner, he thought. And he noted that once Geronimo turned his gaze on his audience, no one dared shout his name again.

GATEWOOD BEGAN THE CLIMB UP to his tent, perched high in Guadalupe Canyon where the Chiricahuas had made their camp. He hadn't expected great fanfare, but he had expected some small show of gratitude. He understood that his manner of proceeding had been idiosyncratic, the enemy army had turned out to be tiny, and the operation had attracted little publicity for want of dead bodies, but the rewards of victory were boundless, in his view: now that Geronimo had fallen, the United States was finally a single country, and every passage between the Atlantic and the Pacific was open and secure.

Granted, things hadn't turned out exactly as President Cleveland had wanted for political reasons, but it seemed to the lieutenant that he had served his country and government more than satisfactorily:

he had just turned the key in the last lock, opening the last door to Andrew Jackson's dream.

He clutched the handle of his cane: his joints hurt, and the muscles in his back ached. The climb got steeper here. He took a deep breath. President Jackson's dream, he thought, was so sinister that its vilification was the only point on which Lincoln and Grant had ever agreed, but most of the country's voters believed that the little piece of the American continent they called the United States should be theirs alone, and it had fallen to him to satisfy that demand. It was no small thing. And the general charged with welcoming the victory hadn't even shaken his hand.

He took off his broad-brimmed white hat as the slope of the mesa grew sharply steeper. He had hurried down without realizing that coming back up without a horse would be a terrible ordeal. He looked up, fanning himself with his hat, then set it back on his head and returned to thoughts of Andrew Jackson. During Gatewood's long and tedious last convalescence in Virginia, he had spent his days boring himself slogging through volumes of U.S. history, discovering that what he was reading began at a certain point to overlap with his life.

Even Jackson never dared to dream that the growing country that elected him would one day stretch to California; much less that his policy of removing all Indian nations to land west of the Mississippi would be adopted as an extermination strategy. The final chapter in this story—playing out across Arizona and the north of Mexico— was also the final chapter in Gatewood's military career. To imagine that it represented a surge in the tide of U.S. history gave his life purpose and maybe even profundity, didn't it? He looked down at the tents, the flags, the men in clean fatigues still standing at attention. Who will we fight now? he wondered.

He turned back toward the hills. The ascent seemed almost vertical: all he could see were stones and brush, almost poking him in the nose. There was no way he could know that once the Chiricahuas were defeated and the country was a monolith of continental unity, the army would have no choice but to turn itself into a machine for occupying foreign lands. Maybe if he had known that what was to come was an empire disguised as a republic, he would have changed sides once and for all. He knew that his military run was done, but he couldn't know that the rest of the officers who had served with him on the Sierra Madre expedition would be sent to Cuba and the Philippines in a murky, pathetic attempt to seize the last sad remnants of the Spanish empire. Many of the youngest 4th and 5th Cavalry recruits would return to the Sierra Madre to chase Pancho Villa during the Punitive Expedition. And many would be officers in World War I, dying of dysentery and cold in the muddy fields of France.

Thinking about President Jackson's dream wasn't helping him with the climb, so he pictured his wife instead, the way she entwined her feet with his in their bed in Virginia. He'd spent so few nights there, and now it was the only place he had left to go: his point of arrival and the place he would wait for death to come.

MILES KNEW THAT HIS FATE had already been decided when he saw his chief of staff waiting for him at the gate of the military command at Albuquerque. The officer hurried up to him before he could dismount. Miles didn't have to dig much. He asked: The War Department? Twenty telegrams give or take, general. The White House? Only two; but there's a bad word in one of the messages from the War Department. What word? *Fuck*. Miles blew out his breath. Let's see them, he said. They're on your desk. The general dismounted without waiting for the stable boy and strode to his office.

```
from secretary endicott to general miles stop
disturbing news received at war department regarding
geronimo detention stop tucson sheriffs office
reports no word received from officers under your
command regarding arrival with detainees stop we
cannot confirm that geronimo is in army custody
until you send us comma soon comma the date you
plan to deliver prisoners to civil authorities stop

from secretary endicott to general miles stop
general miles question mark as you know comma
president cleveland believes geronimo and followers
must be arrested and tried in civil court stop the
white house knows geronimo has been caught and has
received reports of no contact between officers
under your command and office of tucson sheriff
stop any news question mark

from secretary endicott to general miles stop why
no response from the posts under your command in
Apacheria region question mark where is everybody
question mark please send quick response regarding
destination of prisoners stop president is anxious
stop

from secretary endicott to general miles your
chief of staff says you and all troops involved in
apache war operations are at skeleton canyon right
now comma witnessing talks between you and geronimo
in advance of his surrender stop prefer not to
speak to the president until word received from
```

you stop delicate matter comma could end comma for you comma in court martial stop you had express orders comma none of them requesting geronimos surrender comma much less quotation marks talks quotation marks with him stop

from vice president thomas a hendricks to general miles stop dear general miles stop president requests communication with you via these channels stop please be so good as to report your availability the moment you receive this message stop

from molly hoyt sherman nelson to general miles stop a messenger has just come from the telegraph office with a very urgent telegram from the white house asking if i know where you are stop i replied to the vice president that you were in arizona or new mexico stop he asked whether i knew anything more specific and i said no stop as you can imagine comma i fear the worst stop send me a telegram as soon as you return to the fort stop i beg you stop I'm alone with the children and my lunatic mother comma i can't handle such matters stop

from secretary endicott to general miles stop ive confirmed by separate channels that you were or are in quotation marks talks quotation marks with geronimo comma negotiating a surrender that you have no authority to negotiate stop i have what i need to write you up for insubordination stop the president is furious and i am humiliated stop

from the president of the united states grover cleveland to general miles stop may i inform you

```
       comma that this is the first time in two years as
       president of the united states comma that i find
       myself obliged to pay a visit to the telegraph
       office stop it is imperative that you communicate
       with us before you make a mistake that you may
       regret stop


       from secretary endicott to general miles stop
       where the fuck are you question mark
```

GATEWOOD TOOK OFF HIS BONE-COLORED linen jacket once he had reached the top of the mesa. He sat down on a rock. Behind him was the Paso de Guadalupe. Before him, the sweep of the mountains: the Chiricahua range, and beyond it New Mexico, Texas, and the east, where no one would have to surrender anymore because now everything was going to be a single nation under the gaze of one God, all clenched in the white fist of steel that President Jackson had dreamed of.

The Apaches hadn't made camp the night before. They had slept under the sky in case they had to flee. If General Miles was as trustworthy as they hoped and talks were established, they would erect the wickiups. After taking a good look at the mountain, Gatewood returned his gaze to the surface of the mesa. People were sitting on the ground, waiting for news from below, still tense. From where he sat, the reclining men talking in small circles looked like stones in the landscape. The only group to stand out were the women, who stirred the fire, cooking something. He passed his hand over his face. The dull gleam of their hair, their rawhide garments, the glittering shawls embroidered with butterflies so abstract as to be unrecognizable. It will all go to hell, he thought. And in the name of what? A country identical everywhere; a nation where nothing ever changes, a mill for grinding everything into chaff. Utter hell, he said: everything forever the same.

ZULOAGA SAID TO CAMILA: you asked me yesterday whether I was a good man. They were walking toward the river, which was the crux of Mangas's power: his people were mountain and desert folk who could get along in barren lands, pine forests, and plains, but what made the Gileños Apache royalty was their dominion over the river and its valley. They lived to defend it, and when the U.S. Army took it, they would scatter and be lost, becoming like all the other Chiricahuas who no longer had the numbers to stand alone. It was in the river valley that Corredor was awaiting Zuloaga, who was coming to him now with Camila.

I never imagined there was anything like these lands in Nueva México, said Zuloaga, it's as green as Sinaloa, as if we were near the coast. She said: Because of this wonderful country, they can die of old age without having to learn criollo ways; they never go hungry, and they always have horses.

In their conversation the night before, Mangas had offered Zuloaga a place to stay for as long as he wanted in a wickiup hastily built for him. The Apaches had given him freedom of movement so long as he was in their camp, but they asked him as a courtesy not to carry his gun, because no one walked around with pistols on their belts among the wickiups and it would make the warriors nervous. Mangas had explained through his translator that he wasn't in charge; he just made suggestions and each head of family came to his own decision. He had already recommended that they show the lieutenant respect as a citizen of Chihuahua, but if Zuloaga fucked up, he couldn't be responsible. He had also said that if Camila wanted to go back to Janos, she could; she was his wife, not his slave, and if she chose, he would send her back after the baby she was carrying in her belly was born.

Good and evil are the business of priests, said Zuloaga, I don't know whether I'm a good man. I stand on principle. I'm not the best Indian hunter in the north of the Republic, as they say down south, but I am the stubbornest, because I believe that if you have rights, you have to buckle down and do your duty, like all of us. Please, she said, that's pure cant. The lieutenant colonel stuck the fingers of both hands under his belt. We can argue about it later, he said, and he went on: Your husband told me my pigheadedness and foolishness reminded him of his Gileños; it fascinated him that we kept coming on, even though Pisago, out of fear, had taken us on the longest and most difficult path; either we had balls or we were crazy for coming anywhere near Cuchillo Negro's territory, being Mexican, whether Chihuahuan or Sonoran, which is why he sent for me—he was curious and wanted to meet me. She gave him a sidelong glance: Don't call them Gileños, she said, call them Bedonkohes, which is what they call themselves; they'll like you better and it will do you good to call them by their name. You wouldn't believe how the kid up ahead pesters me about that, said the lieutenant.

Why did you go so near Cuchillo's land? asked Camila after they had walked a little farther. Zuloaga hiked up his trousers and belt; he wasn't used to going anywhere without a gun. We were following Pisago, who was supposedly leading us to water; I think everybody knew what was happening except me. She nodded: Same here again—I'm sure everyone knew you were coming except for me; Mangas must have told Cuchillo to let you alone because he doesn't want trouble with Chihuahua, he wants to send the message that I'm here of my own free will. Zuloaga stopped. He took off his hat and ran his hand through his hair. He said: That's what he told me last night, as if he'd been waiting for me to come; he said the child you're carrying will be Apache but also part Chihauhuan, and he wants to keep peace with the governor, wants me to carry the message. So are you a good man, Lieutenant Colonel Zuloaga? I'm going to take his word to the capital, replied the lieutenant. She smiled. So what did you think of him? Who? Mangas. The lieutenant colonel was the type who could carry on a conversation but who turned stiff and unforthcoming when he felt he was under scrutiny. He clammed up. Well, he said, he's a commanding man; the truth is I understand very well why you choose to stay here. Why? she asked. The soldier closed his eyes in impatience at the cross-examination. You weren't about to find somebody like him in Janos. She laughed. I'd have to die and go to heaven, she said. And she went on: As confident and sure of himself as he is making war or talking politics you'd never know it, but in private he's modest, shy, if you can believe it. Now it was Zuloaga who laughed, nervously. Camila smiled: He could be a Casanova. Casanova who? asked the lieutenant. Never mind, she said.

The evening before, still hesitating amid precautions and protocol she could only guess at, Camila had led him to the wickiup she shared with her husband. Mangas was kneeling outside, repairing a saddle with Goyahkla. It impressed Zuloaga that on his knees he was more or less the same height as the boy. The lieutenant greeted the kid, who proudly ignored him, as if they'd never met. Mangas, still young enough not to be bound up in solemnity, or so sure of his authority that he didn't feel the need for ceremonial displays of power, cuffed the boy in the head and said something to him. Camila explained that Goyakhla was being scolded, told not to be rude to guests. The boy made some retort and the chief laughed uproariously. Camila whispered: he says you're his guest, not Mangas's, because he was the one who welcomed you to Bear Creek. In a hail of bullets, thought Zuloaga, but he didn't say anything: he understood that he was there by a trick of fate, and they were treating him well because they chose to.

Mangas held out his hand, still kneeling. Zuloaga bent down a little to shake it, surprised, but when the chief rose fully from his position on the ground, he understood. Even though everyone had said he was as big as a wall, Zuloaga wasn't prepared to see him unfold: the man filled his entire field of vision. The lieutenant took a step back, driven in part by the need to get a good look at him and in part by the feeling that if he didn't there wouldn't be enough space for the chief to straighten up completely. Don't be intimidated, Camila said in his ear. Then aloud: I'll leave the two of you now, and she went off.

The chief was wearing a muslin shirt and trousers, with no adornment at all. He carried a satchel of woven maguey fibers. His black hair was gathered in a knot on top of his head. His enormous face was full of ridges, as if carved with a knife. There was something treelike about him: his skin like burnished bark, his knotty joints—a body devoid of fat. He motioned the Mexican toward a fallen trunk where they could sit and talk.

As soon as he sat down, the lieutenant colonel took a sack of tobacco from his coat and handed it to the chief, who retrieved a carefully carved wooden pipe from the satchel slung across his shirt. Mangas filled the bowl and handed back the sack so the lieutenant could roll a cigarette. As they smoked in silence, two other warriors, much older than the chief, came to sit with them. Zuloaga handed them the tobacco and they filled their own pipes. He passed them matches. One of them began to talk, not looking at Zuloaga but straight ahead, as if confessing to a ghost. The chief put a hand on his shoulder and called Goyahkla.

It was the boy who translated, Zuloaga told Camila the next day as they walked toward the bend in the river where Corredor was waiting for them. And the kid seems more like other Indian captains I've talked to than Mangas: you can see he knows how to have a good time, but he's like the old men, he looks at you without seeing you, if you know what I mean; there's a storm brewing in him. Camila smiled. He's very bright, she said: he learned Castilian quickly. Call things by their proper name, Zuloaga said; it's Spanish in this country.

She shrugged off the jab. The bastard loves shooting, she went on; he goes on all the expeditions as a novice, and he can't wait until they let him take his shirt off and ride in with guns blazing. He's Mangas's godson and the grandson of one of the toughest chiefs there ever was; everybody expects he'll take over some day, but he's still a shrimp. She went on, animatedly: When the warriors decide to ride out and the biggest boys strut in front of them hoping to be chosen as aides and brought into battle, Goyahkla is already quietly saddling the horses and readying the provisions so they choose him; at the rate he's going, they'll make him a warrior at fourteen, like Cuchillo Negro.

Zuloaga opened his eyes wide. Do you know Cuchillo Negro? he asked. Camila stopped walking. He's family. But Goyahkla is Mangas's favorite and mine, too; he's stealthy as a ghost, she said, right now I'm sure he's following us and he's so close he can hear what we're saying. She laughed. So be careful what you say. The lieutenant stopped and scanned their surroundings. He bent down, picked up a good-size stone, and threw it at a shrub. He's coming out now, said Zuloaga, I got him.

Goyahkla's head rose from the brush. There were branches stuck to his back, and every visible bit of skin was plastered with mud. He didn't think it was funny that Camila—whom he regarded as part stepmother, part older sister—had given him away or that the lieutenant had discovered him. He was wearing the aggrieved look on his face that he'd had the night before as he repeated what the old men said, full of complaints about Sonora's behavior and the treacherous war they were always waging against the Apaches. Stop spying and come talk to us, said Camila now; you'll meet a novice like you. Goyahkla turned and began to walk back toward the camp. Camila called after him, her voice as commanding as it must have been when she was a teacher navigating the classrooms of Tepic.

Geronimo! And he turned.

Geronimo? asked Zuloaga. The patron saint of translators: that's what I call him, and I tell him that when it's time to take his warrior's name he should choose it. She shouted again: Geronimo! Come with us, that's an order.

MILES TUGGED AT HIS BEARD after he'd gone through the pile of telegrams in the order they'd arrived. His secretary, standing a few feet from the desk, eyed him anxiously, twisting his cap in his hands. Miles met his gaze and snorted. He got up from his chair and walked to the bureau, opening it calmly and taking out an unlabeled bottle of whiskey and a single glass. He poured himself a healthy slug and downed it in a gulp. Then he poured a more reasonable amount and walked calmly to his desk. He opened a drawer and took out his pipe, some matches, and a tin of tobacco from South Carolina that perfumed the whole room when he opened it. It wasn't until he was filling the bowl of the pipe, tamping down the tobacco with excessive vigor, that he addressed his subordinate again. Muttering the words, unable even to look him in the eye, he said: You wrote to Secretary Endicott and you didn't have the guts to include the reply in the pile, is that right? I didn't include it because it was an answer to a message addressed to me, general, but I can get it if you want. Don't bother, replied his superior. Do me a favor and go straight to the cells, without a word to anyone, and arrest yourself. If the military police ask you any questions, tell them to talk to me, because you're incommunicado. He lit a match and brought it to the pipe. He inhaled. May I ask why? asked his assistant. You told the secretary of war where I was. He's my superior, general. Then Miles looked up and it was only now that the young man realized how deeply angry he was. I'm your superior, too, he said, and in these parts we close ranks. Get out of here and arrest yourself; if you open your mouth, I'll have you court-martialed and executed. His narrowed eyes and clenched jaw made it very clear that he was in earnest. The secretary saluted briskly, put on his cap, clicked his heels, and left the office.

The general got up and opened the door to shout that before he arrested himself he should tell the heliographer to report to his office and not speak to anyone on the way. Then he returned to his desk, ran his hand over his face, and drew on his pipe, smoothing the rasp of tobacco with another swallow of whiskey. Standing in the middle of his office, he began to compose a new imaginary letter, staring at the tips of his boots. Dear Molly: How could I do such a thing? How could I turn those brave men over to the Tucson sheriff? That imbecile who never fought a day on a battlefield and who goes to church all squeaky clean after hanging Negros and Mexicans for kicks? He didn't even have the guts to complain to me before he went crying to Washington. I may have seen more people die and ordered more volleys against the Indians than any other member on active duty, but those were acts of war against enemies who would have done the same to us if they could. I mean, it's not as if I agree with Gatewood; I don't think the Apaches need be treated like some opera company bringing culture to the nation, but what else could I do? Will you still love me when you learn that my career is over? That we'll never move to Washington? And what about the children? This will be in the papers.

Outside, the stable boys were unsaddling the horses to take them to be fed and brushed after their grueling trip. The unit that had accompanied the general to Skeleton Canyon had dispersed by now. He took another swallow of whiskey and felt in his desk for the box of matches. He lit his pipe again, this time calmly and carefully enough that the embers caught. He went on rehearsing the writing of his letter: Maybe my stomach has shrunk from all the Mexican food we eat here, or I've reached my quota of dead bodies, but from the moment I got on my horse to go and meet Geronimo I knew I would not put him to death, and that drunkard Lawton was right: no matter how many presidential orders we receive, we have our honor. Sending them to Tucson would have kept me up nights for the rest of my life. He took another swallow of whiskey. We'll be in Massachusetts for good, dear. The children will have to go to college if they want a career in public service, because they'll be turned away at West Point for bearing my name. He walked to the window. Pressing his fingertips to his temples, he rested his forehead on the cool glass. Will you still be the belle of all the balls if your husband is the laughingstock of the party? Will the mediocre future that awaits us tarnish your pearls? He inhaled smoke, his eyes still closed.

The office door creaked while he was slumped on the windowsill. You sent for me? asked the heliographer. The general half turned. His face was as deflated as a roasted eggplant. We're fucked, he said. The engineer raised his eyebrows. General? he asked. Miles stroked his beard, took a deep breath, and asked whether the engineer had been the one to gather information on his whereabouts. No one but my secretary knew I was going to Skeleton Canyon, he said; no one in this fort or anywhere else, precisely to prevent what's happened from happening. The heliographer closed his eyes. It was my fault, too, he said, with head bent: I ordered all the regiments to be in parade uniform upon your arrival at the canyon; I didn't know it was a secret—I checked with your secretary and he said it was all right. The general rubbed his head. Go back to your machine, he said, and inform all the commanders in the region that communications with the War Department will be going out through my office only from now on. Even as he spoke he knew that this brief would be short-lived, because he would be removed from his post as soon as he reported to the capital. Tell them that anyone who sends a message to Washington without my consent will be court-martialed for insubordination. The heliographer snapped his hand to his forehead with a *yes, sir* that the general found frankly comical. Record the time each command post confirms receipt of my message, the general went on, and when you have the list bring it to me personally, without speaking to anyone at the telegraph office. It might take a while, said the engineer. What I have to do will, too, replied the general, if I'm lucky. The man closed the door after himself, and Miles sucked in another hit of smoke and swallowed the rest of his whiskey. He closed his eyes, twitched his mustache, and got up to pour himself more.

ELLIE COULD BE PRICKLY AND stubborn, but one of her virtues was a charming, exasperating, distinctly gringo variety of enthusiasm. But when her husband said, we're going to the stables, she looked at him in disbelief, and before he could assure her that she would thereby become the only woman in all of San Antonio to see the prisoners up close, with no bars in between, she started off toward the fray.

The attorney let her go; the crush was too tight and she would soon give up. He went to sit with the baby in the shade of a white ash: she had been holding him all this time, and the poor thing was bathed in sweat. The baby's bonnet clung to his skull. Such hair didn't deserve the prison of frills and cotton, McMillan decided, and he took it off. Seeing that the child was still uncomfortable, he removed the gown's outer skirt and then the gown itself: since they had already been to church and they hadn't stopped to visit the baby's grandparents, he could be left in his underthings. McMillan took off his fedora and fanned the child, then he let him crawl on the ground, so what if he got dirty. Years later, when the man who had once been that baby was a respected judge, feared and beloved by the whole state of Texas, he would say he owed the reasonable side of his iron character to his father's liberal impulses. Comanche notions, he called them. The shade and the fanning soon refreshed the baby's shining curls.

Ellie returned looking crestfallen. Did you see them? asked her husband. Impossible, she replied, with a sigh. They're just a bunch of Indians, said McMillan; will you come with me now to the stable door? She looked at their plump piglet of a baby and took off her own bonnet. I'm glad you undressed him, she said. But isn't it better if I wait here for the tram car back so I can go home and bathe him?

Now he was the one to pout. It's Sunday, he said, and I want you to meet Lawton; he's a war hero. She scowled. How do you know him? she asked. I don't; that's what we're here for, to meet him; he's a living relic, the last officer to win the last Indian war. She nodded. That's not what the papers claim, she said. That's why he needs a great lawyer, he replied. Let's go, then, she said, and she gathered up the baby from the ground.

. . .

```
to secretary william c endicott from general
nelson miles stop mr secretary stop it troubles me
greatly to find a pile of telegrams from you on my
desk comma some distinctly unfriendly stop i am
just back from an urgent expedition to the mexican
border comma where i confirmed that geronimo and
all the rebels under his command were detained by
captain elpenor ware lawton and are in united
states territory stop i performed this task purely
out of a sense of professional duty stop lawton is
under my command comma but as you know comma he
received orders from you or from one of your
emissaries comma without any input from me stop i
was simply informed of them stop if the chain of
command is broken from the start comma it seems
to me only natural that the mission will end in
the kind of communications disaster we are
experiencing now stop as you can imagine comma I
can do little but ensure that the captain does his
job comma given that his orders neither came from
me nor passed through my office stop my role is a
little awkward stop i cannot ask a subordinate to
tell me what my orders are stop i appeal to your
```

understanding stop in any case comma i am more concerned about a graver situation that i can only guess at comma regarding which i beg for your confirmation and discretion stop i suspect comma by the tone of your communications comma that i continue to be the victim of slander in the corridors of washington comma and comma worse yet comma that this slander has reached one of my closest subordinates comma who apparently lied to you comma sending imprecise information to the war department due to pressure from some low ranking official in the capital comma just as the dubious local authorities in tucson seem to have done stop mr secretary comma it is not my place to make suggestions but to follow orders comma which I do to the letter when they are clear and delivered to me and not to my subordinates comma but permit me to remind you that information spread by politicians and reporters in arizona and new mexico is poisoned at the source stop as you well know comma the people in these territories are deeply suspicious of the army comma as they are of all federal government institutions stop do they not hate the office of internal revenue question mark are they not always spreading rumors about supposed conspiracies by the department of education to eradicate christianity in the newly occupied territories question mark the only explanation i can find for the communications chaos we find ourselves in comma in addition to the structural problem already indicated comma namely that orders to my captain are not issued by me nor am i aware of their nature since they come to him directly from washington comma is that some lower ranking officer in the war department who sympathizes with the opposition to the federal government in these lands comma has found a way to

broadcast in your office the malicious rumors i
battle here every day comma which ive previously
discussed with you comma and which im sure you've
also heard from my predecessors in this post stop
but here i am comma ready to respond to any
questions from the president comma and confirming
that the apache prisoners are currently under
federal custody and in the united states stop

GATEWOOD WHISTLED, AND THE WOMEN making yucca flower tamales turned to look at him. He asked, in Chiricahua, for someone to help him up from the stone where he was sitting. As always, they made endless fun of him until Osceola, one of Chief Chihuahua's daughters, rose to come to his aid. She approached and held her hands out to him. Gatewood had been in such bad shape for so long that everyone knew how to help him up: first he had to be yanked by both arms, and, once he was lifted from his seat, still bent double, his helper had to take the weight of him on their chest. Then Gatewood would reach up and grip their shoulders as he straightened his legs little by little, arching the small of his back and tilting up his sternum. When the lieutenant's position could begin to be described as erect, his helper had to hug him tightly around his lower back, in the lumbar region, and wait for the moment when there was a crack somewhere amid bones, ligaments, and what was left of his lower back muscles. The crunch was so intensely painful that it almost always triggered something that looked like a brief faint but that he experienced as a hallucinatory period of varying duration. The routine was particularly comical when his helper was a woman: Apache women were strong but they were short and square-shouldered, and he was tall and thin.

The lieutenant looked at Osceola's hands, ready to help, and held out his own, clenching his jaw. She said in Spanish: Ussen gave you the power of great suffering, then she pulled. It felt like a lance piercing his back, parting his spine. He saw sparks behind his closed lids. He felt himself fall like deadweight onto the woman's shoulders while she hugged his hips as hard as she could, still laughing. He had no feeling in his legs. He pushed himself upright from her shoulders while she squeezed to release the knots in his back. Then his brain flickered out like a candle, and he didn't come to until Osceola performed what the others found the most amusing part of the process: she brushed his nostrils with a tuft of hair so that he took a gulp of air and revived.

Before the familiar pain returned, Gatewood had a few seconds, sometimes longer, during which he got his old body back, free from torment. In that instant of clarity and pleasure he felt impregnated by the intimately familiar scent of the woman's hair. All Apaches had that smell, of woodsmoke and buckskin, of sweat and the dry earth that clings to stones, of salted meat and pollen. He kept his eyes closed, trying to store in the caverns of olfactory memory a smell fated to disappear from the world as soon as the negotiations down below were over and the Chiricahuas were packed off on a train to military showers, a military diet, and ordinary attire. When a woman leaves a man, he thought, everybody knows the one thing he can't bear is the loss of her smell. He squeezed Osceola's shoulders again. When he returned to Arizona after his medical discharge, if he ever returned, everything would smell of stew and the henhouse, like the rest of the country. He took another deep breath and let it out. Where is Naiche? he asked the woman in Chiricahua, the pain returning slowly to its realm. She pointed to a group of warriors lying on the ground a little distance away. Over there, she replied in Spanish, unless he had to get up to piss laughing while you were swooning in my arms.

CORREDOR AND GOYAHKLA MET WITHOUT speaking to each other; something went amiss. The Raramuri thanked Camila for the invitation to the ranchería and said he'd better stay with the horses, his tone so blunt and his eyes fixed so seriously on Zuloaga's face that the lieutenant didn't dare argue with him. Goyahkla didn't say a word to Corredor, seized as he was by envy and rage when he saw that the kid he'd been told was a novice already had two pistols in his belt and a good rifle on his horse. Zuloaga understood that certain things were beyond his power. He didn't insist on Corredor returning with him to the wickiups.

. . .

```
from general nelson miles to secretary endicott
stop no mr secretary comma im not avoiding your
questions comma maybe my last message was a little
long and the reply to your question was lost amid
my expressions of bewilderment stop the apaches
are in effective custody of the federal army and
in united states territory stop right now they are
somewhere between douglas and fort bowie in apache
pass stop as you know comma traveling with them
isn't easy comma because they bring along their
wives comma their children comma their elders stop

from general nelson miles to vice president thomas
hendricks stop mr vice president stop it is an
honor for me to inform you and president grover
cleveland directly that the rebels are in federal
custody and in united states territory stop i went
in person to confirm they had crossed the border
after a series of clashes with the mexican army
and civil authorities stop our boys did a great
```

job stop they returned unscathed and in fine form with all the prisoners they were ordered to capture stop despite many provocations suffered at the hands of their mexican counterparts comma always given to trickery and lies stop our boys avoided international conflict while doing their duty stop congratulations comma our honorable federal institutions are still functioning like clockwork stop

from general nelson miles to secretary endicott stop i am unfamiliar with this lieutenant gatewood you mention stop nor am i aware of the alleged apache surrender treaties you refer to stop i cannot make deals with the indians stop only the president or congress possess that authority stop i'm just a general stop i don't make peace treaties stop

from general nelson miles to vice president thomas hendricks stop mr vice president comma it gives me great pleasure to hear that mr president cleveland is standing behind you as we communicate stop send him my respectful regards stop here in the southwest we struggle every day to maintain the integrity and security of the united states comma as well as the dignity of the federal government comma so maligned in these parts comma and we don't always feel heard in washington stop you cannot imagine how happy my boys will be to know that we have a commander in chief who takes a personal interest in them stop regarding the presidents question stop the reply is no comma we do not make deals with the indians stop that is the preserve of the civil branch of government comma just as i myself cannot order the execution

of an enemy who turns himself in peacefully to
the military authorities with the intent of
surrendering to the civil branch stop it would
be a sin and a crime against humanity stop the
dealing of justice is a civil and local affair stop
i say this cognizant above all of mr president
clevelands great regard for the law stop our boys
ventured south of the border stop they risked
their integrity and their lives stop they
accomplished their mission in strict accordance
with the law stop the rest is the job of other
authorities stop

from general nelson miles to vice president thomas
hendricks stop no mr vice president comma i don't
know where they are now stop i returned to
headquarters in new mexico upon confirming that
the apaches were in our custody and in united
states territory stop as i was congratulating the
boys comma i was informed that my presence was
required in the telegraph office comma so i left
my men stop my mind was at ease because I knew
that captain elpenor ware lawton had received his
orders directly from the secretary of war rather
than through me stop

from general nelson miles to president grover
cleveland stop mr president comma geronimo and
his men are in arizona territory stop our duty was to
detain him and we fulfilled it to the letter and
at great expense stop it is now the responsibility
of the state civil authorities to bring them to
trial stop up until the moment i left my boys
comma the tucson sheriff had not communicated with
them stop captain elpenor ware lawton planned to
continue northward to fort bowie because the

apaches were uneasy so near the mexican border stop but the person who can best inform you is the secretary of war himself stop in all matters concerning geronimos detention it was he who gave direct orders to captain lawton comma overruling me completely stop i can only confirm comma proudly comma that my boys successfully carried out secretary endicott's very difficult and almost impossible orders comma orders that someone in the field might not have given comma with no loss of life stop i saw geronimo arrested with my own eyes stop congratulations stop

from general nelson miles to secretary endicott stop you will get no reply from the forts comma mr secretary stop upon returning to inform you that our boys had heroically done their duty i set up the emergency protocols dictated by the manuals and statutes in case of enemy infiltration of communications between the high command and the field commanders comma as warranted stop all messages from active duty officers reporting to me will pass through my office until further orders stop i hope you agree that this is the correct protocol to follow comma given that someone comma possibly in my office comma has engaged in treasonous behavior stop i have already ordered an investigation and i plan to court martial whoever turns out to be responsible for misinforming you stop

from general nelson miles to secretary endicott stop can you truly believe i think of the war department as the enemy comma mr secretary question mark much less the civil authorities of arizona comma whom it is my sworn duty to protect stop the problem is the local papers comma which do not always act in the interests of the nation since they are private enterprises stop it was they who infiltrated my office stop i regret that my messages are not clear stop there's a reason i chose arms over letters comma forgive me stop regarding what you call your specific questions comma i believe I have already responded in full stop the chiricahua apaches are in our custody stop i have no authority to make deals with the rebels stop if they turned themselves in to captain lawton my boys could not have shot them under risk of court martial stop as you know comma we have a president with a very high regard for the law stop there can be no lawbreaking as perhaps there was in past indian wars stop and we are besieged by the press beyond anything that i can recall following the dozens of battles in which ive taken part comma always in the service of the nation and always victorious in the end comma fighting the indians of the great plains stop my boys are soldiers comma mr secretary comma not assassins stop any suggestion to the contrary is highly damaging to the institution of the federal army comma and it offends me deeply stop let us hope that the civil authorities of arizona do their job comma we have done ours comma under very difficult circumstances as it happens comma and in a manner that i do not hesitate to call heroic stop the apache war has been an open wound in our republic ever since we incorporated the southwest territories and captain lawton has stanched it stop it saddens me greatly comma as a veteran of the indian wars and as a commander of the federal army comma that anyone doubts his service stop and no comma i have no idea who this lieutenant

gatewood supposed to have been traveling with the
4th cavalry in the sierra madre can possibly be stop

to vice president hendricks stop theyre en route
stop i can only contact them by heliograph stop
which is a little delayed in the mountains comma
which is where they are stop each message has to
pass through many more stations than on the east
coast stop I am heading out to make contact with
captain lawton right now stop i beg you to inform
the president comma if he is no longer there with
you comma not to give up hope comma its a slow and
laborious process in these mountains comma but I
have it under control stop

Miles rested his forehead on the telegraph operator's desk and gave a long sigh. He raised his head, and with his eyes still closed, he said: at least we've got the upper hand again. He smiled.

The operator was exhausted and tense. Messages from the local forts had piled up while he was focused on the exchanges with Washington. He asked the general whether they should take a look at them and Miles said soon, but now it was time to take a break. Can I suggest something, with all due respect? asked the operator. Why don't you write your wife a note telling her you've returned safely from your mission? I don't mean to meddle in your affairs, but she's clearly very upset. Of course, said the general; in a moment. He threw back his head. Then he got up, took his chair, and leaned it against the wall. He folded his hands on his belly, licked his lips, and sucked in his cheeks. Alarmed by what seemed clear signs of an incipient nap, the telegraph operator asked the commander whether he didn't want to send for the heliographer. The general shook his head, tilting his nose skyward and closing his eyes, and muttered: We have to give Lawton time. He fell asleep.

The general's nap lasted a worryingly long time, from the telegraph operator's perspective. The heliographer didn't interrupt until he had collected confirmation from every fort agreeing that any outgoing message would be routed through the regional command center. He woke the general, shaking him gently by the shoulder, and handed him the list. Miles read it with little grunts, taking off his spectacles every so often to rub his eyes, perhaps to show that he would have liked to sleep a little longer. When he was done, he asked whether this was all of them. Every single one, the engineer replied.

Very well, said the general. He slapped his palms on his thighs, returning his chair to the vertical position. He knew the secret mechanics of the office nap like no one else. A cold breath of tribulation crossed his face for a moment. He glanced toward the window and asked how much light was left. An hour and a half, more or less. Where was Lawton the last time you made contact with him? He was still at Apache Pass. Return to your machine and tell him to head east immediately. The heliographer took a notebook and pencil from the back pocket of his military engineer's fatigues. Tell him to head for Texas through Ánimas so no one can cut him off. In Lordsburg, he must take the train with his whole company and all the Apaches. Are you taking notes? Yes, sir. Tell Lawton he can't stay in Lordsburg; there's a detachment there. Let him camp on the hill at the Shakespeare ranch and post sentinels to wait for the train, boarding by night so that no one sees. He mustn't receive any telegrams; tell him to hide his hands behind his back if anyone finds him and tries to deliver one. He must damage the heliograph before boarding the train. Once he reaches El Paso, have him halt the train and send word to the El Paso sheriff that he's in Texas territory with the Apache prisoners and then immediately have him send me a telegram saying the following: General Miles, I just received your message; we've been marching cross country with the Apaches and we boarded the train in a hurry on our way down from the Shakespeare ranch; I've had no notice of any communications from you. The heliograph was damaged in Shakespeare. We're in El Paso, outside the jurisdiction of the Arizona and New Mexico authorities, who never contacted us. We're boarding the train for San Antonio. I'll expect word from you at the next station or a later one.

The general looked up and met the heliographer's eye. Did you get that down? Yes. To the letter? Yes. When you've sent the message and Lawton has replied, come back here and give me the paper you used to take notes. Yes, sir. Make sure that Lawton himself is present when the message is received and that it's repeated out loud to him as you transmit it; neither he nor any of the heliographers at the other stations should transcribe it. Announce that if anyone does, they'll be arrested and discharged.

IT WASN'T A BAD DECISION to break camp at the Peñascosas cabin in the morning. Our departure was a flurry of stress and chaos, but a happy flurry. Everyone in a rush, picking up, packing, cleaning. The urgency of tidying everything away and making it to the airport on time halted the ticking clock of the parting to come. By seven thirty we were all in the station wagon, the back crammed with our things.

The drive to Tucson was long and hard. The plan was to stop first at the airport to drop off Cruz for his flight, then head north to the San Carlos reservation, where Geronimo had spent much of his adult life. After this last stop on the shaman's path, we would turn northeast, cutting diagonally across northern New Mexico toward Colorado, Kansas, and beyond, returning in long marches to New York, where we would resume our everyday lives.

At first the children tried to convince their brother to come with us to San Carlos at least. I joined in; we could buy him another ticket to fly out of Denver in a few days. He was generous and patient with the kids, as he always is, but unwavering: he was cinematographer on a documentary he was filming with friends, and he had a production meeting with the crew. With me he was unequivocal: Too late, Dad, he said, and I thought of Nana saying it was never too late so long as one Chiricahua remained standing.

MILES TOOK ANOTHER BRIEF NAP, scarcely a few minutes long. When the heliographer woke him again with the news that Captain Lawton was on his way to Shakespeare via Ánimas, he dictated a new telegram, to be sent first to the president, then to the vice president, and finally to the secretary of war, though he knew all three were in the same room:

> captain lawton is in the mountains stop ive sent messages to all my jurisdictions and also to the border posts under my command stop if they halt for provisions or spend the night at any military post he will respond immediately stop its most likely comma however comma that he will spend the night in the open since he is with the apaches comma in which case we will hear from him in the morning when they reach a train station stop

He got up heavily from his chair and asked: What time is it in Washington? Nine, said the telegraph operator. All right, he said, and headed for the door, gesturing to the heliographer to follow. In the corridor, he asked for the man's notes. The engineer ripped a couple of pages from his notebook and handed them to him. Ugly handwriting, the general said, glancing at them then crumpling them up. He put them in his mouth, chewed, and swallowed. They exited the barrack offices and walked down three corridors and across two courtyards to the cells of the military police. They went in.

The general asked for news of his secretary. He's incommunicado, said the sergeant on guard. Can I see him? The three advanced to a vault with a barred gate that was generally used to hold natives and Mexicans; never white men, much less officers.

The sergeant opened the door. The secretary was lying on a metal cot with no mattress. He rose and saluted without a word. The general asked the sergeant: Has he opened his mouth? Not since he told me he was supposed to be incommunicado, sir. Nothing? The military policeman thought for a moment. He asked for water, he said. The general scratched his nose and gave a dramatic shake of his head. Gag him, he said, and chain him to a latrine, because I need this cell. Then he pointed at the heliographer. I want him in here, he ordered. If he speaks a single word or writes on the wall or does anything whatsoever, let me know and we'll punish him, too. Yes, sir. Neither of the prisoners protested.

The general went to his room for a quilt and a chamber pot. Then he stopped by the armory to request two sets of handcuffs and a chain. He returned to the telegraph operator's office and chained him to a chair; the operator put up no resistance. He set the chamber pot under the chair, in case the operator needed to piss, and he left enough slack in the chain securing his hands so that he could lower his trousers. He draped the quilt over his shoulders. We're going to stay here nice and quiet, he said, putting a hand on his shoulder with something like tenderness, until Lawton gets to Texas; if you need to take a shit, hold it in. Yes, sir, said the operator, and he added: Don't you want to write to your wife first? Miles took his pocket handkerchief and gagged the man, shaking his head with perhaps genuine sadness. He patted the operator's shoulder again, looking at his watch: It'll be four in the morning before the captain reaches El Paso, he said; get some rest. He headed to his rooms. On the way, he was already composing another letter to his wife. Dear Molly, he thought, we may have dodged a bullet.

THEIR PATH ALONG THE EDGE of the canal in the shade of a row of ash trees was pleasant but the walk around the quadrangle wall seemed long under the late-summer sun. McMillan sat the baby on his shoulders to keep him cool. He had put his own hat on the child's head, which made the baby burst out laughing and then kept him entertained. At the stable gate they discovered that they would not be alone here either: a dozen reporters armed with notebooks, photographers, and narrow-brimmed little East Coast hats were waiting for someone to heed their pleas. A low-ranking elderly soldier was on guard inside the closed gate. His gaze was fixed on some point in the distance above the reporters' bored faces.

McMillan approached the gate and informed the soldier as discreetly as he could that Lieutenant Parker had said he would send for him. The soldier touched his cap and took a ring of keys from the pocket of his fatigue jacket. From the way he groped for the ring, extracted it, and selected the right key for the lock, it was clear why he had never advanced beyond corporal. McMillan, with the child still on his shoulders, turned to his wife to wave her closer. One of the reporters asked Ellie what they were doing there, and she replied with naive pride that her husband was the lawyer of the hero who had brought Geronimo to bay. Immediately they were swarmed, the reporters asking McMillan questions about his client's case, to which the lawyer had no answers as yet. Was it true that the captain would be court-martialed upon his return to the East Coast? Did he know anything about General Miles's possible resignation? What did his client think about the fact that he hadn't been decorated? Did he plan to send Geronimo back to the authorities in Tucson or keep him in federal custody? The lawyer understood now why the captain's emissary had been so insistent he should visit on a Sunday with his family. He replied that as they could see he was making a courtesy call with his wife and son; would they not respect the Lord's day and let them pass? He ushered his wife through the open door under his upraised arm and then slipped in himself.

The corporal barred the gate again, as if the reporters didn't exist. McMillan didn't glance back even though they continued to lob questions at him as he made his way into the quadrangle behind his wife, the child on his shoulders perhaps asleep now under his hat. The soldier caught up with them and asked whether Parker had said where they should meet. He didn't say specifically, McMillan replied; he told me I should come today if I wanted to meet Geronimo.

Ellie stopped and turned. You didn't tell me we were going to meet him, she said. It was a surprise, he replied, a smile on his face. She shook her head: It isn't the same as watching them through a gate, especially with the baby; he's a bandit, a murderer. McMillan cast a glance at the soldier, who was gazing into the stables as if nothing were amiss. He replied: They're prisoners, unarmed and in army custody; nothing can happen. But what if it does? How many children did Geronimo kill in Arizona? Sonora? Don't you read the papers? McMillan didn't read the papers. He turned again to the soldier, this time clearing his throat to get his attention and then addressing him directly by his rank. How dangerous are the prisoners? he asked once the other man was listening. They don't do nothing, the corporal said; I dunno, though. I'm from here, I fought the Comanches, and you wouldn't catch me alone in a room with one of them, even dead. Ellie raised her eyebrows. With you dead or him dead? Him. McMillan scratched his nose and said: If Geronimo is in town and he's unarmed, I'm not going to leave without meeting him.

It was clear that this was his final word on the subject and no matter what happened he was going ahead. You can stay here if you want, he said, but the baby and I are going: he'll tell his children and his children will tell their children.

HE WAS RIGHT: THE GREAT-GRANDSON of that baby told me the story I'm telling here.

SHE GAVE IN. ALL RIGHT, SHE SAID, but only if the captain guarantees nothing will happen. McMillan asked the corporal: Should we stop at Lawton's office first? The corporal shrugged. The captain's a late riser, he said, and I believe the gentlemen from Washington are going to question him again. He raised his cap and ran his hand through his thinning, sweaty hair before concluding: Thought you were here to help with that. The lawyer had known the captain had problems, but he hadn't realized they were so serious. That's between him and me, he said. Can we see him? The corporal shook his head. My orders are to take you to El Gordo Parker, the skinny fellow who spends all day with the Apaches, he and another fellow, a Mexican—nobody knows why he's here. Anyway, they're the only ones who talk to Lawton; they'll let you know.

The lawyer glanced at his wife, who nodded her agreement. Let's go, he said to the corporal, who replaced his cap and, before they moved on, revealed the depths of his bureaucratic soul: There's one little problem, he said. Geronimo is on display right now, but once we get to the barracks his shift will be over and you'll be able to talk to Parker. McMillan glanced at Ellie again. Let's go, she said. The lawyer touched his son's legs. Is the child all right? he asked his wife. He's fast asleep, she replied. Is he still wearing my hat? He's in no danger of sunstroke, she said, and she looked at the guard. Let's go, she repeated.

IT WAS JUST PAST THREE IN THE MORNING when Miles, in his pajamas and robe, opened the door to the telegraph office. The operator, who was awake, heard him cross the threshold and turned to him with a look demanding urgent action. Did something come? the general asked, ungagging him. From the White House, the operator replied, his mouth like sandpaper from the cloth on his tongue. Shit, said the general, who hadn't had the courtesy even to bring a glass of water. What do they say? he asked. I couldn't read it, replied the operator, my hands aren't free. The commander uncuffed him, checking the chamber pot as he did; he saw with relief that it hadn't been used. The telegraph operator reached for the roll of paper. It's from the president, he said, and he read it: "any news comma general question mark." How long ago did it arrive? asked Miles. Three minutes at most. What time is it in Washington? It just struck five. The general massaged his neck. Let's reply, he said, taking his spectacles from the pocket of his robe, as if he needed them. He dictated:

> weve been waiting by the telegraph machine comma
> mr president comma since our last communication
> stop i dont know what route captain lawton may
> have taken but be assured that the moment he comes
> to a place where my messages can reach him comma
> he will be in touch stop i had hoped they would
> spend the night at a garrison comma but they must
> have slept out in the open comma as they generally
> do when traveling with savages stop perhaps theyve
> followed an apache trail through the mountains
> stop in which case it will take them a little
> longer to reply stop do you want me to go out and
> look for them myself question mark

The general scratched his belly in satisfaction, put his spectacles back in the breast pocket of his robe, and sat down, thinking about sleeping for a few more hours. The telegraph machine hummed again as soon as he was settled. He said: Ugh. When the message had finished printing on the strip of paper, the operator read it to him:

> stay where you are stop as soon as lawton reaches
> a place where he can read your telegram comma
> order him to halt and request instructions stop

The general grimaced. He's pissed, he said. He closed his eyes and slept.

GATEWOOD FELT MODESTLY GRATIFIED THAT Naiche would reach out a hand to be helped up from the ground. It was a typically virile Apache move: asking for help when it wasn't needed, perhaps just to make a connection. The lieutenant had no strength, but even so the Chiricahuas often asked him for help, a gesture of trust that struck him as noble. Jefe, Gatewood said, once Naiche was standing. The Indian put his hand on Gatewood's shoulder and said, in Chiricahua: Chief of everybody but you, Long Nose. He smiled and added: Long Nose, lone wolf. Gatewood returned the smile and repeated the epithet by which the Apache was known in Mexican newspapers: Nanche, jefe de jefes y terror de la sierra. And he went on: Here we part ways and I don't know whether we'll see each other again, so I propose you walk me to my horse. The chief put his arm around the lieutenant's shoulders. It was so long he could sling it around the lieutenant's neck in friendly fashion and still comfortably reach Gatewood's opposite elbow to support him—and Gatewood was a tall man, too.

They soon left behind the rest of the Chiricahuas, who had returned to what they were doing once the daily comedy of Gatewood's struggle to rise was over. The lieutenant broke the silence: This is like death, chief. I doubt we'll see each other again; you'll have to say goodbye to my brother Geronimo for me, too. The Indian replied with words his father had spoken on perhaps a more solemn occasion: True friends always meet again. On this side or the other, he added. The lieutenant lowered his gaze. Not this side, he said, I'll either be discharged or given a desk job on the coast. The other side, then, said Naiche; it won't be hard to find you with that nose Ussen gave you. We won't see each other there either, said the gringo; I'm going to heaven for saving your ass and Geronimo's, and you'll be going to hell for killing all those Mexicans. The Chiricahua shook his head: I expect God's reward for that, so I'll see you there if you up your game. They were approaching the edge of the mesa, and Gatewood still couldn't see the horses. The Apaches had left the animals at the bottom of the slope because it was quicker to descend on foot if they had to flee. The lieutenant twitched his mustache. Not to worry, said Naiche, I can carry you, so long as you blow your nose first.

. . .

> attention stop mr president s stop grover cleveland
> comma at the white house comma from stop g stop
> nelson miles stop as I suspected comma mr president
> comma they made camp in the mountains comma
> outside Shakespeare comma new mexico stop they
> boarded the train without visiting the local
> garrison comma as is the usual practice on
> campaign stop they didnt receive our communication
> until the convoy arrived in el paso stop they are
> halted there comma awaiting your instructions stop

CAMILA SAID: IT'S AS IF YOU AREN'T FROM CHIHUAHUA; it's as if you're from my childhood and you're still a boy. As if you've crawled your way out of a pit and I'm here up above. In my mind, you're not from Buenaventura, you're from someplace that feels remote to me already and your boots are caked with moon dust. Everything got turned around when I was taken. It was awful, terrible: I didn't know I could endure such pain. If I had thought of the ranch, of the tables full of food in Janos, I wouldn't have made it.

They were sitting by the river. Camila scratched her head, casting her gaze over the water, past the fruited trees of the valley, up to the sheltering mountain and its hanging forests. Pines and stones, stony stands of pine. Lieutenant Colonel Zuloaga realized all he had to do was listen; she was bidding farewell to a way of life, but above all to a language she wouldn't use again, so he was quiet, tossing pebbles into the stream that ran steeply downhill here, carrying the pebbles away. His job was to salute her, give her his blessing, thank her for her participation in a given society and history; essentially to tell her, in the name of President Valentín Gómez Farías, that she had permission to leave the Republic. He raised his hat a little to show vulnerability. It wasn't hard. Man of sierra and rifle, he understood very well how Camila and Chief Mangas Coloradas had fallen for each other.

She pulled Goyahkla toward her, as if for protection. The boy understood perfectly and nestled under her arm like a child. The lieutenant colonel could see that Goyahkla was a little in love with her, too, even though he had to call her shumma, mother, because he was Mangas's godson. He watched the boy lie down on the ground and rest his head in her lap. He caught the sidelong look Goyahkla gave him. The boy knew very well what was going on, and he wasn't just enjoying the petting, he was delighting in the fact that she was more his than Zuloaga's. She sank her fingers into his thick, black, very clean hair.

It was truly brutal, Camila went on. At the ranchería everyone knew Mangas was returning with a captive, and the abuela had ridden out to clothe her in proper fashion. I understand that now, but back then I didn't understand a fucking thing. I just watched as it all happened. I was nervous, but I wasn't afraid, there was no reason to be, since I was dressed like an Apache woman and surrounded by warriors. I thought they had accepted me. Fool that I was.

Everyone was waiting for us, curious and outraged, though I only understood that later. Mangas's two wives were well-born, the daughters of other chiefs, and he himself is the grandson of a chief and the chief before that. She looked at the boy, sinking her bony, calloused knuckles into his hair and rubbing his skull. That chief was this boy's grandfather, and father of his uncle Cuchillo Negro, she said. They're Apache nobility.

I was where I was and that was all I had. When Mangas rode up, everybody was outside the wickiups, just looking at me, mothers holding back their children. The women who had been out foraging had returned by now, but they were standing there with baskets still on their backs, the men holding the sticks and balls they'd been playing with. They didn't move until an old man came out of his hut and approached us, beaming. He spoke to Mangas. Now I know he's a healer, but back then he just looked like an old man to me, still vigorous but careworn. Good-hearted, certainly; you met him last night. It was only then that my husband and the warriors dismounted and began to give hugs all around. When the cows and mules loaded with plunder caught up with us soon after, they began to sing and raise a ruckus. I didn't get off my horse. The abuela had touched my leg and I understood it was my place to sit quietly.

The truth is, seeing them with those big smiles on their faces, I relaxed; you've seen it, too—they blaze like suns when they're in good humor. No one was paying attention to me. It's not as if I had been expecting anything, but I could see they weren't savages. They were a bunch of people buffeted by their struggle with the elements, like you. Like us, you mean? Like the Chihuahuans. Aren't you a Chihuahuan anymore, Camila? I don't know what I am, but the point is they were happy to bursting that their boys had come back, bringing beef and other essentials. The Bedonkohes lack nothing, lieutenant, but everything they gather for themselves takes work. Nothing falls from the sky. That's their world, and they're grateful for it.

When the hugging was over the people began to move toward the empty space they always leave in the middle of camp, where you saw they build the fire. It wasn't this camp. We were at a place a little higher up because the cold hadn't really set in yet. It was clear they'd been there for a while: the grass was so trampled it was more like a field of dust. Mangas was the center of attention, everybody slapping him on the back, talking, wanting to be touched by him. Everybody's kids were crowding around him, making an incredible racket.

They led him to his wickiup and he went inside, walking backward as if to thank the people for loving him so much, like a zarzuela singer. The other warriors went their own ways. The people didn't return to the fields but broke into groups; others went into their wickiups, and the cattle and horses left. Then I got off my horse and sat on the ground. I didn't dare come all the way into the camp. It even occurred to me, invisible as I was, that I could take the horse and go. Gallop west, find a mine, beg for help. But what kind of help could I ask for? I looked at my hands, dark and cracked as Apache hands, my Apache skirt, the Apache braid that the abuela had made for me before we returned from the river. I made a bargain with myself: if it got dark and no one had spoken to me, I would go.

It was Goyahkla here who came back for me. Quesque que haces aquí jueras, what are you doing here outside, the chief wants to know, he said to me in his brand new Spanish, the little donkey. From her lap, the boy smiled and said: Donkeys are las mexicanas who let themselves be stolen. Camila pinched his cheeks. What was it like, Geronimo, she asked. Goyahkla frowned, whistling between his teeth. Was fine, he said. Camila said: I was just happy someone was calling for me at last.

The distance to the wickiups couldn't have been more than two hundred paces, lieutenant; I stood and set out to cross to them as quiet as can be, but those cabronas never miss a sound: in the morning, I swear, the wings of bees wake them. A gaggle of old women emerged as I walked. They stood watching me with long-burnished hatred, centuries-old hatred, mi señor, a hatred so brutal there's no explaining how you and I are sitting here alive.

Of course I backed up, thinking about running again, all the way back to Janos. The boy, sensing I was at breaking point, grabbed my hand and pulled me forward as the old bitches, hijas de la chingada, came creeping toward us. They lined up along my path. They didn't dare insult me directly because they didn't know how the chief would react, but they whispered something that sounded like a threat and a curse. Que salga mi indio, I said to myself, please let my Indian come out. If he was man enough to snatch me away, let him be man enough to defend me from these women. By the time we reached Mangas's wickiup, I was surrounded. Maybe I should have leapt inside, pero nomás no pude, I was paralyzed, I grabbed the boy and asked him if something was going to happen to me, but the cabrón didn't understand my Spanish because he was as scared as I was. Goyahkla, in her lap, lowered his eyelids.

Then Mangas's two wives came out and began screaming at me. They threw dirt in my face, spat on me. The others closed in. Goyahkla tried to drag me out, but they kicked him away. As they began to beat me I spied Mangas watching from the door of his wickiup, which I had nearly reached.

They slapped me, yanked my hair, pinched me, wrenched my breasts. They had me so hemmed in as they pummeled my belly and face that I couldn't even bend over to protect myself. At some point one of them tripped me and I fell on my back. You can't imagine how viciously they kicked me in the ribs, the face, the kidneys. I curled up in a ball, but they trampled me. At one point they dragged me up and spreadeagled me, like an animal about to be gutted. There was nothing I could do to defend myself anymore, and I lay there on my back, waiting for death. So much pinche fucking work, I said to myself as I felt the heels of their moccasins slamming into my ribs over and over and over; they kicked me in the neck, trying to break a vertebra, the bitches taking turns. I think I caught a glimpse—though likely I was just told about it later and imagine I remember it—of Mangas's two wives getting hold of a log. Not a branch, lieutenant, a log, cabrón, a big one, the kind we sit on to talk, and they let it fall on my head. If anything else happened to me after that, I can't say.

Mangas got rid of his two wives that same day, or the next, or God knows when, because I knew nothing for some time. Both were kin to chiefs, one Chihende and the other from some other band. Mangas rejected them for their savagery, though the Apaches value women who are merciless fighters. Maybe he was looking for an excuse. What he says is that he wanted me ever since he saw me running in the brush. He liked the way I fought to survive: he always repeats that after we've fucked, he says a man like him needs a woman like me.

And the truth is I don't think either of those two hijas de la chingada would have borne what I went through; they wouldn't have put their whole hearts into it, carrying on no matter what: they were spoiled little ladies, haughty Apache maidens. In any case, he told them they had to leave and their brothers came for them. I'm told they challenged him, and he bested the two together, laughing all the while: the first one quickly, run through with a lance to get him out of the way, and the second with his bare hands, so that his people and the outsiders would know who was boss. You've seen him; he isn't easy to beat. With those arms of his, if he sets his hand on your forehead there's no reaching him with the tip of your knife. They say he returned the sisters himself, each with horses and a share of the plunder from the raid on the ranch, and his wives' brothers were laid to rest like great warriors. He went himself to offer explanations, and no one sought revenge, because it was done right and proper.

I don't know. A little while ago a warrior came through here, a tough bastard; they call him Nana and he's like my husband: a boy and already a legend. Or he's the opposite of my husband, because he's short, but he always wins, too. And he's Chihende. We made room for him and treated him warmly, he stayed a few days and everyone was friends again.

But that's not what we were talking about, said Camila after a long silence. They took me to the abuela's hut. Who knows how long I spent there, but they sang to me, gave me some foul-tasting tea; sometimes I saw a clean, empty field and other times hell itself. She scratched the boy's head. This one and his sister took care of me. Goyahkla rubbed the cat eyes Ussen had given him, crowded nearly up to his forehead by his red cheeks. He had giant, even frightening teeth. Everbody and everbody done wrong, he said, las bi'áás done wrong and los husbands beat them because they casi-casi kill Camila. Everbody and everbody come to my abuela's house and help sing to my shumma. Everbody and everbody thinks she will not live, but the abuela only healing and singing and healing and singing.

Camila nodded, proud of her godson's Spanish, of her own toughness. One day I could sit up, she said, and I saw my legs, they were like matchsticks. I'd never been skinnier or more wretched, and my life wasn't easy in Chihuahua either. The lieutenant laughed. Please, you were a teacher there, you had a ranch. She shrugged. Go on, roll me a cigarette; there are still things my fingers can't manage after what they did to me.

Zuloaga took his time, making a good job of it, rolling it tight and fat. He handed it to her and lit a match. She drew the smoke in. What a lovely custom, she said, lighting cigarettes for ladies. Here I can only smoke secretly, inside the wickiup. Mangas loves it, he says it turns him on to see me smoke like a man. Zuloaga blushed a little. She noticed and delivered another jab: You have no idea how it feels when a man the size of him fucks you all night long, lieutenant, pinche paradise. Goyahkla laughed, escaping from her lap and rolling on the ground. Then he knelt and rose partway, hunching his shoulders. This how my sister and me carries Camila when she gets better, he said, pretending to be a crutch.

Camila went on. So it was: together they hauled me up to get me out of the wickiup at last. All I wanted was to see the sun and be given something solid to eat because I was wasting away, I was frail as a leaf, a pitiable sight. And that was how we ventured out. Not all of my wounds had healed, so we moved slowly. The minute I emerged, there was a new uproar. Goyahkla, kneeling beside her again, laughed. I felt the sun on my face, I closed my eyes, and the howling began. Enough, I said, and I tried to go back in, but the children kept pulling at me and they sat me down on the ground. I looked back at the hut and I saw that the abuela was watching, unconcerned, and behind her was pinche Mangas, who hadn't lifted a finger for me the first time I was beaten and surely wouldn't this time either.

The whole pinche town came to make noise at me. I didn't understand a thing. I begged them in my little girl Apache to give me food and then do what they liked to me, but I was so weak they didn't hear a thing, they must have thought I was praying. And then? asked the lieutenant, who had finally dropped his confessor pose and was genuinely interested in the story she had to tell; the story she needed to tell before she turned Apache forever.

Suddenly the crowd parted and one of the women who had beaten me came forward, still very angry. She was carrying a pretty earthenware platter, surely stolen, with two pieces of meat on it. One was nicely roasted, golden, juicy, the kind of thing we would eat at the sawhorse tables in Janos on Sundays. The other was the raw liver of some animal, oozing blood in a bowl. A fawn, I imagine, because it was small. Goyahkla nodded. A fawn, he said, we catch and tie up for when she is ready. You're a soldier, said Camila, you know the smell of roasted flesh after you've gone a long time without eating, and I hadn't eaten anything in who knows how many days. But I needed not to die, so I snatched the bowl and drank the blood before grabbing the raw liver with both hands and eating it in three bites. Imagine the pleasure I felt as I licked up the blood on the platter, lieutenant. The world went black, I saw stars, and I thought: Now go ahead and kill me, hijas de la chingada.

As I was licking the juices from my forearms, I noticed that the noise had started up again, and everyone flung themselves at the kid and his sister, but they were hugging them, and the abuela came to sit next to me and everyone kneeled beside her and spoke warmly to her. They started up the chants that had so tormented me during my recovery. Behind the whole mass of them came Mangas. He knelt before me, giving me what he imagined were gentle pats on the cheek, ruffling my hair. He shoved Goyahkla and everybody fell around laughing. The chief himself helped me up, his giant hand at my waist, and bore me along to where the people were gathered. The old women took out their little buckskin pouches and scattered pollen on us. We were parting the waters of the hullabaloo when I turned and asked Mangas if I could eat the roasted meat, too.

THE CORPORAL BROUGHT THEM JUST outside the barracks courtyard and waited with them until Parker, Geronimo, and the Chiricahuas accompanying him on his shift came back from the quadrangle. The lawyer decided he wasn't so sure this was a safe place when he realized that all the warriors, not just the ones he'd seen on display, were walking freely around the area assigned them in the fort. We'd better wait here outside, he said to Ellie when he spotted Chief Naiche sitting on the ground among the Indians scattered about the courtyard, too tall for the rather timid shade of the eaves.

McMillan knew the tiger was returning from his shift when he saw the chief stand, stretch his astonishingly long arms, and brush the dust from his buttocks. Unlike the men he'd seen on display, the chief was still in Apache dress, with his knee-high moccasins, tunic, and buckskin jacket. He made a sign to his wife that the man who had just risen was Naiche himself, and he saw that she was already on her feet, straightening her skirts and fixing her hair as if she were about to be presented to an ambassador. It was she who pointed south, drawing his attention to the figures of the prisoners from the quadrangle, who were coming now, followed at some distance by Lieutenant Parker and a man also in military attire, though his uniform was buff-colored; surely the Mexican officer the corporal had mentioned.

McMillan was struck again by how confidently the prisoners moved. One of them was strolling along, hands in pockets, as if on his way to drink beer with friends. The war shaman was telling some story with the measured enthusiasm of one who knows he has his audience in the palm of his hand. The other man was fingering his hat, listening attentively. When the lawyer saw Parker look up, he waved, and the lieutenant took the Mexican officer by the elbow and steered him in their direction.

The officers sauntered over. Parker held out his hand almost absentmindedly. Now we can shake, he said; I'm Lieutenant Parker. McMillan said: I'm the attorney who was recommended to your captain in case there is a civil suit. And this is my son, he added, pointing upward. Parker gave a half smile. The captain can't talk to anyone since Washington ordered the trains stopped, he said as if in warning. Then you'll have to tell me everything, replied McMillan, but tomorrow at my office would be better, if possible. Parker narrowed his eyes. You wouldn't believe what a pain in the ass the War Department lawyers are, he said; worst of the military and civilian worlds combined. McMillan smiled, putting his hand to his son's back to make sure he was still safely balanced. But this is Texas and we do things differently here, he said. Parker returned from the world of legal entanglements with a shake of the head. Pardon me, he said; this is Lieutenant Estrada. He's with us to assure the Mexican government that Geronimo won't be returning to the sierra. McMillan held out his hand. Only then did the lawyer remember that his wife was with him. He turned to introduce her, but she wasn't there.

. . .

```
attention stop mr president s stop grover cleveland
comma at the white house comma from stop g stop
nelson miles stop of course captain lawton is
still under my command comma mr president comma
and i have no reason to suspect insubordination
```

stop you correctly note that the prisoners are no longer under the jurisdiction of the arizona authorities stop from a legal perspective comma the matter is a little more complicated stop in accordance with protocol comma captain lawton notified the civilian authorities in el paso comma texas comma as soon as he arrived with the prisoners stop now that the local justice system has been notified comma we would have to begin extradition proceedings to remove them from texas and return them to arizona stop i sincerely apologize for this mess stop i never thought they would get so far so quickly stop ive already been in touch with the authorities in tucson to put our lawyers at their disposal in case they want to reclaim the indians comma given that the apaches are now under the jurisdiction of the texas justice authority stop truly sorry stop

NAICHE AND GATEWOOD WALKED TO the western edge of the mesa. The chief didn't know that this would be the last time he would see the sun set behind the Chiricahuas. Neither man was overcome by the majesty of the landscape: they were used to it, they believed it would always be there, they had things to do. The lieutenant felt the bayonet of fear in the small of his back just seeing the slope and noting how sandy the ground was: he would pass out from pain if he had to climb down there. The chief reassured him; saying he had a plan for just such a quandary, and without asking leave or giving warning, he seized Gatewood under the armpits and lifted him onto his shoulders. The lieutenant struggled a little but he knew that this posture, which he adopted when riding, would lessen the strain on his lower back and, by extension, his thighs and knees.

The owner of an ailing body always has tricks to dodge the dark angel of humiliation; he has the composure to inconvenience others when necessary. And it seemed to Gatewood that the chief was telling the truth about his plan and even enjoying this peculiar mode of seeing him off.

Naiche was a kind and serious man, as Mangas Coloradas was said to have been. Perhaps less resolute, though he lacked the resources to lead his maternal grandfather's life of constant resistance. But as everybody said, he had an unyielding side, too, like his father, Cochise. He was stubborn or proud, depending how you saw at it. He didn't deal directly with U.S. or Mexican officials. He let Geronimo set up talks and then he would consent or not, without explanation. It was Naiche people followed, not the war shaman. He did have a clownish side, very different from his father's pure flint, that he could draw upon to survive emotionally complicated situations, like the one he was facing now.

Gatewood imagined that when Naiche returned to the camp after they had parted, he would tell everyone how he had carried the lieutenant down on his shoulders; they would make fun of him, but Naiche would be modestly proud of having borne a white-eyes aloft: no one else was big or strong enough. Gatewood lifted his face, feeling the sun on it and turning his attention at last to the dramatic view of the mountains spread before him. He smiled without sadness.

Endings, no matter how foretold, never announce themselves as final, at least not as they're being lived. The last intimate encounter with someone always seems to be the latest in a series: a moment to be repeated, nothing special. No one ever thinks they've sampled someone's saliva for the last time, or that from now until the day they die they'll miss the scent of the swirl of skin behind a particular earlobe. We don't register the last time our children reach for our hand to cross the street, only the first time they don't. When we move to a new city, a new country, we always think we'll be coming back; everyone else will stay frozen, as if enchanted, and the next time we see them we'll give them a hug and they'll still smell of the same lotion, tobacco, burnt coffee. But friends change and move on, buy expensive lotions, stop smoking, give up coffee, smell of green tea when we get back. Or they lose their minds, are confined to mental wards, and die horrible deaths that we learn of by email. There's that last lucid conversation watching some random soccer match with Grandpa and that last meal prepared by Grandma's expert hand, a last phone conversation with the mentor who made us what we are and who one morning slips in the bathtub and dies.

Gatewood knew that if by some chance he made the trip to the Southwest again, the landscape that had left its mark on his mind like the hole a stone leaves in the snow would no longer be the same. Absent the Chiricahuas, there would be ranches, cattle, towns with their churches, hotels, laws, cemeteries. There would be the rattle of carriages and the rustle of silent Puritans on their way to church on Sundays; there would be bells and roosters.

Naiche turned to look up at him sideways, studying him mockingly as he had done since they met. His shiny black hair, short by warrior standards—one of his wives cut it, using a basket to shape it—spun with his body in a perfect spiral as he turned his head to meet the gringo's gaze. Are you ready? he asked, and he stamped the ground with both feet, as if to rehearse the distress of the descent. The lieutenant smiled, part anxious and part amused. Before him was the slope, and at the bottom of the gully were the horses; among them he recognized his own and El Gordo Parker's, with military saddles and kit. Beyond was the end of Skeleton Canyon, the only crack in the tortured huddle of the sierra, and the path to New Mexico.

Ready? Naiche asked. Let's go, said Gatewood, and he had a moment of insecurity, the urge to look all around, cast an anchor for memory. He turned, and what he saw wasn't the colossal mountains and sky of Arizona, but the pinche Chiricahuas, falling all over laughing, watching him play the leading role in the comic scene of the day, the week, maybe the year. They had all known in advance that Naiche would carry him; probably they had even bet on it. Motherfuckers, he thought, and he dug a heel into the chief's ribs—the ribs of the only king, son of kings, and grandson of kings he would meet in his life. He said: Arre, cabrón. The Apache endured the pain, knowing it was deserved and worth it. He replied in Spanish as well: Nomás no uses la nariz de fuste, so long as you don't use your nose as a whip.

The sight must have been a treat from the Apaches' point of view. The pair made up an impossible monster, a centaur of copper and silver, a mythical animal in buckskin trousers and white linen jacket, a flagpole with a fedora on top. Naiche smiled up at his rider again, but his toothy grin quickly turned serious. Does it hurt less, Long Nose? he asked. It doesn't hurt at all, said Gatewood. He felt that something much bigger than his life was unfolding, and the chief understood it and he didn't. Then let's go, said Naiche.

Finally they began their descent. At first the slope was rocky and easy to navigate, with patches of vegetation for footholds. The lieutenant watched the world from a perch higher than a horse, the chief searching calmly for the best spots to set his moccasins; their combined shadow was the needle of a sun dial, a pillar from which gods would no longer descend.

Gatewood felt the rocking motion in his groin and a vague queasiness in his stomach; Naiche felt the officer's thighs on his shoulders and the pressure of his boots on his ribs: the measure of his friend's fear. They reached a stone crest, the start of the steepest part of the descent, where the sand began. Here we go, Long Nose, said the chief, not waiting for confirmation.

The lieutenant clutched the chief's head. The horses were still: by now they must have recognized the men's scent. If they had been able to see them, they might have found it a preposterous picture: man mounted on man. Gatewood turned his head and saw that the Chiricahuas had run to the edge of the slope to watch them descend. They weren't laughing anymore. Who would? Last rites for a piece of the world that as of that day was no longer new. Ussen on the way out and the Great Father in Washington on the way in, history knotting itself up in the final rupture of the American order, the humiliation of those who don't deserve it so somebody can write about it later, as Homer said. History as it is: sad. That is all, America.

. . .

```
attention stop captain elpenor ware lawton comma
wherever he is comma from stop g stop nelson miles
stop dear captain lawton stop this is a direct
order from president cleveland stop you and your
troops and the prisoners must take the train to
fort sam houston in san antonio and wait there for
his emissaries comma who will conduct a series of
interviews to determine what to do with the warriors
and whom to hold responsible and whom to clear in
case a procedural error has been made stop i beg
you to tell them nothing but the truth stop i have
been relieved of all responsibilities in the
region comma so the mission is in your hands until
further notice from my superiors stop i wish you
the best of luck stop don't let yourself be
intimidated comma you are the only hero here stop
```

THE LAST LEG OF THE trip to Tucson was as arid as the stony cactus country we were driving through. The little ones sat in gloomy, hostile silence, the girl huddled next to her big brother and Cosme distant, looking out the window with a surly expression on his face and one hand over his mouth, like his mother when she's protecting herself from suffering, when she refuses to admit that something hurts because there's no choice but to go on.

Cruz didn't say much after decreeing that it was too late. I was afraid to ask what he meant. Too late to prolong the trip? Too late for our life together? Inés tried to engage him in conversation about the documentary he'd be working on, but his replies were monosyllabic, and finally she gave up and began searching for Mexican radio stations.

ELLIE HAD BROKEN AWAY FROM the group of men, curious to get a closer look at the Chiricahuas, who were heading into the barracks courtyard where Chief Naiche stood waiting for them with a smile, in an inexplicably good mood given his state as prisoner king. They weren't what she had expected. They didn't wear feathers, didn't seem fierce or crazy or murderous. They were just men who walked the earth as if it belonged to them.

Ellie, Ellie, her husband called a few times. She turned back toward the group. Rejoining them, she asked Parker flat out: Why are they so happy? The lieutenant shrugged as if to say that in war everything is relative. They're alive, he said; they're on their way to Florida, where they'll be locked up in a fort, but they'll be with their families; it could be much worse. What about the Tucson sheriff? asked Ellie. What about him? asked the lieutenant. Every day in the papers he swears he's going to hang them. Parker stroked his mustache. We didn't arrest them; they surrendered. So? The officer shook his head, trying to explain something for which he didn't have the words. To hang them now would be murder. The lawyer looked skeptical, and Estrada smiled. Can I get closer to them? interrupted Ellie, who hadn't taken her eyes off the Chiricahuas. Of course, said the lieutenant. Is it safe? asked McMillan, and Parker and Estrada laughed.

McMillan watched nervously as his wife slowly but resolutely advanced toward the prisoners. How many people has Geronimo killed? the lawyer asked again, his voice a little higher than usual. He could tell by the way Parker put his hands on his hips in disbelief that he really had once been fat. The lady can talk to them as much as she likes, he said; she could go and talk to them even if they were armed; they're warriors, not murderers; not like you but not very different from me or Lieutenant Estrada here. McMillan was clearly uncomfortable with the situation. Though she'll have to speak to them in Spanish, Parker said.

Arriving at the airport, getting things out of the back, everybody walking to the airline counter, giving Cruz money for the trip so he could indulge himself a little over the next few days. And then the hugs. Long, mostly silent. Don't be a stranger, I said. I'm not the one who lives in a foreign country, he said. I don't think he meant to be cruel; he was trying to be brave. He let me touch his face.

And then the hardest part: the siblings' hug. Amelia's tears, Cosme's grim seriousness—he must have thought he had to set some kind of example for his little sister.

Zuloaga returned to the camp to get his things. Goyahkla had run off with the other boys as soon as they reached the wickiups, so they were alone. He said to Camila: I plan to travel to the state capital and convince the governor to sign a peace treaty with Mangas. She nodded. You'll have done a good deed, she said; and now go, so that you make it to the watering hole by nightfall; you have safe passage, so go without fear. He stepped forward to get a hug from her, if nothing else. She took a step backward and said: What an innocent you are, Lieutenant Colonel José María Zuloaga; come anywhere close to touching me and your head will be blown to pieces before you even get a whiff of me. He nodded in acceptance. Do you really and truly want to stay? She smiled tenderly. I'd rather take a bullet than return to Janos, she said. Ta bueno, replied the officer, and he handed her a small parcel from his saddlebags. This is yours, he said. What is it? she asked. Your boots and clothes, he said, the ones you left outside of Janos the day your husband stole you away. She peeked into the parcel, sniffed the clothes, closed her eyes, and handed it back to him. Give this to my uncle and aunt when you pass through Casas Grandes and tell them I'm happy and healthy, that I'm going to have a son and he'll be one hell of a warrior. What if it's a girl? Then she'll be one hell of a warrior, too; it can be so here, but never there. Isn't that the truth, said the officer. As soon as I've delivered the baby, amigo José María Zuloaga, they'll give me a rifle of my own, or did you really believe I turned Apache just because Mangas is good-looking?

As he descended the sandy slope on Chiricahua-back, Lieutenant Gatewood got a further glimpse of the vision he'd had when he was hauled up from his seat on the stone. After Naiche helped him mount his horse, the lieutenant told him what he'd seen.

I don't have enough Apache to describe it, he said, so I'll tell you in Spanish. I saw the desert, I saw a chingo of Indians returning to Arizona, waves and waves of Indians coming from Mexico and beyond, from the jungles down below, in the farthest south. Big, strong Indians crossing the desert to take back what's been stolen from you. I saw them speaking their own tongues, Spanish and other languages. And they were in Brooklyn and Raleigh and Philadelphia and Atlanta, cities in the old part of the country that you may visit after you're taken to

Florida. I saw their children in schools and parks and hospitals. And truly they were Indians and almost all of them spoke English; they were beautiful gringos the same color as you, and they became army officers and doctors and senators. I saw that this land would become their land, too. Your land. I saw that you would return through them.

Naiche was standing beside him. He had one hand on the horse's reins and with the other he was stroking its mane, cropped military-style. He replied in Apache, language of royalty. You should be telling this to Geronimo, he's the war healer, he could explain what your dream means; or Lozen, but she went down to meet with Miles, too; you should tell them and listen to what they have to say—Lozen has Victorio's ear, she hears for all the Mimbreños still left; don't go, ride up instead, I'll help you dismount and we'll wait for them.

Gatewood rubbed his face and adjusted his hat, shaking his head. No, he said. Why? asked Naiche. Because it's all over, he said. Then here we part, replied the chief, and he held out his giant hand. The lieutenant took it and clasped it in both of his. Where are you going? Naiche asked. Though it doesn't matter. To New Mexico, said Gatewood, I'm going to present my discharge papers there, because if I go through Apache Pass the dead will tug at me. The chief nodded, maybe understanding that everything was finally over between them. You're going through Ánimas, said the warrior, in Spanish. Where else? said Gatewood; that's what we are, nothing but ánimas, ghosts.

The children were in a terrible mood for the whole drive to San Carlos, which was longer than we expected. Cosme sat with his fists clenched all the way, looking for excuses to pick a fight with his sister.

Lieutenant Estrada understood before his gringo colleague that the lawyer wasn't asking silly questions about what the Chiricahuas might do but trying to restrain his wife. He put a hand on McMillan's forearm, saying he would accompany the lady, not to fear. The lawyer thanked him, and as he watched the lieutenant walk after his wife, he asked Parker: Where does he carry his gun? El Gordo replied casually that he had left it in his room because he was on a diplomatic mission. But don't worry, he said, you won't find a more easygoing folk when they're at peace.

Ellie got a good look at the Chiricahuas before they noticed she was there. They were laughing uproariously, and she had no idea that what they were laughing about was the stupidity of the people who had fought to see them from the other side of the fence. She thought there was something toylike about them, with their square frames and straight backs; they were like those automatons that spit out little paper strips with fortunes on them for anyone who deposits a penny in a slot, as if they, too, were made of wood and had been set in motion by the coin of a different god.

Then Chapo, Geronimo's son, saw her approaching—she recognized them all because she had followed news of them in the papers for years. He pointed at her and the other three turned their heads to look. They stopped laughing. The youngest immediately dropped their gazes to the dusty ground. Geronimo and Naiche watched her with something like gravity, or arrogance. When she was five or six feet away, Ellie stopped and lowered her eyes, fixing them on Geronimo's hands, grazed by glory and calloused from holding a gun. They were full hands, dry as dead branches, that made spasms blossom deep in her and rise up to her breastbone. She felt her palms sweating.

The Mexican officer stopped an inch or two behind Ellie, saying something she had no interest in hearing. She moved closer to the Apaches, away from him. She didn't stop again until she could smell the war sweat of the Chiricahuas, a musk like that of the soldiers of Greek verse. She took one last step and looked up, but Geronimo's eyes were on her breasts, barely detectable under layers of cotton, crinoline, and silk. Her aureolas shrank, pleating into so many folds that her nipples hardened. She felt the scrape of her bodice against them. She took off her bonnet and said in her mooing Spanish that it was an honor to meet him. The Apache's smile was forced. He bowed his head and said: The honor is mine. Then he clapped his son on the back. He was about to introduce him when she interrupted, saying: Chapo, it's a pleasure to meet you. And you must be Perico, she went on, nodding at the third man. And then, making a small curtsy: Chief Naiche. The warrior laughed and said something in Apache to the war shaman. He says there's no need for that, translated Geronimo, peering at her as if seeing someone else through her. He drew his right hand from his belt, all the while scrutinizing her face, and held it out to her. She took it between hers with twin jolts of fear and reverence. She could have licked it.

Her husband, who had been watching from a distance, hurried over. Rather than simply noticing his wife's unease, McMillan felt struck by it. No fist to the gut, but the hole left behind when it was withdrawn. He would have liked to mark the ground in front of her with a line of pee. Lieutenant Estrada, who was still a hand's span behind Ellie, stepped forward to introduce him. Naiche was taller than the lawyer, but Geronimo was so much shorter that when McMillan nodded earnestly in greeting, he felt the baby, whom he had forgotten, shift on his shoulders. He straightened and raised his hands to the child's knees. As he did, Geronimo stuck his right hand back in his belt. He wouldn't be taking it out again. He turned his gaze back to Ellie.

McMillan saw now that it wasn't desire in the Indian's eyes; he was weighing her in memory, as if searching for something he had lost a long time ago. Suddenly he said something to his comrades in Apache. Then he turned to Ellie, telling her in Spanish that she reminded him of a woman who had been married to Mangas Coloradas. A woman from Chihuahua, he said, Naiche's grandmother, she died among us. McMillan was listening to Estrada's translation when the war shaman fixed his eyes on him. He felt his penis and balls shrink up into his belly like an octopus. Take care of her, said the Chiricahua, abruptly; she's a real woman.

The child, awake now, was a little storm on his father's upper slopes. McMillan lowered him from his shoulders as a way of changing the subject. He took the hat off the baby's head, saying: This is our son. The baby's tangle of carroty curls, bright as the sun, split the day. The officers hadn't seen Geronimo smile so broadly in all the time they'd spent together. It's red, he said, and Estrada hurried to translate for the lawyer, who was the kind of English speaker proud of not knowing a single word in any foreign language.

For a long time after this encounter with Geronimo, Amyntor Blair McMillan wondered whether Ellie could be the same woman he thought he'd married. Once the warrior turned his attention to the baby, she snatched up the child. So clearly desperate was she to regain the shaman's gaze, so shamefully and humiliatingly desperate, that McMillan didn't recognize his wife. The lawyer wasn't a reader. He hadn't picked up a book since he graduated from college, and he scarcely glanced at the papers. He couldn't understand that it wasn't Geronimo's physical presence but the whiff of glory that had turned Ellie to quivering jelly. Nothing is such a turn-on as a name that will go down in history, but to be aware of it you have to be a devotee of the printed page.

The woman took the baby and set nervously to grooming him: she tidied his curls, straightened his smock and swaddling cloths, popped her finger in her mouth, and spit-polished his face and hands. The baby resisted at first, but soon a tight sphere of complicity descended upon him and Mrs. McMillan. The warriors and officers watched them, seized by nostalgia for a happiness to which they had lost the right. McMillan was a different kettle of fish. He didn't have even the emotional intelligence to realize he was missing anything.

When the baby was more presentable, Ellie stuck out her tongue at him and he responded in kind, which made Geronimo smile again, bright as the day. She looked up at the old man once more, and he came forward until he was just inches from mother and child. She felt her husband stirring behind her and sensed Parker put a hand to the gun at his hip. She saw a seething in the eyes of the war shaman, so near to her now, and she watched him think a little and then relax. He touched the child's chin. ¿Quieres cargarlo? Ellie asked. The Indian didn't move to take the baby, but he ran his hand slowly over its head. He raised his eyes and fixed them on McMillan. It was a look of peace. Were you a redhead as a boy? he asked. Red as a tomato, replied the lawyer, Estrada translating. Everyone was able to breathe again. Take him, insisted Ellie, he's a brave little thing, he won't cry even though you're the meanest Indian in the world. Chapo, Perico, Naiche, Estrada, and the shaman himself laughed. Geronimo looked up at the lawyer again. ¿Puedo? he asked. McMillan, persuaded at last that he was the only player of truly no consequence in this whole drama, turned pleadingly toward the Mexican officer. He's asking whether he can hold the baby, Estrada translated, and added: To the best of our knowledge, he has five children and who knows how many grandchildren. The lawyer glanced back at Parker but it was too late: his wife was handing his son over to the most feared outlaw in all the limitless territories of North America.

Sitting at the desk of the motel room we found in Datil, New Mexico, when we were at the point of exhaustion, I'm going through my notes, unable to sleep. The children and Inés are breathing in unison, maybe a sign that tomorrow we'll be ourselves again and not the overwrought emotional wrecks we've been all day. I notice I haven't written much about the long period that Geronimo's Gileños spent on the San Carlos reservation. After seeing the place today I think maybe my hunch was right. Better to ignore a place, no matter how beautiful, where the Chiricahuas were so unhappy: numbered like cattle, divided, and set against each other over and over, made dependent on alcohol and rations of weevil-infested flour and beef jerky.

Gatewood could tolerate the pain when he was on horseback, so making his way down the rest of the mesa was a little better, though hardly relaxing: the ground was uneven and sharply pitched. In the loose gravel, his horse's haunches swayed like a boat, though its gait was slow. He had his eyes closed and the reins clutched to his stomach, top teeth grinding against bottom from pure terror of the stabbing pain. His doctor in Virginia—a man who cared more about health than stamina, unlike the rotten military surgeons who prescribed whiskey and told him to close his eyes when it hurt—had once pointed out that his ills were confined to his lower back and joints; any trouble with his upper back and legs came from grinding his teeth. This, too, explained his ruined molars, savage migraines, and chronic torticollis.

He reached the bottom of the gully with relief, closing his eyes and doubling over. Being able to stretch his back was an advantage of riding. He felt grateful to be alone at last, even if it was because a whole world had been annihilated in a fifteen-minute ceremony. He took off his hat, tied it by its strap to the saddle band, and sprawled across the horse. He let his jaw slacken, his mouth gaping like a dying fish, and closed his eyes. He rested his head on the horse's neck, stretching his body sideways and letting his arms dangle like a dead man's, with the pommel of the saddle in the curve of his neck, his eyes half-closed. The horse slowed its pace as it felt him relax.

The beast must have missed the other horses, the mounts of Martín and his cousin, Gatewood's perennial scouts. The two men had ridden down with Geronimo to witness the negotiations with Miles, surely expecting a reward—which they would never get—for having served the U.S. Army so well. The lieutenant later learned that Martín, always the clever one, understood the magnitude of the surrender and left Skeleton Canyon before the other Chiricahuas set out for El Paso. He simply got on his horse and rode back to Mexico, with no one bothering to stop him. He became foreman on a ranch and began going to church on Sundays again. In time he migrated to Coahuila because he understood that there would never be peace in Sonora or Chihuahua for the Apaches remaining there, and some people still recognized him. He worked on a ranch called Australia. His sons fought in the Revolution and scattered, their own sons never knowing they came from a line of princes who once ruled the badlands of Arizona, Springfields in hand.

Geronimo reached out and took the baby, who touched his face in amusement and curiosity. Gatewood opened his eyes without lifting his head: he had come to the plains of New Mexico, near Ánimas; the geological mass of the Chiricahua Mountains had been left behind. Before leaving to embark on his daily routine, General Miles freed the telegraph operator. He ordered him to go to the prison vault and release the heliograph operator, too. Tell them to leave my secretary where he is until further notice, he said. He walked out into the first courtyard, hands in the pockets of his robe. Confined to the Fort Sam Houston barracks in San Antonio, Lawton believed he would be exonerated because he had done the right thing, and President

Cleveland was a just man. And he was exonerated, so thoroughly that the Oklahoma town that would later witness the deaths of the warriors who had surrendered to him in the Sierra Madre would be ultimately named after him. What he could neither guess nor foresee was that he would eventually be sent to the toy war in the Philippines, where he would be the only U.S. Army general to die in combat. The Filipino who shot the bullet that blew out his brains was named Geronimo. When Zuloaga returned to the spot where he'd left Corredor, the boy was mounted and waiting. Are you coming to Buenaventura with me, or are you going back to Casas Grandes? asked Zuloaga. He added: At headquarters we're always in need of good gunmen. Let's go, said the Raramuri. The war shaman threw redheaded Phoenix McMillan up into the air and both smiled, a drop of saliva escaping the child's mouth and splashing—slow, viscous, glorious—on the old man's forehead.

At the San Carlos reservation, the children went into their private realm, a world that turns its back on us, all whispers. They've been to Mexico, so poverty neither offends nor frightens them; it doesn't stand for anything but itself. It is neither shameful nor humiliating, because it's always imposed by others. They kept up a constant stream of talk, never pausing or paying attention to anything else as we visited the cultural center and drank soda at a little grocery store, and I tried to strike up conversations with people who ignored me. At some point their games intersected with the play of some children in the town's main square and they tumbled around with them. They took photographs with Cosme's cell phone. When I asked them, back in the car, what it was like to have Apache friends, the girl asked: Were they Apache? Her older brother, in the professorial tone he adopts when addressing his sister, said: Apache, but not Chiricahua.

The lieutenant propped himself up on both elbows on his horse's back. He was bathed in sweat and drool, as only those who've slept hard can be. He reached back for his canteen and took a long drink of water. McMillan, Parker, and Estrada held their breath until Naiche, who had done nothing but idly watch the small drama unfolding before him, burst again into rather mocking laughter. Geronimo said something to him in Apache and held the child close. He turned toward his friends as if to boast he hadn't lost his touch with babies. Then he got up and thanked the child's mother for the loan with a slight nod. The men finally relaxed, and Ellie felt something like a gentle nibble between her legs.

San Carlos is what's left in the wake of the revelation that war was unnecessary. The record of a pointless struggle: endless suffering so we can keep playing ball. What we find at San Carlos is what we find in the Mayan communities of Yucatán and the Aymaran lands of Bolivia: evidence of what we've done to America, soil that fills our mouths when we lay claim to it. We aren't the children of these lands; we're an occupation force. We should be living on our knees. We should have to give it all back. That is all, America, that is all. At the very least we should know your name.

General Miles looked up at the sky. The sun had risen. It would soon be time for reveille. He patted the pockets of his robe, smoothed his hair, and felt in his breast pocket for his pipe and spectacles. He put on the spectacles to check that there was still tobacco left in the pipe, then he put the pipe in his mouth. Fucking Geronimo, my dearest Molly, he thought as he searched for a match in his other pockets, continuing the letter in his head. There's a legend about him, did you know? People say that when he was young his god told him he would be immortal in combat. I believe it's true: never have so many people tried to kill a man, and it turns out Lawton, Gatewood, and I together saved him and got ruined along the way. I don't even understand why.

It was night now, and they were lounging at their ease by the Bear Creek watering hole, having paid their respects to the dead in the canyon where they'd been killed and where El Gringo and Elvira had given them a better burial than they'd ever expected in life. As they were having coffee after supper, Corredor boldly suggested they should go back that very minute and shoot Goyahkla. Why in the world? asked the lieutenant, intrigued but not taking him seriously whatsoever. Didn't you get a look at his eyes? No. They went black with rage when he saw my pistols, said Corredor. Think about it, he went on. If we get rid of him now, we'll save ourselves a heap of dead bodies. Zuloaga smiled. Ta usté loco, he said.

As we got back in the station wagon to set out again, Cosme very formally requested that we please stop just before crossing the border into Colorado. He was in a good mood, or at least at peace, crazy proud of having played for a little while with a bunch of Apache kids. There was connivance in Amelia's clear laugh that accompanied the request: they had a plan.

Gatewood thought he would stop at the cantina in Ánimas to get water and fodder for the horse; he would have a plate of frijoles enchilados con carne, a beer, and a double whiskey to make it to Lordsburg in good spirits. I should ride all the way to Virginia, he said to himself, as he untied his hat. No part of him hurt. He set the hat back on his head, thinking there were things that could only be said in Mexican: Que se vayan todos a la chingada. He slapped the reins.

I honored the kids' request and stopped the station wagon right on the border between New Mexico and Colorado, pulling over to the side of the deserted highway carrying us back to the Northeast, and asked: Now what? Unlock the doors, said Cosme. They burst out of the car, shoving each other and tussling like the two puppies they still are in happy moments. I watched as they planted their feet firmly on the ground and counted to three, giving each other looks of perfect complicity. They raised their hands to their mouths and shouted in unison at the top of their lungs, with the earsplitting force that jolts us awake at night: There are still Apaches, Nana, and we remember your name.

Then Geronimo took a few steps away, holding the redheaded baby even tighter. He whispered in the baby's ear, surely in his own tongue. The children shouted: There are still Apaches, Cochise, and we remember your name. He might have been telling the baby he had powers, the Apaches had powers, and he could help him find his own. Maybe he whispered that his son Chapo was here, but soon he would see Lenna, Azul's child; she was still little, captive in Florida, and he had surrendered because he didn't want her to suffer there fatherless. There are still Apaches, Mangas, my children shouted, and we remember your name. He might have been telling the baby how the white-eyes put children in jail—they still do and no longer feel any shame—and that if the baby came with him he could be a little Apache, even though he had red hair. There are still Apaches, Geronimo, and your name will not be forgotten. He might have been telling the baby how when he was a young man he'd had other children, but the Mexicans had killed them and his first wife in an unholy massacre, a shame to be borne forever by those of us who carry the green passport with an eagle on the front; one of them was an infant when they shot him, his body blown to pieces where he was left lying on the ground. Or he might have told the baby that his life was just beginning as the Chiricahuas were leaving, and it was a pity he had been born too late. The land would endure, but the world had ended.

ACKNOWLEDGMENTS

Three brilliant minds accompanied the writing of *Ahora me rindo y eso es todo* from its beginnings as a free-for-all of ideas and stories until its publication in Spanish: Julio Trujillo (rest in peace, hermano; like Chief Cochise, I believe friends will meet again on the other side), Valeria Luiselli, and Silvia Sensé. If the book is worth anything, it is thanks to those who read it and offered their opinions and unerring observations. Ria Julien and Natasha Wimmer were its first Anglophone readers—I sent the manuscript to both of them the very night I finished it. They've stuck with it throughout with a devotion that I can never repay.

Running around and through the writing process were always Miquel, Dylan, Maia, and—as *Ahora me rindo y eso es todo* turned into *Now I Surrender*—Emilio Guadalupe. I hope that their capacity to marvel at the small things has permeated the pages of this book. The millenary wisdom of Aimé Iglesias Lukin was a centering force whenever neurosis got the better of me during the preparation of the English version of the book, and the many things that Jorge and Juan

Enrigue—always my first readers—had to say about the first edition in Spanish led to improvements here.

This novel, like most I've written, began as a failed short story, and, like many of my projects, it bears the mark of José Emilio Pacheco, to whom I owe so much. He knew of my interest in Geronimo, and while I was studying for my doctorate with him, one day he told me that the father of Martín Luis Guzmán—my favorite Mexican novelist—had been present at one of the Apache warrior's surrenders. I was never able to confirm this—even the most dedicated reader could never read as much as José Emilio—but in an attempt to write a story about Martín Luis Guzmán as a boy seeing his father return from a military campaign in the desert, I began to gather books, articles, and testimonies about the Mexican side in the Apache Wars.

The list of readings that this novel draws upon is endlessly long, but fundamental are Geronimo's autobiography as dictated to S.M. Barrett, the memoirs of Joaquín Terrazas, and the war diaries and correspondence of Charles B. Gatewood. Also very important were studies by Peter Aleshire, Shelley Ann Bowen Hatfield, Antonio García de León, Louis Lejeune, David Roberts, Manuel Rojas, and Robert M. Utley. Along with the many testimonies of Apaches and U.S. and Mexican soldiers, Edwin R. Sweeney's colossal tale of the final years of the Apache Wars, published in three volumes—*Mangas Coloradas*, *Cochise*, and *From Cochise to Geronimo*—is the backbone of this novel. Everything is in there. I spent a lot of time requesting and reading books from the libraries of Columbia, Princeton, and NYU, where generous people found me work as a professor of language, literature, and creative writing, giving me access to the stacks.

Columbia's Butler Library in particular has an amazing collection of local monographs and books issued by Mexican academic institutions that try to make sense of the impossible relationship between the Apache nation and the Mexican administrations of the nineteenth century. When, before I had finished *Ahora me rindo y eso es todo*, my colleagues and friends at Casa Hispánica had no more Spanish classes for me to teach, Julie Crawford granted me another year of economic stability—and access to Butler—in exchange for teaching the great epics of Greek and Latin literature at Columbia. It was in returning to Homer and Virgil that I remembered, thanks to Julie, that what I was writing was meant to be literature, not history or politics. Finally, the Spanish division of the Romance languages department at Hofstra University gave me the stability and peace of mind I needed to finish the book. Benita, Miguel Ángel, Pepa, and Vicente have been irreplaceable travel companions.

Like Julie Crawford, Marie Arana, Zach Mamphilli, and Laura Perciasepe were always attentive to the evolution of *Ahora me rindo y eso es todo*, offering thoughts, readings, and outrageous ideas. Laura wasn't the editor of *Now I Surrender*, as we both hoped she would be while I was writing it, but she was so involved in its writing that for a while she answered to the name "Laura Perciapache." It was Marie Arana who got me to read Harlyn Geronimo's *In Geronimo's Footsteps*, whose spirit and stories were so important for me that they deserve special mention. The transfer of *Ahora me rindo y eso es todo* into English, in the sly and eloquent voice of Natasha Wimmer, was a great effort of reconstruction, not just for Natasha but also for Rebecca Saletan, always deliberate and patient in the face of writer and translator's overenthusiastic efforts to improve the book as she ushered it into English. The observations of Douglas Miles and Karl Jacoby did much to sharpen the final version of the text.

Now I Surrender is a novel, a *novel*-novel. Though it's based on a vast and more or less traceable historical record, it is laced with license-taking and wild leaps for which I—and not the throngs of wiser people on whose shoulders I stood to write this—bear sole responsibility. Thank you to those mentioned in this note and to the many I have surely overlooked.